This can't be happening to me.

I pulled out his shirt from where it was tucked into his pants. *Not me. Not with someone as gorgeous as him,* the analytical part of my mind said as I ran my hands over his chest. *This has to be some sort of mental derangement. I'm going to end up locked in a looney bin if I let this fantasy continue...* My thoughts shriveled to nothing but the purest pleasure when my hands swept across the thick muscles that ran from his breastbone down to his belly, the heat of him sending little shivers of anticipation down my back.

"If you touch me, woman, I won't be able to stop," he growled into my shoulder, his mouth hot on my neck. All the while, his hands moved up the curve of my hips to my breasts.

"Who wants you to stop?" I moaned, arching my back so my breasts pushed harder against his hands. I didn't care if I was acting inappropriately. I just wanted him, despite the fact that somewhere out there, an angry dragon man with pepper-sprayed eyes was probably searching for me.

DAY *of the* DRAGON

KATIE MacALISTER

FOREVER

NEW YORK BOSTON

Copyright © 2019 by Katie MacAlister
Bonus book *Wolf's Mate* Copyright © 2017 by Celia Kyle

Cover illustration by Craig White. Cover design by Elizabeth Turner Stokes. Cover copyright © 2019 by Hachette Book Group, Inc.

Forever
Hachette Book Group
1290 Avenue of the Americas, New York, NY 10104
forever-romance.com
twitter.com/foreverromance

First Edition: March 2019

Forever is an imprint of Grand Central Publishing. The Forever name and logo are trademarks of Hachette Book Group, Inc.

The publisher is not responsible for websites (or their content) that are not owned by the publisher.

The Hachette Speakers Bureau provides a wide range of authors for speaking events. To find out more, go to www.hachettespeakersbureau.com or call (866) 376-6591.

ISBNs: 978-1-5387-6110-6 (mass market), 978-1-5387-6111-3 (ebook)

Printed in the United States of America

OPM

10 9 8 7 6 5 4 3 2 1

ATTENTION CORPORATIONS AND ORGANIZATIONS:
Most Hachette Book Group books are available at quantity discounts with bulk purchase for educational, business, or sales promotional use. For information, please call or write:

Special Markets Department, Hachette Book Group
1290 Avenue of the Americas, New York, NY 10104
Telephone: 1-800-222-6747 Fax: 1-800-477-5925

To my darling Michelle, best agent in the world, for keeping me sane when I badly wanted to become a professional hermit.

DAY *of the*

DRAGON

CHAPTER ONE

Archer Andras was not having a day that would be awarded any gold stars for excellence.

It started off bad and gradually went downhill from there.

"Who is it?" Miles asked that morning when, squatting next to a shallow tide pool, Archer turned over a waterlogged body and looked down into a face he knew.

"Davide." His lips tightened as he touched the gray powder that ringed the man's eyes, nose, ears, and mouth. He didn't have to smell the residue to know what it was.

"Christus Rex," Miles said softly. "Has he been—"

"Yes." Archer stood up and gestured to the other four storm dragons who stood awkwardly holding a canvas stretcher. "Someone blasted dark power through him."

"*Someone?*" Miles's jaw worked for a few seconds while the four men laid a blanket over their dead tribemate, then lifted him onto the stretcher. "I think we all know who is responsible for this, just as he's been responsible for the others. The question is, what are you going to do about it?"

"The same thing I've been doing," Archer said, the grimness in his voice originating from the cold fury that gripped his soul. Not even his fire warmed him—he felt as icy as the gray-green water that lapped at the tide pool. "Try to protect my tribe. Find those who attack us. Build more defenses." He gestured toward the house that sat on a slight rise above the narrow strip of beach. "Take him to the basement," he told the men. "We'll hold the pyre after his family has been contacted."

"The shadow dragons have much to answer for." Ioan, one of the stretcher bearers, watched Archer, his eyes filled with anger. "They *must* pay for this murder."

"They must pay for all the murders," Miles responded automatically. He waited until Ioan followed the men to the basement before grabbing Archer's arm as he headed toward the house. "How many more members are we going to lose before you get off your ass to do something?"

Archer's dragon fire rose, but he kept it leashed,

simply pausing to give the man next to him a long look. "You forget yourself, cousin."

Miles's jaw worked again. They were alone now, the other members out of earshot. "You have to do something," he said at last, his voice gritty. "You have to draw him out. This is intolerable."

"Do you think I'm not aware that my own tribe is being decimated, slowly but surely, one dragon at a time?" Archer snarled, slamming his cousin up against the white stone wall of the house. "They are *my* family, Miles, as surely as you are. It is *my* family that is being killed, *my* family's homes that are being destroyed, their businesses ruined, their protections smashed. I feel every indignation suffered by *all* the members of my tribe, from you, my oldest friend, on down to the newest dragon to find solace in our numbers. I am doing everything I can to keep them safe and happy, but I can't work miracles."

"If you can just lure him out—"

"How?" Archer released Miles, frustration heightening the sense of impotence that followed such attacks. "I have tried for over a hundred years, and to what end? I can't fight someone who hides in the shadows."

"Then perhaps you shouldn't be master of the tribe." Miles spat the words out, giving Archer a hard shove on the shoulder, making him stagger back a couple of feet.

Heat flashed through Archer, and for a moment he considered teaching his cousin a lesson, but he ended up shaking his head to himself, feeling that there had been enough death. Miles was obviously just as frustrated as he was.

"You have done little enough to stop the wholesale slaughter of our tribe. If *I* were master of the storm dragons—"

"But you are not," Archer said slowly, the note of warning clearly evident in his voice. His eyes were narrowed, the icy cold of grief not even touching the dragon fire that always burned inside him. "Do you lodge a formal protest against me?"

He held Miles's gaze until the younger man dropped his eyes in an act of submission. He knew just how much it cost Miles, but he had little choice. The storm dragons had been together for a relatively short time, only slightly over a hundred years, and as their first master, Archer had to be firm to those who would gainsay him. Without a strong hand to lead the often fractious dragons, they would devolve to a lawless band who scraped by on the fringes of both the mortal and immortal worlds.

He'd be damned if they returned to that.

"No, I do not wish to protest against you," Miles said, holding the subservient demeanor for the required length of time before looking Archer in the eyes. "I don't have designs on your job."

"Good." Archer smiled suddenly and punched Miles lightly on the arm. "Because it's a nightmare I wouldn't wish on my worst enemy, and certainly not on a cousin of my blood."

The corner of Miles's mouth curled, acknowledging the affection in Archer's voice. "There has to be something else we can do. Someone, somewhere must have a way we can defeat him. Maybe if we parlay again?"

Archer walked toward the house, feeling unusually defeated. "We can try setting up another parlay with Hunter, although I don't expect it to go any different than the past ones."

"Perhaps this time—"

Two dragon patrols approached.

"It will be no different than before," Archer said, his eyes on the dragons. "The shadow dragons will profess innocence in the deaths of our members. Hunter will deny any charge I level against him. We will go away from the parlay dissatisfied and frustrated, with no resolution."

The patrols bowed and moved on, leaving the two men to enter Archer's house. They strode along the stone tile until Archer reached the second-floor room he called his office. The entire side of the house facing the ocean was made up of floor-to-ceiling retractable glass doors, allowing him to drink in both the light and the salty tang of the sea air. He loved this house, loved the view, loved the way the light seemed to lift everything to a brightness that filled him with joy. That was his blue dragon sire's blood in him, making him crave days spent surrounded by glorious sunshine, while the heritage of his green dragon mother ensured that he loved the endlessly restless sea just as much.

Miles's phone gave a chirp when Archer sat down

at his laptop, pulling up the tribe records to locate Davide's family so that he could tell them of the tragic loss, noting Davide had been a member for only two years. His heart was sick with the knowledge that there was little he could do to avenge the death, at least nothing that he could do that would not bring more heartache and death to the tribe.

"This is interesting," Miles said slowly, looking at something on his phone. "And it might be just what we're looking for. You remember that manuscript that surfaced in Venice late last year?"

"No." Archer pulled up Davide's record and was relieved to see he had listed no family members, not that he believed Davide was truly without kin. So many ouroboros dragons had cut ties with families when they went outlaw and were removed from the family records and shunned by all.

Except the tribes. Archer glanced at the database count and took a small amount of pride that seventy-eight lost dragons had found their way to him.

"I told you about it around Christmas. A parchment had been slipped into the lining of an old sixteenth-century grimoire. It's mostly indecipherable, but a note at the top of the manuscript leaf was written in Latin, claiming it was the true telling of the Raisa Medallion." Miles's gaze was full of unspoken comments as he looked pointedly at Archer.

"There is no Raisa Medallion," Archer said, turning back to his laptop. "The manuscript is either a recent fake or an antique fake."

"You don't know that for certain," Miles pointed out.

"I'd know if my mother created a dragon artifact imbued with unimaginable powers and bestowed it upon me, making me the first dragon hunter," Archer said. "In case it escaped your notice, I am not a dragon hunter. I am a dragon. Nothing more."

"Your mother gave only half of the artifact to you," Miles said, still reading his phone. "According to lore—"

"I don't need to hear fairy tales, thank you," Archer said, trying to forestall the inevitable, but once Miles got a bit in his teeth, he didn't let go.

"Raisa, daughter of the green wyvern, was cast out from the sept when she declared she was mated to a blue dragon. Namely, your father."

Archer flipped browser windows to check on some of the tribe-held businesses. "I know who my parents are. You don't need to remind me of that."

"You may know who they are, but you weren't raised by them, and you refuse to even look at any of the mentions I've found about the Raisa Medallion."

"I have no need to concern myself with something so distant in the past. The present is what matters."

"And yet the past is what drives the present. If your father hadn't been cursed at the behest of the green wyvern, he wouldn't have become part demon. And, of course, you wouldn't be what you are without him being what he was…"

Archer tried to stop listening. "How the sire came to be has nothing to do with it."

"He was a brilliant alchemist," Miles pointed out. "If he hadn't been, he couldn't have made the Raisa Medallion, which is what we're talking about. I don't argue with you simply to hear my own voice, Archer—this history is important to us. Not just the dragon hunters that your father created, but also *us*. Storm dragons."

Archer sighed before saying, "The difference between us is that you believe the tales about the medallion, whereas I know they are nothing but vague references to events that never happened."

"You're just being stubborn," Miles answered, clearly annoyed that Archer wasn't rising to his bait.

"No, I'm being realistic. This is a fantasy, Miles, nothing more than the imaginings of a deranged maniac's mind, one determined to rewrite history to satisfy his ego. I am *not* a dragon hunter!"

"You're awfully good with a sword," Miles said with a smile.

"My father was an insane, homicidal blue dragon who stole my mother from her family, impregnated her, and then slaughtered her when she swore she'd take her own life before submitting to him again. Those are the only important facts about my parents," Archer said, pushing down deep the little kernel of pain that never failed to manifest when he thought of his blood family.

Much better to focus on the one he had made.

Miles continued as if he hadn't spoken. "Well, that and the fact that your mom gave you and your brother pieces of the medallion."

"And then promptly abandoned those sons while they were still babes, leaving them without protection, family, or anyone who gave a damn about them." Archer closed the lid of the laptop, stood up, and gazed out the retractable door, now open so that the room seemed to extend seamlessly onto a wide balcony. He wriggled his shoulders to loosen them up and thought briefly of taking a swim in the infinity pool before he had to deliver tribe justice to two newer members who didn't understand that his word was now their law. He sighed, wondering if the day would come when the tribe members would settle down into a peaceful existence. He had a horrible premonition it wouldn't be in his lifetime. "There were no medallion pieces, Miles. Whatever you think you've learned is just a story, nothing more."

Archer closed his mind to the sorrow that was his family. He'd worked hard over the centuries to reach the point where he could think about his twin without raging, although the fact that just as soon as he had started the storm tribe, Hunter had formed a tribe of shadow dragons—and quickly became the most feared of all the ouroboros dragons—still rankled.

"It's time you opened yourself to the truth about your parents," Miles said, glancing over to where Archer stood, arms crossed, leaning against the edge of the open door while looking out to sea. "You may not believe any of this is real, but the facts speak for themselves. You and Hunter should be the first dragon hunters, but you're not. There's a reason for that, and this Venetian manuscript could tell us what happened all those centuries ago. Why you and Hunter were separated. What happened to your parents. We need the manuscript so we can have it translated. It might give us the edge we need."

"Even if it did contain a true history, it can be of no use to me. The medallion wouldn't have any power over our enemies," Archer said, rubbing the tension in the back of his neck before turning to go down the hall his bedroom. If he had to mete out justice, he'd do it in something other than jeans and a T-shirt that had seen better days. "It's all just history of long-dead dragons."

"Ah, but you don't know that for sure, and that's where things get interesting," Miles said, still reading from the phone as he followed his cousin. "The manuscript is here. In California, Santa Mar to be exact. A local bookseller bought it at auction and smuggled it out of Italy and into the U.S. last week."

"And what do you expect me to do?" Archer asked, peeling off his grubby clothes and marching nude into the bathroom to shave the day's stubble from his face. "Buy the damned thing? I told you that it's fiction. Not real."

"You don't know what it says." Miles smiled. "And, yes, I thought you could buy it. Then we'd have it translated, and we'd be able to find the Raisa Medallion."

Archer didn't like to roll his eyes when faced with things he thought unworthy of attention, but he did so this time, lifting his chin so he could shave around his Adam's apple. "What the hell would we do with the medallion even if it was real?"

Miles was silent for so long that Archer lowered his chin and caught his cousin's gaze in the mirror. "Can you think of a better way to bring him to heel? To make him pay for the deaths?"

Archer considered that for a moment but shook his head and rinsed off the wickedly sharp straight-edge razor. "You forget one important point."

Miles made an annoyed gesture. "I know, I know, there's no proof it's real, but if we can just get our hands on it and translate it—"

"No." Archer finished shaving, then wiped his face clean of any errant bits of shaving cream. "You forget that if it is real, and if it has as much power as you believe, then nothing in this world or the next will stop every dragon in existence from trying to get their hands on it."

"It has importance only to dragon hunters," Miles said, dismissing Archer's comment. "Hunter will lust for it, to be sure, but others? I don't see what good it would do them."

Archer's shoulders twitched as he donned clean clothing. "Do you really think that the Raisa Medallion, if such a thing exists, will be allowed to remain untainted by those who would use it for dark purposes?"

"Only a demon hunter could wield it," Miles objected.

"Or a demon."

Their gazes met.

"Then we have to be the ones to acquire it," Miles said, his eyes somber.

Archer hesitated, wondering if it was worth the effort to continue fighting the idea. What was the worst thing that could happen if he agreed to Miles's suggestion to buy the manuscript? He would be removing it from the grasp of those who might seek to abuse it. There was also a certain amount of satisfaction to be drawn from the knowledge that he was keeping for himself an item Hunter was sure to covet. "Very well. I'll buy the damned thing."

"As a matter of fact, you already have," Miles replied, grinning. "I came to an agreement in your name a few minutes ago, while you were waffling over the idea. I expect a call from the bookseller about when we can collect it. Are you free this evening? We could run into Santa Mar and pick it up."

"I suppose, although I ought to be working on rebuilding some of the tribe businesses that are failing—"

"You know how the saying goes: all work and no play makes the dragon as dull as a mortal. We'll have dinner, find a few females, and let them feel the beast inside of us."

Archer came perilously close to rolling his eyes again, but agreed to meet his cousin in town later in the day. After all, he mused to himself as he took his seat in the living room, now used to hold tribal meetings, it wasn't as if anything was going to come of Miles's grand plans.

The Raisa Medallion was a piece of fiction. It was just that simple.

Anything else would be unthinkable.

CHAPTER TWO

"GIRL, WE NEED TO FIND YOU A MAN, STAT."

The words danced around me, not penetrating the dark wall of my thoughts for a few beats. The second they did, though, I looked over at my friend Laura. "What? *Me*?"

"Yup." She fanned herself with a flattened Junior Mints box as we trailed the last of a late-night crowd out of the movie theater and stood for a moment on the sidewalk. The air was downright turgid, with no breeze, making me feel like an invisible beast was licking me with a thick, sticky tongue.

Sweat started between my shoulder blades and trickled its way down my back. "What are you talking about? Why would I need a man?"

Laura arched an eyebrow at me. Beyond her, Bree, the third member of our party, watched her closely, then arched her brow as well. "Dude," she said.

I hadn't known Bree long, unlike my bestie-since-grade-school Laura, but she seemed pleasant enough, if a bit...eccentric.

Luckily, I'm all over eccentric.

"You clearly need a man because you didn't once drool during the movie." Laura fanned herself harder and pulled out her phone. "Thus, you are out of practice. Where's that ride? He should be here by now."

"I try to make a habit against drooling in public," I said calmly, but backed up when a group of men stumbled out of a bar next to the theater, heading toward us with steps that were none too steady.

"We just sat through an hour and a half of the most gorgeous manflesh alive today, and you didn't sigh once. Or squirm in your seat. Or even make a single risqué comment," Laura said, snapping when one of the drunk men bumped into her. "For chrissake! You don't own the sidewalk, asshat!"

"Asshat!" Bree repeated, shaking a fist at them. The man gestured rudely before staggering after his buddies. "I like that. Hats of asses. I'm going to remember that one."

"So far as I'm concerned, Hollywood can take their policy of inflicting story arcs and plot twists and emotional depth on superhero movies, and dump it all in favor of ninety minutes of buff, shirtless men parading around flexing at things. Damn. Evidently the driver was in a minor fender bender." She looked up and down the street. "We can try to get someone else, or we can go to Pemm Square and pick up a cab at one of the fancy hotels."

"I don't mind a walk," I said, hoping no one heard the lie in my voice. Since I had made a promise to myself that I would work at tackling my fears, I added in a voice filled with false confidence, "It would probably be faster to walk."

"Smart thinking," Bree said, nodding. She had two round blobs of long blond hair wound onto the top of her head like little anime animal ears. "Plus, if we walk, we can find a place that has booze. I like booze. Booze is good."

"Booze is very good," Laura agreed, and marched determinedly up the street.

"Uh...you do know you have to be twenty-one to legally drink, right?" I asked Bree. She looked like she was about eighteen. Nineteen, tops.

"I'm older than I look," she answered, then flashed a huge smile at me before whirling on her heel and dashing after Laura.

I pushed down the little wriggle of uneasiness that we'd be out and vulnerable to comments by the uninhibited folks who frequented the area at night. My stomach felt like it had twisted upon itself.

A couple of women stood together kissing, breaking apart when I hurried past to catch up to my friends, one of them saying to the other, "Holy jebus, did you see that girl?"

I shut my ears to it and caught up just as I heard Laura saying, "—you had a bad experience with your ex, who I completely agree was an asshat—"

"Hat of asses!" Bree interrupted, grinning again. "Lots of hats. More asses. What did he do?"

"Cheated on her royally," Laura answered before I could.

"Cards?" Bree asked, her nose wrinkling as she slid an arm through mine. "Or sexually?"

I sighed. Evidently tonight was going to be one of those nights where everything made me uncomfortable. "He two-timed me with someone he worked with, but that was a long time ago, and we weren't really that...together."

"Rat bastard still broke your heart," Laura tossed back over her shoulder to us.

I said nothing. There wasn't anything to deny.

"Wow. What did you do to him?" Bree asked me.

"Do to him?" I shot her a curious look. "You mean revenge? If so, nothing. I was pretty...well, devastated, to be honest, because I trusted him, and he broke that trust."

"She cried for weeks," Laura said, pausing to wait for a light to change. "He really did a number on her psyche. I wanted to geld him, but alas, the California Bar doesn't look kindly on its members emasculating the general public. No matter how much they deserve it."

"I know a curse to make pubic hair grow really heavy," Bree offered, giving my arm a squeeze. "I'll teach it to you if you want."

I slid her another look, unsure if she was joking or not. Her expression was filled with concern. "Er... thanks, but as I said, this was all a long time ago. Eight years, as a matter of fact."

"Eight years in which you haven't dated at all," Laura pointed out.

"There's nothing wrong with being by yourself," I protested, trotting across the street with Bree still glued to my side.

"Nothing wrong with it if you are truly happy, but you aren't, and don't tell me you are because I've known you for more than twenty years, and I know sad when I see it."

"I'll know the right man when I find him," I said with much dignity. "I've always been a fall-in-love-at-first-sight sort of girl. I just haven't found someone to fall for yet."

"Out of all the men in Northern California? Methinks the lady protests too much."

"Methinks so, too," Bree agreed.

"Bah," I said, trying to dismiss her comments.

Before I could dredge up a suitable topic to change the subject, Laura continued. "Good Lord, woman, we just saw the most delectable men in skimpy superhero costumes, so you can't tell me your motor isn't running at least a little bit. I had to shift into third gear when the Hemsworth guy had that water scene. Mmrowr."

"Mmrowr," repeated Bree, who nudged me, clearly expecting me to reply in kind.

"Rowr. The difference is that those sort of men

aren't realistic," I objected as we turned a corner, a fetid smell of rotting garbage wafting up from side yards. The night being as hot and muggy as it was, people sat on the steps of the houses, smoking, laughing, kissing, and in one instance, barbecuing. We climbed the hill that led to a popular area that housed two of the most prestigious hotels in Santa Mar, a growing suburb along the northern California coast. The air seemed to get thicker and moister with every step we took. I plucked the damp gauze of my dress from my sweaty chest, wishing I'd turned down Laura's offer to see a movie and meet her new neighbor.

"Superheroes? Of course they aren't real," Laura said.

Bree looked thoughtful. "I liked the one who wore that plastic suit and flew around shooting people. If I could do that, I'd get so much more done every day."

We laughed, but there was a note in her voice that had me sliding her a questioning look before saying, "Actually, the superhero part was what I found the least unreasonable. What doesn't ring true at all is the idea that men who look like those actors, with their perfect hair, and six-packs, and general drop-dead-gorgeousness gave the time of day to the common people on the street. That just doesn't happen in real life."

Laura, who was still walking slightly in front of Bree and me, cast a glance back as we rounded another corner. Ahead of us was the first of the exclusive hotels, the Merit, in all its art deco glory. In front of the curved drive sat a long row of cars, everything from a stretch limo to a couple of sleek, expensive sports cars, and even a handful of more mundane cars and taxicabs. "Why wouldn't they talk to people? That's who they were saving, silly—the people in Metropolis. Or whatever town they were supposed to be in. I didn't hear much of the actual dialogue since I was too busy drooling over the eye candy."

I shook my head. "Men who look like that—like actors or models or just guys blessed with really good genes—aren't interested in people like us."

Bree watched me with bright eyes but said nothing. I had a feeling that since Laura and I were in our early thirties, and she was obviously much younger, she was feeling her lack of experience with men and dating.

"Don't be ridiculous. Of course they do! Handsome men pay attention to me all the time."

I was silent, feeling even more like I was an outsider looking in. Laura was lovely—of course it made sense that the sort of man who wouldn't give me a second glance would still notice her.

"Oy. Now the app says the nearest driver is forty minutes away." Laura slipped her phone into her purse and waved a hand at the hotel. "Let's go in and have a drink while we wait. The bar is bound to have AC."

Bree clapped her hands happily and did a little hopping skip as she followed Laura. My stomach tightened even more when I followed my friends, hesitation making my steps lag. There were beautiful people everywhere—women who were dressed in club wear, all glittery short dresses that exposed a lot of boob and leg, with gorgeous hair, perfect makeup, and impossibly high heels. The men swaggered next to them, clad in equally elegant attire, reeking of money and expensive cologne. They were very aware of themselves and each other, clearly entranced by their partners, their faces showing both satisfaction at the eye candy on their respective arms and a smooth self-confidence that made my stomach drop.

And then there was me. Sweaty, odd me, standing out like a thumb at a toe convention.

Behind me, a car purred to a stop, no doubt about to disgorge another gorgeous couple. I took a step forward, rallying my courage and telling myself to just go into the hotel and not worry about anyone else.

A sudden sharp blow to my back had me stumbling forward a couple of steps, knocking my purse out of my hand.

A man who was a couple inches taller than me, with shoulder-length reddish brown hair, stood with his back to me as he helped an elegant woman out of the car. She had the long legs and poise of a model or actress, her thigh-high slit dress moving around her like it was made of water. Another long leg emerged from the car, causing the man who'd obviously bumped into me to help out a second lovely example of what I could never be, followed by a second man.

The first woman flicked an annoyed glance my way before slapping a smile on her face and clinging to the first man's arm as they glided past me. I bit back a testy comment about people who didn't have the decency to apologize when they bumped into someone, and bent down to pick up my purse, but another hand was there already.

"Oh. Thank you," I murmured, taking my bag from where it was offered by the second man's hand. He was taller than the first, with shoulders that seemed impossibly broad. He didn't say anything, didn't even look my way, just nodded and allowed the second woman to latch on to his arm before they, too, glided their way into the hotel.

"At least that one had some manners," I murmured to myself, irritated at my moment of weakness.

So what if I didn't have a man who treated me like I was the best thing in the world? I didn't need adoration. I might have an appearance that kept me from swanning into expensive hotels like the two women I'd just seen, but that didn't mean I was dirt under their feet.

With my chin held high, I entered the hotel lobby.

"The glamorous people are going to do their thing no matter what I think. Although I would like to point out that I couldn't have predicted their reaction to me any more accurately," I told Laura and Bree ten minutes later as we sat at a small table in the emptiest of the three hotel bars. Bright neon blue light that traced down the bar cast a weird glow on everyone, but the noise was of a volume that would allow us to converse without having to yell. I took a sip of my gin and tonic. "It proves my point exactly."

"What, that some guy who bumped into you didn't stop to chat?" Laura gave a one-shouldered shrug. "He probably didn't realize he'd done it."

I remembered the strength of the blow to my back. I had no doubt he'd felt the collision.

"Plus, and I'm not excusing his rudeness in not apologizing and picking up your bag, because politeness costs nothing, but you have to admit that sometimes you aren't aware of where you are. Spatially, I mean."

"Huh?" I asked, plucking out a bit of ice from my drink and crunching it.

She waved a vague hand. "You do insist on walking with your head down like you're a hideous monster who is going to stop traffic if anyone catches sight of your face."

"You're not a hideous monster," Bree told me frankly, somehow having managed to possess herself with three different beverages, all of them of the sweet, fruity variety. She fanned three straws and sipped from all three at once. "I've seen a behemoth that was hit by a truck and that stopped traffic because it was so hideous. Well, also its intestines caused three cars to flip, and they blocked the road, but you can believe me when I tell you that it was hideous. You just have"—she plucked a piece of pineapple spear off a plastic swizzle stick from one of the drinks—"patches of white on your hair and eyelashes, and weird-ass eyes."

"Bree!" Laura said sternly, consulting a list of bar

snacks. She didn't even look up while she chastised the girl. "We don't said *weird-ass*. It's *differently eyed*. And streaks of white hair are super trendy right now. Besides, Thaisa has a genetic thing going on. Polioni. So it's not like she can help it."

"Poliosis," I corrected, taking a big pull on my drink. I welcomed the sweet, sweet burn of gin as it slithered down to my stomach.

"Right, and it's not like she has a third arm or something." Laura waved a hand at me while she drained her margarita, and caught a waitress's eye before signaling for a refill.

"Do you want a third arm?" Bree asked me, leaning toward me.

I gawked at her. "Why on earth would I want that?"

She shrugged. "It would keep peeps from looking at your hair and eyes."

I blinked at her a couple of times and tried to send a "she's had too much already" eyebrow semaphore to Laura, but the latter was still consulting the menu. "Thanks, but I think I'll pass."

"Your choice," Bree said, craning to see what the people at the table next to ours had ordered. "Snacks! Mama needs snacks."

"I'm getting some. I think we could all use something to soak up the alcohol." Laura glanced up to smile, considered me for a minute, then reached a hand across the table and gave my fingers a squeeze. "I think your eyes are very pretty. Unique, yes, but the browns and golds and the other colors in them are lovely."

"Thank you," I said, returning her smile, a little ball of warmth easing my knotted stomach a little. Then again, it might have been the gin. "You are a good and valued friend."

"I'm not just saying it— Hi, can we have another round, please? Oh, and some wings. Er . . . and a blooming onion. Thanks. I love those things," she said in a confidential tone to Bree. "So bad for you, but damn, they go down good."

"I don't know what you're talking about," Bree said, her face animated, her eyes sparkling with joy. The two little balls of hair on top of her head fairly vibrated with happiness. "But I like watching you talk."

"Years of arguments before the bench, my dear," Laura said. "What were we talking about?"

"The fact that handsome men like the one who ran into me don't have the time of day for the average person," I said swiftly, changing the subject away from my appearance. I knew what I looked like—I didn't need Bree and Laura to dissect the weirdness that was my genes.

"Right. Let's go over this point by point," Laura said.

I laughed. "Your lawyer is showing."

"You're just jealous because you're stuck inside all day poring over moldy books while I get to wear power suits and have expensive lunches on the lead attorney's dime." She accepted the beverages and food, and plucked a sodden chicken wing from a plate before shaking it. "Your hypothesis is that handsome actor types don't seek interaction with those of us of more average looks."

"That's correct, Your Honor," I said, stifling a little giggle. *That* definitely was the gin.

"More booze! Excellent!" Bree said, making obnoxious slurping noises as she hastily guzzled the last of her three drinks in order to make room on the table for the fresh glasses. "I had a boyfriend last week, but then I found out he was just using me."

"Oh, Bree," I said, patting her hand. "I'm so sorry. Men are dogs."

"They truly are," Laura agreed, and shoved the plate of wings toward me. "Eat, Tha."

I picked a piece of celery from the plate that didn't appear to be smothered in the gloopy red sauce. "Did you dump him?" I asked Bree, more than happy to move the subject away from my life.

"I had to." She leaned close to my head and said breathily, "Fallen angel."

I blinked at her a couple of times. "Pardon?"

"He was a fallen angel." Her nose wrinkled. "Nephilim, you know?"

"No, I don't," I said slowly, and waited for her to focus on the food before sending another round of eyebrow semaphore to Laura. This time she caught my look, but totally misinterpreted it.

"What? Oh, sorry, I got sidetracked by the food. What proof do you offer to validate your hypothesis?"

I sighed to myself and took another sip of my drink, ignoring the second one that sat untouched. As I was about to speak, a small group of people entered the bar, pausing at the entrance to glance around. There was something about the way the two men stood, looking as if they owned the place, their body language speaking loudly of arrogance and confidence. I nodded toward them. "Your Honor, I would like to enter into evidence Thigh Dress, Sparkle Bosom, Auburn Man With No Manners, and his friend Tall, Dark, and Possibly Dangerous, who at the very least isn't beyond picking up a woman's purse even if he doesn't bother to look at her when he gives it back."

Laura turned around to look at the foursome. Bree put both hands on the table and leaned across the glasses and plates to stare at them. "Holy shitsnacks," Laura said, getting up and hurriedly moving over to my side of the table, taking the empty chair next to me so she could look without being obvious. "That red dress Sparkle Bosom is wearing is gorgeous. The thigh one isn't half bad either, but would you look at those men? Hoobah! Which is the one who ran into you?"

"Auburn Hair," I said, picking up a menu and pretending to look at it so I wasn't staring so obviously at them. The women in the party didn't seem to be any too taken with this bar, but Auburn Hair gestured toward the back, and the ladies slunk forward with the sort of forward-hip-action runway walk that I associated with fashion shows.

"Man, he's something, isn't he? And the tall one isn't bad either."

"I like Tall, Dark, and Dangerous," Bree said, still

perched over the table. "He's pretty. I like the way his hair swoops back. Men who have swoopy hair like that are usually really good lovers."

I blinked in surprise at her, not saying anything, other than agreeing with her assessment that he had nice hair. It was glossy, straight, and swept back from a slight widow's peak. My fingers suddenly itched to touch it.

"I like them both," Laura said, making a little purring noise softly to herself as the foursome strolled toward us, clearly heading for a bank of booths behind me.

"Bree," I whispered harshly, trying to get her to sit back in her chair lest they see her gawking, but she just stayed where she was, her face filled with merriment.

"Oh, my Lord." I half covered my eyes, too embarrassed for words as they approached us.

"Erp!" Laura said with a hiccup, and hid behind another menu.

The two ladies passed, the look on their faces reading smug enjoyment of being the center of attention. Auburn Hair was hot on their heels, saying over his shoulder in what I recognized as the archaic Old East Slavic language, "Take your enjoyment tonight. It will ease the sorrow." The tall man trailed them, and it was he who gave Bree an odd look from the corner of his eye as he passed by.

"Hi," she said, grinning like a maniac. "Nice tail."

The man paused for a minute, his eyes first widening in surprise, then narrowing on her. Through the screen of my fingers, I could see that he had pale blue eyes, *very* pale, so pale that it was really just a ring of blue color on the outer edges of the irises, fading almost immediately into an icy gray just barely tinged with color.

As the man's gaze slid over Laura and me, I hurriedly slammed shut my fingers, making sure they covered up the half of my eyebrow and lashes that lacked pigment. To my intense relief, he walked on without saying a word, joining his buddy at the booth behind us.

"See?" Bree said, giving the four people a little wave before sitting down. "He noticed us. Thus and therefore, you were wrong, Thaisa."

"Holy shit, Bree! I can't believe you did that," I murmured under my breath, my eyes filled with oodles of meaning when Laura moved back to her original chair. "And to say something about the man's ass... that's sexual harassment, you know."

Bree's eyes widened until her resemblance to an anime girl was almost overwhelming. "I didn't say anything about his butt. I said he had a nice tail."

"He didn't have a tail." I felt obligated to point out the obvious.

"Not in this form, but you never know what he gets up to when no one is looking," she said sagely.

Once again, I had no answer to that comment. I looked to Laura for help with her neighbor.

Her eyes slid past me to the men for a moment; then she took a long pull on her drink and shrugged. "Well, you have to admit, Bree did get TD and Dangerous to look at her. That does officially disprove your hypothesis."

"Bree looks nineteen, is adorably cute, and could charm a lifelong misanthrope," I pointed out.

Laura thought about that for a moment, eating another chicken wing. "Yes, but you didn't include that exception in your opening statement."

"We reject your evidence," Bree said, nodding, then suddenly squirmed in her chair as she dug through the pocket of the black-and-white-striped jersey short skirt, pulling out a handful of what looked like a wad of fabric scraps. "I forgot, I have presents!"

"Er..." I said, watching as she deftly separated the bits of colored fiber, pulling out an object that I immediately recognized from my childhood.

"Friendship bracelets!" she announced, presenting Laura with a diamond-pattern cloth bracelet, done in rainbow colors. "Here is one for you, Laura, because you are my neighbor, and friend, and you take me out to watch movies and have booze."

"Wow, I haven't seen one of these since we were in fifth grade," Laura said, laughing, but immediately slipped it on. "You remember when we spent that summer making them, Tha?"

I made a face. "My gran has boxes of the embroidery thread we bought stashed away in her basement." Pain stabbed at me as I spoke. "She did have, anyway."

"And here's one I made for you, because you are my new friend." I looked up to see the little blue and green circle she held before me.

"Oh. Uh...thank you." She dropped the twisted cloth bracelet onto my palm. From the middle of it, a dark, tarnished little metal charm dangled, about the size of a dime, but oval in shape, with a crudely scratched sun visible on one side. "It's very pretty, but you don't have to give me anything, you know. I'm happy just to have you as a new friend."

She just grinned. "Sasha said I should give it to you because you never know, right?"

"Sure," I said slowly, at a loss as to what and who she was speaking about. "Do I know who Sasha is?"

"No, but that's all right. You get me instead. I hope you like it." She looked expectantly at the bracelet.

"It's lovely," I said, quickly putting it on so that I wouldn't hurt her feelings. She had to be slightly squiffy, but I decided to just embrace her oddities and not worry about trying to understand her conversational leaps.

"Now," she said, beaming at us both. "Our friendship is sealed and cannot be broken. Zizi's pink nipples, is that right?"

I looked where she was pointing to a big clock hanging above the bar.

"It looks like it's accurate," Laura said, who had her phone out and was tapping on it, obviously sending a text. "Quarter after midnight. Yup, that's right."

"Gotta go. My ride is here," Bree said, leaping to her feet. "People to do, things to see. Thank you for the movie. See you tomorrow!"

Before Laura or I could say anything, she was off,

racing through the bar like a gazelle, all artless long limbs and fluttering clothing.

"Wait, she has someone picking her up? I didn't see her texting anyone. She's had a lot to drink.... Maybe we should go see who this ride is," I said, half rising.

"Damned prosecuting attorney. If she thinks she can pull that shit on me— Hmm?" Laura looked up from her phone, a faint puzzle between her brows.

"Bree," I prodded her, gathering up my purse and slipping the strap across my chest.

"What about her?"

"Who is her ride? She's so young, and she's had an awful lot to drink. I wouldn't want someone to take advantage of her." I pulled out my wallet and dropped a few bills on the table. "I'll just make sure she's okay, then wait for you outside, all right?"

"Sure. Just give me five to ream this prosecutor a new hole; then we'll see if there's a ride to be had."

I hurried out, pausing to look back, curious to have one last glance at the fabulous four. The lights were dim in that part of the bar, but I could see Auburn Hair holding out a hand to Thigh Slit, obviously taking her to the minuscule dance floor. My gaze slid over to the other couple. Sparkle Bosom was leaning across the tall man, angling herself so that her breasts brushed against his arm. His face was turned toward her, where he was quite clearly giving her all of his consideration.

I heaved a little mental sigh, wondering what it felt like to have the complete attention of a man like him, being the most important thing in his life. "Someday, maybe," I said aloud, trying to cheer up my suddenly glum spirits. "It's not like it's out of the question that at some point, I'll find a man who makes me happy."

As the last word left my lips, the tall man turned and looked straight at me, his eyes almost glowing in the dim light as his gaze caught mine.

I stumbled backward, blinking, fighting the urge to run, a few seconds later giving in to my brain's panicked demands that I get the hell out of Dodge. I turned and hurried out to check on Bree, feeling as if I'd been seared down to my soul by those eyes.

It was a disconcerting experience. One that, oddly, I wouldn't have minded repeating.

CHAPTER THREE

THE RIDE FROM THE MERIT HOTEL TO ROSSE, THE
suburb to the west of the Bay where I lived, was slow,
even given the fact that it was after midnight and the
local bridge was fogged in.

"—and I told her that there's no way I'm letting him
testify, because the prosecutor will crucify him. It'll be
a bloodbath, a literal bloodbath, if she gets him to admit to the conviction eighteen years ago. Boy, this is
taking us forever to get home. What are you doing?"
Laura, now slightly snockered, turned in the darkness
of the back seat of the car we'd eventually managed to
hire, the bluish white lights along the roadway flashing
on our faces and down onto our laps. Unlike Laura, I
wasn't fretting about the time it took to get us home;

the slow pace allowed me a few seconds for each pool of light to illuminate the book that lay across my thighs. "Are you writing down what I'm saying?"

"Of course not," I said, waiting for the next patch of light before adding a description of Bree's behavior in the bar, and after a moment's thought, a note that the man who'd picked her up, the one I'd managed to question before he drove away, did indeed look sober and not at all like a white slaver. Or worse. "I know Bree is just your neighbor, not a close friend, but do you think we did right letting her go off to spend the night with Ramon? He looked nice enough, but she's so young…"

"Bah. How could she have bought the bungalow next to mine if she was too young? I think she just has one of those perpetually young faces. You sure you didn't write down anything I said? Because if anyone found out I was talking about a client, my goose would be cooked."

"I changed everything you said so that it was non-identifiable and pretty generic," I said, smiling. "The last thing I want to happen is for you to be defrocked, or whatever they do to lawyers."

"Disbarred, and let me see."

I hesitated a second, but there was nothing I'd recorded about the evening's events that she didn't know, so I handed the journal to her and pointed to the evening's conversation. Good friend that she is, she just read those parts and handed the journal back to me without glancing at the rest. "Thanks. I hate to be suspicious, but I've had too much to drink and I don't want that to haunt me."

"No one but you and Gran know I journal every day, so I doubt if the prosecutor is going to demand anything I've written about you," I pointed out.

"You don't know her. She's positively psychic at times. What were we talking about?"

"Bree and her evidently new boyfriend, Ramon."

"Oh, yeah, that. I'm sure she's fine, but call her in the morning if you are worried. Do you mind if I get dropped off first? Like I said, I've had a bit too much to imbibe, and if I see Edgar, I'm likely to punch him in his smug face, and I really don't want to end up having to deal with an assault charge. Judges tend to frown on that sort of thing."

"Your ex-husband is, I'm happy to tell you, on the East Coast on a big buying trip. He's not due back for another ten days."

"Oh?" She brightened at that thought. "So the cat's away, eh? Maybe we could have lunch tomorrow. Or dinner. I want to talk to you about this need you have for a man."

"Laura, please—"

"I am determined to see you happy, even if I am miserable. Lunch tomorrow?"

"Can't, I'm afraid. Edgar's acquisitions have been arriving almost daily, and I have to log and catalog them, not to mention translate anything that is within my purview, and then there's taking pictures and scanning, and a million other things. As well as dealing with anyone who comes into the shop. I just sold one of the items today for some big money, so tomorrow I will have to make sure that it's packed up properly for the buyer."

"That's what you have Jamie for," Laura said. "Is he still pimply and awkward and prone to standing in corners staring at you with his Adam's apple bobbing up and down like he's a human-ostrich hybrid?"

I laughed at the description of my boss's nephew. "He's gotten a bit better about the standing in corners and staring bit, but other than that, he's pretty much the same."

"Dinner, then. Surely you can do dinner? I really want to talk to you about finding you a man."

I sighed, but agreed. "I'll see Gran at five, but if you can hang on until six, I should be free."

"Awesome." She sat back, and within five minutes, she was snoring. I continued writing, feeling that my day was never complete till I'd taken down the thoughts and happenings of the last twenty-four hours.

By the time I made it home, it was almost one-thirty in the morning. I tipped the driver, and after a quick glance around the street, slipped along the side alley where the stairs to the apartment above the shop were located. I trotted up the stairs as quietly as possible, so as not to waken the other occupant of the top floor, an elderly woman beset with insomnia, and made it into my apartment with a sigh of relief.

I slipped into a filmy pale blue satin negligee before stopping by the bathroom to do my nightly ablutions. I stared at the mirror for a few minutes, trying to see myself through Laura's eyes, but in the end, I just shook my head and clicked off the light, intending on going straight to bed.

A thin line of light showed under the door that opened on the stairs leading down to the shop. "Oh, Lord, if Jamie's left the lights on, Edgar will be furious." Pausing only to punch in a security code at the top of the stairs, I hurried down the wooden staircase barefoot, the satin nightie making the faintest whisper of sound as it swept each step behind me.

The light in one of the back rooms was on. I tsked at Jamie's slipshod store-closing habits and clicked it off, making my way around tables of secondhand books, a couple of knockoff copies of objets d'art, and a back wall filled with vintage posters cling-wrapped onto large pieces of cardboard. When I opened the door to the office, two things struck me at once: the first was that it wasn't very smart to go downstairs in the middle of the night when I was alone and unarmed, not even so much as my trusty bottle of pepper spray to hand, and the second was that the man with the pretty pale blue eyes was much better on closer inspection.

Not that I recognized him at first.

"Hey!" I yelled, startled to find two men in Edgar's office, one digging through the crate of items that had evidently arrived after I'd left to meet Laura and Bree. "What the hell do you think you're do— Awk!"

The two men whose backs were to me spun around, and I recognized the auburn-haired man who'd run into me at the hotel, but before I could finish my sentence, his friend, the tall man with silky black hair, had me pinned up against the wall, one arm across my neck.

"I think this might be it," Auburn Hair said, searching Edgar's desk, tossing aside a small heavily patterned rug before pulling out a black portfolio and opening it to peer inside. "It was beneath the prayer rug."

"That's...not...yours..." I wheezed, and tried desperately to remember the instructions in a self-defense book I'd read years ago. "It's been sold!"

"I know," he said, flipping open the archival portfolio.

Desperate to save the very old leaf of an illuminated manuscript that I'd sold to a collector earlier that morning, I grabbed both of my captor's arms and jerked my knees up, aiming for his noogies, but he was too close to me, his thighs blocking my attack.

"Dammit," I snarled, wondering if I had it within me to gouge at those pale, startlingly beautiful eyes.

"Stop struggling. I mean you no harm," Gorgeous Eyes said, giving me only a swift glance before looking over his shoulder at his friend. Despite him understanding the archaic Slavic language that his friend used at the bar, he had an English accent tinged only slightly with East European. "I'm only taking what is mine."

I made a fist and tried to get enough of a swing to punch him in the face, but flat against the wall as I was, I knew such an attack would be ineffectual at best. "You call pressing yourself against me in a wholly inappropriate and extremely repugnant manner while your friend steals things causing no harm? Wait…what? What's yours? What are you talking about?"

"The Venetian manuscript. The one you sold to me via my cousin." He turned to look at me then, his pale eyes bright with anger. "Do not pretend you don't know what I'm talking about. Or is it that you now wish to demand more money for it after we agreed to a price? I don't care how many other offers you have received for it—we agreed on a price, and I do not take kindly to a betrayal of our agreement."

"Your cousin?" I racked my brain for the name of the collector who had jumped on the manuscript listing the second I had it on the website storefront. "Milo somebody-or-other?"

"Miles. You will honor the agreement he made in my name. When you did not reply to my messages, we decided to get the leaf before some ill befell it," Tall, Dark, and Scary said, the lines of his face as hard and unyielding as his body, still pressed so intimately against me. I was suddenly very aware that the heat of his body sank through the thin layer of satin that was all that separated my skin from him.

"I think you're confused," I said, finding it a bit difficult to get air into my lungs. He must have realized that, because he moved his arm off my neck, shifting so that he held both of my hands pinned to the wall alongside my ears. "I'm not trying to do your cousin out of anything."

"Did you get it or not?" he asked, watching as Auburn Hair examined the small page of vellum.

"Yes, this is it." Auburn tucked the parchment into a leather attaché case and gave his friend a nod.

"I've left the payment you asked for upon on your desk," Handsome Eyes said when he turned back to me, his anger almost palpable. "Tempted though I am to withhold it after you clearly have received other offers and wish to sell it to a higher bidder. Unlike you, I honor my word."

"I would never do that," I said, outraged at the accusation, my mind partially distracted by the feel of him against me, so hard and foreign and...male. I was no shy virgin despite having had limited association with men, but never had I found myself pressed against one in a manner that made me very aware of the way his chest rose and fell against mine. "I didn't know you were coming by to pick it up, and I certainly didn't make any agreement to sell it to someone else."

"I'll be outside," Auburn Hair said, glancing at me as he passed, his gaze impersonal and clearly unimpressed, saying in Old East Slavic, "Do you need help...cleaning up?"

"No," the man holding me said in the same language. I wondered if they were scholars, too. That made sense if they had bought the leaf. "This won't take long."

My eyes widened as the meaning behind the words

struck me. Was this handsome, dangerous man not going to believe me? The second he said he'd bought the item his friend was stealing, I'd relaxed, chalking their unorthodox visit up to sometimes overly enthusiastic collectors. But now... was he hinting he intended on killing me?

"I swear to you, I wasn't trying to sell your leaf!" I struggled in earnest now, trying to punch and claw and scratch him. I might not be any great addition to the world, but I refused to leave it without so much as a whimper. "I haven't done anything wrong."

"You are only going to hurt yourself doing that," he commented, his hands like iron holding my arms helpless. "If you did not intend to sell the manuscript, why did you not respond to my messages?"

"I've been gone all day," I panted, trying desperately to get my hands free, my fingers curling into claws. "Not that it's any of your business, but my boss is out of town, so I spent the day with friends."

"Did your employer take other offers? Is that it?" His eyes lost a bit of their anger, speculation coming into them.

"God's nostrils, are you hard of hearing? I did not take another offer!" It skittered through my mind that I wouldn't put it past Edgar to get a couple of collectors bidding against each other, but since he left the selling of items to me while he was off on buying trips, I figured he hadn't had time to do that with this particular item. "I was going to contact you tomorrow—today— to find out if you wanted me to send it to you or arrange

for you to pick it up. Now, let go of me!" I twisted, attempting to get out of his grip, but it was useless, and
we both knew it.

"Not until you calm down," he said, the last of the
anger in his eyes fading, replaced with amusement that
I found highly insulting. "You will harm yourself trying to squirm free."

"You bastard! You're not any better than a common
criminal, treating me like this!" I tried again to get my
knees up, but the movement just made him step forward until one of his legs was pressed between mine.

I froze at the intimate position, my brain staggering
to a halt at the feel of his hard thigh between mine. I
knew—in the sane part of my mind—that I should be
terrified, that women who were in my situation were at
risk of a sexual assault, that I should be fighting with
every ounce of my strength, but the sense of peril that
I expected simply wasn't there.

"Criminal? Perhaps," he said with a slight twitch at
the corner of his mouth, "but common? I won't say
I'm as rarified as you are—" His gaze moved from my
eyes, to my lashes, to my eyebrows, on up to my hair,
now pulled back in a ponytail. "But I assure you that I
am in no way common."

"Your leg," I said through ground teeth, trying to
hang on to what dignity I had left. If I could just
get some distance from this beautiful, forceful man, I
could think properly.

"My leg?"

"It's between mine."

He looked down, which I realized gave him a clear view of my cleavage. I took a deep breath to protest the fact that he could see clear down to my stomach, but that just made my breasts squish against his chest even more than they already were. "Is it? I'm afraid I can't see past your…er…"

"It is." My breath was coming hot and fast, something else I couldn't control. I wanted to yell and scream and hide in a dark room where I would have time to think, but he kept distracting me by breathing, his chest moving against mine in a rhythmical manner that made my breasts feel heavy and very interested in him. "It's…it's rude. I realize you're angry because I wasn't around to get your messages saying you wanted to pick up the leaf, but assaulting my person by shoving your leg between mine, and rubbing your chest on me, and holding my hands is…it's intolerable."

"And yet, I find myself of the opposite opinion. You smell like a field of sun-warmed flowers. Spicy flowers," he said softly. His head dipped down until his mouth was an inch from my ear, his breath hot on suddenly sensitive flesh. "You have a beautiful neck."

My mind came to a screeching halt when it struck me that he was flirting with me. Flirting! With me! What was so wrong with my life that I couldn't find a man who didn't run screaming from me unless he was the sort who pressed women against a wall and smelled their necks? "I…uh…thank you. I think. Now, release me."

He chuckled, the rumble of it in his chest making heat pool low in parts that hadn't felt such things in years. "You sound offended. It was a compliment, little flower." His breath steamed my neck as his lips just barely brushed a spot beneath my ear that was suddenly a full-on erogenous zone. "So sweet. So smooth and silky."

Thrill rippled down my back, making my breasts even heavier, a strange, restless feeling sweeping over me. I wanted to rub against him, to breathe in his scent just as he was breathing in mine. To bathe in the heat he was radiating... With a snap, I came back to reality, swearing at myself and heartily ashamed that I was evidently so desperate for a man's attention that I was getting my jollies from what was clearly a dangerous situation. "Right, that's it, I'm putting myself in Laura's hands at the first opportunity."

"I don't know who Laura is, but if you are of that persuasion..."

He let the words trail off, his eyes filled with a steamy heat that I felt myself respond to despite everything that should have sent me running screaming from him. "I'm not gay, if that's what you're asking," I heard myself say.

"Ah. I can't help but be pleased by that," he murmured, his breath back on my neck.

It struck me then that far from a compliment, what he had said was really an insult. I jerked, relieved when he released my hands at last. I didn't wait for him to react, though—I jammed both of my palms onto his chest and shoved as hard as I could. "Do you really think I'm so stupid?"

He didn't budge so much as an inch, but his head did come up, his eyes narrowed on me.

"Or maybe you think I'm just naïve." I tried to shove him back again, but he held me where I was, both of his hands now on the wall next to my ears, using the strength of his body to keep me pinned in place.

He looked confused. "About what?"

"Your *compliment*," I snapped, giving the word the sneer it deserved as I spoke it. "What you really mean is that my face is so freaky, my neck is nice by comparison. Well, I'm sorry that I'm not drop-dead gorgeous like you are, but some of us have to live with what the genetic shake of the dice throws us."

He frowned, two glossy ebony brows pulling together as he considered my face once again. I swear his eyes darkened, the blue leaching inward from the outer rim. "When did I say your face is freaky?"

I couldn't help myself. I knew it was stupid to stand there in nothing but a thin negligee, arguing about something unimportant when I should, at the very least, be trying to reach the panic button on the desk, but there was something about this man that enraged me. Annoyed me. Irritated and infuriated and intrigued me. "Oh, come on. My neck is lovely? *My neck*? You were clearly offering me a pity compliment because there was nothing nice you could say about my eyes or hair or anything else that men normally comment on when they want to flatter a woman, and that, Mr. Your Leg Is Still There, is the epitome of rude."

To my surprise, a little smile tugged up the corner of his lips. He leaned in until his breath fanned on my lips, his mouth a fraction of an inch from mine. Heat swept up my chest in a flush that made perspiration prick on my palms. When he spoke, his lips brushed against mine. "I've changed my mind. You aren't rare... You are utterly unique."

"Are you...going to...You're not going to..." I wanted badly to ask him if he was going to release me, but I couldn't catch my breath. It was like the heat from his body sucked out all the air from my lungs.

"Kiss you?" he asked, his lips moving gently on the corners of my mouth. "Ah, flower, you tempt me, but unique as you are, I would hate to see your petals wilt under my heat."

I stared into his eyes, now completely blue, and tried to think of something to say, tried to remember that I should be doing something to stop him, to regain control over my body, but my mind was too overwhelmed with the sense of him. The pressure of his leg between mine combined with the way his shirt rubbed against my breasts made me feel like I was standing in a shower of flame, effectively shutting down my ability to reason.

And then he was gone, the soft click of the door—along with the sudden chill that prickled the hairs on my arm now that his body was no longer pressed so intimately against mine—the only sign he'd been there.

"Dammit," I said, staggering over to Edgar's desk chair. "Damn *him*."

The satin of my nightgown rubbed over my now highly sensitized breasts as I sat down, giving me a full-body shiver. "And damn my lack of control."

Lying on top of a stack of packing manifests that I'd placed on Edgar's desk over the last few days was a yellow certified check. The amount was enough to make me wish I owned the shop, instead of just working at it as Edgar's researcher and general lackey, but my gaze moved quickly to the name of the strange, sexy man who had paid such a staggering amount for a leaf out of a medieval manuscript.

Archer Andras. I stroked a finger across the name, mentally going through Edgar's customer list. I had a pretty good memory where such things were concerned, and I'd never seen such an uncommon name. Without thinking about it, I found myself picking up the small prayer rug and folding it before placing it on the desk, digging through Edgar's inbox until I found a manifest I'd placed there that morning.

LOT 15A-VENICE. Sold to E. Wendell, Ross, California, USA. Contents: (1) prayer rug, 0.76 m x 1.22 m, wool and silk, c. 1811. (1) blow pipe, 15 cm x 4 cm, wood, c. 1788. (1) manuscript leaf, 188 mm x 137 mm, vellum, dated by scribe on colophon leaf 1474.

"Manuscript leaf," I murmured, putting the small wood blowpipe back in the box where Auburn Hair had removed it during his search. "What the hell was on the leaf that Mr. Handsome Eyes Archer was willing to pay triple the amount Edgar spent on it?"

I pulled up the low-resolution pictures I'd taken of it

that morning, but there was nothing that rang any bells in my scholar's brain. The top had a scrawled hand in Latin, while the rest was in code. I'd planned on trying to crack the cipher, since that was my hobby, but the leaf sold before I had time to really look at it.

What was so important about it that the two men broke in to get it rather than wait until the morning?

I was still mulling over that question eleven hours later when Edgar called to check in. As usual, he dominated the conversation, barely letting me get a word in.

"Be sure you pack the set carefully. Dr. Monroe chewed me out over the last set of books you sent him, and demanded I give him a discount on this sale. I didn't, of course, because that's not how you get ahead in the world, but I don't want him annoyed any more than he is. Did you get the items from the last two auctions?"

"I think so. We received a small box of jade figurines on Wednesday, and one shipment came yesterday morning. A small box of books came last night, while I was out."

"You were out? Why were you out?" he asked suspiciously. "I won't have you taking unauthorized time off! I pay you to be at the store to receive the shipments and process them appropriately, not gallivanting about wasting my time and money! You can be replaced, you know! There are other unemployed scholars, hundreds of them, just aching to have a cushy job like yours! You remember that the next time you try to cheat me!"

"Edgar, I'm not cheating you," I interrupted, knowing it was no use to try stopping him until he was good and ready to listen. Which, sadly, was hardly ever. "I didn't leave early. I didn't know there was a carrier coming, or I would have stayed with Jamie."

"You're paid to receive those shipments and get them online!" he snarled into the phone. I held it a foot away from my ear, sighing heavily. "I don't care how long you have to stay, I won't have my valuable property being left on the doorstep because you're out sucking off some man."

"Edgar!" I said, shocked by his vulgarity. "I was not out with a man, not that it's any of your business. I left at my regular time, and as I said, I had no idea that another shipment was coming—"

"See to it that you know when the next one comes in," he snapped. I thought about asking him how I was to expect to do that when he didn't share shipping information with me, but I had a more important subject to bring up. He continued before I could tell him the good news about the manuscript. "There's a prayer rug in the shipment that I want you to process, but be careful with it. It's supposed to be imbued with demonic powers."

"It's what?" I asked on a gasp, staring at the innocuous-looking rug that sat folded neatly next to the stack of papers I was idly rifling through. I picked up a stapler and used it to move the rug over a foot.

"Just process it as usual, but don't touch it unless you have to. The seller said that his daughter summoned a demon using it, which is why he tossed it into the auction lot. Had to get rid of it so the stupid girl wouldn't keep using it. Pull up a list of demonologists, and send them the info on it, but don't give them a price. We'll see what offers come in before I decide what to ask for it."

I eyed the prayer rug. "Someone summoned...*a demon*?"

"I've told you not to worry about anything odd like that. The people who are involved with the Otherworld aren't interested in freaks like you; they just want objects of power," he said, obviously not minding that he had just insulted me.

I ignored the mention of his pet conspiracy theory—that there was a group of supernatural beings who mingled among normal people—and gritted my teeth for a moment over the sting of his insult. "Just as you like. Oh, I sold the manuscript leaf that came yesterday. It was snapped up almost immediately. In fact, the buyer came by late last night to pick it up—"

"What? What the hell did you say?" Edgar's voice rose an octave. "What the fuck did you do with my manuscript?"

"I sold it. For the maximum amount," I said, knowing that Edgar's policy of setting an initial price that was way above what an object was worth should make him happy. I decided to leave out that the men had taken me by surprise and the odd reaction I had had to Archer. "The buyer came with a certified check and took the leaf away with him last night."

"WHAT THE HELL DID YOU DO?" he screamed

into the phone, loud enough that it made pain lance my eardrum. "You stupid bitch! Are you telling me you sold that manuscript? For how much?"

I told him, wondering what was going on. My palms pricked with sweat at his reaction, worry flaring to life within me. "It's well above what you normally ask—"

"You stupid bitch!" he repeated, screaming in my ear. "Who did you sell it to?"

"A man named Archer," I said quietly, my stomach twisting on itself again. "The price was good—"

He raged even harder, calling me names that I pretended not to hear. I gritted my teeth while he worked off the worst of his bile.

When he paused for a breath, I spoke as calmly as I could, despite shaking and feeling sick at the attack I'd just survived. The irony that Edgar could make me feel a hundred times worse than Archer's unexpected visit didn't escape me. "You didn't tell me *not* to sell the manuscript, Edgar. I had no idea you wanted to keep it—"

"Get it back," he snarled, his voice low now, but his breath came as fast and rough as if he'd just run a marathon. But it was the undertone of pure, unadulterated threat that left goose bumps prickling along my arms. "You will get it back, or I will break every bone in your body, and when I'm done with you, I'll break your precious grandmother. Do you hear me? Get the fucking thing back, or you will wish you had never been born."

I was shocked into silence. Edgar was not the best

employer by any stretch of the imagination, but there weren't a lot of jobs available for someone with degrees in art history, medieval history, and art restoration. Especially for someone who shunned museums with staff members constantly staring and commenting about people who looked different.

"What was the problem with selling it?" I asked, sick with fear. "If you had told me you didn't want it sold—"

"I could get ten times that amount, that's what the problem is, you stupid slag! You have until tomorrow to get it back. If you don't...well, you brought it upon yourself. And your grandmother. Don't forget that. If she suffers, it'll be your fault." His voice seeped horror from the phone, making me shiver.

He hung up before I could do anything more than sit in a stunned state of shock and disbelief. He hadn't really threatened Gran, had he? He knew how vulnerable she was, how frail, and how hard I worked to keep her in the care facility where they treated her with compassion. Driven by a need too horrible to face, I called the facility and asked to talk to my grandmother.

"Thaisa? Isn't this your day to visit?" one of the carers asked. "I will hold the phone up for her, but I'm afraid she's having one of her foggy days."

"That's okay. I just want her to hear my voice, even if she doesn't realize it's me," I said, and spent the next ten minutes prattling mindlessly, talking about nothing and anything and not getting any response other than a few unintelligible murmurs.

"I'll see you in a few hours, Gran," I said at the end of my time. "I'll bring you some puzzle magazines, all right?"

"Puzzle books?" My grandmother stopped mumbling to herself. I could almost see her eyes light up. "I like puzzle books."

"I know you do. I'll bring some tonight. Love you."

"What am I doing with this phone?" I heard her ask the attendant, who said a brief goodbye to me before hanging up.

I have never been a forceful person, preferring reason rather than passion, and never have I acted in an aggressive manner toward anyone, but as I sat there on Edgar's chair, sightlessly staring at his desk, resolve was born deep in my belly. I would do whatever it took to protect that dear, lovely, gentle woman. If it meant demanding that handsome Archer give back the manuscript, then demand I would. And when I was done, when I had given Edgar his damned manuscript leaf, I would quit. I would rather live on the streets and give the care facility every cent I earned from some menial job rather than continue with a man who could so callously threaten a harmless old woman.

The door opened, and a laconic Jamie wandered into the office, picking at his teeth. "Hey, Thaisa, there's a man here who wants to buy that Spinoza set, and the check is for over a hundred bucks. Can you come approve it?"

A red wave of anger washed over me, foreign to my normally less volatile nature, the strength of it forcing me to my feet. I slammed my hand down on the desk, snarling, "And if that bastard ever messes with me again, he'll be the one who will suffer. I'll kill him myself before I let him so much as touch a hair on Gran's head!"

Jamie's eyes widened, and he backed out of the office, his Adam's apple bobbing frantically. "Holy shit! Okay, I'll tell him he has to use plastic!"

The anger ebbed away at his words. I looked up but saw only Jamie's back as he scurried out to the cash register in the main room. "What? Did you want me, Jamie? Oh...hell!"

CHAPTER FOUR

MY PHONE RANG WHILE I WAS SNARLING ARCHAIC
obscenities at a website that refused to give me what
I wanted unless I paid a large sum.

"What?" I snapped, answering it absently without
even looking to see who was calling. Immediately,
guilt pinged me. "Er...sorry, hello."

"Wow. If you worked for anyone else, I'd ask you
what bee got up your butt, but knowing the man for-
merly known as my husband, I don't have any doubt
he's been working your nerves. What's the matter,
Tha? What's the bastard done to you now?"

"Oh, Laura," I said, a sudden rush of tears making
my eyes swim as self-pity swarmed all over the anger

that had been my constant friend the last few hours. "He really is a bastard."

"Uh-oh." Her tone, which had been light, sobered instantly. "He totally is, but you almost never admit it. What's up? Wait, can you tell me in...er...two and a half minutes?"

"I don't...I guess," I said confused. "Why the time limit?"

"I'm on a plane and we're about to take off. I've been called to the Portland office for a couple of days. What did Edgar do to make you so upset? You sound like you're crying."

"Not quite, but it's a close thing." I swallowed back the lump of tears that made my throat ache. "He threated to hurt Gran."

She said something very profane. "Call the cops."

"I can't. I mean, I did, and asked if a verbal threat was enough to get a restraining order against him in Gran's name, and the police said no, mostly because he's on the other side of the country, but if he continues, then I can lodge a harassment complaint. But other than that, they won't do anything."

She swore again. "Why is he being such a dick?"

"You remember last night at the bar?" I asked, trying to pick out what I wanted to tell her. For some reason that I didn't understand, I felt almost reluctant to explain how Archer had held me against the wall. I decided that hiding behind my embarrassment at my reaction to his body being pressed against mine was a sign of cowardice and blurted it all out in one garbled sentence. "The man with the pretty eyes, the tall one not the auburn-haired one, he was in the office when I came home, but he wasn't alone. He had the other guy here, too, and they were rifling through some items that Edgar had sent here, and when he saw me, he pushed me up against the wall and squashed me against it with his body, saying that I'd tried to trick him and not give him a manuscript he bought, but I was going to send it to him today, so I let him take it and holy hellballs, was he hot, really hot, not just sexy hot but physically hot, and I think you're right after all that I'm going to need a man because if I could get so hot and bothered by one man leaning on me, then what does that say about my life?"

"Wow. That was a hell of a sentence. Dammit, can I just…Fine. Sorry, Tha, I have to turn off my phone now. I'll call you as soon as I'm free, okay? I just wanted to tell you that I can't do dinner tonight after all, but Bree said she'd fill in for me. Love you!"

The phone went dead before I could respond.

I glared at the laptop screen, frustration making my skin feel itchy. "Why is nothing going right today?"

The door of Edgar's office creaked open just enough for Jamie to stick his nose through it. "Uh, Thaisa? It's my lunchtime. I was going to get a burger, but if you don't want to come out and watch the store—"

"No, that's okay," I said, glancing at the clock and stretching as I stood up. "I didn't realize it was so late. You go off to lunch, and I'll do my research out at the register."

Jamie was still a bit skittish about me after the morning's episode, despite my copious apologies about my behavior. He flashed me a few nervous looks while he got his skateboard and headed off to a burger place near a local skate park. I went out to the front desk, but there were only two people in the store, and I could tell at a glance that they were browsers, neither one likely to buy anything. I settled behind the cash register and pulled out my phone, about to continue the Internet search on the term *Archer Andras California*, but at that moment the shop phone rang.

"The Illustrated Grimoire," I answered, making a face to myself at the search results.

"Good afternoon," a smooth voice said, one that instantly had me setting down my cell phone. It had a husky quality, and a mix of an English and Irish accent. "Do I have the pleasure of speaking with Thaisa Moore?"

"Speaking," I said, a little prickle of awareness skittering down my back.

"Excellent. My name is Vehar, and I understand that you are the finest scholar on the subject of medieval Europe to be found in Northern California. I wish to discuss a little project with you."

"I'm...I'm flattered," I said, uneasy for some reason I couldn't pinpoint. "But I assure you that I'm far from being the finest scholar. There are any number of good ones at the university—"

"Ah, but they are evidently away attending a conference in Frankfurt. And you, fortunately, are here.

Would you be available to meet with me? Say this evening?"

"What does your project entail?" I asked.

"The translation of an obscure French work dating to the late fifteenth century. I believe it to be a fable, but alas, it's written in a cipher, which I understand is your specialty."

"It is." If I convinced Archer to let Edgar have his manuscript back, then I could quit and thus would need the income a freelance job would provide. "I would be delighted to look at your manuscript and am available this evening. Er... are you in the Santa Mar area?"

"Indeed I am. Since I am aware women of your standing are no doubt loathe to meet with a stranger in a private home, shall we meet in a public venue? There is a club whose atmosphere I can recommend, one where we might discuss the details of the project."

"Thank you, I appreciate you picking a public place." He gave me the address and suggested nine as a meeting time. I did a fast check on the club, decided the overwhelmingly good reviews meant it would be a safe place to meet, and agreed to do so. "I'll be there," I promised, my mind already returning to the problem of finding Archer.

"I look forward to seeing what you make of this," he said in that silky voice that sent another peal of warning bells off in my head. I couldn't quite pinpoint what worried me about this man but figured so long as I was aware of what was going on around me in the club, it would be fine.

Besides, I had much more important problems to tackle than a man who made me vaguely uneasy. A half hour later, I was still struggling with a search for Archer's information. All I found was a man bearing that name associated with a coastal town a half-hour drive from me, so I knew it had to be the correct Archer, but how was I supposed to find his house number without paying for that information?

Suddenly, I remembered the e-mail printout and ran to fetch it.

"Got you now, Mr. Sexy Eyes," I said, going back out to the register, almost immediately disappointed when the e-mail lacked a physical address.

"Really? That sounds good, unless all you have are eyes." Bree sat on the counter next to the register, swinging her legs and leafing through a small book the size of a modern-day cell phone. My eyes widened not just at her outfit (hot-pink velvet corset and bloodred tulle skirt), but also at which book she was holding.

"Bree!" I dropped the e-mail printout and sprinted to her, doing a little dance in front of her. "That's the *Liber Salomonis*! How did you get that? It was locked up in the case. Please, be careful with it. It's very old, and very fragile."

"It's not a very good grimoire," she said, flipping through a couple more pages, almost giving me a heart attack at the thought of what the oils on her fingers would do to the fragile pages. "There are loads of mistakes here. Take this…" She pointed at one of the pages. I eeped, and ran back into the office to grab a pair of the cotton conservation gloves I wore whenever touching fragile objects.

"Their suffumigation of Hermetis is all backward. They have the days mixed up, and the four Nota Orationem are just dead wrong. Ha! Dead wrong! Pun!"

"Let me just take that from you," I said, gently prying her hands from the book, sighing in relief when there was no visible sign of damage. I placed it back in the climate-controlled case that sat next to the register, propping it back up on a stand, a discreet price tag next to it on the archival cloth that lined the case. I made sure it was locked tight before turning back to Bree. "I don't know how you got that out of there, but please don't do it again. The books in the climate cases are all very fragile, and extremely valuable. This one is such a prize that Edgar doesn't want to sell it. Unless, of course, someone has the price of a small house; then he'd probably let it go."

"I don't see why anyone would want it when it's just wrong about so many things," Bree said, pulling another book onto her lap. This one was slightly bigger. "Let's see how badly this *Liber Iuratus Honorii* gets things wrong."

"No!" I squawked, all but snatching the book out of her hand. I gave her a long glare before I replaced it in the second case, also climate controlled and also locked. "That is a very rare copy I only just finished transcribing."

"Really?" Bree tipped her head to the side as I counted the books in the two cases. They were all present. I don't know how she'd gotten them out of there while leaving the cases locked, but so long as they weren't hurt, I wasn't going to lecture her.

Not overly much, anyway.

"Yes, really. That's what I do—I translate the works that Edgar finds. A lot of them are copies made by scribes who intentionally—or unintentionally—slightly tweaked the original text, and it's actually quite interesting to see what changes were made, and speculate why. In that *Iuratus Honorri*, for instance, I found a section talking about making a type of amulet that I've never seen referenced anywhere else."

"Dragon amulet," she said, nodding, and to my utter amazement, recited, " '*After this ye shall know that the first seven-cornered star be made of azure, the second of vert, the third of crimson, the fourth of night, and the round circle of or.*' That was the forming of the dragon race, although I've not heard of gold dragons."

I gawked at her. "How... Where did you... Have you studied—"

"Laura says I'm supposed to take you to dinner," she said, jumping down off the counter. "Did you want to talk about the dragon from last night?"

My mind felt like it was circling around and around. I couldn't get over her knowing about the passage on amulets that I'd never seen anywhere else. "The what?"

"I'm assuming you must have seen him again." She reached out and touched one of my earlobes with a finger, holding it up to show me. "Dragon scales."

"What on earth are you talking about?" I asked,

shaking my head and wondering if Edgar had finally driven me stark, staring mad.

"Could be a dragon hunter, but their scales don't usually shine like this," she said, considering her fingertip. "Hey, let's do Chinese."

I stared at her in confusion, finally shaking my head a second time. It didn't help any more than the first time I tried to clear it. "I would be happy to have dinner with you tonight, but I have to see my grandmother first. Chinese is fine. There's a good restaurant out by the home my gran is in, so we could meet there."

"I'll come with you," she said, beaming a happy smile at me. "Old ladies love me! What time?"

"Er…" I was at a loss as to how to tell her politely that my grandmother had few visitors, most of whom she didn't recognize. "I suppose it would be all right for you to come, but my gran gets confused easily, and I wouldn't want her upset."

"I'll bring a puppy," she promised after I told her the address of the home. She hurried toward the door, pausing long enough to look back and say with absolute sincerity, "Everyone loves a puppy, right?"

"No animals are allowed at the home—" I started to say, but with a little wave, she was through the door and dashing down the street. "Except service animals," I finished, suddenly exhausted, like I'd gone five rounds with a boxer.

I touched my earlobe, then examined my finger. There was nothing on it but the faintest shimmer of iridescent glitter, and I was sure that had come from the dash of powder I'd put on my face that morning in lieu of cosmetics. "That girl is downright loopy!"

The rest of the day crawled by. I sent an e-mail to Archer asking him to contact me immediately, packaged up a couple of orders that Edgar had indicated needed to go out, was in place to receive the day's arrival of two silver goblets and an ugly little statuette depicting a man riding a frog, and spent the rest of the time trying to force the Internet to give up its secrets on one Archer Andras.

By the time I was due to leave, I was thoroughly frustrated and had sent two more e-mails to Archer with increasingly agitated demands that he contact me as soon as possible or provide me with a number where I could reach him. After reminding Jamie that he was in charge of the store and leaving him with strict instructions to make sure the doors were locked, the alarm set, and lights were turned off, I decided that I'd just have to pony up the money to the background check site in order to get Archer's contact information.

Bree was waiting when I got to the assisted living home where Gran lived. To my utter relief, the puppy she had brought was of the stuffed toy variety, a cute golden retriever with huge eyes that reminded me of hers. What was even more of a surprise was that Bree was absolutely right—she was the hit of the home, flitting from one elderly resident to another, all bubbly personality and bright chatter. Gran clutched the toy puppy that Bree had given her, cooing over it and stroking it just as if it were a real dog, making me feel ashamed of myself for a few minutes that I hadn't thought to give her such a gift.

When we left an hour later, several of the more mobile residents gathered around the door to wave us off, extracting promises from Bree to visit them again.

"That was fun," she said, taking my arm as we wove our way around people doing their evening shopping. I had donned a pair of sunglasses as I usually did in daylight hours, finding solace in the way it hid so many of my oddities. "I like your gran. She's very smart."

"She used to be, yes. She's a bit more...vague... now, but when I was little, we'd work books of cryptic puzzles together. Our favorites were the ciphers. Gran was a whiz at them. Bree..." I hesitated, not wanting to ruin what had been a surprisingly pleasant evening so far, but at the same time, victim of my own curiosity. "How did you know about that passage from the *Liber Iuratus Honorii*? I only translated that a few months ago and haven't sent it to any of the academic groups yet."

"Oooh, this place has almond chicken. Mama loves almond chicken," she said, peering at the menu posted on a restaurant window. "We can get loads of that, unless you don't like it."

I followed her into the restaurant, smiling when a harried young woman nodded and pointed us to a table near the window. "As a matter of fact, I try not to eat too much meat, but I suppose a little chicken wouldn't hurt. Is there a reason you're changing the subject, or do you just not want to answer my question?"

"Why would I do that?" she asked, taking great enjoyment in loudly slurping the cup of tea that she'd just poured. "Now, what are we going to do tonight?"

"Actually, I have plans." I decided to let go of the fact that she once again hadn't answered my question; I had more important things to focus on, like getting a hold of a certain pale-eyed man. "I'm sorry if you thought we were going to go to another movie or do something fun like that, but I'm afraid I have a project I'm trying to deal with, and an unrelated appointment for a little medieval cipher-breaking job at nine, so I won't be able to spend time with you."

"Oooh, is your project something fun? I can help." She clasped her hands and watched me with bright, interested eyes.

"I doubt if you can. I need to get in contact with a man—"

"Wow, that was quick," she interrupted; then she looked out the window and suddenly waved enthusiastically at a woman who was slogging her way up the hill. The woman looked startled at being so greeted, and with her head down, hurriedly charged past. "Did Laura find you someone, or did you find a man yourself?"

"I...er...found one myself. I guess. Although it's not a romantic thing. Do you remember anything about last night?"

"Lots. I jumped Ramon's bones, then he jumped mine, and then we slept."

I paused in the act of pouring myself a cup of tea

and gawked at her for a moment, before deciding that was too rude. "I meant earlier, when we were together."

"Ah," she said, her eyes narrowing on me. "The bar at the hotel."

"Yes, actually. The two men that we…uh… commented on, in particular."

"Dragons," she said, nodding.

"They were actually in the office— What? Dragons? What about them?"

"The two dragons you had the hots for." She poured herself another cup of tea, examining the little bowl containing packets of various types of sugar.

I took a deep breath, wondering if Bree took drugs. She didn't seem to exhibit any signs of an addiction, but there was really no other way to explain the sorts of things she said, unless she was mentally ill, and I'd discounted that idea earlier at Gran's home. She had been nothing but charming and caring to a bunch of elderly, confused people. "Okay, I'm going to say something that is borderline insulting, and I apologize for it in advance, but are you all right?"

"Sure thing. Why do you ask?" She tipped her head to the side to consider me.

"Dragons," I said succinctly.

"Yeah. The one you snogged last night. Wait, *snogged* is the right word, isn't it?" A little frown creased her forehead. "It means kiss, right? I saw it in a movie, and next to hats of asses, it's my new favorite phrase."

"It does mean that, but I didn't kiss a dragon last night. I didn't kiss anyone, as a matter of fact," I answered, pushing aside the memory of Archer's hot breath steaming the shivery spot behind my ear. Just thinking about that made my thighs feel weak. "Even if I had, I would have kissed a man, and not a mythical being with wings and a penchant for virgins."

"Yeah, about that..."

The waitress arrived with our food just at that moment, which made Bree—who had ordered five different dishes that she wanted to try—cheer.

I waited until she had a loaded plate (and wished I still had the sort of metabolism that allowed me to eat anything and everything without a care), before suddenly blurting out, "How old are you?"

She looked up, sucking in a noodle, her nose scrunching as she clearly thought. "One thousand, seven hundred...No, that's not right." She set down her fork and counted on her fingers, her mouth working silently. "One thousand, eight hundred, and forty-two."

"Not in days, silly, how many years are you? Wait." I did my own mental addition. "That wouldn't even be right if it was days. Did you count in weeks?"

"Years," she said indistinctly around a mouth of food.

"I see." I just stared at her, my gut filled with sadness. If it wasn't drugs, then clearly she had a mental illness, one that left her delusional. But it wasn't my business to point that out to her. I made a promise that I would be supportive and helpful if she wanted either, but I wouldn't push her to seek help unless she made noises along those lines.

"How old are you? In days?" she asked.

I pulled up my phone's calculator. "Discounting leap years, thirteen thousand, one hundred, and forty days."

"Cool," she said. "Do you have a date to snog the dragon tonight after seeing the cipher dude? Or can we hang together because we're besties and Ramon has practice with his band?"

I had just sworn to myself that I would be supportive and helpful, and here I was already wishing to tell her I was busy later. "I don't mind spending time with you, but what I have to do is going to be extremely boring. I have some computer research to do, although perhaps you might like to browse through some of the books in the shop while I do it. The ones that aren't worth a fortune. I don't know about later..." My uneasiness rose again at the memory of that man's silken voice in my ear. I thought for a minute, my eyes on her, trying to weigh the comfort of having someone with me to the practicality of her annoying a potential customer.

In the end I decided that I had enough on my plate without the cipher breaking, so if I lost the job because the client didn't like Bree, it wouldn't really matter. "All right," I told her. "You can come with me to the club to meet the cipher man."

"Awesome! I'll be your protector and keep you safe," she said, flexing one arm.

"Mmm-hmm."

"What are we doing before that? Your project that you have to do?"

I ignored the loud slurping sounds as she guzzled sweet and sour soup, saying carefully, "The two men we saw in the bar last night showed up in my boss's office later on. The tall one, whose name is Archer, bought a manuscript leaf from Edgar, and he came to claim it. However, Edgar...well, Edgar is being a hat of asses and changed his mind about selling to Archer, which means I have to get the manuscript leaf back. I'm trying to find Archer's house or a phone number without having to pay a month's salary, that's all. It'll be just me and the laptop, so if you have more exciting things to do..." I let the sentence drift off, hoping she'd lose interest.

"So, you're trying to find this Archer dragon dude?" Her nose scrunched up again as she chewed a massive mouthful of kung pao beef. "Why pay all that money for something that you can get easily?"

"Easily?" I shook my head. "I've spent the whole day investigating how to get Archer's contact info. You know how the news stations always say it's dead easy for anyone to find out anything about you online? That's absolutely not true about Archer. There's almost nothing about him. Nada. Zip."

Bree belched, giggled, and excused herself, then, evidently sated after consuming all the food before her, looked around the restaurant. "There's more than one way to skin a behemoth." She looked thoughtful for a moment. "Four ways, actually. Come on, if you're done, let's go see what you have in your shop that can help you."

"In the shop? Wait, Bree...dammit." I hurried over to settle the bill, more than a little peeved that I was stuck paying for everything she consumed, before running up the street after her.

By the time we reached the shop, I was out of breath from the hills in our neighborhood. I unlocked the front door, turned off the alarm, and flipped on a couple of lights before collapsing onto Edgar's chair in his office. "No wonder you can eat anything you like," I panted, picking up a sheet of paper to fan myself. "One more block would have killed me."

Bree was nosing around the room, poking into the various items Edgar had bought that were waiting for processing. She set down a bone goblet and moved over to the desk. "What's that?" she asked, pointing to where I'd stuffed the prayer rug into a large plastic bag.

"A demonic prayer rug." I turned on the laptop and returned to my Google search for info on Archer.

"Really? Cool!"

"It's not real, obviously. I mean, the rug part is, but the demon bit is just a story," I said, giving her a look that said she ought to know better. "Edgar spun some song-and-dance about it summoning a demon, but it's not the truth. He only does it to entice buyers."

She took the bag and dumped the rug onto the desk, holding her hand over it for a second before snatching it back and shaking it, as if she'd been stung. "Why do you think that?"

"Because demons aren't any more real than dragons are. Hmm. I wonder if a private detective would be cheaper?" I tapped a few keys, making a face at the rates listed.

Bree got a giant pair of fire tongs that were leaning in the corner of the room and used them to pick up the prayer rug, hauling it over to the center of the office before spreading it out on the floor. "You spend your days translating grimoires and other magical texts, and you don't believe in demons?" She shook her head. "That just don't make sense, son."

I glanced at her, thought about it for a few seconds, then admitted she had a point. "People a few hundred years ago believed in a lot of stuff that isn't real. What are you doing?"

"Setting up the demon rug. Normally I frown on calling up demons because the place I work for discourages that sort of thing, but since you're stuck and need a little push getting to the Archer dragon, then we'll risk it. You have some salt?"

I blinked at her a couple of times, unsure if I should take her aside and have a mental health talk with her now or if that was too invasive. "I . . . yes. Are you talking about drawing a circle of salt?"

She grinned. "Who better to summon a demon than a woman who has read all the instruction books?"

"Bree . . ." I was silent for the count of six, half of me feeling my online search was a waste of time and the other half genuinely worried about her mental state. On the other hand, I was tired of feeling frustrated and helpless. I hadn't gotten anywhere trying common sense and the organized method; maybe it was time to try the unorthodox and unrealistic. "You know what? Let's do this."

"That's the attitude! You get the salt and gold, and I'll get the dead man's ash."

"We don't have any—" I stopped when she pulled a small glass jar from behind a couple of Edgar's personal book collection. "Oh. I guess we do."

"Your boss knows how to do things right," she said, opening the jar and sniffing at it. "This stuff is fresh. You'll have to draw the circle. I'd get into all sorts of trouble if I did it."

"Sure, why not. I've got nothing better to do until nine. Thank God Jamie has an addiction to hard-boiled eggs and likes them salty." I fetched a small bottle of salt from Jamie's snack drawer and trotted back to Edgar's office, where I smoothed out the prayer rug, noting as I did so that some moths had gotten to it at some point. It was a muddy sort of red, with little yellow threads running through it, but mostly it was so faded and dirty that the original pattern couldn't be determined. "Right, drawing a circle made of salt now."

"You want me to call the quarters, or do you want to?" she asked.

"Don't I have to?" I asked, drawing a thin circle with the salt.

"If you were using something modern, yes, but this is an old rug, so it will expect things done the old way," she said, standing and spreading her arms out wide and turning to face east. "Apprentices were always used to call the quarters while the practitioner did the actual summoning. Bide ye with us, sylphs of the air, to guard and protect us."

I sprinkled the ash Bree found in the salt circle, being careful to touch it as little as possible. I didn't truly believe the rug was evil in itself. Still, I acknowledged as I scooted my way around it, I was just superstitious enough to be wary of it.

Bree turned to the north, and recognizing the calling of quarters that she'd used, I mouthed with her, "Bide ye with us, stones and rocks of the fields, to guard and protect us."

She turned to the west. "Bide ye with us, naiads of the depths, to guard and protect us."

I sat back on my heels and eyed the circle, mentally running down the instructions given in many of the old grimoires, making sure it was complete and whole. I didn't want Bree using an improperly drawn circle as an excuse why nothing had happened.

I stood and turned south with Bree, unable to keep from saying with her, "Bide ye with us, dragons of the embers, to guard and protect us."

"What demon are you going to summon?" Bree asked.

"I don't know. I suppose I could look at a list in one of the *Liber*s."

"There's one that's been hanging around Santa Mar a lot lately," she said, sitting cross-legged next to the rug. "Naamah."

"Sounds as good as any. Naamah. I think I know

that name." I dug through my memory, pulling out a
name that I'd read in one of the grimoires. "She had a
fling with Adam after he dumped Eve, and bore him
demonic kids."

"The plagues of mankind!" Bree said, nodding.
"She used to hang out with Henry the Eighth."

"Uh...sure," I said, and fetched a photocopy of a
valuable grimoire held in the British Museum. I drew
the symbols related to the demon Naamah. "Last
thing...blood."

I dashed upstairs to my bathroom, grabbed a safety
pin that held the curtain closed, and after dipping it in
some rubbing alcohol, pricked my thumb with it, carefully nursing the drop of blood as I made my way back
to Edgar's office. Carefully, I dabbed the drop of blood
on the circle of salt.

"Okay, that should be it. Ready?"

Bree nodded and, grabbing a small fire extinguisher
that had been tucked in the corner with the fire tongs,
stood at the ready.

"You think we're going to need that?" I asked her,
standing so I could hold my hands over the circle.

"It's just in case Naamah is testy about being summoned. She used to have the best resting bitch face
ever."

I pursed my lips, keeping back comments that I
knew would not be welcome, and instead said, "I con-
jure thee, Naamah, by the power of thy lord Oriens, to
appear before me now without noise and terror. I command thee, Naamah, to my will by the virtue of my

power. By my hand thy shall be bound, by my blood thy shall be bound, by my voice thy shall be bound!"

Bree frowned. "I don't think that's quite—"

I was about to turn to see what she was saying when something amazing happened. The air inside the circle seemed to thicken, like it was made of clear gelatin that clumped up, twisting upon itself until it started to take shape.

The shape of a handsome man with blond hair that had been slicked back, a shirt open to the waist, and a pair of black leather pants. The man's eyebrow rose in obvious question.

"Holy shit," I said, my mouth agape as I stared at the man, then looked down at the photocopy of grimoire pages still held in my hand. "Holy everlasting shit. What...uh..."

"Hello, Naamah," Bree said, sauntering forward, the fire extinguisher still held in her arms. "I see you're a man now. How are the kids?"

"Busy as ever," Naamah said. "You know how it is with plague-bringers...there's always work to be had somewhere."

My gaze swiveled from the man who stood on the prayer rug, his dark eyes glinting with something that I took to be pure evil, over to Bree. "You know...uh... know this person?"

"Demon. I told you, she...sorry, he...used to hang around Henry's court."

The man smirked. "Those were good days. Happy days."

"I can't…" I shook my head. "I can't believe this is happening. How…"

The man…no, not man, demon…rolled his eyes and gave a big martyred sigh. "Great. Another witless person has summoned me. You'd think the Otherworld would educate its denizens better. You want me to hold your hand? Fine, although I'm only doing this because Oriens is having in a lecturer on diversity awareness issues, and attendance is mandatory for those in residence. What is it you desire of me, oh, master?"

I just stared at him, my brain still struggling to wrap itself around the fact that everything I'd studied for the last twelve years, everything I'd translated, read, and summarized was true.

Demons are real.

"We want information on the Archer dragon," Bree told the demon, giving me a nudge with her elbow.

"You know the rules," Naamah said, covering his mouth while he yawned.

"You have to ask the questions," Bree told me. "It's a demon rule."

"Huh?" At last my brain chugged into action, decided that if this was the way things were going to be, then it would be better to go with the flow and stop balking and wasting time.

Gran's well-being was at risk, after all.

"Right," I said, anger firing up at the memory of Edgar's threats. "Demon Naamah, I command thee to…er…" I turned to Bree and whispered, "What can a demon do that I can't do?"

"Find the Archer dragon," she said.

"His last name is Andras, not Dragon." I looked speculatively at the demon. "I command thee by my voice, my hand, my blood to locate the address and/or phone number of Archer Andras. According to the info I did manage to find, he's in a town on the coast, although that might be outdated information. Can you do that?"

The demon rolled his eyes again, then gestured toward the circle. "Release me, and it shall be as you demand, oh, mighty mortal master."

"Oh, sure." I quickly released the quarters, then rubbed out a bit of the salt circle, breaking it so the demon could leave it. "Do you need anything to do the job?"

"Well, since you ask"—the demon bent and picked up the prayer rug, folding it and tucking it under his arm before strolling out of the office—"this will do nicely."

"Um?" I asked, looking at Bree.

"Go after it," she said, making shooing motions.

"Is he leaving? Hey, Naamah? Where are you going?"

I ran after him, catching up just as he was about to open the front door. "You can't just leave!"

"No? Watch me."

"You're supposed to do as I bid you! All the books say that! I give you a command, and you have to do it," I argued, following him onto the sidewalk.

"Says who? I'd say farewell, but you know how it

is." He gave a little bob of his head and tapped his chest. "Demon. We don't do nice."

"You can't just leave!" I squawked again, unsure of what I was to do in that situation. Should I run after him? Command him to stop? Send him back to hell, where he belonged?

"Demons, man," Bree said in a "what are you going to do about it?" tone.

"Can he do that?" I tried to remember what the grimoires said about the abilities of demons in the control of the summoner. "Shouldn't he have to do everything I say?"

"If you had added the line about that to the summoning, yeah," Bree said, doing a little spin and throwing her hands up to the night sky. "You left it out. I wondered about it at the time, but since you didn't include it, he's not bound to you."

"Well, hell!" I said.

"It's called Abaddon, actually."

I stared at her.

She grinned. "It's what mortals think of as hell, but I don't suppose you care an awful lot about that now."

"No, I don't. That man...that *demon* has got Edgar's rug." I closed my eyes in mingled horror and sorrow. "And I just let him walk off with it."

"Don't worry," she said, punching me lightly on the arm. "We aren't helpless."

"We aren't? I sure feel that way." A headache started to bloom in the back of my head. I rubbed it, wondering if I could disappear with Gran sufficiently that

Edgar would never find us. I glanced at my watch. "Crapballs! I have to get going if I'm going to make that club by nine. Dammit, this would happen to me right now."

"There are a couple of dragon hunters who live on this coast. We'll call them after your cipher appointment."

"You have dragons on the mind, kid," I told her, my stomach sick at the thought of what I'd done. The information in the grimoires was real, demons were real, and I'd just let one steal Edgar's rug. He was *so* going to kill me when he found out.

"Dragon hunters take care of demons," she said with a shrug. "You need one to get your rug back. Where is your cipher dude meeting you?"

I looked at a note I'd made on my phone. "We're meeting in about twenty minutes at some place called T and G."

Bree clapped her hands and did a little jig. "That's great!"

"You know it?"

"Of course I do." She pulled out her phone and punched in a text message. "It's *the* spot to see and be seen."

"It is?" I asked, my stomach now turning over with the knowledge that I'd just gone from the frying pan to the demonic fire. Not only had I summoned a demon—which was loose doing who knew what—but I had to show up at what sounded like a fancy club without having time to change into anything a little nicer. I glanced down at my black-and-white polka-dot retro sundress, trying to smooth wrinkles out of the bodice. "That's just what I need. I wish the client had told me it was a chic place. Oh, well, I'm just meeting him there. It's not like I have to work in that sort of a chaotic environment."

"You'll fit in perfectly there," Bree said, sliding her phone into her bag. "It's the West Coast version of a famous club in Paris. This one is called Theurgy and Goety."

"White and black magic?" I asked absently, my mind whirling around as to what I could possibly do to salvage the horrible turn my life had taken. Run away with Gran? I didn't have the funds for that. Plead for mercy from Edgar? I gave a shudder. He didn't have any. Get the police involved? How on earth would I explain a demon stole my evil prayer rug?

"There's bound to be someone there who will be able to tackle Naamah once you talk to your cipher dude, and we get your thingie back from the Archer dragon."

"Manuscript leaf," I said sadly. "At least Edgar can't kill me twice for losing two things. Oh, Lordy. What am I going to do?"

Bree, who was still twirling, stopped and stuck her fingers in her mouth and blew an earsplitting whistle. A car that was crawling past a cross street came to a screeching halt and turned down our road, pulling to a stop in front of us. "This is Ramon's brother Sanmal. San, this is Thaisa. We need to go to T and G pronto. Thaisa has an appointment at nine."

"Dude," the young man with a wispy brown mustache and goatee greeted me.

"Hi, San. Thanks so much for the ride, not that I knew Bree had you lined up. Um…I don't know if we can make it there in time." I followed Bree into the back seat of the car, not seeing any other option open to me.

"Duuude," he drawled, laughter in his voice. His foot hit the gas, and I was flung backward on the seat, barely making it into my seat belt before he hit the road for the coast, lights flashing past us at an alarming rate.

I closed my eyes and prayed to whatever deity was obliged to listen that we arrived in one piece, although I didn't have much hope left. The events of the last two days had pretty much left that commodity in incredibly rare supply.

CHAPTER FIVE

ARCHER REALIZED HIS BROTHER WAS IN THE CLUB THE second he stepped across the threshold.

For one, all conversation, laughter, and even the low drone of music that always provided an undertone to Theurgy & Goety stopped at his entrance.

But it was the sense of black power sending inky tendrils into his soul that warned him that Hunter was near. He strolled in, noting the number of dragons present, and quickly donned an expression of indifference. One of the men at the end of the bar turned as he approached, and Archer beheld his own face. Hunter had the same high cheekbones that came from their Slavic father, the same faint cleft in a gently blunted chin, the same black hair with its slight widow's peak, although Hunter wore his hair down to his shoulders, where Archer preferred a shorter cut.

Only Hunter's eyes were different, a pale green that looked like frosted moss. "Archer," Hunter said, dipping his head in greeting.

It took Archer a moment to control the dragon fire that flamed to life at the sight of his brother. "Hunter," he finally managed to get out, a ring of fire bursting into being at Hunter's feet.

His brother raised an eyebrow at the sight of it before stamping it out.

Archer thought of all the things he wanted to say—the impotent sorrow at the deaths of his tribe members, of the despair that filled him whenever he thought of his future, of the burning pain that seared through to his heart—but mindful of the dragon members present, he simply turned on his heel and walked to the far end of the club, taking a booth that was hastily vacated by a group of trolls in surfer wear.

Miles followed, muttering under his breath as he joined Archer. "What is *he* doing here? I thought he was in Hungary. Wasn't he in Hungary? Why is he back now?"

"The manuscript," Archer said, very aware of everyone watching even the slightest interaction between his brother and himself. "If you heard about it, he must have as well."

"Do you think he knows you have it? He'll try to take it if he finds out," Miles said darkly.

"If he doesn't know now, he soon will." Archer felt

itchy, like ants were crawling on his skin. He turned his head to find his brother was watching him, lifting a glass in a silent toast. Archer turned back to Miles without acknowledging the gesture. "Where's the man you said would be here? The translator?"

Miles half stood and glanced around at the people mingling in the club. Most of them were seated around small tables, but there was a dance floor in the back where denizens of the Otherworld clumped together, their bodies moving in time to the thump of the music.

Small groups of people chatted, gossiped, flirted, made deals, and exchanged information all while holding drinks of various varieties and potencies, the air thick not with smoke, but with the earthy incense used to cleanse the air of less savory scents that sometimes lingered upon beings of dark powers.

"I don't see him," Miles said after scanning the occupants. "He may be late. He said he had to get some books from the university since he wasn't sure what he'd need."

"Are you sure he's worth the money he's charging?"

Miles shrugged. "The university said that most of their people are away on a medieval literature conference, but this man was available. Other than him, there are only one or two independent scholars who might have the chops to tackle something as rare as our manuscript. I figured you'd want the best."

Archer said nothing. He didn't relish spending precious money on having the leaf translated, but since he'd paid a small fortune to buy the damned thing, he figured he might as well know what it said. If for no other reason than to shut Miles up on the subject of the Raisa Medallion.

A waitress brought them a dusty bottle and two glasses, her eyes wide when she glanced at Hunter before saying to Archer, "The Vandringsmand sends his compliments and would like to remind you that the club has been duly warded and guarded with banes against violence and magic, but not dragon fire, and thus requests that any differences you have with other dragonkin be settled outside the domain of the T and G."

"You may tell Altus—" The words stopped dead on his lips when two women walked into the club, a tall girl who looked vaguely familiar and the delicious flower who had so tempted him the night before.

"Yes?" the waitress asked.

"Tell him if there is any dragon fire to be found tonight, it will not originate with the storm dragons. Miles, do you see who just came in?"

The waitress hurried off as Miles twisted in his seat, his eyebrows going up. "Interesting, but not up to our standards, do you think?"

"Your standards and mine are quite a bit different in that regard, as you well know," he said mildly. "That's the woman from the bookshop last night."

Miles looked again. "Ah. The odd-looking one."

"She's not odd-looking," Archer said, feeling a little stab of annoyance.

"To each his own, although you have to admit she

has nothing on the fair Catriona you enjoyed last night. At least, she certainly seemed pleased when she left this morning."

Archer ignored his cousin's pointed comment. He'd fully intended on spending the night allowing the busty Catriona to do everything she'd whispered that she wanted to do to him, but after fetching the manuscript, he'd spent the night alone.

Unbidden, his eyes returned to the flower. She moved to the other side of the club, disappearing into the mass of people. "She e-mailed me three times today."

Miles's smile became wolfish. "I'm surprised she can read."

"Not Catriona—the woman from last night."

"What did she want? Ah. A good vintage. 1902." Miles opened the bottle of dragon's blood, the heavily spiced red wine that dragonkin favored. He poured them each a glass, then tossed back his before consulting his phone.

"To talk to me about the manuscript, evidently." He frowned as the patrons of T&G milled around, blocking her from his view. He wondered what she was doing at such a place. Was she here on a lark? To gawk at the members of the Otherworld who gathered each night? To meet a man?

She hadn't struck him as being anything but deliciously mortal, as quirky of mind as she was of appearance, but that appealed to him. If he'd known she was not as fragile as he first assumed, he might have indulged in the kiss that she so clearly wanted. He certainly had been on the verge of giving in to desire, but only the realization that she was mortal kept him from claiming her mouth as his body had demanded.

Just thinking about her mouth, the smooth silkiness of her neck, and the scent of a field of flowers that seemed to cling to her had him hardening. He gritted his teeth and told his erection that now was neither the time nor the place for such things. Before he realized what he was doing, he was striding down the length of the bar, aware of his brother off to the right but his eyes focused ahead, on the bodies as they parted before him, until he stood at a table where his flower and her companion sat, looking with wide eyes as the waitress explained the rules of T&G.

"—and members are not allowed to summon demonic beings, bane hounds, or old gods. All imp remains are to be placed in the appropriate bucket located in the bathrooms, and the Vandringsmand, Altus Deye, asks that all patrons keep any minions, Abaddon-based or otherwise, under full control at all times. Blessed be, and welcome to Theurgy and Goety," the waitress said in a singsong voice.

"Er...Vandringsmand?" the flower asked, looking confused.

"It means *wanderer* in Danish," Archer said, pulling out a chair and inclining his head toward it. "Do you mind?"

Her eyes widened when she saw him, a variety of emotions flitting across her face, starting with surprise, followed quickly by pleasure, a flush making her cheeks a shade of pink that delighted him and ending in a wariness that he didn't care for nearly as much. "Certainly," she said, glancing at the woman next to her. "Er...I don't think we've done the introduction thing. My name is Thaisa, and this is Bree."

"Hi," the younger woman said, grinning at him. "You're just the person we're looking for."

"Then I am delighted that I chose to come here tonight." His gaze shifted to the flower, her oddly striped eyelashes fluttering over eyes that he thought at first were filled with guile, but now he knew to be as fathomless as the ocean itself. She had some genetic oddity that made her irises multicolored, the lower third a rich, deep brown with amber lights streaking inward from the edge, while the rest of the iris was gray with glittering black flecks, like wet hematite. It was an unusual look, those piebald eyes, but he liked it. It expressed her character well, he decided, remembering her outrage when she thought he'd insulted her.

"Yeah," Thaisa said slowly, her gaze still wary. She gave her head a little shake as if she was dismissing a thought, and squared her shoulders. He had the sense that she was girding herself for battle. "Regardless, I'm happy to see you again. I've e-mailed you numerous times today—"

"Three," he corrected, then checked his phone. "No, just the three."

Her lips thinned. He liked her mouth. It was normally full and sensual, the color of a barely ripened strawberry, and he could easily imagine the sweetness that lurked within.

"None of which you bothered to answer," she pointed out.

He acknowledged that. "I've been busy. I planned to respond later, when I had time."

"Indeed." For some reason, she seemed to be annoyed at him. He much preferred her soft and warm, clad in a satiny bit of nothing as she'd worn the night before. The memory of her breasts, plump, soft, and so enticing as they heaved on his chest was a memory that had risen in his mind more than once in the last twenty-four hours. "I can see you're very much in demand, although I don't see your eye candy tonight." She made a show of glancing around the club before looking back at him.

He enjoyed the way she tried to intimidate him with a pointed frown. "Eye candy? You mean Catriona?"

"Was that Sparkle Bosom's name?" Thaisa gave a ladylike sniff and adopted an expression of such indifference that it made a little burble of laughter rise within him. Was she jealous? Usually he disliked jealous lovers, since they demanded constant shows of affection, but Thaisa was different. She wasn't even his lover, and she seemed outraged. Delightfully outraged, her personality just as unique as her appearance.

"Sparkle Bosom is particularly fitting," he allowed, remembering the amount of glittery powder Catriona had bedecked herself with. It was one of the reasons why he didn't regret spending his evening alone. He much preferred a woman who smelled like herself, not like chemicals.

A woman like Thaisa, who reminded him of a field of carnations nodding gently in a late summer breeze, their spicy scent hanging heavy in the air.

Thaisa looked confused for a moment, then said, "So, she's not here?"

"No." He kept his lips from twitching with the amusement of watching her trying not to be jealous. Archer was no stranger to mortal females fawning on him—his appearance, he knew, was viewed with favor by them—but he never put much stock in it. He was as he was, and there was little he could do about it. It was much better to just get on with things without worrying about how he appeared to others. "As you see, I am all alone tonight. Other than my cousin Miles."

"Oh." She looked slightly mollified before glancing around. "I'm afraid I don't have much time to talk to you—"

"Why?" he interrupted.

She looked askance for a moment. "Why don't I have much time?"

"Yes. Are you here to meet a man?" He cast a glance over at her companion, the one named Bree, who sat with her elbows on the table, her chin resting on her palms, her eyes watching him with obvious amusement. "You are looking for a threesome?"

"Oooh," Bree said, looking thoughtful.

"Hell, no! I don't share!" Thaisa said, her eyes wide

with astonishment. She blushed then, her gaze skittering away from his. "That is to say, I don't do three-somes. With anyone. Not that...you know...you'd be asking me."

"Party pooper," Bree said, then stood and waved. "Be right back. I see an old friend." She bumped into Archer while trying to avoid the waitress, scooting around him to weave her way through the crowd. "Whoops, sorry."

"Why wouldn't I ask you?" Archer wondered what Thaisa would say next. He wasn't entirely sure if he liked the air of the unexpected that clung to her. Unlike Catriona and all the other women Miles rounded up for him, Thaisa and her conversation didn't follow the normal pattern. Usually women cooed over him, expecting compliments in return, with a light sprinkling of conversation (most of which was overtly flirtatious). But Thaisa...He didn't know what she'd say next. It left him feeling oddly unbalanced, not a wholly unpleasant experience.

"Because you're gorgeous," she blurted out, her blush darkening. "And I'm..." She waved a hand at her face.

"Lovely?"

She made a face at him, her eyes going from embarrassed to angry in a flash. "There's no need to be patronizing, Mr. My Neck Is Nice."

"I wasn't patronizing you, and your neck *is* nice," he said, looking at the long length of it, wanting to nuzzle it all over again. He wondered if she would react to that spot behind her ear that had seemed to give her such delight the night before.

She took a long breath and lifted her chin as if she wanted to fight him. He liked her chin. He liked how it seemed to take umbrage at the things he said.

"I think the less said about last night the better."

"If you aren't here to meet a man in order to have a threesome—and I will be honest that they are not something I particularly enjoy—then why do you have limited time?"

"I have an appointment with someone, not that it's any of your business."

"A man?" he asked, annoyed that he cared so much. What the flower did was nothing to him.

Except he did want to kiss her.

"Yes, he happens to be a man," she said, clearly exasperated. "I don't know why you're grilling me about this! It's nothing to do with you!"

"You're the one who brought up last night." His eyes dipped to her neck, then her breasts. "I have no problem talking about how you enjoyed my attentions."

"Gah!" she shouted, slamming her fist on the table. "Dammit, stop pretending to flirt with me!"

"I wasn't aware I was pretending anything," he said calmly, enjoying the way her loss of temper made her eyes sparkle with a light that were he a mortal man would make him very wary.

"You don't think propositioning Bree and me with a threesome is flirtatious?" She took a deep breath, making her breasts almost overflow the curved front of her dress bodice. He eyed it speculatively, mentally pushing the act of tasting those breasts to the top of a newly formed Things He Wanted to Do to Thaisa List. "You obnoxious, stereotypical, sexist—"

With an effort that gave him much pleasure to watch her make, she managed to get her temper under control, taking another deep breath that he fully appreciated. "I'm sorry. That was out of line. I shouldn't have called you obnoxious, although men who go around propositioning women... Well, we'll let that go."

It must have cost her a lot, but she rallied a smile. It was ragged, and her eyes still shot daggers at him, but it was a smile, and he gave her full points for it.

"Although I am short on time, I do need to talk to you about the manuscript you bought. I don't suppose you'd like to sell it back to Edgar?"

"No," he said without hesitation. "If he thinks he can squeeze more money out of me for it—"

"It's not that," she said, pausing to bite her lower lip. He looked at her lip. He wanted to bite it, too.

"A situation has arisen, one that I hope you can help me with." She toyed with a coaster that the waitress had placed on the table, stroking it in a way that had Archer wishing her hands were on him instead. "Evidently Edgar had a change of heart about selling it, and he's annoyed that I let you have it."

"That is his problem," Archer said, his mind caught up with the idea of just what areas of his body he'd like Thaisa to be stroking at that moment.

"Yeah, well, unfortunately, it's also my problem."

She hesitated again, then said quickly, "I don't suppose you'd like to have just a copy of the manuscript? If you are only interested in the text, that is, although I don't know if that has much historical value per se. It looked to be an excerpt from a morality tale from the bit I saw. But I'd be happy to pay for photography and a really nice print of it."

"The leaf is mine," he said, idly wondering if he could manage to hold back his fire while kissing her. He didn't have a lot of experience kissing mortal women—usually he had to forgo that aspect of sex. "I hold what is mine."

"I understand that you purchased it fair and square from Edgar, but...well, I don't like to play the pity card, but I would really appreciate it if you could let me have it back. Naturally, I would return your check to you."

He shook his head.

She looked like she might lose her temper again. Another flush darkened her cheeks, her eyes glinting their mixture of light and dark. "I would be happy to add a...well, I guess you could call it an inconvenience fee, although Edgar doesn't leave much in the store account, and I have my gran's rent due next week...but if I could sweeten the pot, so to speak, I would be happy to do so."

He let his gaze roll over her. "A negotiation? Hmm. What do you have to offer?"

She made an abrupt gesture. "A little money. Say...maybe twelve?"

"Thousands or millions?"

Her mouth dropped a little. He couldn't stop himself from reaching across and pushing her chin up, taking the opportunity to rub his thumb over her lower lip, the one she kept biting.

The one he wanted to taste with an ever growing desire.

"Hundred!" she said, batting away his hand, giving him a good glare to boot. He wanted badly to tell her how much he liked watching her be indignant but suspected she wouldn't take it as the compliment he meant it to be. "I can just barely scrape up twelve hundred if I tell Gran's people they'll have to wait a bit... but I think they'd do that." She thought for a moment. "They like Bree. Maybe if she visited a few times, they wouldn't kick up a fuss."

He shook his head again. "Money is good, but I'd need a lot more than what you're offering. Do you have anything else to barter?"

If she had been a dragon, smoke would have been wafting from her nose, he thought as he watched her fight an inner struggle. Ire, fury, anger, and all their variations battled with pride, and something fleeting that made him feel uncomfortable. He lifted his chin, scenting the air, catching just the faintest hint of it.

"I have..." She stopped, her jaw working a few times, her knuckles white with her grasp on the table. "I have me."

She was afraid. He searched her face but saw no signs of the fear that he had scented a moment before, but it had been there, and it troubled him. As much as he enjoyed teasing her to see her temper flare, he didn't like the idea that someone had scared this delightful little flower.

"Are you now propositioning me?" he asked, pushing down his fire. What sort of a bastard had frightened her?

She looked like she wanted to punch him in the face, as she'd tried repeatedly to do the night before. "Yes."

"I see. That is an offer much more suitable for such a valuable object." He didn't have time to involve himself in a mortal's dilemma. He had more on this plate than he could handle now, and to even consider finding out who was giving her grief and making them think twice about ever bothering her again was folly, pure folly.

"Well? Do we have a deal?" She swallowed back her anger and tried to arrange her face into a pleasant expression. "I get the manuscript back, and you get... er..."

He smiled suddenly, the decision made even before he could debate it. He stood, catching her chin in his hand and tipping her head back, leaning over her to say, "You will grace my bed, flower, and soon, but it not be in exchange for the manuscript. I do not give up what I hold."

His lips brushed hers as he spoke. He was going to stop there, not wanting to risk harming her before he knew if she was immortal or not, but then she opened her mouth under his with a soft exhalation, and the next thing he knew he was kissing her, his tongue sweeping into her mouth to taste her, to tease her, to encourage her to taste him. He held his fire back with an iron grip, not wanting to frighten her, but it was a near thing when her tongue made gentle, fleeting little dabs at his. He pulled back then, aware that if she continued, he'd throw her over his shoulder and take her to the nearest bed.

"You'll hear from me," was all he said before turning and stalking down the bar to where Miles sat with three women, extremely aware that his erection was less than happy with him.

CHAPTER SIX

"MISS MOORE?"

A man's voice slid across the fog that held my brain in a grip of lust, desire, anger, and a bone-chilling fear. "Hmm? Oh, yes, that's me."

"You permit?"

"Please," I said, gesturing toward the chair. I tried to drag my mind back from the land of Archer's lips, and Archer's gorgeous eyes, and the way Archer's hair swept back from that little widow's peak that made my knees go weak, and the touch of his thumb on my lip, and dear God, the way his mouth took possession of mine just like it had a right to charge in and boss my own tongue around. I felt hot, flushed, and ruffled, as if my clothing were two sizes too small. I cleared my throat, squelching down the fear and other feelings that threatened to overwhelm me, and donned my most professional manner. "You must be Mr. Vehar? Have you...uh...been here long?"

And did he see Archer kiss the wits right out of my head? My cheeks burned with the idea that all the people around us saw Archer give me what was clearly a pity kiss.

Although it sure didn't feel like there was a lot of pity in it.

"I haven't been here long, no, although my name is not Vehar. I am Poe, Damian Poe, no relation to Edgar Allan." The man who sat opposite me smiled, his mild blue eyes friendly, his manner that of a politely distant professional, someone like a dentist or a chiropractor. "Mr. Vehar asked that I discuss the job with you, since I have a familiarity with the manuscript."

"I see. I'd like to hear about the project." I looked as attentive as I could.

He steepled his fingers. "Have you heard of something called the Raisa Medallion?"

I thought for a moment. "I can't say that I have."

"I would be surprised if you had, to be honest. It is an artifact whose existence has long been in question." He told me a tale about a precious necklace that had been broken in two, the two halves lost to time. It sounded like something from an old fairy tale, but I let him talk, making a few notes in a small notebook as he did so. "The existence of the medallion has come to the forefront with the uncovering of a recent manuscript."

I shifted in my chair, something in the back of my head wanting attention, but I couldn't pull it forward to look at it.

"The manuscript is reported to give the details about the medallion, so naturally, there are a number of individuals—both scholars like yourself and private collectors—who are very interested in the information to be found within it."

"I don't think I've ever seen anything like that," I said, intrigued.

"It is, I'm told, quite unique. Our belief is that the manuscript contains clues as to where to find the two pieces of the medallion."

Another ping went off in the back of my head. This time, I recognized it for what it was. I wondered if Edgar's leaf was from the same manuscript? It was hard to stretch coincidence to two such ancient leaves being discovered at the same time.

"We're hoping you can help us," Damian said, smiling in a friendly, guileless manner.

"I will certainly do my best."

"Excellent." He stood, and moved around to pull my chair out for me. Slowly, I got to my feet, mildly flustered by the action. "Perhaps you would care to look at a facsimile of the manuscript?"

"Facsimile?" I asked, frowning. Although it wasn't unknown at all to work off such things, most scholars worth their weight wanted the real thing to study, since there were so many minute clues on the vellum itself, things that couldn't be duplicated by photos.

"Yes. I have a copy here," he said, pulling a sheet from his pocket. "You will see that it is mostly in ciphered code, which we are unable to break."

I glanced at the page, my eyes widening. "That's... *that's* the document? Are you sure?"

"Quite sure," he said, taking my arm and guiding me toward the door.

I didn't want to make a scene by demanding he let go of me, but neither did I wish to be hustled off. For one thing, Bree was floating around somewhere in the club, and for another, the worry that had been my constant companion suddenly kicked up to high, making me pull back when he reached the door. "I'm sorry, I can't go with you right now. I have a friend here—"

"She's waiting in the car for you," Damian said, his nice eyes shining with a light that I didn't really like.

Panic flared to life within my belly, and I twisted my hand out of his grasp, but at that moment, three men who had been lurking at the end of the bar moved over to form a semicircle behind me, effectively blocking me off from the rest of the club.

"Whoa, now," I said and, realizing I couldn't get past them, turned to make a dash for the parking lot, but Damian grabbed me by one arm while another man, one who reminded me of a linebacker, grabbed the other. "What the hell do you think you're doing?" I asked, trying desperately to get away from what I worried was now an outright abduction.

A fourth man joined us as I was more or less frog-marched out to the car. "Astul! Damian! My dear Miss

Moore, you have my profound apologies for this harsh treatment."

The voice that reached me as I was tossed into the back of a waiting limo was as smooth as melted chocolate, and just as rich.

"You...oof...God's wounds, get off of me!"

"Sorry," a breathy voice said in my ear. The weight that had squashed me onto the floor suddenly lifted when Bree rolled off me. "This is my first kidnapping, and I didn't know they were going to throw me in. Whatever happened to people luring you into a van filled with candy?"

I pushed my hair—which had come down from a simple French twist in the violence of my abduction and subsequent struggle—out of my face and got to my knees, hands immediately helping me onto the seat as the car jumped forward.

"I can see I will be having quite a talk later with Damian and Astul about their method of treating ladies. Are you harmed? No? Excellent. And you?" The man with the beautiful voice assisted Bree onto the seat next to me. "I can only offer the both of you my most profound apologies for my tribe's overly enthusiastic attempt to fulfill my request for your company."

I opened my mouth to lambaste the man who'd hired me, but did a double take when I got a good look at him. He had a familiar widow's peak, familiar jawline, familiar cheekbones...basically, familiar everything, with the exception of his hair and his eyes. Where Archer's were gorgeous frosted blue, this man's were a pale green, like moss caught in a piece of ice. "What…uh…who…"

"Hey, look, dragons." Bree looked at the two men opposite us, the duplicitous Damian, at whom I leveled a really quality glare, and a second man with no apparent signs of a neck and arms so beefy they could barely cross over a massive chest.

"Bree," I said with a warning in my voice, pulling her back next to me when she would have gone to sit on the other side of the limo, scooting over until I had her pinned between the car wall and myself, the better to keep her away from the bad men. "Now is not the time for that."

"There's always time for dragons," she said. "Except for that one. He just looks mean."

She pointed at the man with no neck. He growled at her.

I shot Bree a warning look, but she just growled back at the man.

Mr. Smooth Voice leaned back, one arm draped casually across the top of the seat. "The regrettable method used to ensure we have privacy while speaking with you aside, it is my great pleasure to meet you in person."

"Just who are you?" I asked, more than a little annoyed at how we'd been treated. I realized I should have been scared, or terrified that we were about to be sexually assaulted, murdered, or sold into slavery, but oddly I was more annoyed than anything else. "Are you related to Archer?"

"I am," he said, inclining his head in assent. "I'm sure I can count on your good nature—both of your good natures—to accept my most profound apologies for my need to speak to you so urgently, but this is a delicate matter, and delicacy is *not* my brother's specialty."

Brothers—that made sense. Something inside me, some antagonistic inner fire that had seemed to ride me for the last day, rose immediately despite the man's smooth manner. "This is kidnapping, you know."

"My very dear Miss Moore!" he said, his eyebrows rising. "I would never hold you against your will. You had agreed to meet with me at T and G, and my associate did just that. I assumed you wish to get started immediately on the little job I have for you. Ah, but like my men, I have left the niceties aside." He placed a hand on his chest and made a little bow. "I am Hunter Vehar."

"What a very graceful introduction that was. I hope you enjoy making such pretty bows to your fellow cellmates once you're convicted of two counts of kidnapping!" I snapped, very aware of his charm. Still, I couldn't help feeling like he was a carbon copy of Archer, and that the copy wasn't quite as fine as the original.

"My dear Thaisa—do you mind if I call you that? I assure you that both you and your friend are safe in my care, and since I could see my brother was attempting to seduce you into providing what he wanted, I intervened as soon as I could."

"Archer wasn't trying to seduce me," I said, more than a little embarrassed that he saw Archer kiss me. "He just…he was just saying…uh…"

"My dear, you do not need to tell me about the methods my brother uses," he said, putting his hand on mine. I slid mine away after a few seconds. "He is known throughout our community for his habit of attaching women to him, and when he's had what he wants, they are left to their own devices."

I wanted to dispute that statement, but the memory of Archer with Sparkle Catriona on his arm the night before came all too swiftly to my brain. And yet…if they were dating, why wasn't she with him now?

"Alas, when it comes to the ladies, Archer is un-refined, his manners not at all what the gentler sex enjoys, and if you will allow me to give you a piece of advice, you will stay away from him."

I shook my head, more to myself than to address what Hunter was saying, mustering up as much polite-ness as I could. "He didn't seem unrefined to me. He certainly doesn't lack the sort of moral compass that makes him kidnap people, for example."

"Touché," Hunter said, smiling ruefully.

"I really must insist that you stop the car and let Bree and me get out."

"You do not know Archer as I do," Hunter said, his eyes shadowed. He ignored my demand to be released, just as I guessed he would.

Worry rose in my mind. Hunter might say he meant us no harm, but there was something about him that had my brain urging me to escape. I glanced around to see how hard that was going to be. The privacy barrier between the driver and the rest of the limo was down, but there were only two of us and, excluding the driver, three of them.

"My brother has attacked my tribe since the day it was formed," Hunter said, looking out the window as lights flashed past us. We had to be on a coast road, heading north. "The shadow dragons have only ever sought to be left in peace, but his tribe refuses to tolerate our existence and seeks to destroy us all."

If we came to a stop somewhere safe, I mused, and I punched out the silky-voiced Hunter, would I be able to get Bree and myself out of the car before the man shaped like a brick bakehouse tried to stop us?

"Long have we tolerated his strikes against us."

I eyed Damian, who was watching something on his phone. Maybe if I lunged at him first, slamming him into Mr. Beefy, and had Bree take out Hunter... but no, I wouldn't risk her welfare like that. Not to mention the fact that she probably wouldn't do as I ordered and would end up sitting on his lap touching his chin and jawline that was almost, but not quite, as nice as Archer's.

"I knew when my brother accosted you in the club that I had to move quickly to get you out of his grasp lest he force you to a regrettable situation."

I'd just have to use my pepper spray. But how to get all of them fairly quickly... that was the problem.

"The storm dragons are not known for their fair dealings with others, be they dragonkin or mortals."

Hunter first, I decided. Then Beefy, then the sneaky Damian. Although maybe Beefy should be first, since he's likely to be the one who posed the most threat. A sense of what Hunter was saying filtered through to my brain at that point, causing me to turn and look at him. "The storm what?"

"Dragons." He gave me a long look. "You are surprised to hear me speak ill of another tribe? The ouroboros dragons are not like other dragons who sit safely in their septs. Our tribes are born of the lawless, the outcasts, dragons who left their families in order to seek a life beyond what they would have otherwise, and while they are fiercely faithful to their tribe, they do not tolerate well those who would attack us."

"Dragons," I repeated, feeling as if I'd been struck a physical blow. Slowly, synapse by synapse, my brain pointed out that if demons were real, why shouldn't dragons be the same? "Archer is a dragon?"

Sympathy filled Hunter's pale eyes, his fingers resting for a moment on my arm in an obvious attempt to provide comfort. "He neglected to tell you? That surprises me. From what I know, he is more than willing to tell anyone who will listen to him the sad tale of his life, how he was so badly treated, ostracized by both dragons and mortals, how he was denied the status of being the first dragon hunter. I assumed he had played on your sympathy by urging you to provide him succor."

Mr. Beefy snorted and murmured, "Succor," like it was a dirty word.

I looked at him, then at Damian, and finally back to Hunter, my brain chewing through everything and coming to one conclusion.

"Hold, please," I told Hunter, holding up a finger. I turned to Bree and whispered, "He's a dragon?"

"They all are," she answered, her eyes bright, but her smile having long faded. "I'm glad you finally decided to believe."

"It just didn't seem possible...They don't *look* like dragons."

"Pfft. Who would want to stomp around in dragon form when human is so much easier?"

"Point taken." I turned back to Hunter, who was waiting patiently. "Right. You're a dragon."

His eyebrows rose, his mouth curving in a little smile. "I wasn't aware that was in doubt."

"That means Archer is a dragon."

"A very inferior sort, yes. I am the master of the shadow tribe. As I just mentioned, my brother leads the storm dragons."

Thickset Man said a rude word in a Czech dialect. I considered Hunter, trying to decide if this new world paradigm changed my plans. "You have a copy of Archer's leaf."

Hunter's eyebrows rose a little. "You know about that?"

"I do. I sold him the leaf." I felt as if I was caught up in sticky web of confusion, with little tendrils spreading away from me, wrapping around everything I knew, connecting them all...but in a pattern I couldn't quite see. "Is that what you want me to decipher?"

"Yes," Hunter said, flashing a smile that softened the lines of his face. "If you would be so kind."

My inner voice warred with my sense of reason. On the one hand, it sounded like Archer's people had not treated Hunter's very nicely. But did that mean anything to me? I wasn't part of their world. I was a simple medieval scholar with an expensive grandmother and a crappy boss.

I said nothing, only listening to Hunter with half of my attention while I worked through my tangled thoughts.

"There isn't a problem working from a photocopy, is there?" Hunter asked.

This had gone far enough. I didn't know who was telling the truth about whom, but I did know what was right. "I would be happy to discuss the matter with you, but only if you turn around and take us back to T and G. I'm not comfortable being whisked off to an unknown destination, especially since I did not consent to this journey."

"Yeah. And you didn't even offer us candy," Bree said.

Hunter sighed. "I thought I explained the circumstances to you. I assure you that I'm thinking only of your own safety."

And that's what pushed me over the edge: the way he justified ignoring my request. Archer may have

been pushy about kissing me, but he didn't cross this
sort of a line.

"Let us talk about pleasanter things," Hunter said
smoothly, smiling. I could feel the effect of his charm,
but it just left me chilled. "I assure you the photocopy
is legible. I examined it myself, so unless there is a reason for you not to work with it, you should be able to
get started immediately."

Bree and I had to get out of there, out of the car, out
of Hunter's control. The whole dragon thing aside—
and I was feeling rather proud of myself that I moved
past the impossibility of the idea into acceptance—I
wouldn't have remained in that circumstance with any
other man.

Except perhaps Archer.

The car continued north, now leaving behind the
suburb communities and heading into a more forested
area.

"There are times when original documents are too
fragile or otherwise unavailable to be examined, leaving physical copies, photocopies, and photographs a
valid source of translation," I said carefully, trying to
assess my options. Bree and I didn't have a great many
choices, but I wasn't going to just sit here and let Mr.
It's For Your Own Good take us who-knew-where.
"But what you're asking isn't quite ethical. So far as
I know, this leaf has never been deciphered and translated. It only came up to auction last month, and from
the notes my boss left, it was unknown. I've never
seen mention of a morality tale dating to that time,

and medieval fiction has been a particular interest of mine."

"You refer to the note in Latin at the top of the leaf?" Hunter asked, making a gesture at Damian, who promptly handed over the photocopy. "I admit to being a bit rusty, but does this not say that herewith is the true and accurate tale of the Raisa Medallion?"

I took the paper he handed me, studying it when he turned on the overhead light. Bree leaned over my shoulder to peer at it. "More or less, yes. There's a bit here about it being told to the scribe by a wanderer who was near death, and something partially obliterated that I believe refers to a deathbed confession."

Momentarily distracted from planning an escape, my gaze slid lower on the paper, to the strange symbols that filled the page with few breaks, indicating individual words or sentences. These were no letters from any known alphabet, but odd little curls and slashes that clearly were the shorthand of some long-dead scribe. I let my eyes glide along the lines, not trying to take in the individual symbols but rather to establish a pattern of frequency. My fingers itched for the notepad I always had at my side when deciphering or translating. A symbol popped out to catch my attention, and then a second, the pattern of their occurrence sliding into place in my head. If I could find a few more, I might be able to start working on the shorter words—

"As you can see, it's quite fascinating," Hunter said, sliding the paper out of my hands and tucking it away in his jacket pocket. "Already, you have been able to glean more from it than I could. I look forward to see-ing what you can do with the cipher."

I met his gaze, which as far as I could tell was absent of malice. That didn't sway me, though. "Why would you kidnap us over something so unimportant in the grand scheme of things as this little leaf?"

He made a face. "That word again! I assure you that I have no such intention to detain you against your will."

"Fine," I said, nodding toward the window. "Then pull over and let us out."

"Here?" He rolled his window down and stuck his head out a little bit before pulling it back in. "We are skirting the national forest border. There are few houses for miles. I wouldn't mind a walk along a dark road by myself, but I am master of the shadow tribe. You are a woman. A particularly delightful woman, but still, one who might be vulnerable to attack. In addi-tion to that, we will be at my house within half an hour, where I assure you will be far more comfortable than walking back to the T and G."

I knew before he even started talking that there was no way I would be able to convince him to let us go.

An audacious plan came to me, one that I would not, in the normal course of my life, even remotely con-sider, but I really didn't have a choice.

I slipped my phone out of my pocket, resting it on the seat between Bree and myself, crossing my legs to hide the movement of my left arm as I typed out a mes-sage in a text box.

GET READU

"I hate to disappoint you, Mr. Vehar—"

"Hunter, please. Only my banker calls me by the other name." His smile radiated warmth.

WHEN CAR STOP WE RUNAWA Y

"Hunter, then. I hate to disappoint you, but I am not going to be able to decipher that leaf. It belongs to Archer, although I'm hoping to convince him to...Well, that's neither here nor there. The fact remains that the leaf is, so far as I know, untranslated, and it doesn't belong to you. It would be grossly unethical to translate it without permission of the owner."

Bree, who thankfully had not stared at my fingers typing blindly, pulled out her own phone despite the fact that I wasn't actually sending her a text message.

Hunter frowned. "I realize that my brother must have spun you some sort of tale—"

My phone burbled. I sighed, trying not to roll my eyes. "Excuse me a moment." I made a big show of picking up my phone, just like my fingers hadn't been resting on the screen.

WHY??? Bree texted.

"It's nothing important," I said, smiling at Hunter as I carefully set the phone back down between Bree's leg and mine, typing quickly THIS IS WRONG

"Thaisa, I can guarantee you that I would not ask you to do anything illegal, and although I'm aware you're not comfortable providing me with a translation of the cipher, your reputation—and indeed, *you*— will not suffer in the least. Quite to the contrary, in addition to the payment we discussed on the phone, I am happy to provide you with a sterling professional reference."

My phone burbled again. I glanced at it. OK. WHICH WAY DO WE RUN? I VOTE INTO THE TREES. ANIMAL SCENTS TO THROW THEM OFF, YOU KNOW.

I tucked my phone down on the seat, saying loudly as I toyed with the strap of my purse, slowly sliding my hand inside it, my fingers blindly searching for the pepper spray that I kept for solitary trips home on the bus. "Sorry again. Everything is *all right* now." I glanced at Bree to see if she got the meaning. She waggled her eyebrows, which I took as an affirmative.

"Is there some problem?" Hunter asked, glancing toward his men. "I assure you that I won't allow anyone to speak ill of your decision to help my tribe."

It was on the tip of my tongue to ask him what on earth a medieval morality tale had to do with dragons, but since I'd only just come to grasp the idea that dragons were real, and walking around in human suits, I decided to let that go. "No, no problem. Er…where are we?" I peered past him as if trying to get my bearings. He glanced out the window, which, as I hoped, caused the other two men to glance as well.

I threw myself forward, slamming my purse into Damian's head, knocking him sideways while I shot the pepper spray into the face of his burly companion before turning it on Damian.

The latter screamed and fell to the floor, clawing at

his eyes, while Beefy took a swing at me that caught me on the jaw, sending me flying backward. Hunter was across the space of the limo, jerking me forward, his face black with anger, but Bree rose over him, a bulky object in her hands, which she brought down onto the back of his head. He went down, falling on top of where Damian was on the floor sobbing and cursing profanely.

Mr. Beefy grabbed me by the throat, his face bright red, his eyes mere slits, but another dose of pepper spray had him crying oaths in a guttural tone, blindly grabbing for us.

The car swerved dangerously as the driver realized what was going on, fishtailing when he slammed on the brakes, half turning toward us.

"Run!" I yelled to Bree as I gave him a dose of the pepper spray as well, making sure I stomped hard on Beefy's hand when I scrambled over the top of the two prone men. Bree leaped from the car and ran. I stumbled and almost fell onto the road, but was up and running after her in a second.

"Woohoo!" she yelled, doing a little joyous leap, waiting so I could catch up. I grabbed her arm and ran down the road for a few feet, my adrenaline pumping so hard I couldn't hear anything but the blood in my ears. This section of road was devoid of houses. To our left was a thinly forested incline that had more tree cover as the ground rose. On the right, a sharp drop-off swept down to a small community on the coast, the lights of the houses and streetlamps wavering slightly in the summer evening. Ahead of us, in the distance, I could see the lights of a car driving toward us.

"Woods!" I yelled to Bree, instinct driving me to get away from anyone who might be a threat. We leaped the metal barrier intended to keep cars from plowing off the road, and bolted into the tree line, slapping branches out of our way while we headed for deeper cover. Bree was ahead of me, her long legs eating up the distance, leaving me to follow the tree branches that were jostled by her passage through them.

"What did you hit Hunter with?" I gasped in pain as a branch slapped me in the face.

"Art deco ashtray," she said, stopping to wave a blocky chunk of amber-colored glass. "I was going to give it to Ramon, but when you attacked those dragons, I thought I'd just see how sturdy it was. It's *very* sturdy. You go south." She pointed to my right. "I'll go east."

"I think we should stay together—" I started to say, but a roar of anger from the road had me shutting up, and instead of following Bree up a steep, slippery incline, I spun off to the right, concentrating on running as silently as possible without slamming face-first into any obstacles. It was darker in this section of the forest, the scent of pine and damp earth strong, the shadows cast by the trees too dense to see into. Enough moonlight glinted through that made it possible for me to move with a reasonable amount of safety, although I cracked both shins on numerous rocks and fallen tree trunks. My face stung with scratches when I tried to squeeze myself up to trunks in an attempt to disappear, even though I knew my harsh breathing, so loud in my ears, must be audible to anyone searching for me.

A stitch of pain grew in my side, causing me to slow down. I paused next to a tall cedar and held my breath for as long as I could, trying to hear signs of pursuit. I thought I heard the rumble of voices in the distance, but it was a fleeting noise that wasn't repeated.

It wasn't easy listening over my pounding heart, and after a minute, I decided that I must have put enough distance between Hunter and me, and knelt behind a jagged rock to catch my breath and wipe the wetness from my face.

Just as I was able to breathe without gulping, I heard a loud crack, the sound of something stepping on a dried branch. Fear gripped my gut, my adrenaline spiking a second time. I knew exactly how a trapped animal felt, panicked and desperate to get away from whatever was out there in the darkness.

"Thaisa."

My stomach gave a lurch at my name, carried to me on the wind. I stared into the darkness of the wood, trying to pinpoint where the sound had come from. Dammit, Hunter must have recovered from the pepper spray faster than I thought.

"I know you are here. Do not run from me."

I got to my knees and peered over my rock but didn't see anything moving. Carefully, I eased to my feet, hoping Bree had gotten away safely. I didn't worry that if she made it to a town, she'd get herself back to safety, and given how fleet of foot she was, I figured she had a much better chance of escaping than I did. I looked around, saw three redwoods clustered together about thirty feet away, and carefully edged forward, my hands in front of me blindly as I stepped as lightly as possible.

"I mean you no harm."

I snorted at that obvious lie, immediately slapping a hand over my mouth while praying that Hunter hadn't heard the noise.

Three more careful steps and I was at the redwoods. I clutched their rough bark with a silent sob of relief, finding comfort in the inky shadows cast by their substantial forms.

"Do you know that dragons love the hunt?" Hunter's voice was conversational as he delivered that tidbit of information.

My eyes widened at that. The voice sounded closer, but given the number of trees around me, I couldn't tell from where it came. I thought it was to the right. I crept around the trunks of the three redwoods, trying to peer through a moonless section to find a target of potential safety.

"It stirs the primal beast in us. Mates run, dragons hunt—it's considered a type of foreplay."

I stared in surprise at the darkness behind me. What the hell was Hunter hinting at?

Ahead of me, a cedar that listed at a forty-five-degree angle off a mound of dirt beckoned to me. I held my breath and hurried toward it.

"The end of the chase is always highly pleasurable."

His voice sounded farther away now, from the south.

"I tell you this even though we are not mated. I know you are frightened. You have nothing to fear from me. I do not harm mortals."

That definitely sounded farther away. I breathed a sigh of relief and turned to slip underneath the angled trunk of the cedar, but just as I reached it, a man loomed up out of the darkness.

I sucked in my breath to shriek, but before the noise left my lips he was on me, his hand over my mouth, pushing me back against the redwood. I bit his hand and started to struggle.

"Pax!" he said, his breath heavy in my ear as he leaned into me. I froze for a moment; then his scent teased my nose, a familiar scent, one of a woodsy, lemony soap that I remembered from the previous night.

I pulled his hand from my mouth and squinted at the silhouette that loomed over me. "Archer?"

"Yes. Did he harm you?" His breath was hot on me, his hands running over my person as if he was checking me over for injuries, the gentle little touches sending my libido into overdrive.

"No, I'm all right." I sagged into him in relief, not understanding why I felt safe with Archer when he evidently did all sorts of horrible things to Hunter's people. "But what are you doing here?"

"When I saw my brother take you, I had to try to save you. He would use you ruthlessly in order to hurt me."

"That was nice of you," I said, somewhat breathlessly, my brain spinning in a circle with my awareness of him as a man. He was big, so big, and very masculine, and yet, rather than run from him, I wanted to fling myself on him and revel in his strength. In his heat. And oh, glorious day, in the differences between our bodies.

How on earth had I gone from frightened half to death to incredibly turned on in the space of a few seconds?

"You must not go anywhere with my brother again. It isn't safe," he insisted, taking a step closer to me.

My body cheered, my girl parts thrilled that he was back in our life.

"You're awfully close," I said, my brain so overwhelmed with his nearness that it just let my mouth blurt out whatever it wanted. "Every time I take a breast I can feel you."

He looked down at his chest, where it was a hair's breadth away from mine. "Pardon?"

"My breath," I said, trying frantically to get my mind to work. It was a lost cause. It was too busy squealing to itself about how close he was, how I wanted desperately to touch him, and most of all, how I wanted another chance at kissing him. The kiss we'd shared in T&G had almost melted me, and I had a feeling Archer had restrained himself during it. My mouth went a little dry at the thought of repeating the kiss without an audience or restraint. "Every time I take a breath, I can feel your chest."

There was enough light from the moon to see that his eyes darkened, outright darkened. One minute they were pale ice with just a hint of blue, and the next, they glittered like blue topaz in the shards of moonlight that bathed us. "Who are you?" he asked in a low growl that I felt deep inside me.

"I'm just a researcher," I said, something nudging my awareness. Something that I wanted to talk to Archer about, although I'd be damned if I could remember what at that point.

He leaned in, breathing in deeply, his chest rubbing on mine. I tried not to moan aloud. "This is madness."

"Yeah," I agreed, unable to keep from putting my hands on his arms. Beneath the shirt, his muscles felt like banded steel. "But pretty nice madness, you have to admit."

His breath brushed my ear, then my jaw, his hands clenched at his side. "This should not be happening. You are not a dragon. And yet, I find myself responding to you as if you were."

I whimpered softly when his mouth skimmed my jaw, moving over to suck my lower lip for a moment.

I don't know if it was the sudden life-and-death dash from peril that had my body clamoring for Archer and his touches, for his kisses, hell, for *all* of him, but whatever the reason, I was left with an overpowering need to touch and taste him. I knew well that I had shifted into a mental state isolated from common sense and reality, but that didn't seem to be of any importance.

This can't be happening to me, the analytical part of my mind said as I ran my hands over his chest, pulling out his shirt from where it was tucked into his pants. *Not me. Not with someone as gorgeous as him. This has to be some sort of mental derangement. I'm going to end up locked in a looney bin if I let this fantasy continue...* My thoughts shriveled to nothing but the purest pleasure when my hands swept across the thick muscles that ran from his breastbone down to his belly, the heat of him sending little shivers of anticipation down my back.

"If you touch me, woman, I won't be able to stop," he growled into my shoulder, his mouth hot on my neck all the while his hands moved up the curve of my hips to my breasts.

"Who wants you to stop?" I moaned, arching my back so my breasts, which had somehow gone from blobs of flesh that hung off my chest and occasionally made it hard to jog to demanding little strumpets whose focus was solely on Archer, pushed harder against his hands. I didn't care if I was acting inappropriately; I just wanted him, despite the fact that somewhere out there an angry dragon man with pepper-sprayed eyes was probably searching for me.

Archer consumed my thoughts, and just as if he read my mind, his mouth was there on mine, his arms moving around to pull my hips tighter against him.

When he nipped my lower lip, asking for entrance to my mouth, I didn't hesitate. I let him in, welcoming the taste of him and the wonderful way all the hard lines of his body fit against my curves. His hands seemed to stir little fires with the touches he trailed down my back. The night air prickled on my flesh when he pulled down the zipper of my dress, making me shiver again.

"You are so soft, so very soft," he murmured, pulling back his tongue where it had been bossy with mine. I've never found tongues to be overly romantic, but with Archer the experience was different. His tongue was just like him, pushy, arrogant, and very, very hot. I slid one leg up the side of his, pulling the rest of his shirt out of his pants and hurriedly tugging it over his head.

"Chest," I said on a breath, spreading my fingers across his pectoral muscles, delighting in the heat of him and the way the little hairs there tickled my fingers. I didn't need to be able to see to know he had a genuine six-pack—the ripple of muscle moving from his chest to his stomach made my legs feel wobbly.

"Yes, it is," he said, sliding the straps of my dress forward, quickly dispensing with my strapless bra. If I thought my breasts felt good in his hands with clothing between us, the touch of his fingers on my bare flesh just about made me spontaneously combust. And then he dipped his head, taking one nipple in his mouth, and I arched back, my mouth open in a silent gasp while I tried to process the sensation. It felt like he was bathing my breast in fire, the heat of it almost too much to take.

"Ah, flower, you have no idea what you do to me," he murmured against my breastbone as he kissed a hot line over to my other breast, his breath and mouth steaming my flesh in a way that left me restless and yearning for more. So much more.

"You almost...just a little to the left, please...oh, God, yes, right there... You almost gave me a heart attack. I thought you were Hunter. Would you do the other? It's suddenly jealous."

He turned his attention to my other breast, which was indeed trying to catch his attention, giving it due consideration before moving upward again, nibbling on my shoulder, and then higher, to a spot behind my ear that made my legs buckle, literally buckle. He chuckled as he hoisted me up, pressing me into the tree, his mouth burning a brand on mine. The bark itched against my bare back, but at that moment, I didn't care about that, or that we were out where Hunter could find us. I just wanted Archer. All of him.

"The hunt...it makes us wild...Christus Rex, tell me you are not mortal, because I don't think I can hold it any longer."

"I...I..." My mind couldn't seem to form a coherent thought that wasn't focused on Archer's mouth and hands and the way I wanted us to fit together.

His mouth was on mine again even as he pulled my legs up and around his waist, one of his hands sliding around my hips to find my underwear.

I nipped his tongue when it got bossy with mine again, squirming against him when his fingers found sensitive flesh, dipping inside me in a way that had me groaning into his mouth. I knew what was about to happen was wrong, that I should be running from this sensual, seductive man just as hard as I had run from his brother, but as he snapped the narrow satin straps of my underwear, all I could think of was pressing myself closer to him.

And when he surged into me with a primal growl, I flexed my hips, welcoming him with a thousand little muscles that tightened happily around him.

"You are hotter than my fire," he panted, his hands on my hips, holding me as he licked my neck, then kissed me again. "I don't think I can hold it—Christus, tell me you can handle it—it will kill me if I stop."

"Give it to me," I murmured, not knowing what he was asking, but so wild with the feel of him moving inside me, I wanted more. I wanted all of him. "More," I pleaded, and bucked against him when his movements became shorter, his thrusts wild now. I tangled my hands in his hair and tugged, my body demanding everything he had to give.

With a primal noise deep in his chest, fire swept through me, roaring through my veins, pushing the tightness inside me to the point where I thought I would simply break into a million little pieces. Flames lit my mind as they coursed through my body, making me a beacon of sexual ecstasy, and with a cry, I embraced it, welcoming the flames, reveling in the way his fire wrapped around us both, pushing me over the edge into an orgasm unlike anything I'd ever experienced.

He bit my shoulder, his shout of completion muffled by my flesh even as he pressed hard into me, his hips flexing a few times while he found his own release.

His breath was rough in my ear, my heart pounding almost as loud. We stood like that for a few minutes, his chest heaving against me even as I struggled to get my own breath, to make sense of what had just happened.

Slowly, I unhooked my legs from around Archer's hips and slid down him until I could stand.

"Wow," I said, panting as I looked at him, the shadows hiding all but his eyes, which were now a brilliant, glittering sapphire. "That was...that was amazing. I can see why you guys are immortal, if that's the sort of sexy times you get up to. I don't think I could survive many interludes like that."

Archer stared down at me, disbelief chasing astonishment in his eyes, followed by a sharp speculation.

"No," he said, shaking his head, his hands still on my hips. "You are not...you cannot be mortal."

"I am. Um. Would you mind—thank you." He released me when I bent to snatch up my bra, shaking it out before putting it back on, and pulling up the bodice of my dress, turning my back to him while I pulled my hair out of the way. "Zip, please?"

"You took my fire," he said, obliging me before tucking himself back into his pants and retrieving his shirt. "No mortal can do that. Only..."

"Where did my underwear go?" I asked, squinting through the darkness.

He found the pair where it was dangled from a waist-high fern and handed it to me. I made a face at the damaged undies, now unwearable, and tucked them into my purse.

His eyes narrowed on me, his pupils elongated, like a cat's. Suddenly he was on me again, his face buried in my cleavage, breathing in deeply.

"What are you doing?" I asked, wanting to simultaneously push him away so I could sit somewhere quiet by myself and think about what happened and to grab his head while demanding he do it all again.

"Learning your scent," he murmured, moving up so that he spoke against my collarbone. "You smell... right."

"That's my deodorant," I said with a shaky laugh. "It's supposed to be super good under times of stress, and running for my life through a forest followed by sexy dragon time evidently qualifies as that."

"Come," he said, and taking my hand, turned and started off, just as if he expected me to trot along behind him without a word.

CHAPTER SEVEN

"HEY!" I SAID, TRYING TO PULL MY HAND BACK FROM
where Archer held it in a steely grip.

My body was still humming with the aftereffects of
our sexual encounter, leaving me with an overwhelming desire to curl up and purr.

Archer tightened his fingers and gave me a little tug
forward, not saying anything.

"Look, I didn't like it when your brother tossed me
in his car without bothering to ask if I wanted to go or
not, and I don't like it when you use the same high-
handed tactics. Although what we just did against the
tree...hoo! Yeah, that was *very much* all right."

He wound around trees and rocks much more suc-
cessfully than me, still saying nothing.

"How did you find me out here? And how did you make your voice sound like you were in front of me when you were standing behind me?"

"I'm a dragon," he said finally, a steady pressure urging me ever forward. "When I saw the shadow dragons searching the side of the road, I knew you must have escaped." He paused and pulled me up for a hot, fast kiss that melted my resistance. "You are more resourceful than I gave you credit for. I am pleased that my mate would take appropriate actions to get away from the shadow dragons."

"I never go anywhere without my pepper spray," I said, giving up and allowing him to lead me through the forest. The nightmare scene of painful shin-breakers and frightening shadows had faded once he had found me and was now a distant memory. I could still taste Archer, the memory of his mouth on my breasts leaving them heavy and wanting. Hidden parts of me were lying back exhausted, panting dramatically while already making plans for a repeat performance.

Archer stirred more than just sexual appreciation, I decided while following him through the woods. Hunter made me nervous, but Archer made me feel... I shook my head at the word that came to mind. *Safe.* How could I feel safe with him, a man I'd just met, a man who wasn't even really a human being?

It made no sense. Maybe I was under his thrall? Did dragons have thralls? I made a mental note to research that later and decided that I was temporarily insane. I wasn't really safe with Archer. The only person I ever felt safe with was my gran, and no sexy, large, really handsome dragon man was going to change that.

As I was arguing to myself, the words he'd spoken made a few synapses spark. "Wait a minute, your *mate*?"

"You took my fire. It surprised me, too. Ouroboros dragons don't often find mates, since our genetic ties have been broken, making it difficult to find someone compatible with us."

"You are using way too many words that sound like they *should* make sense, but don't. Let's take the big one first, this mate thing. If you think I'm some sort of a dragon—"

"Not yet," he said, glancing back at me, his eyes now their normal pale, iced blue. "Soon, though."

"But I'm human!" I protested.

"Yes. That is why it is so unexpected."

"That's like…cross species. Isn't that impossible?"

"Unlikely, but not impossible. Originally, dragons did not mate out of their septs."

"Come again?"

"Extended family groups. Ouroboros dragons do not have such bonds, but that meant mates, those who were genetically matched with us, are few and far between."

"Again, can I point out I'm human?"

"I know what you are," he said, his voice grim as he marched slightly ahead of me, his fingers holding tight to my hand.

I was about to continue questioning him when a thought fought its way through the postcoital haze that wrapped around my brain. "Bree!" I squawked, guilt flooding me that I had forgotten her so easily.

"Who? Oh, the sprite?"

"No, Bree. She's the girl who was with me tonight. The one who likes to stare at you and say inappropriate things—your tail! *That's* what she meant! She knew you were a dragon when we saw you at the hotel bar. That little... I'll have a thing or two to say to her, but, Archer, we have to find her first so I can say those things. She's somewhere in the woods. We split up in order to make it harder for Hunter to find us."

Archer swore under his breath but dropped my hand and stopped. "Which direction did she go?"

"To the east."

He pulled out his cell phone and spoke quickly into it, speaking Proto-Balto-Slavic, another old language, this one the progenitor to modern languages currently in use in Eastern Europe. I'd done part of my master's research in that language, but I was amazed that Archer and his friend knew it along with Eastern Slavic. "The sprite is in the woods, evidently running to the east. No, they left, but knowing the shadow dragons, Hunter will make a show of returning. I don't expect them to take long to do so. Find her fast."

I was about to ask him if he'd done research in medieval central Europe but lost my train of thought when he took my hand again and helped me over a fallen trunk, saying, "Miles will find your friend before the others do."

"I appreciate that, but she's my responsibility." I

looked around, confused as to where we were. "I appreciate you sending your friend—I assume Miles is the man with the auburn hair who was with you last night—but she's *my* friend, and I can't let her run around a forest on her own, especially if Hunter and that huge man with no neck are out there looking for her."

"They won't be," he said, making an exasperated sound in his chest before taking my hand and tugging at it again.

"How do you know?" I was still peering around the trees, although I did reluctantly let Archer pull me down a game trail. Ahead of us, barely visible down a steep ravine, I thought I saw a glimpse of light.

"They are cowards. As soon as they saw us, they left." His voice was completely neutral, not gloating, not angry, just as if his brother was of no matter to him.

I stopped worrying about Bree for a minute to eye the man who was holding branches ahead of me so they wouldn't whap me in the face. "He doesn't have very nice things to say about you. I take it you two are on the outs?"

"To date, forty-one members of my tribe have been murdered," he said, and this time, there was emotion when he spoke, a deep anguish that I felt more than heard. "You could call that being on the outs."

I stopped for a third time, causing him to look back in question. "Your brother killed your...er...I'm not quite sure on dragon nomenclature, not that I even realized you guys were real until half an hour ago, and frankly, I think I'm doing an exceptional job of not making a bigger deal about it, but to be honest, I raised a demon earlier, and that kind of took my paranormal-being cherry, if you will. Am I babbling?"

"Yes," he said, and pulled me forward another ten yards, then paused and looked down a long, forty-five-degree slope made up of dirt, small shrubs, and ferns. Given that there were rocky cliffs on either side, it looked like the only way to the road unless we took another path.

Archer didn't say anything; he just turned to me, swung me up in his arms, and started down the slope.

"What the hell!" I squawked, twisting my body around him so that once again my legs were around his waist, his head smashed into my breasts while I clutched his hair in a death grip. "Ack! Stop! You'll break your neck! Or mine! Ack ack ack!"

His arms cartwheeled, and I felt the vibrations of him speaking into my boobs but couldn't understand what he was saying when he continued forward, more or less sliding down that slope, dirt and small rocks and bits of plants cascading down before us. Amazingly enough, he managed to keep his balance until he reached the last yards of the slope, at which point he tripped over a large rock and fell forward. I only had a fraction of a second to realize I was going to be between him and the road and braced myself for what was sure to be a very painful experience, but Archer twisted in the time it takes for one second to pass to another, with the result that I landed on top of him when he skidded a few feet on the road.

"Oh my God, oh my God, oh my God," I chanted, my heart pounding while I scrambled off of him, trying to simultaneously catch my breath and run my hands over him to make sure he wasn't hurt seriously. "Don't you ever do that again! Are you hurt? Did you hit your head? Holy shit, Archer! We could have both been killed! Or at least seriously injured. Are you bleeding? I don't see any blood, except…Oh, man, I have a clump of your hair." I showed him the small wad of hair that was still clutched between my shaking fingers.

"So I gather," he said, rubbing the side of his head before sitting up. He winced and tried to look over his shoulder.

"Did you hurt your back? How did you twist like that? That was impressive, although I don't know how you— God's boils!" I'd crawled around to see his back and stopped at the bloody, gruesome sight that met my eyes. The slide along the asphalt with me riding him had resulted in a hideous case of road rash, the entire upper back of his shirt shredded, his flesh bloody and black with dirt. "Oh my God! Okay, don't move," I said, my hands shaking as I pulled out my cell phone. "I'll call 911."

"There's no need," he said, getting to his feet. He winced again but offered me a hand. "It will heal soon enough, although I would like to point out in my defense that if you hadn't climbed me like I was a ladder and tried to smother me with your breasts, I would have been able to see. Come. My car is this way."

I stared at him in astonishment, amazement, and other a-words of surprise that I couldn't think of at that moment, because I was so agog with the fact that he thought he could just walk off a major injury like having his back skinned off. "Agog," I said, my brain picking something ridiculous to focus on because it just couldn't cope with anything else.

He cocked an eyebrow at me as I got to my feet.

"It's my third a-word for what the hell do you think you're doing? Archer, you can't just pretend your back isn't a bloody mess."

"I'm not pretending anything. It just isn't of importance at this moment. Are you going to come with me, or do I have to pick you up and carry you? That act will definitely not be pleasant for my back, but if you insist—"

I punched him in the chest. Not hard, because the poor man had to be in immense pain already, but enough to let him know I didn't appreciate his bossy attitude. "Listen, I'm really sorry that I climbed you like a ladder, but I...It just seemed...Oh, hell, I just wanted to be held if I was going to die." A little flush swept upward to warm my cheeks. "Regardless, I am not the sort of person who likes to be manhandled, and that includes being picked up and hauled around like I'm a sack of potatoes."

He flashed a wolfish grin at me, an expression that flooded my stomach with heat and pleasure. I reminded myself that I'd only just decided that I didn't feel safe with him despite the most mind-blowingly fabulous sex, but it didn't do much to stop me from wanting to fan myself.

"Trust me, flower, I do not think of you as a sack of potatoes. Come along. I don't wish to remain here while my brother has time to return to reclaim you."

"Reclaim me? What is that supposed to mean?" I trotted alongside him, his long legs making me move faster than I would have normally, but since I was scanning the tree line for signs of Bree, I didn't object.

His fingers twined through mine in a way that made my stomach do happy little flutters. Dammit! I just lectured myself, and yet here I was happy fluttering just at the touch of his hand.

With much sternness, I pointed out that just because we had a hookup in the forest didn't mean his talk of being a dragon mate was valid. Or important.

Or desired.

The horror of the kidnapping, following my relief at being found by Archer, simply pushed our libidos into overdrive, that was all.

My inner voice made a comment about how sad it was when one had to lie to oneself. I thought mean things at the voice.

"What are you doing?" Archer asked me.

"What do you mean?"

"You're growling."

My blush lit up my cheeks again. I was glad we were in a section of the road without a light. "Just...uh...telling my inner voice that she could go to hell."

He shot me a look I couldn't identify in the darkness. "You are a *very* unique woman."

"Yeah," I said on a sigh. "I've always been weird. Speaking of unique, Mr. Mythical Beast, I have a bunch of questions."

"Ah," he said, nodding to where a black sedan had been pulled off the side of the road. Ahead, I could see the skid marks where Hunter's limo had come to its abrupt stop, but of the limo—or Bree—there was no sign. "Here are the keys. Wait in the car. Lock the doors. If my brother returns before Miles and I do, leave."

He shoved a set of car keys into my hand before starting for the trees.

"Oh, you are so not doing this," I said, and ran after him. "I don't mind you helping me look for Bree, because despite what a particularly snarky part of my mind says, I'm not stupid, but Bree is my friend, and I feel responsible for her."

I heard him muttering under his breath but couldn't catch what he said.

"People who deliberately say rude things too quiet for others to hear are cowards," I said, following him across a downed trunk that spanned a ditch filled with inky ferns.

"I said that I was going to regret having such an acute sense of smell."

I frowned as we went deeper into the tree line. He paused at the crest of a hill, moving forward when I pointed to the direction I'd last seen Bree fleeing. "If that's a slam against my deodorant, I'd like to point out that the Archer Log Flume ride we did down that hill could push even the most effective of products beyond its limit."

"I was referring to your scent."

I took a brief whiff of my armpits. "Well, I am sorry if I—"

"Christus Rex, woman, I am not insulting you," he snarled, pulling me to his chest, his nose buried in my neck. He breathed in deeply, a low, rumbling noise coming from his chest that had an answer deep inside me. "Your scent drives me insane. It's not just a field of flowers. It's..." He took another deep breath as I fought the urge to slide my hands up his chest. I might not be too shameless to go at it with him in the relative privacy of the forest at night, but I drew the line to sex on the road. "It's like you are bathed in sunlight. Golden, warm flowers that make me want to bury myself in you again—"

I fought it, I really did fight it, but I turned to a puddle of goo against him, my still very happy girl parts deciding that if he wanted to go another round, they'd be up for it. Luckily, his phone gave a little hiccup just as he started nibbling on my earlobe.

The conversation was short. "Miles has your friend." He turned on his heel, and we hurried back toward the road. "They are near the road, hidden, but they saw the shadow dragons on the move, no doubt to try to reclaim you."

"There's that word again."

He said nothing, but I saw another wince of pain when he reached back to help me scramble down a boulder. I decided I'd distract him from the discomfort of his back with some of the thousands of questions that had popped up in the last few hours. "About this mate business—what we did back there was pretty awesome. More than awesome, really, but I should tell you that I'm not looking for a romantic partner. I'm perfectly happy as I am. So if whatever it is to be a mate means we're dating—"

"We aren't dating," he said, his words cutting into my soul. For a moment I was stunned by the baldness of his words, even though I'd just told him that I wasn't in the market for a man.

How stupid is it to feel hurt by that after I just said I was not looking for a relationship? Unreasonably, I *was* hurt, and that just made me more annoyed at myself because I hate it when I act inconsistent.

"You're growling again, flower."

"Sorry." I gritted my teeth for a couple of seconds instead. "I have a really sarcastic inner voice, and she's riding me hard tonight. Naturally, I wasn't implying that you would be interested in dating me—the interlude in the forest aside, judging by Sparkle Bosom, you're into a totally different sort of woman than me—but since we're agreed on the 'steamy forest dragon sex is awfully nice, but it's not going to go any farther than that' situation, I guess I don't understand the mate reference."

He slid me a fast glance. "Why do you do that?"

"Do what? Ask questions? I like to have things orderly in my mind." I sighed.

"Curiosity, I understand. I enjoy satisfying my own. But you insist on denigrating yourself, and I do not understand why. Is it because of your genetic difference?"

I touched a finger to my affected eyebrow, automatically smoothing it. "I'm not denigrating anyone. I have a very healthy self-image. I just have no false idea of what I look like. We have this weird dichotomy in our culture—either people feel it's perfectly fine for them to make unsolicited comments to me, or they try to boost me up with inclusionary statements meant to make me feel like I'm utterly gorgeous when I'm not remotely. So, yes, my situation makes me more aware that people find my appearance freaky than someone who lives their life without such things."

"I, too, have different genes. I do not use it as a crutch as you do."

"Hey," I said, frowning at him. "Unless you've lived through the insults that I've had to endure, you don't get to make those judgments."

He stopped when we hit the road and took my chin in one hand. "And yet you hide behind dark glasses during the day and tell me that I couldn't find you sexually arousing simply because you have different coloration manifesting itself in unimportant ways. This despite the steamy forest dragon sex."

I slapped his hand from my chin, annoyed that he more or less called me a coward. "Says the man who looks like a freakin' *GQ* cover model! What do you know about having people stare and make comments and laugh at you because you are different?"

His jaw tightened so hard I was amazed he could get words out. "My parents abandoned me when I was a babe because I was not what they wanted. I grew up without a family, without a clan, on the outside of both the mortal and immortal worlds. I had no one, no one to care for me, no one to claim me. I don't even have a name that is my own. You think I don't know what it is to be different from everyone else? That has been every hour of every day in all the seven hundred years of my existence."

Anguish was raw and rough in his voice, a pain so deep it made tears prick at the back of my eyes. "I'm sorry. I'm so sorry. I didn't know you were abandoned. That's beyond tragic. But…but you have a name…Wait, did you say seven hundred years?"

"Archer was my job, not my name." The edge in his voice was as sharp as a razor. He strode past me, bone-deep sorrow trailing behind him.

I stood for a moment trying to process the hell he had lived through, wanting to cry. My parents had died when I was very young, but at least I had my gran and a name of my own. I ran after him, not touching him but feeling like a gigantic self-centered fool. "Not that it in any way compares to what you lived through, but I don't hide behind my sunglasses. I just…just take a break from people staring at me. Also, can we go back to that seven hundred years bit? Because that really boggles my mind."

"If you had some truly unfortunate quirk, like six breasts or a couple of arms growing out of your head, I could understand your attitude, but not this. I expect better from you." He continued walking as if he hadn't just said the most outrageous things.

And suddenly, I was annoyed again. "Look, I get that you had a hard life. I'm sorry about that. I can't do anything about it other than . . . well, I guess I can help you pick out a new name if you'd like one. One that's truly yours, one that you feel reflects who you are. But that aside, you don't get to say rude things to me just because you had it harder than I did growing up. And because we got hot and bothered together."

He said nothing.

"After all," I pointed out, still mildly miffed by his attitude toward me, "you may not have had an easy life before, but you have to be sitting awfully darned pretty now if you can spend the sort of money you spent on a manuscript leaf. You spent more than five years of my wages on a piece of vellum and a bit of gold leaf."

He snorted.

"Don't you snort at me so dismissively, dragon boy." I broke into a trot to keep up with him.

"Master. I am a dragon master, not a boy."

"Some of us have learned to overcome the shit life gives us, you know."

"And you think I have not?" His eyes were as pale as the moon that hung heavy in the sky.

"I think you have probably done exactly that, but somewhere along the way, you forgot what it was like to be less than perfect. Maybe people started doing things for you because you have a pretty face. Soon you expected it, for no other reason than you were a handsome man. I work for one of your type. Edgar is a bastard, but he's a handsome bastard, and don't think he doesn't use that for everything he can get. You're a hundred times more gorgeous than him, so I can just imagine what goes on in that mind of yours. You may have had a rough start to your life, but I bet it wasn't long before all you had to do was snap your fingers and you'd get what you want. The world isn't that kind to the rest of us, Archer. Some of us were born struggling with what we were given, and we remain struggling all our lives."

"Is it my fault that others did not work to prosper as I did?" His voice still had an edge to it, but it hurt less, like he was thinking about what I said.

A warm glow spread within me. Only my grandmother had ever truly listened to me. "Of course not. You are to be commended for what you've made of your life. Even if thinking about it being seven hundred years long is a big of a mind blower. And just so you know, we're going to sit down with a digital recorder one day, and I'm going to interview the hell out of you about what you lived through. You're a historian's wet dream."

He made a face but continued to walk. Despite my irritation, I wanted badly to take his hand, but the comment about us not dating had me hesitating to make such a familiar gesture. I knew that to some men, sex—

while being the most personal of all interactions—was purely functional, with little meaning beyond that. Perhaps Archer was like that. Perhaps he wouldn't like it if I assumed that because we'd had an extremely good time in the forest, I could take his hand whenever I wanted. Or brush a strand of hair back off his brow. Or just stand close to him, so I could feel his heat.

I edged a little closer to him, so my hand would naturally touch his while we walked, just in case he wanted to hold my hand.

"I do not understand what point you are trying to make," he said, his voice back to its normal rich, deep tones. His brother might have gotten all the silkiness, but Archer's voice seemed to thrum deep inside of me.

"I think that perhaps you could view the plight of others with a little more compassion. Not all of us are able to do with our lives what you did with yours." My hand bumped his again. Dammit, why didn't he take the hint?

He said nothing.

"I hate to pry, so feel free to tell me if this is too personal, but I told you I had a wicked curiosity, and I don't understand how your parents could abandon you as a baby. What was it they wanted you to be that you weren't?"

"A dragon hunter." He looked moody now, his face all harsh shadows and angular planes. "We were to be the first, but we didn't come out...right."

"You were supposed to hunt your own family?" I asked, aghast.

"No. Dragon hunters are dragons who hunt demonic beings. They have mastery over such beings beyond what others do. My parents once dreamed of a race that would serve the mortal and immortal worlds alike, each dragon hunter a perfect balance of dragon and demon, the dragon to provide the strength and resolve and the demon to give the ability to defeat others of its kind. But we were not born with a balance."

I was almost afraid to ask. "What happened?"

"I am a dragon," he said simply.

The implication hit me like a plank to the face. "So your brother is—"

"Yes." He skewed me a hard look. "That is why you must not heed anything he says to you. There is no dragon in him, only darkness."

"How tragic." I felt an odd sort of sympathy for Hunter. Until I remembered how he refused to even consider letting Bree and me go. "For parents to do that... it's just unthinkable. How about Devon?"

He shot me a confused look. "What about it?"

"As a name. It's a nice name. I've always liked it. You could be Devon."

"No."

"Okay. Charles."

"No."

"You're right, that's way too average for you. Um..." I spread my fingers wide, so they would be extra pokey when my hand moved against his. "Phoenix?"

"That is a city, not a name."

"It could be both. Tristan?"

"No."

"Gerard. Martin. Fahrvergnügen."

The look he gave me was priceless.

"All right, we'll give up on that for a while," I said, all but stabbing him with my little finger. Was the man dense? Clueless? Numb in the hand region? "Why don't you tell me about your storm dragons?"

"What do you want to know about them?"

"How many people are in your group?"

"Tribe. More than seventy."

I made a fist and swung it into his hand. "I have to say, this is all really fascinating from a scholarly standpoint. I recall mentions of dragons in some older texts, but I never had any idea that they were referring to a race of actual beings."

"We have existed almost as long as man has."

"Dammit, Archer!" I stopped and glared at him.

He walked on a few steps, then turned back and looked at me with an obvious question in his shadowed eyes.

"Are you going to hold my hand or not?" The words were blurted out before I realized it.

He looked at my hand, then back up to me. "You just finished telling me you don't want a romantic partner."

"Gah!" I yelled, and stomped forward past him, ignoring him when he held out a hand for me. Infuriating, irritating... I bit back all the words I wanted to call him, knowing I had no one but myself to blame.

"I am a strong, independent woman. I do not need a

man. I am perfectly happy as I am. Hot forest dragon sex is not of vital importance to my happiness. I have my gran, and that's the only person I need in my life."

"You are not at all what I expected," Archer said, once again at my side (damn his long legs). His voice held mingled notes of both amusement and annoyance. "Not that I thought to ever find a mate."

"You haven't. I'm human."

"I have seen other dragon's mates, ones from septs. They do not argue with their dragons."

It was my turn to snort derisively.

"They are supportive. Undemanding." He thought for a moment. "They follow their dragon's wishes."

"Then it's a good thing I'm not your mate, because I am *so* not any of those things."

"I believe this will end up being good," Archer continued in a meditative tone. I refused to look at him. I did notice, however, that he didn't try to take my hand again. For some reason, that made a hysterical little giggle well up inside of me. "It will keep us from being bored with each other over the centuries."

"You're quite, quite insane."

"No, but I suspect you may drive me there."

I gawked at him for a moment, but his lips twitched. I smacked him on the arm. "I can't think of anything worse than spending the rest of my life with you."

I regretted the words the instant they left my lips. I felt Archer withdraw from me even though he didn't physically move away. I tried to stop him to apologize and explain what I meant, but he kept walking.

"I'm so sorry. Archer, stop." I dashed in front of him, my hands on his chest. "I'm sorry, that came out wrong."

"You do not need to apologize," he said in a stiff voice fraught with dignified injury.

"Yes, I do, because I blurted out only part of what I was thinking. The whole thought was that I can't think of anything worse than spending my life with a man who is so handsome, and so interesting as you, because women will constantly be throwing themselves on him. On you. I'm not..." I struggled for the words, ashamed that I had said something that had hurt him but not wanting to bare my dirty secrets.

"You're not what?" he unbent enough to ask.

"I'm...oh, God's wounds! I'm jealous, okay? I'm a horribly jealous person. My ex-boyfriend told me that was why he hooked up with other women, because he couldn't stand me being so possessive. And with you being so sexy you could steam a nun's socks at fifty paces, and chock-full of historical information that could probably fill an encyclopedia, I'd be a raving lunatic trying to deal with all the women who would be sucked onto you like you were a magnet and they were a bit of iron. Don't you see? What we did in the forest was the best sexual experience of my life, and to be honest, in the top five of overall life experiences. Okay, top two, but we can't do it again because then I'll start to get attached to you, and after that...well, it's not pretty."

He stared at me for the count of six, then tangled

his fingers in my hair, pulling my head back so that my mouth was angled up to his. "You are my mate. I am yours. I will never give you cause to be jealous, just as you never give me a reason to doubt your fidelity." He kissed me, his mouth hot and hard and not at all gentle. But when I slid a hand up his chest, he made that noise in his chest again and wrapped us in fire.

"Does that make things clearer in your mind?"

I blinked, touching my lips when he pulled away from me. "Huh?" My brain was a muddled mix of thoughts of him, of his fire and his body, and how much I wanted to repeat the forest scene. It was then I noticed my fingers were on fire. "My fingers are... on...*fire*," I said, so shocked I didn't know whether to scream or cry. Oddly, the heat didn't hurt. It felt like a gentle warmth, one that almost tickled.

"Dragon fire will not hurt you," he said, seeing the panic in my eyes. "Your ability to control my fire is another sign you are my mate."

"It's so...hoo. I don't know if I can get used to this," I said, watching the flames flicker.

"Come. The car is just around this bend."

I stayed where I was, watching the fire. It was mesmerizing.

He sighed, came back to me, and patted out the fire, then took my hand and led me forward.

"That was seriously awesome. But, oh, man, I am so in over my head."

"Yes, but all will become clear to you with time."

The car loomed up before us, reminding me there

were more important things going on in my life. I gave him a long look and gestured toward his back. "Do you want me to drive? You're hurt. It can't feel good to lean back against a seat."

"I've had worse injuries," was all he said, opening a door for me. I hurriedly got my seat belt on, noting the lines of pain around his mouth when he did the same. He might claim that it was no big deal that he'd torn off half the flesh on his back, but it had to be almost unbearable.

I rallied another subject suitable for distracting him from the pain that I could still see in his face. "I get that Hunter is Mr. Bad, but why do you keep saying he wants to *reclaim* me?"

"He took you." He frowned as he drove, his eyes watchful. "He must have some nefarious plan for you. He can't know you're my mate." He stopped, then glanced at me. "Unless you told him."

"Of course I did." I stared out the window, watching the shadows slip past us. "I tell everyone I meet. Did you not see the billboard on the outskirts of town announcing our matedom?"

He said nothing.

"As a matter of fact, your brother hired me to do a job." I slid him a thoughtful look. "He has a photocopy of the leaf you bought from Edgar, you know."

The car swerved for a moment.

He swore in Magyar, the language of Hungary. "He showed it to you?"

"Yes." I made sure he had control of the car before

I continued. "He hired me to decipher it, but I told him I wouldn't. Which brings me back to the subject that I broached earlier tonight—"

"He hired *you*?" Confusion was written all over his handsome face, visible by the glow of the dashboard lights. I spent a moment admiring the line of his jaw, wishing I could run my fingers along it, and kiss the shadow of stubble. "Why?"

"Because deciphering medieval codes is one of my hobbies." I looked out the window again, having another mental argument with my libido.

He didn't say anything for a few seconds, but he shot me a couple of curious glances. Finally, he said, "Miles researched translators but did not mention you. Do you decipher manuscripts professionally?"

"Sometimes. There's not a lot of untranslated texts out there, but every now and again I get a crack at one." I smiled to myself. "Have you heard of the Voynich Manuscript?"

"Yes. It is undecipherable, most likely nothing but a collection of symbols that have no actual meaning."

My smile grew a tiny bit smug. "Not *entirely* undecipherable."

He shot me another questioning glance. "You broke the code?"

"Part of it, yes. There's another man who was making some headway with another section, and we had just agreed to join forces when Edgar made me stop. He said it was a waste of time working on projects where I wasn't bringing in money to the shop." Anger fired in me at the memory of the fight we'd had over that, but since I knew now my time with him wouldn't last beyond me giving him back Archer's leaf, I let the negative emotions go. "And speaking about that, your leaf—"

"I must make a call." He touched a button on the dash, causing his phone to go into speaker mode and dial a number. "The woman he stole is a scholar," he said in Proto-Balto-Slavic. "She can translate the leaf."

His buddy whistled into the phone and answered in the same language, "That's a stroke of luck, since the man I contacted said he had a family emergency. I guess it's a good thing you all but steamed her knickers off last night, eh?"

My eyes widened. Archer slid me a fast look before answering, "*He* has a copy of the manuscript."

"How did he get that?" Miles swore. "He'll come looking for her, then."

"Yes. We must keep her safe. From him."

"Agreed. Take her to bed. She'll follow you anywhere after you fuck her a few times."

I bit my lower lip and looked out the window again, tears of embarrassment pricking the backs of my eyes. That bastard. Both of them! So that's why Archer was so happy to have forest sex. He just wanted to make me fall for him so I'd do whatever he wanted.

At which my inner self pointed out that he didn't know what I did before I told him just half a minute ago. I stopped trying to set fire to Archer with my mind.

"She doesn't deserve such crudeness," Archer told his friend in a gritty voice, causing me to peek at him. Did he just defend me in some weird way? "Keep your mind on your responsibilities, and do not interfere with mine."

"I suggest using your tongue," Miles said with a laugh. "Her twat may not be very pretty, but at least you won't have to look at her face."

I imagined a dartboard with Miles's face on it. It didn't give me enough satisfaction. I substituted Miles's face itself for the dartboard and smiled.

Archer said a rude word and hung up. "They should be just ahead," he said after a couple of seconds of silence.

I alternated between needing to crawl into a corner so I could have a good cry and beating Miles over the head. I absolved Archer of all suspicions, since it was obvious he wasn't of the same mind as his foul-mouthed, and fouler-minded, cousin, but regardless, I couldn't help but wonder if there was another reason he might want me to have the hots for him.

We rolled to a stop at a turnout. Waiting next to a sign describing the view were two shadows, which quickly detached themselves and hurried over to the car.

Archer hit the door locks so Bree and Miles could get into the car, but rather than climb in the back as I expected, Miles pulled open my door, gesturing at me, clearly expecting me to get out.

"Get in the back," Archer told him, frowning. "They could be right behind us if they are in the area."

"You know I hate riding in the back." He reached for my seat belt while Archer swore under his breath. I slapped Miles's hand off me, undoing the buckle myself and snatching my purse off the floor as I got out of the car.

He smiled and held the back door open. Bree was about to get in when I made a fist and punched Miles in the nose as hard as I could. His head snapped back, sending him staggering backward a few steps until he stumbled over a rock and fell.

"Come on, Bree." I grabbed her wrist and started off toward the road.

"Oh, good one, Thaisa!" She peered over her shoulder, giggling. "He's up again. Ouch, I think you may have broken his nose."

"Good. I wash my hands of the pair of them. We'll walk home." I disregarded the fact that walking home was not the wisest move in the world. Somehow, we'd do it. Even if Hunter tried to nab us again. I had my pepper spray, after all.

"Oooh," she said, glancing back again. "I didn't see this coming."

I didn't either, but it felt good. It felt very good.

Except the part where I walked away from Archer.

CHAPTER EIGHT

ARCHER COULDN'T BELIEVE HIS EYES, BUT AS HE lunged out of the car, his back screaming at the movement, he had the oddest urge to laugh. Of course Thaisa had punched Miles in the nose for no reason. He was coming to expect the unexpected from her.

She might not be the ideal dragon mate, but he realized that an ideal mate might be intolerably boring.

He was in front of Thaisa before she could do more than storm off a few feet, her friend in tow. "What do you think you're doing?"

"Not following you around after fucking you a few times, that's for sure," she snarled in the old language, the one used by early dragons.

Surprise chased chagrin as he took her by the arm,

spinning her around to face him. Her eyes were angry, but worse, shiny with tears. "You understood?"

"Very much so," she answered in Magyar at the same time Miles got to his feet, his hand bloody where he held it to his nose. She switched to East Slavic to add, "I speak eight different variations of archaic Western, Middle, and Eastern European languages, as well as four extant ones."

Archer couldn't stop from shaking his head, laughing as he did so. "I might have known you would understand such archaic languages. Come, my fiery flower, you have made your point. No, do not try to prick me with your verbal thorns. We are not safe here, and I can almost feel my brother's tribe breathing down my neck."

"What the hell?" Miles asked nasally, stopping before them to glare at Thaisa. "I didn't deserve that!"

Fire whipped through Archer at the look his cousin was giving Thaisa, fire and an unreasonable urge to add more injury to Miles's nose. "Apologize to her," he ordered, taking Thaisa's hand in his, twining his fingers through hers so that he could rub her fingers with his thumb.

Miles stopped feeling his nose, a smear of blood visible underneath it. "The hell I will! I've done nothing wrong."

"She speaks the old languages," he said in Proto-Balto-Slavic. "My phone was on speaker when I talked to you."

Miles's gaze swiveled to Thaisa. "Shit."

"Why, yes, that is my exact impression of you," Thaisa said in a voice that fairly dripped with honey. Archer didn't blame her for being angry, but this was not the place to placate her ruffled petals.

Miles muttered an apology while Archer led Thaisa to the passenger seat, ignoring his cousin's glare as he did so.

A frosty silence settled over the car when he headed south, to his home. He slid Thaisa occasional glances, but she sat with her arms crossed, staring pointedly out the side window, not saying a word, not even acknowledging his existence. He wanted to apologize for what his cousin had said but decided that was better left for a private moment.

His back still hurt like it had been raked by lion's claws, but the pain was beginning to ease, indicating the healing process innate to all dragons was working. He wondered if perhaps a little twinge or moan of pain might not exact some sympathy from Thaisa but decided he was above such pathetic manipulation.

If only she'd stop ignoring him. He didn't like that at all, especially when he was blameless. At least where Miles's rude comments were concerned. He dwelt instead on the memory of her responsiveness in the forest, when she had tantalized him, initiating a chase guaranteed to drive his control to the edge even though he now knew she was ignorant of such things.

He thought of telling her just how much he enjoyed her heat, the way her breasts heaved against him, of the lure of her mouth, and how the moment when she embraced his fire had driven him past all that could be borne.

No, he'd wait for a private moment to tell her those things, too.

Dammit. Why was she punishing him by pretending he wasn't there, sitting right next to her, obviously waiting for her to tell him the most outrageous things that came to her mind. He wanted to hear her growl at herself. He wanted to answer the many hundreds of questions she evidently stored up, but most of all, he wanted to see his dragon fire reflected in her sated, passionate eyes.

"I don't see why you have to cater to the woman," Miles said a half hour later from where he sat in the back seat. He was speaking in Zilant, a language used exclusively by dragonkin centuries ago, before English became the standard language of communication. "Just because she overheard a few things. At least she can't understand this."

Archer began to see why so few ouroboros dragons were mated. It wasn't that due to their mixed genetic backgrounds there were simply no compatible males or females; it was because mates had to be the most exasperating, confusing, and downright irrational beings on the planet.

Thaisa continued to ignore Archer despite his many encouraging glances her way.

"Hey, that's Zilant, isn't it?" Bree asked. She nudged Miles. "I've heard about it, but never actually heard it, if you know what I mean."

Miles shot her an outraged look before saying—still in Zilant—to Archer, "Is no language safe with these two?"

Archer slid yet another look at Thaisa, who still seemed annoyed. He didn't blame her for being insulted, but she was his mate. She had to know he would have words with Miles later about the proper way to speak to and about her.

He reached for one of the hands that was so tightly tucked across her chest, but she merely shot him a fulminating glare and twisted so that her back was toward him.

"I don't know," Bree told Miles with a grin. "Is there?"

Miles glared at her. "I knew it! Archer! Did you hear that?"

Why hadn't Thaisa told him that she was a scholar earlier? He toyed with the idea that she had led him along deliberately, playing him until he couldn't resist her neck and her hips and the way her breasts pressed into his chest, and all that silky skin that beckoned him, making him hard just thinking about filling her with dragon fire—and himself—but after a few minutes mulling that over, he dismissed the idea. Thaisa wasn't devious. She might be irrational, she might have a delightful quirky nature that she didn't seem to appreciate, but her eyes were never shadowed with deception, and her countenance was as open and sunny as her personality.

She was going to make his life a living hell.

"How did you learn to speak Zilant?" Miles demanded to know of Bree in that language. "You're not a dragon. Only dragonkin are allowed to speak it. I insist that you stop this instant."

Archer's vision for the future never included a mate. He had spent his life alone, on the fringes, never belonging, never bonding with anyone, not until he found Miles and decided to form a tribe. And now here was this woman, this mate who drove him to distraction with her wonderfully different eyes and the warmth that seemed to wrap around him like his fire.

"Dude, I don't know what you're talking about," Bree told the now irate Miles. "Chill!"

"You didn't understand me?" Miles asked suspiciously, still in Zilant.

"Of course not," she said, flashing Archer an impish grin before pulling out her phone.

Miles sat back, looking smugly pleased.

Christus Rex, he would not allow his mate to wrap him around her little finger! If she wanted to sulk, so be it. He was master of the tribe, master of her, and if she thought she could get around him with a few hurt feelings and tears, she could think again.

"Why did you decide to specialize in medieval history?" someone asked Thaisa. He was surprised to find the words came from his mouth.

She turned back to look at him, sniffed as if she wasn't going to answer him, but suddenly unbent, sighing before she turned around to sit properly in the seat. "I thought it was interesting. You must feel the same way if you bought the leaf."

"Wait a minute," Miles said in English, suspicion dawning on his face. He frowned at Bree. "Wait just one minute. When I asked you if you understood me, you said you didn't."

"That's right," Bree said.

"Ah. Yes. There is a reason I bought the leaf. Mostly because Miles had a theory about it." He let her see how pleased he was that she had stopped ignoring him and tried to take her hand again. She pulled it out of his grasp. "It has to do with an old fable."

"The Raisa Medallion? Your brother told me about that, although not why you guys are so interested in it. It's just a story, right?"

Warmth blossomed on his thigh as Thaisa placed her hand on his leg in a possessive move. Instantly, blood rushed to his penis, ensuring that he would spend the rest of the drive home feeling as if his trousers were two sizes too small.

"The medallion is supposed to be the one my parents divided between my brother and me."

"God's shiny pink butt! That was about you? The story that your brother told?"

"It is a fable only. There is no truth to it other than my parents abandoned us."

"No wonder you don't want to give back the leaf." Her hand was warm on this thigh. Very warm. His fire, usually smoldering quietly inside him, roared to life at the touch. He flicked the air-conditioning to a level higher.

Her fingernails were on fire again.

"What did you mean by it?" Miles asked Bree.

Thaisa looked at her hand, her eyebrows arched. Archer's body interpreted the look she gave her hand—located so near his genitals—as an outright act of sensual teasing, and accordingly, he hardened even more.

Dammit, now his trousers were three sizes too small. If she kept touching him like that, he wouldn't be able to walk at all.

"What did I mean by what?" Bree murmured, the tinny sound of a mobile game coming from her phone.

Archer lifted Thaisa's hand and placed her index fingertip inside his mouth, extinguishing the little dollop of fire.

She gasped, heat shimmering in her eyes. *His* heat.

He repeated the process with another finger, swirling his tongue around it.

She moaned softly to herself.

"What did you mean by saying you didn't understand me, when you had to do just that in order to know what I asked?"

"Are you on crack, like, right this very moment?" Bree asked, giving Miles a look that said he was being unreasonable. "Have you eaten some funny mushrooms? Some hemp-flavored noms?"

Archer repeated the process with Thaisa's next two fingers, thinking seriously about unzipping his fly so as not to injure himself while his trousers continued to shrink.

Thaisa quivered.

"I am not the crazy one here!" Miles said, his hair standing on end like he'd been running his hands through it.

Archer, with a sidelong look at Thaisa, took her final finger into his mouth, the dragon fire on it absorbing into him. He gently bit the pad of her finger. She clutched the car door with her free hand, her eyes huge and misty with desire.

Desire for him. He released her finger and smiled.

She reclaimed her hand and slumped back on the seat, giving odd little twitches.

His penis attained a hardness equivalent to marble. Or titanium. He could probably use it to crush rock.

"That's it. I'm done talking to you," Miles said, and turned away from Bree, leaning against the side of the car, closing his eyes in an obvious signal he was going to sleep.

"Quitter," she said in Zilant.

Miles hissed something rude.

"What..." Thaisa cleared her throat. "What were we talking about?"

Archer had to think for a few minutes. "Your desire to translate ancient medieval texts."

"That's right." She pounced on the subject, her breath a bit ragged.

He smiled. She might tell herself she wasn't his mate, but it was obvious she was halfway to being in love with him already. As his mate, it was right and proper that she should love him, whereas he, the master of the tribe, would show her respect and a reasonable amount of affection, but nothing too consuming. He cared for all the members of his tribe, so really, it would be no extra trouble to ensure she was happy and free from cares, and in return, she would love him with all the passion he saw growing every time he looked into those lovely, mysterious eyes.

He shifted in the seat again, making a mental note to have a tailor attend to the lack of room in his trousers.

"Wait, I thought you said you were taking me home?" Thaisa said when he pulled off the highway and took the turn that led to the coast, and his home. "Ross is another seven miles to the south."

"We are going to my home, not yours."

"Really? First your brother kidnaps Bree and me, and now you do exactly the same thing?" She punched him in the leg, right where she had previously placed her hand.

His erection strained his fly.

"What is with you dragons?" she continued to rail, her color high. "Dammit, don't make me pepper spray your pretty eyes!"

"I am not kidnapping you. I am simply taking you to my house because I didn't think you'd care to be alone in your apartment above the shop. The address of which, I need not point out, my brother must know if he contacted you."

"Oh." She thought about that for a moment. "I didn't think of that, but that's a good point. Although you could have asked me first. I could stay at a hotel. Or with a friend. And what about Bree?"

"You would be in great danger by yourself," he said simply. "You may not like the fact that I did not ask for your opinion, but it is your safety as well as others' I am thinking of. That includes Bree, since my brother knows she is with you, and thus he might use her to force you to come to heel. Who is Gran?"

"Your brother said almost the same thing about my safety, although I will admit I believe you a whole lot more than I do him...Hmm? Gran is my grandmother. Why?"

"You said she was the only person you needed in your life. Does she live with you? We will detour to pick her up if so."

She gazed at him with astonishment. "You'd... you'd fetch Gran to keep her safe?"

"Of course. You are my mate. She is your relative. My protection extends to her as well."

"I..." She seemed to have a hard time speaking for a few seconds. "I'm...Archer, I think that's just about the nicest thing anyone has said to me. But you don't have to get back on the highway—Gran lives in a home for Alzheimer's patients. They have locks on all the doors and only let in people who have relatives there, so she's quite safe." She stopped suddenly, her face troubled. "For the most part. Archer, we really need to talk."

"I agree," he said, pausing at the gate that protected his home from intruders and punching in the access code. A clutch of palms provided a privacy screen, but as he drove along the curved drive to his house on the beach, he heard Thaisa's intake of breath.

He stopped outside the garage so that she could get the full impact of the house, pleased that she liked it.

"Holy hand grenades," she said, getting out of the car, her eyes huge while she took in the white stone house that sat two stories high, floodlights scattered along the pathways and foundation softening the clean, sharp lines. The air was still warm with the heat of the day, but the breeze that rolled in from the water brought with it the salty tang that Archer loved. "That's where you live? That's...wow. Just wow."

"I designed it," he said, enjoying the way her pleasure shone on her face. "This side isn't as nice as the one that faces the ocean. I will show it to you in the morning. You will enjoy it."

"I'm sure I will. I've never known anyone who had a beach house," she said, absently taking the hand he held out for her.

It flitted through his brain that he'd never been one to enjoy touching a woman outside of the sexual act, but there was something about Thaisa that had him re-thinking that policy. He liked the way she curled her fingers around his, how she bumped his hand when she wanted him to touch her but was too shy to initiate the contact. It made him feel...He shook that thought away. He felt respect for her, as was proper with a mate, and that was enough. "Miles, cease pretending to be asleep. I want a security detail on the perimeter in the next ten minutes. Send out a warning to the tribe that the shadow dragons may strike them in an attempt to hurt me. The grounds and house will be locked down immediately."

"Pretty!" Bree said, getting out of the car and taking a picture with her phone. She stretched and yawned. "Gotta go, though. Abdul has to be at work early, so I can't stay for the house tour."

"Abdul?" Thaisa looked over her shoulder as Archer led her to the entrance. "I thought your boyfriend was Ramon? And what about San?"

"I have lots of boyfriends." She giggled.

"It's not safe for you. You will stay here so you cannot be used in order to get to Thaisa," Archer said to Bree.

"Really?" She tipped her head and looked at him, a light in her eyes that he thought at first was mocking but quickly realized was amusement. "You think they're going to hurt *me*?"

He opened his mouth to say he disliked having to repeat himself, but reconsidered. "Even sprites can be hurt," was what he finally said.

"So they can, but I am not a sprite," she answered, glancing back at the road where a small minivan pulled up and tooted a weak horn. "Not anymore, anyway. Laters, taters!"

"Wait, Bree!" Thaisa started to go after her when she ran up the driveway. Trajan, one of the tribe members who worked for him taking care of all things mechanical, emerged from the guesthouse that sat back from the gate and sent a questioning glance toward Archer. "It's really not a good idea for you to go scampering around out in the public. Not if Hunter is a demon in man clothes! You should stay here with us."

Archer nodded at Trajan, who pressed the button that opened the gate. Bree jogged through it, pausing at the top of the drive to turn and wave at them. "I'll be fine. Call when you want help controlling your demon," she yelled at Thaisa, waving her phone in the air before jumping into the van.

"What the...my demon? You mean Naamah?" Thaisa frowned and would clearly have gone after Bree if Archer hadn't put his arm around her, steering her into the house. "Sometimes I think she says the most outrageous things possible just to get a rise out of me."

"That is possible," he said, his attention divided between her and the measures he must put into place. If word had gotten out about the manuscript being in his possession, then he had to ensure the safety of his tribe against the attack that was sure to come. "I've found that most members of the Court of Divine Blood have an impish quality about them. This is the living room. That is the dining room. Normally the doors would be open, but for safety's sake, we will leave them closed."

"What on earth is the Court of Divine— Oh!" Thaisa came to a halt at the massive wooden slab table that dominated one half of the open area, the other being the living room. "Those windows—are those windows?—those are amazing! Is it a glass wall?"

He looked with satisfaction at the retractable glass doors that replaced most of the walls on this side of the house, affording a floor-to-ceiling view of the ocean, with only occasional interruptions where stone-covered steel girders supported the structure. "It is, in effect. They can be opened or closed as I desire."

"You get to move the walls...that's insanely wonderful." She dropped his hand to step through the opening onto a broad patio that sat between the house and the infinity pool. Beyond it, the garden rolled down to the natural barrier fence that separated the beach from the grounds. He eyed the fence, noting with satisfaction the two men who lurked in the shadows. He would go out and speak to the patrols later, after he had Thaisa safely settled.

"This is like something out of a magazine," she said, her face shining with delight. "I can't believe you live here."

"It will be less impressive once you have been here awhile," he answered, taking her back into the house and up a broad flight of white stone stairs. "Although I hope you never lose the pleasure I take in it."

"It's just gorgeous." She looked somewhat dazed before she stopped midway up the stairs. "Once I've been here awhile? Archer, you're not asking me to move in, are you?"

"You are my mate." He wondered why she fought that idea so much. Although he'd been surprised when she first took his fire and returned it to him, he had quickly acclimatized himself to her new role in his life, and moved on to planning how best to keep her protected. "Of course you will move here. Mates live together."

"I'm *not* your mate. We're just friends with benefits. Really hot benefits," she said, pulling her hand from his and marching determinedly up the stairs. He allowed himself a moment to admire her ass, wondering how long it would take her to accept the inevitable.

If she thought he was going to let her go, she was mad.

"The subject is not open to debate," he told her, knowing full well she would object.

"Like hell it's not! You can't just make statements about me like that!"

The glare she cast over her shoulder at him was really one of the best he'd ever seen.

He ogled her ass a little more, unable to keep from watching the swing of her hips. Those hips, he mused, could convince him to do much.

"I mean, I admit that we have something—" She stopped at the top of the stairs to face him, making a gesture with her hands held about a foot apart. "We do the steamy forest sex well, and your fire is kind of fun to play with, but that doesn't mean we have a future together."

"If you are going to reference my appearance again—" he started to say, feeling her objections were headed to that subject.

"No, of course not, I'm not that shallow!" she interrupted, then thought for a moment before conceding.

"All right, I *was* going to say that, but it's only part of it."

"I've already reassured you that we will both be faithful to each other," he said briskly, gesturing to the left. She moved in the direction he indicated, a frown pulling down her eyebrows. He liked her eyebrows. They were straight slashes set in an otherwise pleasantly round face, the coloration on her left brow and eyelashes giving her an intriguing air. She was unlike any other woman, but she didn't seem to celebrate that fact. "I cannot change how I look any more than you can."

"The difference being that you're insanely gorgeous," she grumbled, then stopped and faced him. "I know you're tired of hearing this, and I know I should get over it, but I can't! You're so handsome, and…gah! It's like you do it on purpose! Look at you!" She waved a hand at his torso. He looked down at himself, not seeing what the problem was. "Standing there in that lovely blue shirt that matches your eyes when they go sapphire, with your chest taunting me, and your jaw with that bit of stubble that I just know is going to be soft and wonderful, and do not even *mention* your mouth!"

"All right," he said, wondering how the hell he was supposed to make her happy short of defacing himself. "I won't."

She stared at his mouth, licking her lips and blinking a couple of times before she continued. "And then there's your hair!"

"Do I need a haircut?" he asked, wondering if she was ever going to get over his appearance, amused despite himself.

"No! Just the opposite! It's too damned perfect! It's silky and shiny, with a little bitty widow's peak. It's just a little bit long so that a couple of strands sometimes hang over your forehead, and I *love* men with shiny black, slightly long, widow's-peaked, forehead-hanging hair, and you're just standing there flaunting yours at me like you have that right!" Her breasts heaved in her dress as she panted a little. "It's too much, Archer! It's just too much!"

He would have enjoyed looking at her breasts, but he felt that it was more important to let her know she had his full attention. He didn't understand why she was so distressed, but she would no doubt feel better once she worked this odd fit out of her system. He brushed back a bit of hair that had fallen over his brow.

Her fingers spasmed, and she took another deep breath, her breasts swelling above the bodice of the dress, but he kept his eyes on hers. It almost killed him, but he did it. "Well, I'm not going to take it, do you hear me? I'm not going to take that from hair!"

Without warning, she reached out with both hands and vigorously ruffled his hair until it felt like it stood on end. "I'm going to mess it up and then it will stop calling to me to touch it, and touch you, and wonder what it feels like sliding across my belly, and on my thighs, and slicked back wet from a shower. There!"

He waited.

Her eyes narrowed on him. "Dammit! Now you look like you just got out of bed after making love all night, all tousled and steamy and sexy as hell!"

Before he could respond, she turned on her heel and stomped down the hallway, tossing over her shoulder, "Which room is yours?"

He pointed toward a pair of double doors.

"Fine," she snarled, jerking open a door across the hall from it, one of the three spare bedrooms his house afforded. "Is this one being used?"

"No."

"I'm taking it, then." She glared at him from the doorway, her eyes all but spitting fire at him. His fire, he noted. "And don't think I'm going to come crawling to you in the middle of the night, licking your chest, and touching your thighs, and nibbling on your jaw that you insist on keeping right there where anyone can ogle it, and letting my breasts have their way with you, ending in incredibly hot, fire-laden sex, because that thought isn't even on my mind!"

She slammed the door shut before he could reply.

He rubbed his jaw, thought about shaving, and then with a long look at the door, changed his mind. He retreated first to his office, making sure all the members of the tribe had checked in and taken precautions, then went out to verify the perimeter of his own house was protected.

Now that the knowledge of the manuscript was likely spreading, there would be an attack, Archer thought with grim knowledge. His most precious possession was at risk, and there was no way in this world or the next he would anyone to do the unthinkable.

Thaisa was his. That was all there was to it.

He just hoped that someday she would also realize it.

CHAPTER NINE

I WAS SOUND ASLEEP WHEN THE SMELL WOKE ME UP.

"Wha'?" I pushed my hair off my face and rolled from my belly to my side, squinting into the darkness of the room. A faint glow from lights that caressed the outside of Archer's fabulous house stole in through blinds I'd left partially open, enough for me to see that someone was moving across the room. The second I opened my mouth to ask Archer what he thought he was doing creeping around my room while I slept, I realized that the smell wasn't at all his. This was dank and smoky, like leaf mold under a long dead bonfire.

"Ah. You are awake? Excellent. I have come to warn you."

I clicked on the light and stared with surprise at the last person I expected to see. "Naamah?"

The blond man smiled and sat on the foot of my bed, adopting a conversational tone. "As you see, it is me. And I have something of much importance to impart."

"It had better be that you are giving me back my boss's demonic rug."

He just looked at me.

I sighed. "So you thought you'd…what…just pop in and wake me up?" I pulled pillows up behind me, leaning against them while pulling the sheet up over my bare breasts. "At two o'clock in the morning?"

"Deep night," he said with a little tip of his head. "It's when demons are at their best. I'm here to warn you about the dragon."

"Archer?"

"He is manipulating you."

I blinked a couple of times, hoping I'd misheard him. "Hunter? Yes, I can totally see him as a master manipulator, but Archer? No."

"There is an internecine war. You are now caught in the middle of it."

"I don't believe it."

"Nonetheless, it is true."

I thought for a minute. "Okay, let's say what you're right, and Archer is trying to use me. How? What does he want? And why?"

"He is a dragon. He prizes treasure over all else, including people."

"It's possible, but not probable. Proceed."

"He will seduce you to do his bidding because he seeks the medallion so that he might destroy the other tribes."

That totally did not sound like Archer.

"The medallion is just a story," I argued. "It's not real."

The demon smiled, and I felt a bit of my soul tatter and fall to the ground. "Isn't it? If that is the case, why do two dragon masters want it so badly?"

"Yeah," I said slowly, my vision turned inward. What *was* going on with that manuscript? I made a mental promise to eyeball the original just as soon as I could...before giving it back to Edgar. "I still don't understand what you're doing here."

He shrugged. "You summoned me. Until you release me, I must protect you."

I shivered at the thought of being protected by a demon, an actual being of hell. "That's...nice."

His lips pulled back in another smile.

I looked away quickly. "I'll make you a deal—if you bring me back that prayer rug, I'll release you and you can go back to doing whatever it is demons do."

"When I can devote myself to protecting you?" he answered. "Perish the thought. I just thought I'd warn you that he's using you for his own purposes, and once he's done...poof! You'll disappear."

"You're insane," I said, a little skitter of worry making me continue the conversation, rather than getting rid of him, as I knew I should. "What purpose would he have to use me?"

Naamah made a face. "I can't just come right out and state the obvious. We give hints. You have to figure out the rest."

"I don't have anything that Archer wants," I said. The demon was just trying to get into my head.

But why would he bother to do that?

"I'll pop off now, shall I? Unless you wanted to indulge in a little deep night wrestling?"

"Huh?" It took me a few seconds to come back from a dark vision of Archer manipulating me for some unknown purpose.

Naamah leered at me, his gaze on my breasts hidden only by a thin sheet. "I am fully equipped in this form to pleasure females."

I kicked at him from under the blanket. "Ew! No! I don't know how you got past Archer's security, but I don't want you here. You can take your warning and stick it where the demon don't shine. Oh, wait—give me back the prayer rug first."

"Why should I?" he asked, getting to his feet, adopting an injured expression. "You summoned me, and yet now you don't seem to want me in your life."

"Oh, get over yourself already. Where is the rug?"

He shrugged. "I don't have it with me."

I was annoyed, really annoyed. The demon had woken me up from a nice dream where I was licking ice cream off a certain sexy dragon's chest, and for what? To pester me with some cock-and-bull story about Archer using me? I had a feeling there was an ulterior motive for his presence, but I was damned if I could see what it was. "Well, get it. I want it back. It's not yours."

He strolled to the door and opened it, glancing back at me. "Possession is nine-tenths of the law, I believe."

A little chill touched my back with his words. I really did not want to tell Edgar I'd lost two of his finds. "I summoned you, though, and according to all the books I've studied, that means you have to do what I say."

"Isn't that sweet—you believe what you read," he said, smiling.

"It was good enough to summon you."

"I let you summon me because . . . well, because it suited me." He smiled a third time. It sent chills down my spine. "If you had used a different spell, one that was proper and not so far from the original by being retold time and again before being written down, then perhaps the situation might be different. But as it is . . ."

The silent *shoosh* of the door closing as he left sent another ripple of chills down my back. Or was that the threat so obvious in Naamah's voice?

"I have to get that manuscript back," I said to my now-empty room. "And that means Archer just has to return it." He didn't seem inclined to do so, however. Could that be because he was using me, as Naamah said? Maybe he planned on booting me out the door as soon as I translated the leaf . . .

"No," I told myself, pushing down the worry and doubt. "He's not like that."

He's a man, an inner voice said.

"Dragon," I corrected it, then realized that didn't make it better. A man I could understand, but a dragon in man shape?

I shook my head at my own murky thoughts. I would drive myself insane if I started doubting my own judgment. Holding firmly to the thought that I couldn't be deceived so easily, I settled back to go to sleep.

I was just drifting off to the memory of my fingers in Archer's hair, the look of surprise in his eyes as I rumpled him in an attempt to make him a tiny smidgen less attractive (it was a lost cause—the man refused to be anything other than so handsome he made my toenails steam) when the house shook.

"Earthquake," I murmured, too familiar with the little ones to be worried. The sound of a muffled explosion following immediately thereafter, however, had me on my feet and running to the door, yelling, "Archer!" before I realized I was out of bed.

My heart felt like it was held in a vise, my stomach turning over with fear, and panic, and a desperate need to make sure Archer was not harmed. I was at the door when I remembered I was clad in nothing but my underwear. I dashed back to the chair where I'd set my clothing and jerked my dress over my head before racing out of the room.

Voices called from outside the house. Archer's bedroom door was open, but when I skidded to a halt in the middle of his room, expecting to see a vision of bloody horror, I found the bed empty. I ran quickly down the hall, flying down the stairs, my heart in my throat as a little chant started up in my head, praying to whoever would listen that Archer was all right.

My bare feet hit the marble floor between the dining room and living room, and I stopped, my mouth an O of horror as I viewed what was once one of the retractable glass walls that separated the living room from the patio. Archer stood in nothing but a pair of jeans, his hands on his hips while he surveyed the remains of one of the massive glass panels. One part of my mind was happy to see his back had healed, but the rest of my brain was shrieking. Shattered glass lay over the three beige and blue couches that made up the living area. Two men stood outside the now empty wall where the glass had hung on a slider, talking rapidly to Archer in Magyar.

"It had to be a rocket launcher," one of the men said, shaking his head. The other, a tall, gaunt man with a shock of copper hair, wrung his hands, and said in the same language, "We didn't hear them coming. They must have drifted in with the tide so that we wouldn't hear the boat's engine."

"Set up a patrol offshore," Archer ordered his men before turning to face Miles when the latter entered from the dining room. "If they come back, blow them up. Anything?"

"No sign of them," Miles reported. "They must have had a fast boat...that or they are holed up somewhere nearby."

"Was it your brother?" I asked, amazed that anyone

could hate his twin so much that an attack by rocket was the result.

"Do not come any closer, Thaisa." Archer frowned at my bare feet. "There is glass everywhere. You will cut yourself."

"The same might be said about you," I answered, picking my way carefully through the tiny square chunks of glass. The wall must have been made out of safety glass, similar to windshields, since it didn't splinter in the normal pattern. "You don't have shoes on, either. What is going on, Archer?"

He tsked and marched over to where I was carefully nudging aside a glass-covered pillow that had been blown off the couch by the explosion. "Why do you not listen to me? I talk, and you do not listen. No, do not take one more step. I don't have time to pick glass out of your feet."

Before I could do more than give him a sour look, he scooped me up and started toward the stairs. I won't say I didn't have a moment where my inner self squealed girlishly over the fact that he could hoist me up as if I were light as a feather—which I most definitely was not—but I managed to wrestle my brain away from the fact that my arm was pressed against his naked chest and focus on what was important. "Why did your brother bomb you? Was it the manuscript? Or is he just pissed that I ran away? It's me, isn't it? Oh, Archer. I'm so sorry."

"This isn't your fault," he said, setting me down on the stairs, his eyes as pale as the moon as he looked down at me.

The heat from his body drew me. I placed my hands on his chest, sick with the knowledge that his beautiful house had been attacked all because I had escaped from Hunter. "It is. If I hadn't run from him—"

"You would now be in his power, and he would be using you," he said with innate arrogance that seemed to touch everything he said. "Stop looking guilty. You have not precipitated this attack."

I couldn't help myself. I tried, I really tried, but he was filled with fury, a hot, burning anger that I suspected was directed toward his brother. I wanted desperately to temper that anger but didn't know how, so I simply stroked my fingers along his jaw, my inner parts sitting up and taking notice at the soft whiskers that tickled my fingertips. "Perhaps not entirely, but I know I'm partly responsible. I sprayed him with pepper spray, Archer. Bree beaned him with a heavy solid glass ashtray that she carries with her for some reason that I don't understand, since she's not a smoker, but that's neither here nor there because she did have it and bashed it down on Hunter's head, and that's why he's attacking you. Because he's annoyed at me."

"Much as I believe that all who see you will desire you, the truth is less simple." Archer's hands were reassuring on my bare upper arms. "Go back to bed, flower. There will be no more such attacks tonight."

"How can you possibly say that?" I shook my head, letting my fingers drop to his collarbone, just the touch of his sleek, satiny skin making the embers inside me grow into a fire that threatened to consume me.

"Because I know my foe. We have been antagonists for many centuries," Archer said with a grim smile before catching my hands and kissing the flames that danced on the ends of my fingers. "Return to bed. I want you rested before you tackle deciphering the manuscript."

"About that manuscript," I started to say, but he dropped my hands.

"We will talk about it later. Go to bed."

I thought of arguing more with him, thought of telling him how sexy he looked with his rumpled hair, bare chest, and little pillow crease lines on one cheek, but knew he would feel obligated to handle whatever increased security he'd put into place, and I couldn't be of any help with that.

Accordingly, I walked up the stairs slowly, trying to resolve the feelings that swirled around inside me. Naamah had to be wrong. Oh, sure, Archer wanted me to translate the leaf, but he wouldn't have made such a big deal about me being his mate if that was all he wanted from me.

No, Naamah was wrong, and my gut instincts were right. By the time I reached the top, I had another of those epiphanies similar to the moment when I realized that dragons were real.

This time I faced the fact that I couldn't just wash Archer out of my hair. We may have only just met, but I felt like I'd known him forever. That sense of familiarity, of the rightness of him, helped push down the doubts Naamah had raised. Archer may irritate me with his attempts to dominate me, but deep down, I knew I was safe with him. He was the only person other than Gran who made me feel that way, and that had to be more proof that Naamah was just trying to stir up mischief. Archer was far too gorgeous for my comfort, and I knew, *knew* without a single shred of doubt that I'd have to cope with every woman who saw him immediately wanting him, but even that didn't stop the feeling that Archer was now vital to my life.

I stopped at the door to my room, thinking long and hard, knowing I was on the verge of something big. One step into my room, and my life would go down one path. A step in the other direction, to the door opposite, and I'd be taking a gamble that I couldn't be sure wouldn't leave me devastated and emotionally destroyed.

"I might have issues, but I am *not* a coward," I said aloud. I turned and entered Archer's bedroom.

His bed sat on a big platform covered in light gray linen, the bed coverings also in various shades of gray. The room was sparsely furnished, with a tall white armoire, a couple of gray striped chairs next to a gas fireplace, and a small desk and chair. The wall facing the ocean was solid glass, the balcony beyond it tempting me, but with the mental images of the damage downstairs uppermost in my mind, I resisted the urge to sit outside.

I looked back at the bed, noting that Archer preferred to sleep on the left side, nearest the door.

"That's good," I said to no one, moving around to

the far side of the bed. "I'm a right sider. We won't have to arm wrestle over who gets what side."

My inner self gave another girlish squeal over the idea of Archer's arms, of his long fingers (I've always found men's hands sexy), his biceps, as well as the feel of that warm, silky skin beneath my fingers.

And mouth.

And breasts.

After a moment of indecision spent staring at the bed, I examined the bank of closets that filled one side of the room. One end held suits, the sort you see in pictures of Fortune 500 board meetings. I leaned into them, breathing deeply, catching a faint scent that made my entire body feel warm. Another section held sportier clothing, while farther down I found a few T-shirts. I pulled out a blue one that matched his eyes when they were full of desire and buried my face in it, my toes curling into the carpet as the lemony, woodsy scent of Archer sank into my blood. I removed my dress before slipping the blue tee over my head, after which I visited his bathroom—also done in shades of white and gray—dimmed the lights in the bedroom, and climbed into his bed.

I lay on my back, looking at the shadows playing along the ceiling, planning what I was going to say to Archer about the manuscript, wondering about the decision I'd made. Had it really been only a little more than twenty-four hours since I'd first laid eyes on Archer? It seemed like a lifetime had passed, one filled with ups and downs and a whole lot of steamy dragon lovin'.

My inner skeptic was a bit surprised that I had made the decision without thinking about it for a whole lot longer, certainly not before getting to know more about Archer, but I knew myself well enough. I always did fall for men hard and fast, and it seemed this time was no different.

Archer was, however.

Archer…If he had been hurt…My throat ached with unshed tears at the thought.

I must have fallen asleep despite intending to stay awake so I could seduce Archer, because I became aware that I was dreaming again, this time with me lying on my stomach in a field filled with butterflies that fluttered above me, touching me with the lightest brushes of their wings.

Sunlight heated my flesh, while underneath, the grass tickled my bare skin, making me feel restless and oddly needy. Why wasn't Archer here enjoying this with me? I wondered, wanting to turn over so that the sun could warm my underside, but the weight of the sunlight held me down, a solid weight that stroked me with fingers made of fire.

The fingers drew intricate patterns up my legs, swirling and teasing, moving higher to my knees, then higher still to my thighs. Pressure inside me caused all of my deep, intimate parts to weep tears of desire, a familiar tension starting in my belly and spreading out with little ripples of pleasure. The fingers urged my legs apart, the lines of fire that followed them burning a path straight to the place I wanted them most. When one of the fingers dipped inside me, curling downward, I almost screamed with the pleasure of it all.

Warmth swept up my back in soft, long strokes, following gentle nibbles.

A second finger joined the first, and I dug my hands into the grass beneath me, my breath caught in my throat, my lungs unable to pull in more air.

"One more?" a deep voice seemed to wrap around me, drifting in and out of the dream. I moaned in response, my hips bucking when a third finger joined the two that filled me, a thumb flicking over flesh so needy that it made me see stars despite the heat of the day.

"It pleases me that you are so responsive," the voice said as my body coiled like a spring about to be released, pulling me out of the dream. Archer's body was hard and hot over my back. He surged into me, the invasion making me scream with mingled shock and ecstasy. "If you knew what you did to me, flower... The scent of you wraps me up so tight that I will never be free of it. Tell me you don't want me to stop. Tell me you're ready. I will try another time to pleasure you longer, but I must claim you... must do this now..."

"I was ready when the dream started," I said, panting and grabbing the sheets with both hands when he pumped into me with strokes that were not at all gentle. "Do it now, Archer. Fill me. Fill me with your fire, fill me with... Yes! Fill me with that swivel move again!"

He slid an arm under my belly, jerking a pillow under it, which allowed him a different angle of penetration that had me moaning nonstop until I trembled on the edge of an orgasm.

"Filling you is my...Christus, mate, don't tighten up any more, I won't be able to last...it is my intention."

I couldn't help myself, all my intimate muscles tightened around him as he thrust hard into me, the angle allowing him to touch sensitive spots I didn't even know I had, sending me spiraling into a climax that literally made me shake with the power of it.

Fire filled me as he joined me, sweeping up my body, lighting more than just my skin on fire—my soul burned in an inferno of passion and desire...and something that I didn't want to look to closely at.

It took a long, long time for me to come down off that orgasm, and when I did, I found myself draped over Archer's body, his delicious chest heaving, damp with perspiration, and as hot as the fire that still simmered inside of me.

"The bed is on fire," I said, trying to breathe without gasping.

His eyes were closed. He lifted a hand, immediately dropping it back just as if he didn't have the strength to hold it up. "It will die down. All the furnishings in the house have been fireproofed."

"Handy, that," I said, pushing myself off his chest to look down at him. "That was...Holy moly, Archer, where did you learn to do that thing with the pillow? That was the most amazing sex I've ever had, and I thought nothing could top the forest interlude."

The corners of his lips curled. "Are you asking me to recount my sexual experiences?"

"Huh?" I reached across him and patted out the fire that burned along his hip.

He opened his eyes. They were midnight blue, the color slowly leaching out of the irises even as I watched. "You asked where I learned about using a pillow."

"Oh. Sorry, that was more a rhetorical question than anything." I thought for a moment. "Have you...uh... used that particular technique a lot?"

One of his glossy black eyebrows rose. "Are you jealous at the thought of my previous lovers?"

"No. Of course not." I made a dismissive gesture. "What's there to be jealous of? What's in the past is in the past. I wouldn't expect you to be jealous of me having had a lover before. Lovers, plural. Many lovers."

His eyebrow rose a little higher.

"I just made myself sound overly promiscuous, didn't I?"

"Yes, but I understand. You are jealous. That is right and natural. I do not like to think of the man to whom you gave yourself, but I am able to accept the knowledge that you allowed another man to touch your body, to stroke your breasts and hips and thighs, to kiss your neck in the spot that makes you tremble, to claim your mouth for his own, tasting of your sweetness, of the hot, burning sweetness..." His voice trailed off to a rocky finish.

"You're on fire," I said, looking pointedly at his

hands—which were now fisted and burned merrily where they lay alongside his hips.

He cleared his throat, and the flames extinguished. "I do not wish to make you more jealous than you are, so we will not discuss where I learned to use the pillow."

"Uh-huh. How did you know I just had the one boyfriend? The only one who knows that is my friend Laura. Oh, and Bree. Dammit, did she tell you?"

"I have had no conversation with the sprite, no."

"Oh." A suspicion came to my mind. "You didn't do a background check on me, did you? Oh! You did! I can see it in the guilty expression that's plastered all over your handsome face!"

His eyes opened wide for a few seconds; then I was on my back, his hands stroking up my belly to my breasts. "We will do this again, properly this time, without so much haste. You will not entice me as you did when I found you in my bed."

I froze where I was happily trailing my fingers around his biceps, feeling as if his words had hit me in the gut. "Did you not...I thought...oh God, you didn't want..." I couldn't finish the sentence. I was so embarrassed, I wanted to pull the blanket over my head and never face Archer again. I rolled out from under him and reached for the T-shirt and my underwear, which he must have stripped off me while I was dreaming. "I'm so sorry. I would have never— Oh God. How can I be so stupid?"

"What is this?" Archer stood before me, his body so

gloriously male it took my breath away. "Why do you cry? What did I say?"

"I'm mortified," I murmured, angrily dashing tears from my eyes. "I thought you wanted...I thought you were inviting me to...to..."

He frowned in confusion at me for a moment, then plucked the T-shirt off my body, picked me up, and put me back in his bed. "I look forward to the day when you cease underestimating your worth." He crawled over me to slide into bed next to me, before wrapping an arm around me and hauling me up against his body. "You are my mate, little flower. We are bound together. My home is yours. My bed is yours. Your body is mine."

I laughed a hiccupping laugh through the tears that still spilled over my lashes, my heart lightening at the knowledge that I hadn't just made an epic ass of my-self. "Nice switch there, Mr. Domineering."

He grinned, the sight of it making my toes curl with happiness even though he'd done a little investigating of my background. I guess, given the situation, that wasn't such a grievous crime. At least, I was willing to forgive it, since I'd tried to do the very same thing to him.

"It is the way of dragons. You have much to learn, but I will teach you. If I ask you what made you come to my bed, would you misinterpret it?"

"That depends," I said, placing my hand on his chest. Immediately, my fingernails lit with his fire. I tipped my head back so that I could admire his jaw and chin. I had the worst urge to bite that chin with its faint cleft. "Are you asking out of curiosity, or because I'm the latest in a long line of women that you've unexpectedly found in your bed?"

"The former."

I was silent for a few minutes while I tried to put into words my decision. "It was the explosion. When I thought you might be hurt, I realized that I may have only known you for a day, but you were important. To me. And if you were that important, then what was the use in pretending you weren't?"

He made a satisfied noise, rolling onto his side so that I was pressed against his chest, that glorious chest, with one of his legs over mine. "It pleases me that you understand what it is to be mated. Later today, you will be bound to the tribe so that all will know you are mine."

"You know, a little bit of possessiveness is fine," I told him, pinching his side. "But too much is annoying as hell."

"Then it is good that I give you the exact right amount," he said, his breath ruffling my hair. His body relaxed against me, surrounding me with the sensation of warmth and security and a sense of belonging that until that moment, I didn't realize I craved so much.

"Han."

"Hmm? Are you hungry?" he asked sleepily.

"Not ham, Han. It's kind of a cool name. Maybe you're a Han?"

He said nothing, just pulled me tighter. "I do not expect you to name me because I was never given one of my own, flower. I have long been resigned to my past."

"I know, but it hurts me thinking about it. How could your parents abandon you like that? How could any parent abandon babies?"

"My mother died soon after we were born, or so I was told."

"And your father?"

He was silent a moment. "It is said that he did not survive her death."

"I'm so sorry. How horrible that must have been for everyone." I tipped my head back and kissed his Adam's apple, wanting to leech the pain from him, but knowing it went too deep for me to ever fully remove. "But you were babies—surely there must have been others who could have taken you in?"

"I grew up in the keep of a mortal, just another unwanted child left to fight the hounds for scraps of food. Later, they put me to work. I doubt I would have survived had I been mortal."

Tears burned my eyes as I had a picture of Archer as a small child running wild, unloved, with no one who cared whether he lived or died. I shifted so that I could slide my arms around him. "I can't make your horrible childhood any better, but I want you to know that you will never be alone again. I will always be here for you, no matter what."

He rolled onto his side, a puzzled frown pulling his brows together. He wiped the wetness on my cheek. "You weep for me?"

"Of course I do," I said, choking back a sob as I clutched his head to my breasts. "You poor, hurting man. When I think that no one cared...that no one even bothered to give you a name of your own...oh, Archer, I could just beat the ever-living shit out of all those medieval people!"

He pulled himself out of my grip, kissing each breast, then resettled himself with me tucked into his side, cocooning me in warmth. "This fierceness is pleasing. No one has ever wanted to beat the ever-living shit out of an entire keep of people on my behalf."

"I would do it in a heartbeat," I told his chest, allowing myself to relax and melt into him. "Just get me a time machine and watch me."

He chuckled, a sound that made me feel very at peace and one with the world.

Perhaps, I told myself, life was finally coming together for me.

CHAPTER TEN

"ARCHER, WE HAVE TO TALK."

He looked up from his laptop, noting Thaisa had what he was coming to think of as her determined expression on her adorable face. Perhaps it was the way her straight brows pulled together or the lift of her chin as if she expected him to argue with her.

That little lift of her chin made him want to say the most outrageous things to her.

"I'm working. The manufacturer of my doors refuses to see reason about my request for an immediate replacement, and I do not intend to let them dismiss the fact that they must put my claim before other orders. We will talk later, at the binding ceremony."

She glanced at the laptop before nudging his shoulder. "I'm sure you'll be your usual bossy self with them and get them to do what you want."

"Yes, but it may take a little time until they see reason." He pulled her hand from his shoulder, kissed the knuckles, and released it.

"This is important, Archer," she said, tugging at him again. "And it won't take long, assuming you…" She gave a little cough and murmured something so softly, he couldn't hear it clearly.

"Assuming I what?" he asked absently, responding to the latest refusal of the manufacturer, his fingers flying over the keys. If they insisted on being obstructive, he would simply fly to Arizona and discuss the matter in person.

"Are…uh…understanding of the situation."

"I am always understanding. I am a dragon."

"I'm not quite sure why you think the two things go together," she said with humor rich in her voice. "It's been my experience that the opposite…but I don't want to argue with you. I just want to explain why it's important that you sell the manuscript back to Edgar."

"That again?" He frowned when a snippy e-mail from the manufacturer's CEO popped into his inbox. "I told you that I do not give up what is mine." He turned to her, unable to keep from sliding a hand under her skirt and up the satiny length of her thigh. "I thought you were going to start working on the leaf?"

She stepped back, out of his reach. He frowned at that. "I was, but then Edgar texted to say he was flying back today and he'd better find the manuscript waiting for him. You don't understand how important this is to me, Archer—"

"No, I don't. Do you not like my touch any longer? Is it because I did not pay homage to you as you deserve this morning by licking my way up your legs to your woman's parts, tasting the true essence of you, making you squirm with desire until I sink myself in your heat, welcoming those little sounds you make only when I'm deep inside of you and watching passion make your eyes shimmer with my dragon fire?"

She blinked at him a couple of times, grabbing the back of his chair. "Wow, that was…licking? That sounds really nice, not that I've ever been big on oral sex before, but I'm willing to give it a shot if you are."

"Flower," he said sternly, even as he closed his laptop and stood up, finding once again that his trousers were too small in the cock-and-ball department. "You are new to being a mate, so I will show you patience now, but you must understand that I have responsibilities other than making you moan and demand my fire. I am master of the tribe. I owe my consideration to others, as well as you."

Thaisa giggled. "That lecture would sound a whole lot more imposing if you didn't have your hands on my butt right now."

He squeezed the warm, round cheeks that filled his hands, thinking seriously about sliding his fingers under the thin underwear that hid all her secret delights, but he couldn't shirk his duties just to give her the pleasure she was due. "Later," he promised, unable to keep from kissing her delectable lips. She moaned and slid her fingers through his hair, tugging on it. "Later I will give in to the demands of your hips and thighs and woman's parts. Especially the woman's parts."

"Don't forget my breasts," she said, squirming against him in a way that would ensure his jeans were tighter than ever. "They don't want to be left out of the fun."

"I would never shirk my duty to them," he agreed, his hands cupping them. He loved the weight and feel of them, loved their taste, and the silkiness of her skin.

"Fire?" she murmured, pulling on his hair.

"Mate, you cannot interrupt me when I am busy with tribe business—" The rest of the words were cut off when he gave in to her request and let his dragon fire wrap around her, filling her before returning to him. He felt the warmth of his fire in his hair and knew her fingertips were alight again, and for some reason, the simple fact that she was so affected by him pushed him over the edge.

With a growl that started deep in his chest, he gave in to the urge natural to all dragons to join with the one mated to them, and swept an arm across his desk, knocking a couple of books and a sheath of documents to the floor before lifting Thaisa up onto it, his mouth demanding on hers. She whimpered her acquiescence, her fingers tugging at his shirt until she got most of the buttons undone, jerking the material until it came free. He slid his hands up her inner thighs, parting her, spreading her legs and pulling her forward so that she was on the edge of the desk.

"Should we—the window—" Thaisa panted, her hands stroking his chest in a highly distracting manner. He wanted to tell her to stop so he could concentrate his full attention on her, but her touch gave him too much pleasure to even think of stopping it.

"What about the window?" he murmured, enjoying the way she shivered when he dipped his head and licked the valley between her breasts. He pulled down her zipper, his hands removing the bra she insisted on wearing in order to keep her breasts hidden from him, her body trembling when he brushed his thumbs across the hard nipples. She was so easy to pleasure, so receptive to his every touch. He felt a sense of smugness about the way he could overwhelm her with just a touch of his fingers.

"Someone could see us." She gently bit his nipple before swirling her tongue over it. He froze, the pleasure that spread out from his chest causing a tidal wave of dragon fire, sexual ecstasy, and desire, all twisted together.

"Privacy window," he gasped, desperately wanting to give her the slow burn of pleasure to be found in foreplay but unable to maintain control of his passion. It was simply too much. She was too much. With a savage oath, he jerked her underwear off and freed himself, his mouth on the spot behind her ear that he knew she loved. "I can't wait, flower."

"Good," she said, half gasping and half laughing when she reached between them, stroking his length until he thought he might just die from the pleasure, before positioning him exactly where she wanted him. "I've always been quick off the mark, so— Ooph!"

He lunged into her, very close to the edge. He gritted his teeth as he tried to slow down, tried desperately to think of something that would distract him and give him time to bring her to pleasure, but his mind was filled with her, with the sensation of her silky skin under his mouth, of her fingernails gently raking a line up his spine, of the way her intimate muscles tightened around him, gripping him with what felt like a hundred fingers. Then she made that noise, the little hum that warned she was going to give in to her climax, and it was all over for him. He moaned her name into her shoulder, his body pumping life into her even as his dragon fire spun around them, setting the sheaf of papers on the floor alight.

She spasmed around him, her fingernails digging into his ass, pulling him closer as wave after wave swept through her. Her breath was ragged and hot in his ear, and he knew at that moment what it truly meant to be mated. He'd always assumed a mate was like a competent second-in-command, a pleasure to have, someone with whom he wanted to spend time, but not vital to his life, not so deeply ingrained in his soul that he would never be able to separate himself from her.

He was wrong.

"Mate," he said, his voice guttural, imbuing the word with everything she meant to him.

"Yeah," she said, her voice shaky. "That was a hell of a thing, wasn't it?"

"Now you see why it's important that you not dis-
turb me when I'm working," he said, pulling himself
from her with a real sense of regret.

"Uh-huh." She leaned back on one arm, lifting a
wan hand when he stamped out the fire on the floor and
shook the ashy end off the papers. "You don't happen
to have a wheelbarrow, do you? If you could kindly roll
me into it and wheel me somewhere I can recover, I'd
be grateful."

He felt a sense of male pride that their lovemaking
had such a profound effect on her. As he bent to re-
trieve the tattered remains of her underwear that had
fallen to the floor, he stumbled backward and fell on
his ass.

"My poor undies," she giggled, sliding off the desk,
whereupon her legs buckled and she fell onto him. "I
just got them mended last night, and now look."

"We will get you more," he said, taking possession
of her breasts when she tried to pull up the bodice of
her dress.

"You don't need to. I have plenty back home. Speaking of which, I should head there soon. Jamie's okay
with opening the store, but with Edgar flying back today, I should be there. Zip, please. Archer, I really need
that manuscript."

Reluctantly, he released her breasts and allowed her
to put her dress to rights, zipping it up when she turned
for him. He couldn't resist a little kiss on the back of
her neck, just in the spot he would place the tribe mark
later, at the binding ceremony. "You seem to be under

the impression that I like repeating myself. I do not. The manuscript is mine."

She accepted his hand when he got to his feet, wobbling against him as if her legs were still weak.

He was smug about that, too.

"Right," she said, taking a deep breath. "I didn't want to tell you this, because I know the sort of reaction you're going to have, and it's my problem, thus I feel obligated to cope with it on my own, but since you're clearly in dragon possessive mode, I have to. Edgar made it quite clear to me that if he does not get the manuscript back today, he will…well, he will harm my gran."

"I will not allow that to happen," he told her, holding her hips until he was sure her legs were steady again. He buttoned the part of his shirt that still had buttons and sat back down at the laptop. "I have already taken the matter in hand."

"In hand how?" Her brows pulled together.

He fought the need to kiss the little wrinkle that formed between them. "I have verified that the facility in which your grandmother resides has a high quality of care. In addition, the financial situation of the home is reasonably solid, so you will have no worries that they will cease functioning for monetary reasons. The staff's background checks do not reveal anything of concern, and finally, I have urged the company responsible for their security system to upgrade it at no cost to the facility. Two guards will watch over your grandmother for as long as they are needed."

Thaisa's jaw had sagged after his first few sentences, and it seemed to take her a bit before she said, "You did all that for Gran? Overnight?"

"Not by myself. I delegated some of the work. The background and financial checks were done by Miles."

She stared at him for a few seconds, and then to his surprise, her eyes glistened with tears. "You did all that just to make sure Gran is okay. I'm speechless. No one has ever done anything even half as nice for me as what you've done in a few hours."

"You are my mate," he said simply. Although he hadn't put protection for her grandmother in place just so Thaisa would look at him as if he were the most wonderful being who ever walked the earth, he'd be a liar if he didn't admit to relishing the warm glow of gratitude in her eyes. "As for your former employer— he has no further role in your life. If you wish to return to your apartment to gather your belongings, I will send Miles with you."

"See, that's exactly what I knew you were going to say. While I'm...well, I guess I'm okay with the idea of moving in with you, since this house is beyond fabulous, and I'd be an idiot to turn it down in favor of my tiny little apartment, but you can't just say things like Edgar doesn't matter anymore. He does matter, to me."

Archer shot her an outraged look.

"Not in that way," she said quickly, poking him in the arm. "For the most part, I like my job. It's interesting, and I enjoy doing it. And before you come over all high and mighty and annoy the crap out of me by telling me that I don't need to work because you'll support me—I was planning on quitting just as soon as I have you return the manuscript. Edgar has gone over the line this time, and I will not put my gran at risk just because he's a selfish, uncaring ass."

He looked at her, at her face with the eyes that held so much life in them, at her delectable mouth, at the little chin that, even as he knew it would, lifted a fraction of an inch. He thought about what it would mean to return the manuscript, and every atom of his being protested. And because she was his mate but was unlearned, he explained how it was. "Dragons do not give away the treasures they possess. It goes against our very natures. Do you understand, now?"

"I do," she said, looking exasperated. "You bought the manuscript fair and square, and there's no reason you should have to give it up to Edgar, except he made it quite clear—in language that told me I needed to quit my job after this—that if he doesn't get it, there will be trouble. A lot of trouble. And people will suffer."

"You do not understand yet," he said, shaking his head and returning his gaze to the laptop screen. "But you will one day."

He was aware of her standing next to him, fuming, little noises of frustration escaping her. Because he didn't like her to be unhappy, he asked, "Do you wish to work on deciphering the manuscript before you go to your apartment? If you tell me when you wish to collect your things, I will inform Miles so that he will be ready to escort you. I would go myself, but evidently I have to fly to Phoenix to make the manufacturer understand the urgency of this situation."

"Gah!" she said impotently, and he had the sense that she only just kept herself from stomping her foot in frustration.

He looked at her and waited.

"Fine!" she snapped, whirling around as she spoke. "I'll take some pictures and spend three hours starting to decipher it, but no more. After that time, you have to let me take it back to Edgar."

"I do not *have* to do anything," he said mildly, amused despite himself when she slammed the door to his office. He would not tolerate such an obstreperous attitude from one of his tribe, but Thaisa's defiance of his most reasonable statements gave him pleasure. He knew it would take her a bit of time to settle into their ways, but he was confident that she would eventually see the light.

CHAPTER ELEVEN

BY THE TIME I SAT AT THE DESK ARCHER HAD GIVEN over to me in order to work on the manuscript leaf, I was muttering under my breath and wishing I had one of the grimoires with me so that I could slap a couple of curses on a certain dragon.

Then I thought of how kind he was being about Gran, and my anger melted away into appreciation. "Edgar isn't Archer's problem, he's mine, so it's not fair for me to expect Archer to take care of it," I said into the phone. "Especially when he's being so generous by sending his own people to guard Gran. This is my problem, and I need to just handle it, right?"

"Right," Bree agreed. "What do you want me to do?"

"You said to call you if I needed demon help, and I do. What better way to get Edgar to see that he can't threaten Gran and get all up in my business than to have my pet demon scare the living crap out of him?"

"I like it!" she said. "We'll teach him to talk nasty about Gran. His hat of many asses will learn a thing or to when Naamah visits, right?"

"Right. Maybe you can help me find a spell or something to make Naamah give up the prayer rug. Can you meet me at my apartment at"—I checked the clock above the desk—"say noon? I want to get a good three hours in on this manuscript so I can see what all the fuss is about."

"Roger wilco, over and out, you betcha, Charlie," she said.

"Time to weed the World War Two movies out of your Netflix queue," I told her, and hung up.

I settled down to study the small sheet of vellum, using a pair of metal tweezers to touch it since Archer hadn't thought to get protective gloves. He did have a magnifying glass, which I used to go over the leaf, both sides, to look for signs of hidden writing. Most medieval manuscripts didn't have what is colloquially called "invisible ink," but I had seen one that had used a combination of alum and lemon juice to write literally between the lines of what was otherwise innocuous religious text.

This leaf was clear of that, however, which meant I could sit and let the code talk to me. Once again, I let my gaze slip along the carefully drawn lines, the symbols clearly written by the hand of master, but without meaning.

Yet.

Slowly, as I let my focus go a smidgen soft so that the symbols almost burred, frequent ones started popping up to catch my notice. Patterns of them swam in and out of my view, shifting and moving until they started to make sense. I noted the ones that were likely to be the most popular vowels, looking for small words first, since those would let me tackle the longer words.

My fingers danced over the pad of paper I'd borrowed, time seeming to slip past me without intruding on my concentration.

"How is it going?"

I jumped at the voice behind me and turned to find Miles.

"My apologies," he said with a smile. "I didn't mean to startle you, but Archer said you wished to pick up your clothing at noon, and it's close to that now."

The last thing I wanted was Miles hanging around while I consulted with Bree about how to use Naamah to the best effect. He was bound to tell Archer what I was doing, and I didn't need Archer getting bossy on me. Again.

Plus there was something about Miles that made me a bit…the word *suspicious* hung in my mind, but I didn't like to commit fully to it. I just had a sense that something about him was slightly off.

Regardless, I summoned a smile and gestured toward the manuscript. "Actually, I think I'm going to stay here and work on this for a bit longer. I can have Bree pick up whatever I need." The last was a lie, but I added a little wattage to my smile in order to compensate for any tells toward that end.

"Ah," he said, coming over to stand by the desk. "As you like. How is the deciphering going? Getting very far?"

I slid my hand over the notes I'd made, feeling that Archer should be the first one to know what the leaf revealed. "Oh, you know, *far* is a relative term. I have identified some vowels and consonants."

"That's excellent!" He looked pleased, peering down at the leaf as if the translation would leap off the page. "You can fill in the missing letters of the words once you have a few letters, yes?"

"If you know what language was originally used to make the cipher, yes," I said, picking my words carefully. I disliked lying on principle and knew I wasn't any good at it. "If you don't know that, then it makes it much more difficult."

"I see. So it will take some time?"

"These things do," I agreed, then unable to stop myself, asked, "Why are you so interested in this, Miles?"

"Why wouldn't I be?" he countered, surprise in his eyes for a moment before it was followed by speculation. "It's an important relic belonging to dragonkin, and it holds immense power."

"According to the lore Archer told me, this medallion was given to him and his twin, so even if Archer had it, the power would be his. Or do you intend to use it for yourself?"

The last sentence was spoken lightly, but his face turned red with anger. "You seem to forget that Archer is my cousin," he said, biting off each word.

"You wouldn't be the first family member to want to topple a relative who was in power," I pointed out, picking up my pencil and tapping it on the tablet of paper.

"That's ridiculous," he snapped. "I seek the medallion for one reason alone, to fulfill its prophecy."

"The prophecy whereby you end up with Archer's tribe of dragons?" I couldn't help but ask. What bothered me about Miles was the feeling that he was wearing a mask, one that hid his true self.

For a moment, I thought he might hit me, but he got his anger under control. "I love my family. I don't want to overthrow them," he finally said. "Kin are everything to ouroboros dragons, and I have never given Archer a reason to doubt my devotion to him and the storm dragons. If you wish to accuse me otherwise, then I will ask you do so in front of Archer. He will stand up for my character."

"There's a fine line between love and hate," I said softly.

Miles's frown was almost as intimidating as Archer's. "A fact I'm very well aware of. If you are finished unjustly accusing me, I must go attend to the perimeter guard. Archer will be leaving soon. I will alert Trajan that your friend will be coming with your things."

The second the door closed behind him, I ordered a car to pick me up, then stood for a moment with several sheets of notes in my hand, wondering what I should do with them. Archer was out with his men making sure everything was good on the grounds before he headed to the airport to deal with the window manufacturer—I spent a moment trying to wrap my brain around the idea that he had his own jet that he used whenever he had to fly somewhere, wondering if I'd ever get used to that sort of lifestyle—so I couldn't ask him if he had a safe.

I *really* didn't want to risk leaving the notes lying around where just anyone could read them before I had time to talk to Archer about them.

"Hi, Ioan?" While I was downstairs covertly looking for a spot to hide the notes, I ran into one of the dragons that Archer had introduced me to that morning, saying he was in training to be one of what I assumed were an elite level of his personal guards.

"Thaisa," Ioan said, smiling when he tucked away his phone. He had a slight Eastern European accent and was evidently one of the newest members of Archer's tribe. "Archer is just about to leave for the airport. Did you need something?"

"Yeah, you wouldn't happen to know if he has a safe, do you?"

"A safe?" He frowned. "Dragons don't normally use safes. We have lairs, and I know Archer has one, but I'm afraid it is up to him to show it to you."

"Oh. Okay. Hmm."

"I can ask him—"

"No, thanks. I know he's anxious to go out and yell at the window people."

"I will be happy to tell him you are desirous of seeing his lair, if you can wait until later to see it," he said. He reminded me of a puppy who was trying hard to please, hopeful of nothing more than a friendly word and a gentle pet on the head.

"It's not that important. Thanks anyway." I went into the kitchen to talk to the other dragon I'd met that morning. "Genn, I don't suppose you have any supplies?"

Archer's housekeeper was tall and svelte with blond hair down to her butt, not at all what I imagined a housekeeper to look like. In fact, one glance at her had my jealousy ready to fire up, but Archer told me in a whisper that she was romantically attached to another dragon and that I could stop growling.

"Supplies?" she asked. "What sort?"

"Lady supplies. Er...pads."

"Ah." She gave me a little nod. "I think I have something you can use, yes."

Ten minutes later I entered the room across from Archer's, which I had claimed as my own. I didn't want to look too closely at why I felt like having my own room was necessary—my brain was just happier with it. I tucked the copy of my notes into the pillowcase of one of the pillows on the bed, while the originals I folded into a flat wad, and using a small pair of scissors, slit open a feminine hygiene pad, into which I hid the notes. I slid the pad back into its wrapper, and stuck it in the bottom of the box before putting it in the attached bathroom.

"That ought to keep it safe," I said to myself, counting on the fact that most men felt a bit funny handling such things.

While waiting for my ride, I spent a few minutes staring out the window at the glorious view, wondering how I had ended up there when just a few days ago my life was one of normalcy and unimportance.

"Everything okay?" I asked Jamie when I went in the front door of the shop. There were a few customers, one of whom I knew to be a collector of rare books.

Jamie was slumped on a stool behind the register but sat up straight when I came in, almost falling off his perch. "Oh, Thaisa. I thought you said you weren't going to be in until later?"

"I changed my mind." I glanced around, but everything seemed to be under control. "Did we get any more shipments from Edgar?"

"No, but he said he's coming back early to take care of a problem." Jamie's watery brown eyes watched me as I headed for the office. "He said to make sure that you were here."

"Oh, I'll be here," I said, getting a good, firm grip on my resolve and telling myself that my days of being intimidated by Edgar were over. I was mate to a big, bad dragon, and I had a demon at my command.

I ran upstairs, did a fast packing of my clothes and

must-haves, and hauled the suitcases downstairs to the office.

"So, according to *Explicatio Triginti Sigillorum Demonitica*, there's a way to blight someone with hairy moles. How about we mole up your boss's face?"

To my surprise, when I returned Bree sat on the edge of Edgar's desk, holding yet another one of the valuable books from the front case. This time, however, I didn't have a hissy fit. I simply fetched a pair of white cotton gloves and handed them to her.

"Tempting as it is to make him one giant hairy mole, I think we're going to need something a bit more intimidating. He should be here in the next four hours. And while we're talking about curses, you seem to be very familiar with this sort of thing." I gave her a long, considering look. "You want to tell me why it is you understand an ancient dragon-only language, why Archer told me you were a sprite, and why you seem to know what I'm going to do before I decide to do it?"

She grinned and set down the book. Today she was dressed in a plaid, pleated miniskirt, black lace stockings, and a pink peasant top underneath a black leather bustier, her long blond hair wrapped around her head in a braid. "I wondered when you'd ask. I used to be a sprite, so the Archer Dragon was right about that."

I softly drummed my fingers on the desk. "And a sprite is…?"

"We help people. Mortals, mostly, although we do also work with immortals who need a little assistance."

"That sounds like it was a good job. You aren't one any longer?"

"Nope." Her grin grew. "But you can still think of me as... as someone sent to help you for a little bit."

"Mmm-hmm. Help how?"

She shrugged. "However you like."

"Can you magic up the leaf so I can give it to Edgar?"

"No, but I can help you give him boils."

"Tempting, but ew." I thought for a minute. "What about Gran? Can you have a protective bubble put around her so that anyone who wants to do her harm can't get to her?"

"Dude, if I could do that, all the animals of the world would live in happiness," Bree said. "Sprites aren't untapped sources of magical wonderment, although we can make the most amazing glitter bombs, guaranteed to leave the recipient picking bits of sparkle out of his or her asshat for years."

"Enticing as that thought is, I don't suppose I should have you glitter bomb Edgar. As for your offer of help..." I thought about that for a few seconds but decided I was in no position to spurn any assistance, no matter how mysterious the person making it. "Since I'm over my head in this whole new world I didn't know existed, I'll gladly accept your offer of help."

"Good. I'd hate to see anything happen to the Archer Dragon. He's nice. He likes you a lot."

"Why do you call him that?" I asked, suddenly suspicious.

"Archer Dragon?"

"Yes. Dragon isn't his surname. It's Andras."

She shrugged again and hopped off the desk, spinning around and doing a little jig. "But that's what he is, isn't he?"

I watched her for a few seconds, wondering just what it was she knew. "If we all went by descriptive surnames, you'd be known as Bree Drives Thaisa Batty," I said slowly, slipping on the gloves she'd peeled off so that I could pick up the *Demonitica*.

Bree giggled. "How do you know that's not my surname?"

I let that pass. "Right. Let's consult the experts, although this time I'm going to cross-check any spells we cast, because evidently I used a third-rate one from the *Liber*, and look how that ended."

My phone buzzed while we were making lists of things we could have Naamah do to Edgar if he didn't back off with the threats.

Where are you?

I didn't recognize the number, so I ignored it. Sometimes I get texts for a person who used to have my phone number before it was assigned to me.

I demand that you answer me. Why are you not home? Miles said you disappeared.

Archer? I answered, squinting at the phone.

Why did you leave unprotected? Trajan says a car picked you up. Who are you with? Is it Hunter? Another man? You will tell me where you are!

"Whoa. Someone must have had a hard time with the window dudes," I murmured, texting back: I'm at the shop with Bree. Only man here is Jamie, and by calling him a man I'm being generous. Calm your tatas. I have some things to talk to you about after I deal with Edgar.

My phone rang. I sighed the sigh of the put-upon and answered it.

Heavy breathing met my ears for a few seconds before Archer ground out, "You are new to being my mate. I have tried to make allowances for this."

"Good, because I've been your mate for exactly"— I looked at the clock—"twelve hours. Calm down, Archer. You're going to have an aneurysm if you keep breathing like that."

"If I do, it's because you are trying to kill me." The anger in his voice lessened a bit. "Why did you lie to Miles?"

"I didn't so much as lie as kind of mislead him."

He breathed at me. Loudly. I could almost hear his teeth grinding.

"Okay, maybe I did lie a little, but, Archer, I'm not a child and I'm not foolish. I'm not going to give your brother the chance to kidnap me again."

"You do not know the danger you are in by being away from my protection. The protection of my tribe," he said. Anger was most prominent in his voice, but beneath it, there was a touch of something that sounded a lot like...pain.

"Archer, listen to me," I said, turning around and moving over to the hallway for a modicum of privacy. "Are you listening?"

"I want you to stay right where you are. Miles will be there shortly. Lock the doors. Do you have firearms? A Taser? Is your pepper spray with you?"

"No, you're not listening. Archer, stop what you're doing."

"I'm driving from the airport."

"All right, keep driving, but stop talking and listen to me. I'm fine. I have Bree with me, and I'm in no danger. There is no reason for Miles to come. Edgar will be here in a few hours, and I have a plan."

"What plan?" He sounded suspicious.

"One that poses no threat to me," I reassured him, feeling simultaneously silly for pandering to his excessive worry and warmed by the fact that he wanted to protect me from the world. "What time is the dragon thing?"

"What dragon thing?"

"The ceremony you said that will introduce me to all your tribe members."

"It is set for six."

"Okay. I'll be back by then."

His voice was warm and gruff and utterly wonderful in my ear, making me wish he was there in person, his breath steaming all my ticklish spots. "I don't like you dealing with your ex-boss on your own."

"But I'm not on my own," I said in a soothing tone. "I have Bree here, and after all, we worked well together to get away from Hunter."

That was the wrong name to mention.

"You are vulnerable there. I'll send Miles—"

"Hang on." I moved up the stairs until I was at my apartment door. "Are you alone?"

"No. Ioan is with me," he said.

"Am I on speaker?"

There was a little click. "Not now."

I took a deep breath. "I have some concerns about Miles, Archer. I know he's your cousin and you trust him, but he's giving all sorts of worrisome signals. For one, he's super interested in the manuscript, and for another... well, I just don't trust him. Something's up. I think he's hiding something."

Archer was silent for so long I looked at my phone to make sure the connection hadn't dropped.

"You have no reason to distrust him," he finally said, his voice oddly neutral.

"I know I don't. And I don't want to cause problems between you, but I can't help feeling that he has a hidden agenda."

"He has always been devoted to me."

"Good. I...er...I set up a little test. Just to make sure. I made a false copy of my notes and hid them where they wouldn't be too hard to find. If they're disturbed, well, we'll know he went looking for them."

This time the silence lasted for almost a minute. "I would need more proof than that before I acted on it."

"There's more." I made sure no one was near the stairs. "Miles asked me how much of the leaf I've deciphered."

"He told me that you had some letters, but until you could ascertain the language, you wouldn't be able to fill in words."

"Yeah, that's what I told him. Actually, I deciphered it all and finished the translation. I was checking it over when Miles disturbed me, and I...er...I may have let him think I hadn't done very much on it."

"And?" He kept his voice as level as he could, but I heard a note of excited curiosity in it.

"It reads like a creation tale, but I don't think it is. I'll read you the transcript later, when we're alone and we can discuss it."

"Can you not give me a summary now?"

I debated telling him everything but decided I needed time to explain my thoughts. "Sure, but there's a lot more we need to talk about. Basically, the leaf tells about the time when the sun-mother was broken—I think that symbolically means your mother, and physically the medallion itself, which I gather was made in the shape of a sun—and the pieces of her were scattered to the stars, forming a couple of constellations."

"That is...unexpected." He sounded disappointed. "There is no dragon lore about the stars. There was nothing about where the pieces of the medallion are now?"

"No. There's a bit about the balance not being brought to the world until the pieces are together in celestial harmony, but nothing along the lines of 'look five paces under the tall tree' instructions. What it says is a lot more...interesting."

"The leaf is as I thought—worthless," Archer said. "Miles will be disappointed, but I am not at all surprised."

"Oh, it's not worthless, but we can go over that later. I'll let you know when we're done here, okay? We can either get a ride out to your house—"

"I will pick you up as soon as I am back in California."

I smiled to myself, deciding that while it might take me some time to get used to his overprotectiveness, it might take him time to realize he didn't have to treat me like I was a complete idiot who was unable to take care of herself. "Five-thirty sounds good. Bye."

"Mate."

I raised my eyebrows. He was speaking in Western Slavic, one of the lesser common languages. I assumed Ioan didn't have that one under his linguistic belt.

"Yes?"

"You will not do anything foolish. I have confidence in you to attend to the situation with your ex-employer, but I do not have the same confidence that you will not inadvertently place yourself in danger. You have value to me. I do not wish to lose you."

Western Slavic didn't have a lot of words to convey affection, so I didn't take the stilted, formal words at face value. "If you keep saying such nice things to me, I think I could very easily fall in love with you," I told him, a happy glow filling me at the idea.

"That is as it should be," he said in his arrogant voice, the one that made me want to hit him on the head, then grab his ears and kiss the fire right out of him.

"We're going to have a talk later about you falling madly in love with me, too, you know."

"I believe the phone connection is fading," he said in English, speaking loudly as if he couldn't hear me.

"Uh-huh. You can hide, Archer, but I'll find you."

"It's definitely going. Only static now. Do not do anything foolish," he said, then hung up.

I smiled at the phone. He was *so* going to get with the Love Thaisa program, even if I had to drag him there kicking and screaming.

Forty-two minutes later, Bree and I waited in the front of the shop, a circle drawn on the floor, scribed with the seven symbols of the demon Naamah (a step I had missed when originally summoning him), salted, and sealed with blood. I held the *Demonitica* in one hand and the Chalice of Charlemagne (a misnomer, since it was created approximately three hundred years after Charles the Great's death) in the other. Bree said it had the power to protect anyone who imbibed from its silver depths, so we'd both had a bit of Jack Daniel's from it while waiting.

It was a long wait, and we might have had a wee bit too much protection, but in my defense, I was nervous about attacking Edgar with a demon, and thus may have relied a bit too much on liquid courage.

A car pulled up, and the familiar shape of Edgar

emerged, stalking into the store with an attaché in one hand.

"Edgar Lee Wendell," I said formally when he entered the store, the little chime above the door tinkling happily. Bree explained that names have power, and to invoke Edgar's full name would give me power over him. Accordingly, I pointed the *Demonitica* at him. "By the power granted to me by the state of California—no, wait, that's not right. By the power granted to me by the demon Naamah, I command thee to stand where thy is. You are. Hell, which is it?" I turned to Bree.

She weaved a little where she sat next to the circle, then toppled over. "Thou."

"I command thee to stand right thou there," I said, pointing to a spot just beyond the circle.

Edgar paused, his gaze sweeping across the room, taking in the circle, Bree now struggling to sit back up, and me. "What in Christ's name is going on here? You're drunk! Where the hell is my manuscript? By God, you'd better have it or I'll make you rue the day you were born."

"Right. You wanna do this the hard way?" I shook the *Demonitica* at him, then carefully tucked the chalice under my arm to flip open to a page. "We can do it the hard way. I'll just summon my demon friend here, and he'll make mincemeat of you."

Edgar said a word so foul I wouldn't sully my mind with it, then said over his shoulder, "If you have the money, she's all yours."

"Words that give me the greatest of joys," came the reply in a lovely, velvety soft tone.

My eyes widened when Edgar strode past me, revealing Hunter and four men clustered close behind him.

"Well, crapbeans," I said, flipping a few pages in my book to see if there was anything to handle getting rid of a dragon I didn't want.

"It's a pleasure to see you again, Thaisa," Hunter said, strolling in and kissing my hand. "This time, however, I believe I shall make sure that you don't perform another of those really quite miraculous escapes."

"How do you think you're going to do—"

Pain exploded in the back of my head, and my thoughts drifted away into an inky abyss.

CHAPTER TWELVE

THE CALL CAME JUST AS ARCHER AND IOAN WERE driving home from the small airport not far from his house.

"She's been taken," Miles said, breathless and panting, the moment Archer answered.

Fire roared to life in him, fire and rage and a desperate need to lash out at whoever had dared to touch his flower. Ouroboros dragons didn't often shift into dragon form, their genetic makeup keeping them in human form, and although Archer was one of the few who could shift, he had never felt his inner beast as much as he had at that moment. "Who?" he snarled, his fingers so tight on the steering wheel that indentations remained once he had released it. "Who took her? Who dared touch my mate?"

Even as he asked, he knew the answer. Fire swamped him, setting the leather seats alight. Mindful of the gas tank, he leashed his rage and tried to focus.

"It's not what you think. Hunter has her."

"Hunter?" His fury lessened, but only by a small amount. If she had been hurt, if anyone had harmed her...He bit back the need to shift now to rage and storm until he had her safe again.

"She went to her apartment. About five, Hunter and her boss found her at the shop."

Ioan watched him warily as Archer lurched from the car, waving Ioan to the driver's seat. He felt as if he'd been kicked in the gut by a horse. Several horses. A whole herd of them.

His Thaisa, the flower that brought him such joy, such warmth, in obvious danger. Why had he not removed her from the shop? Why had he let her talk him into her plan to tackle her employer? He was sick with the knowledge that he had only himself to blame for what might happen to her. "Where are you?" he asked, taking the passenger seat. Ioan started the car, looking to him for instruction.

"On my way up the coast. You're closer to Hunter's place. I can meet you there."

Archer said something, what he didn't remember, but he assumed later it was an acknowledgment of that plan. He wondered for a few moments if he was having some sort of a fit—his mind felt like it was covered in molasses, slowing the thought processes down, leaving him frustrated and impotent against the need to find Thaisa.

He couldn't risk her. Not even for the peace he so desperately wanted. Hunter wouldn't slaughter her, but there were others...He closed his eyes against the mental images of the lifeless, broken bodies that had been left outside his compound, bodies of storm dragons that weren't even remotely as dear to him as Thaisa.

His mate.

The love of his life.

He didn't even blink over that idea; he just accepted it without wasting energy to wonder when or how she'd managed to work her way into his heart, becoming as necessary to him as the air that filled his lungs. He pushed away the mental images of the sorts of heinous acts that had been conducted upon the innocent.

If she was harmed...if the unthinkable had happened... Archer steeled himself against pain that made him want to scream his anguish into the evening sky.

He would die to protect Thaisa.

"Where to?" Ioan asked as Archer strove to control the pain and fury and frustration that gripped him in iron fingers.

"Shadow dragons," he answered, spitting out the words.

Ioan, wisely, said nothing, just drove west, toward the coast town where Hunter had a large holding.

Archer said nothing during the drive, focusing on creating a plan. Once he made sure Thaisa was safe, he would take care of the threat to her. He didn't know how, but he would. There was simply too much at stake to let it continue.

Miles was nowhere to be seen when Ioan pulled into a clearing hidden from the road, near the entrance to Hunter's twenty-acre compound.

"Do we wait for Miles?" Ioan asked. He was one of the newer members of the tribe, and Archer knew he was nervous, never having seen battle. He would have liked to introduce Ioan slowly to the art of defense against deadly opponents, but he had no choice.

"No," Archer said. He opened the trunk of the car and took out a long metal box. The light was starting to fail, twilight stealing across the sky as the sun sank over the gray-blue water. Faint blue fingers stretched into the peach and rose that flushed the sky, reminding Archer of Thaisa's cheeks, rosy with the afterglow of a sexual climax.

"How much training have you done?" Archer asked the younger man. He removed from the box a wickedly sharp sword wrapped in black silk. Blue gems were set into the hilt, but one socket at the crossbar was empty.

It was a dragon hunter's sword, an *élan vital*, supposedly his birthright, but Archer was no dragon hunter. It lacked the espirit infused in the blade that gave dragon hunters an extra boost to their power. Regardless of the sword's weakened state, he hefted it, testing its balance.

"I've had six weeks of training," Ioan said, looking nervously at the sword. "Miles said I show promise but that I don't think ahead and don't anticipate future moves."

Archer pulled another silk-wrapped bundle from the metal box, holding it. He wouldn't sacrifice a member of his tribe. "If you do not feel confident…"

"No, I am," Ioan said with a sudden gulp, squaring his shoulders. "I am quick on my feet and fast with a blade. I will guard your back."

Archer nodded and handed him a lighter sword and scabbard. While Ioan armed himself, Archer slipped a scabbard onto his back, sliding the sword home. He strapped daggers to either ankle, under his pants; then, after a moment's thought, he pulled out a Taser, made sure it was charged, and tucked it his pocket.

"How are we going to get inside the compound?" Ioan asked quietly when Archer strode down the road toward the large gate that opened into the drive. Hunter's ten-foot walls were dotted with glass and razor wire, Archer knew.

"We're going in the front door," Archer snarled, standing at the gate and loosing his carefully leashed fury. Dragon fire swept through him hot and fast, encouraging his rage to run just as free. Ioan backed up a few steps, his eyes huge, as teal scales rippled up Archer's arms. His body shifted into a sleek, lethal shape that bore little resemblance to the dragons revered by mortals.

He stood still for a moment, embracing the power that filled his dragon form, the primal nature of the true dragon being that dwelled within him giving him a sense of invincibility. Rage threaded through the emotion. Behind that gate his mate was being held captive, taken from him. The air around him grew thick with static as he swore to himself that all who dared harm her would perish.

He pulled the sword from his back as he kicked open the gate, his tail whipping to the side to catch the guard who ran out to stop him, sending the man flying into a massive cedar tree. Two more men erupted from the shrubs that lined the fence, but they went flying as well, slamming into the stone fence with a crunch that spoke of broken bones.

"I didn't know you could do that," Ioan said, his voice reverent as he followed Archer. "I've never seen anyone actually shift. I've heard of it, of course, but to see it…it's amazing."

Archer hesitated for a moment, scenting the air, trying to catch any indication that others were guarding the front gate.

"My brother grows lax, thinking himself secure in his fortress," he said in a low tone. He shifted back into human form and ran silently along the edge of the drive. The trees on each side cast shadows that stretched into inky pools while the sun sank into the horizon.

He knew from past parlays at Hunter's compound that the main house sat on a cliff above a rocky stretch of the coastline, flanked by a number of outbuildings. The drive twisted, revealing the long, low lodge that Hunter called home. Three cars sat in the front of it, beyond which a couple of men smoked, the glow of their cigarettes as obvious as the smell of their smoke on the air.

"Mortals?" Ioan whispered. Dragons, as a rule, did not indulge in the vices of alcohol and drugs.

Archer breathed in, identifying the smell of oil and exhaust from the cars, earthy notes from the rich soil of the beds along the porch that ran the length of the house, and...nervousness.

"Mortals," he said with a nod. "Don't kill them unless you have to."

He strode forward, the sword in its scabbard on his back, his fire once again controlled, but he nursed it, keeping it alive with anger, knowing he would need to draw upon it for strength for what was surely to come.

The two mortals didn't notice any threat until Archer was almost upon them, and then one squawked and tripped when he tried to back up, stumbling backward onto the three steps that led onto the wide porch. The other immediately pulled a gun out of his pocket, pointing it at Archer with a noticeably shaking hand.

"What the— Who the hell are you?"

Archer took the gun from the man, simply took it out of his hands, popped the clip, and threw the gun into the bushes before pocketing the clip. "If you want to survive the night, leave," he told the men, marching up the steps without pausing to glance at the man who was still scrambling backward in his attempt to get out of the way.

Two dragons burst out of the door, swords in their hands, dragonkin preferring blades to more modern weapons. Archer had the first one down before Ioan pulled his sword out of the scabbard. The second dragon spun at Ioan, one hand drawing a spell in the air, the symbols hanging black for a second before fading, but Archer took care of that by the simple act of slamming the hilt of his sword into the man's head, knocking him unconscious.

Archer stepped over him, pausing when he entered the main hall of the lodge. Hunter had chosen to decorate the walls with weapons, everything from broadswords, to two-handed axes, morning stars, glaives, and even a few bows. One caught his eye, a lovely bow with silver chasing on the body in the form of fantastical dragons. It had been a long time since he had felt the pull of a bowstring, and without thinking, he snatched the bow off the wall, testing the draw before sliding a full quiver of carbon arrows over one shoulder.

He marched to a big common room and found three dragons around a table, playing cards.

Archer nocked an arrow and sent it flying at the first dragon, striking him in the thigh. The dragon stumbled and fell, looking in surprise at the arrow that pierced his leg clean through. It wasn't a fatal wound, but it would stop any attacks. The other two dragons pulled knives and leaped forward. Archer caught one of them in midstep, the arrow burying itself in his knee. The dragon screamed and slashed at him. Archer leaped onto the table and fired again, but the shot went wild when he was knocked forward by a man who had come in behind him.

The man with the thigh wound pulled out his phone, typing in a code that sounded an alarm in a distant part of the lodge.

Ioan managed to knock the knife out of the other dragon's hand, and delivered a roundhouse kick that sent the man crashing into a wet bar, before spinning around to assist Archer.

The dragon who'd come up from behind leaped on Archer's back, trying to pull his sword out of the scabbard. Archer snatched another arrow, spun it around, and stabbed backward with it into the man's shoulder. He dropped to the ground, screaming.

"Where are they?" Archer growled, hauling up the man with the arrow in the knee who was attempting to crawl behind the bar. "Where is your master?"

"I am a shadow dragon," the man snarled, his face a twisted mask of pain. "I do not answer to—"

Archer stabbed his other thigh with another arrow.

"Upstairs!" the man gabbled, try to get away from him. "In the meeting room."

Archer dropped him and stalked out of the room, snatching up arrows from a second quiver on the wall before taking the stairs three at a time. At the top of the landing, double doors were closed, a black-and-silver image of a dragon inlaid into the wood. He shifted into dragon form and kicked open the door with a powerful blow, the force so great that one of the doors was torn off its hinges. The doors flew forward straight at four dragons wielding swords.

They went down with a crash.

He stormed into the room with another arrow nocked, aimed right at the throat of the man who sat at the center of a long, glossy ebony table.

Hunter pursed his lips at the sight of the broken door and the four felled men. "You couldn't have just turned the doorknob like a normal person?"

"Where is she?" Archer snarled, pulling the bowstring back to his face, his index finger at the corner of his mouth as he sighted Hunter.

"A bow? Really?" Hunter shook his head as he stood slowly. Another man sat at the table, a man with dark hair whom Archer did not recognize, but since the stranger was mortal, he was unimportant. "And not even the nice compound one that has all sorts of fiddly bits on it that my lieutenant tells me is most proficient."

"You took my mate," Archer growled, letting the bowstring slip a quarter of an inch. A little movement of his fingers was all it would take for the arrow to fly.

"Yes, I did. Have you stopped to wonder why?"

"I don't need to," he said, and let the bowstring slide off his fingers.

Hunter didn't move until the arrow was less than a foot from his throat, at which point he gestured, drawing a symbol in the air, one that glowed black.

The arrow dropped as if it were made of lead.

"Are you done with the dramatics?" Hunter asked.

"Not just yet," Archer said, and pulled the sword from his back, drawing first on the power of his dragon fire, then on the storm that raged within him. Electricity crackled down the sword, the runes that ran the length cold and lifeless, but the energy of the storm snapping and sparking off the metal in little blue-white tendrils.

"You really want to do this now?" Hunter shook his head and stood, shifting into the form of a smoke-gray dragon, pulling his own sword. Like Archer, he bore the blade of a dragon hunter, this one set with green gems. The main socket was just as empty as Archer's, the runes etched on the blade invisible with the dull black miasma that seemed to wrap around it. "I should have known that you would jump to the most extreme conclusion—"

Archer didn't wait. He pulled hard on his dragon fire, holding his sword before him with both hands, the blade pointed down. Static from the air, and earth, and sparks of life of all living things around them gathered into him. He held it for a moment, thinking of Thaisa, of the slow smile she gave him when he had loved her within an inch of her life, of the way her eyes turned liquid with desire when she touched his chest, and of the fact that she was the only person who had ever shed tears over him. He thought of the warmth that filled him when she was near, and took all those emotions, all the hate and love and fears and worries that had been bound upon him during the long course of his life and slammed them forward at the same time he stabbed the sword into the oak floor.

Hunter, taken off guard, was catapulted backward, straight through the wall in an explosion of electricity. The noise was deafening, reverberating painfully in Archer's ears as he jerked the sword up. He peered through the hole, saw the prone form of Hunter in the room beyond, and spun on his heel, striding past an openmouthed Ioan.

"THAISA!" he bellowed, returning to human form before leaving the room.

"Archer?" The voice was muffled but he turned and raced down the balcony that overhung the central hall, trying door after door until he came to one that was locked.

"Get back!" he yelled, and sent a fireball into the door. It cracked and sagged. He shoved it open, his heart coming to life again with the sight of Thaisa and Bree sitting together on a bed, their hands bound behind them with plastic ties.

Instantly, he was overcome with the need to claim her, to breathe in her scent, to stroke his hands down her curves and bury himself in her heat. He wanted to drive away what surely were horrible memories of the abduction and planned on doing so just as soon as he could get her alone. He knew her, however. She would likely shriek with joy at the sight of him there to rescue her. He paused at the door to allow her to shriek, and possibly fling herself on him, overcome with the power of her emotions.

"What are you doing here?" Thaisa asked, not at all looking like a woman who had just been rescued from a lethal circumstance. She didn't shriek. She didn't even leap to her feet with cries of gratitude. "Is that a *bow* slung over your shoulder?"

"We are going to have a talk about the proper way to greet me when I rescue you from certain death," he said, stalking forward. He pulled a dagger from its sheath and cut her ties while Ioan hurried over to do the same for Bree.

"Certain death? What certain death?" she asked, looking confused.

"Where are your expressions of gratitude? Where are the kisses pressed to my face saying without words just how thrilled you are that I have saved you from the clutches of my brother? You're not even crying, are you?" he asked Thaisa, pulling her to her feet and burying his face in the crook of her neck. She smelled heavenly, like the freshest of lavender pressed in the warmth of the sun. The scent cut through him with the accuracy of a razor, but he welcomed its pain. It meant she was alive, whole, unharmed, and still his. "Why are you not even now trying to entice me to kiss you, and touch your breasts, while you rub your hips against me to show me how grateful you are to see me again?"

An interesting parade of emotions flitted across her lovely face, everything from surprise to amusement to irritation. He couldn't keep from brushing a thumb across a lightly freckled cheek, gratitude filling him that he was in time. His flower would continue to bloom.

But only for him.

"I'm not crying because there's nothing to cry about, although I am glad to have the zip ties off my hands. I'm not going to entice you to kiss me since I see you're very likely to do that yourself." Her eyes were dewy with rising passion as he let his thumb rub over her lower lip. Her delectable, sweetly curved lower lip. He loved that lip almost as much as he loved her obstinate little chin.

"Yay, rescue time," Bree said. "Hi, Archer Dragon. Hi, other dragon whose name I don't know."

"I'm Ioan," his tribesman said, bowing.

Thaisa gave a little start while rubbing her wrists, looking at Bree as if she'd never seen her before. "You know all about this, don't you?"

Bree tipped her head to the side, blinking innocently. "Hmm?"

Thaisa looked thoughtful for a few seconds. "No, you couldn't know. Only I know about this, and I don't even understand it."

"Come, mate," Archer said, holding out his hand for her. "You are upset by the abduction. We will return home, and I will kiss your breasts and thighs and woman's parts until you squirm beneath me, demanding my fire."

"The problem is the mother…who in it is the mother?" she murmured to herself, then looked up, his words penetrating her thoughts. A delightful little blush made her cheeks rosy. "Archer! Yes, we can do all of that, especially if you do the thing with your fingers again, but now is really not the place or time to discuss such things."

"No, it is not," a voice said from the door. The mortal who had been with Hunter strolled into the room just like he owned it.

"Who are you?" Archer asked, moving between Thaisa and the man.

"That's my boss, Edgar," she said, moving to his side. "An annoying man who evidently promised to sell Hunter not only your manuscript, but also me to translate it. The bastard."

Archer tried to shove her behind him, but she just bit him on the shoulder blade and moved to his side again. He contented himself by pulling her up tight against him.

"You are the dragon she gave my manuscript to?" The man stopped in front of him, his expression sour. "I can't believe you'd have the bad taste to screw that hot mess, but I suppose to each his own."

Archer glanced at Thaisa. "Why is this obnoxious man here?"

Thaisa glared at the man. "I told you—he sold me to Hunter so he could use me as a trade for your manuscript. He said he came along to see he wasn't done out of what was due him. He's a hat of asses."

"Many asses," Bree said, moving to the other side of Archer. She smiled at Ioan, who looked startled, then pleased.

"You weren't supposed to come until we sent you the ransom note," Edgar snapped, looking put out.

Archer had the worst urge to run him through with his sword, but he took pride in the fact that in all his long years, he had killed only one mortal in anger and that was a man who had been brutally tormenting a dog. Archer did not tolerate people who mistreated creatures who could not fight back.

"He wants the manuscript," Thaisa reminded him.

"He can't have it."

"I told him that, too, but he seems to think he has some power over us."

"He is incorrect." Archer dismissed the mortal, turning to give Thaisa a gentle push toward the door. "We will leave now, flower."

"I don't think so," Edgar said, raising his voice. "Naamah, I summon thee."

"You didn't *really* have to summon me," a demon drawled, strolling in through the open doorway. "I was right outside the door. Where you told me to wait, I should point out. I don't know if this fulfills your demand I make a grand entrance, but it's what you're getting. I have other people to serve tonight, you know."

Edgar's eyes narrowed on the demon, who rolled his eyes and said with great exaggeration, "What is it you seek from me, oh great and mighty master of demons?"

"See thee that dragon there?" Edgar commanded, pointing a finger at Archer. "Kill him!"

"What?" Thaisa shrieked, and would have lunged at the mortal but Archer shoved her behind him, gesturing for Ioan to protect Bree.

"Oooh! A fight!" Bree said. "This is going to be awesome!"

"Are you insane?" Thaisa yelled.

Archer kept his eyes on the demon, who, with another roll of his eyes, took a few steps into the room.

"There is no way Archer fighting a demon is going to be awesome," Thaisa continued. "It's pure horrible. Wait, did Edgar command my demon? Can he do that?"

"Archer is a dragon hunter," Bree said in a soothing tone. "The first one, actually. I think. Hey, Archer Dragon, are you the eldest, or was Smokey the first one out of Mom?"

"Bree!" Thaisa squawked. Archer narrowed his eyes on the demon, who had been carefully removing his suit coat, sliding off his tie, and rolling up his shirt-sleeves.

The mortal Edgar sidled around behind the demon, pausing in the doorway before marching through it. "Get on with it! I don't have all night, and I have to see what happened to the men I left on guard just in case that dragon you killed didn't leave orders to have his people pay me."

"Naamah," Thaisa said in an acid tone, clearly upset at the demon. That she had so little fear both amused and horrified Archer. But what really had him sending her pointed looks—looks she ignored—was the way she repeatedly moved to stand next to him with her hands on her hips, glaring at the demon. "I command thee by the powers granted to me by the *Demonitica* to ignore Edgar and listen to me instead."

"Sorry, sweet cheeks," Naamah said with a smirk. "You didn't summon me properly, and the other one did."

"Do not speak to the demon," Archer commanded. "He will confuse you with lies."

"He already tried that," Thaisa replied with a pointed look at the demon. "In the end, I didn't believe him."

The demon made a face at her. "Ah, but it gave you a few bad moments, didn't it? What do you expect to do with that?" He gestured to the sword that Archer pulled from his back. "That *élan vital* has no espirit. Therefore, it has no power against me."

"True," Archer said, sliding the sword back and whipping around the bow, releasing an arrow just as the demon lunged, his fingers lengthening into claws. The arrow stuck in the demon's shoulder but didn't slow him down. He leaped on Archer, his mouth suddenly filled with wickedly sharp needlelike teeth, snapping at his neck.

"Get them back!" Archer yelled at Ioan, who grabbed both women and shoved them farther into the room.

Archer had a glimpse of Thaisa's face, her eyes wide with fear. The sight of her, his glorious mate, being frightened was enough to kick his fury into high gear. Fire whipped through him, generating the electrical charge that snaked down his hands. He spun, slamming the body of the bow into the demon's head, which sent him flying backward. Archer had an arrow nocked and released before the demon hit the wall. Second and third arrows slammed into the demon's chest immediately after.

"God's gallstones!" Thaisa gasped in wonder. The demon tried to rise, but Archer pumped three more arrows into his chest, pinning him to the wall.

The demon snarled an oath before going limp.

"See? Awesome," he heard Bree say. "Although I've never heard of a dragon hunter using a bow."

"That's because I'm not a dragon hunter."

"Really? You have the sword, dude," Bree said. "I kinda think you are."

He glanced at the women, checking to be sure they were all right. Thaisa's face was filled with amazement as she looked from him, to the demon, and back to him, the light of admiration in her eyes making him feel damned heroic.

"What . . . what happened to Naamah?"

"The demon's form has been destroyed. He was sent back to his master."

"Oh. Good. That was beyond incredible, Archer," she said, moving over to him, her hands fluttering across his chest as if she was making sure he wasn't harmed. "You were like something out of the movies. It was seriously outstanding. You're more superhero than the superheroes."

He leaned down and said softly, "If you keep looking at me like that, I will take you to the nearest bed and bury myself in you until you scream my name in ecstasy. Three times. Possibly four if I can survive your lustful demands upon my poor body."

"Oh, yes, please," she answered just as softly.

He was just about to answer her when a voice called from outside the room. Miles appeared in the doorway, clutching a few sheets of lined paper in one hand. "Hunter? There's a couple of unconscious dragons in the other room. You in here? What happened? I didn't think I'd make it here before Archer, but he must have gotten stuck in traffic. Why did you take the woman? I told you I'd find the transcription she made, and I have—"

Miles's gaze turned into the room, the words drying on his lips.

CHAPTER THIRTEEN

I COULDN'T BELIEVE WHAT I WAS SEEING. MILES HAD betrayed Archer?

I shook my head with the shock of it all. Oh, I'd warned Archer that I was suspicious of his cousin, but to see proof of that suspicion, to be staring right at the face of the man whose betrayal would no doubt cut Archer to the quick...I couldn't stand it.

"You bastard!" I yelled, and would have leaped forward to do who-knew-what to him had Archer not caught me around the waist. "You utter and complete rat bastard!"

Miles stood before us, his hands limp at his sides, his face frozen, but his gaze moved from me to Archer and then to Ioan.

Archer tensed, and I knew he was about to attack his cousin.

"No, Archer, no!" I said, and plastered myself across his chest to stop him. His eyes were filled with confusion. I took his face in my hands, pleading with him. "Don't attack Miles. I know you want to. I know that he betrayed you, and I know I said that he was acting weird, but that's no reason to kill him! Not when there's been so much death already."

Archer slid a gaze over toward Ioan. "Ah." He cleared his throat and added in a voice of pure menace, "Release me, mate. He has betrayed us to our enemies."

Oddly, his fire seemed to subside rather than kick up. I half expected it to explode around us in an inferno of hurt and rage, but Archer's control must have been ironclad. I released his face and gave him a smile to let him know how proud of him I was that he could fight what must be an almost overwhelming urge to smite Miles on the spot.

"He betrayed me, flesh of his flesh," Archer continued, his voice ringing with righteous indignation. "He betrayed the tribe. He has bound himself to those who would destroy us."

Iron control or not, if he continued on, he'd end up doing something that he'd regret for the rest of his life.

"My love," I said softly, my hands on his chest now, stroking him slowly and carefully like one would a wounded animal, being careful to keep myself between him and the still-frozen Miles. "I know you're hurt. I know you want to punish him for what he's done, but you must not do this."

Archer stood immovable, all the hard lines of him crying for my caresses to ease his pain. I kept my hands flat on the swells of his pectorals, my fingers gently stroking.

"Why?" he asked, breathing hard, his eyes glittering like snow on a blue gem. The words fell from his lips like jagged little shards of glass. "Why should he not pay the price of his betrayal?"

Bree giggled.

I shot her an outraged look, mouthing, *What the hell?* to her. She just giggled again, and whispered, "It's just so awesome."

I glared at her for a moment before whispering back, "You really need to get a sense of decorum."

"And miss this? I haven't seen such a good show in forever."

"Don't listen to her," I told Archer. "She's on drugs or something. You can't attack Miles because he is your family."

"He is no kin of mine," Archer said, all but spitting out the words.

"Archer—" Miles spoke at last and took a step forward, his face twisted with some emotion. Guilt? Pain? I couldn't decide which it was, but there was no anger in his eyes, no sense of triumph. I had a flash of intuition that what I had guessed about him was very, very wrong, and knew at that moment that I had misled Archer with my hasty conclusions. With a look at Ioan, Miles squared his shoulders and said, "I— This looks bad, I know, but I have a reason for being here."

"Is it treasure?" Archer asked, his voice gritty. My fingers continued to stroke his chest despite the fact that he appeared quite calm. "Power? What? What did he offer you to turn against us, your own tribe?"

"Nothing—he didn't offer me anything, because I have not turned from you. From the storm dragons."

Archer turned away, disgust written all over his handsome face. "It matters not. From this moment, you are no longer a storm dragon."

Miles staggered to the side a step, just as if he'd taken a blow. I thought for sure he would plead, to try to explain why he was there, clearly about to hand over what he thought was the transcript to Hunter, but instead he just stood there for a moment, his eyes on Archer. His gaze slid to me, then to Ioan, after which he made an abrupt little bow, then turned and walked out of the room.

"Archer—" I started to say, confused. Why did I feel like nothing I saw was real? Why wasn't Archer's fire threatening to burn down the place?

"No. We have no time for this." He took my hands from his chest and collected up the arrows left after the demon's body had dissolved into nothing. I wanted to ask him about that, figuring that must be a thing with demons since no one expressed any surprise but decided now was not the time to ask distracting questions.

"We really do need to talk," I told him when he gestured for me.

"No, we don't." His jaw was set, but his control was amazing since I didn't sense more than just a faint heat of his dragon fire.

I made a frustrating gesture, recognizing the obstinate mood he was in. "Dammit, you annoying man! Yes, we do!"

"This is neither the time nor the place for a discussion," he snapped, marching over to me until his toes touched mine, the heat from his chest bathing me in a warmth that melted all my bones. "Not now, flower! Not when I've defeated my brother and endured the betrayal of the one person I trusted above all others."

"Oh, man," Bree murmured to Ioan, who stood next to her. "He's very good at this, but Zizi's tasseled nipples, he did not just say that, did he?"

"He did, but he is upset," Ioan said softly. "He has been betrayed. We all have. We must have vengeance, just as Archer avenged himself upon the master of the shadow dragons."

"Hmm." She looked at Ioan with her head tipped to the side and moved a few steps away from him.

"The *only* person you trusted, Archer?" For a moment, I felt as if someone had slashed through me with the big herking sword he had strapped to his back, wondering how I could bind myself to a man who didn't trust me with his heart, but the knowledge of what pain he must be suffering from Miles's betrayal did much to soften the harsh words that wanted to burst out. "*Really*?"

He looked stricken for a moment, closing his eyes briefly. "And now I have driven you from my side with hastily spoken words. This day could not get any worse."

"I agree that I've had better days, but I don't think this one has completely gone to the dogs," I told him, leaning forward so my lips caressed his as I spoke. "Because we've only been together a few days, there are some moments when I, too, forget that I am no longer alone in this world. I forgive your hasty words, my delicious, sexy dragon. So long as you immediately amend your statement to 'one of the people I trust.' Otherwise..."

His eyes warmed to topaz blue, his hands hard on my hips as he pulled me tighter against all the hard planes of his body. "I do not deserve you, mate, but I will get down on bended knee every day in thanks that you are in my life. I did not mean what I said—I trust you with my life. There is no one who I trust more—"

"I know," I said, kissing him on the corner of his mouth. "I'm in love with you, too."

An indescribable expression flitted across his face, and I think he would have admitted the truth but at that moment, a familiar blight returned.

"Well, isn't this just grand. I asked him to do one thing, one simple thing," Edgar said from where he glared at us in the doorway. He stomped over to swear at the smear of oily black smoke on the wall and floor.

"And he couldn't even do that. What the hell use is it to summon demons if they can't kill one dragon?"

"Hats of asses," Bree said, frowning at him.

"A whole boatload of them," I agreed, then turned to Archer. "Can we get out of here now? There's something you need to know, and I don't like telling it to you here—"

"And have me be accused of being a poor host?" Hunter skidded to a stop at the door, Miles at his heels. But it was Hunter who kept my attention—his hair was tangled and standing on end as if he'd stuck his finger in a power socket, while black singe marks ringed his eyes, ears, nostrils, and mouth. He looked like a deranged cross between a porcupine and a raccoon.

He walked into the room, not with the grace and power that I'd seen when he kidnapped me—both times—but oddly stiff and graceless, as if he'd been pulled through a wringer. Backward.

"I thought you were dead?" Edgar asked him.

Hunter shot him a look of pure dislike, and to my surprise, Edgar backed up. "Why are you still here, mortal?"

"I want my money."

"You'll get it when you bring me the leaf."

"I gave you the woman. You owe me for her," Edgar argued.

"If I ever see you near my mate again, I will kill you," Archer said simply. "The same applies for her family. Do you understand?"

Edgar started to sneer, but Archer pulled his sword

and Edgar—never stupid when it came to self-preservation—snarled to Hunter, "I'll send you my bill!" before taking himself off.

I slid a glance toward Archer, wondering just what he'd done to his brother. Archer looked very satisfied with himself.

Hunter lifted his big, black sword and pointed it at Archer. "I have a bone to pick with you, brother. Since when did you learn to harness electricity?"

"I am master of the storm dragons," Archer said dryly. "What did you expect?"

"Not that!" Hunter snapped, running a hand through his hair. A clump of it came off in his hand. He glared at it for a moment before transferring the glare to Archer. "I thought it was just a name you picked because you liked it. No one told me you could do"—he waved a hand toward the back of the house—"that."

"What did you do?" I asked him.

Archer smiled. "Took care of him."

"Well, I'm not going to have it! Not in my own home," Hunter said, shaking his sword at Archer before lifting a hand and drawing a symbol that he flung onto Archer. It glowed black on him for a moment.

Miles started to move, but Hunter spun around to throw the same symbol on him.

Archer snarled an extremely rude oath in Magyar and tried to leap forward, but whatever Hunter did kept his feet rooted to the large, colorful Native American rug that covered much of the floor. "What did you do to me, you bastard?"

It was Hunter's turn to smile. "Took care of you."

"Don't worry, I got this," I told Archer quietly, and took a step forward.

He grabbed my arm. "You do not!"

I leaned into him. "Bree and I spent all afternoon reading some grimoires. I'm chock-full of things like banishment wards, and destruction spells, and something to make pubic hair go berserk." I patted him on the arm to reassure him that all was well.

"Regardless, you are not to take one more step forward. Thaisa! I just told you not to!" Archer tried to grab me again, but I was just out of his reach.

"Right, it's on now," I told Hunter. "No one messes with my...my..." I stopped and looked back at Archer. "What are we? We're not dating, so you're not my boyfriend."

"I'm your master," he said with lofty disregard of how that would sound.

"You *so* are not," I said, giving him a glare.

"You are my mate," he amended.

"That's what *I* am, but what are *you*? What do I call you when talking to people?"

"That is not people," Archer snapped, pointing at Hunter and struggling to free his feet from where they were stuck to the rug. He managed to twist one free and was trying to drag the other one forward so he could grab me. "That is a homicidal, deranged demon."

"I like that!" Hunter said, pausing in the act of drawing another symbol. "I'm not the homicidal one here, brother."

"You kidnapped my mate," Archer yelled at him. "You took her from me!"

"And you know full well why I did so," Hunter answered with great dignity. "Stop making such a big fuss about it. I've treated her with the utmost kindness."

"You call binding her hands behind her back *kindness*?" Archer asked, outrage dripping off every word.

I sent him a look of appreciation of his concern for my well-being. "There are times when your protective nature gets you a big gold star for the day, and today is one of those days. If you wouldn't grab me and try to stuff me behind you, I'd kiss you."

"She was bound because she came out of the Taser-induced insensibility almost immediately, and in the first five minutes after she woke up, she tried to pepper spray me twice, as well as attempted to hit me on the head with an ashtray that damned sprite already used once on me. She did manage to bite my wrist hard enough to make it bleed, and kicked me in the nuts with such strength that it's likely I will never have children," Hunter said, glaring at me, a little smoke curling out of his nose.

I put on my innocent face. "You Tased me. Besides, those who kidnap should expect to be fought."

"Well done, flower," Archer said, giving me a look of approval.

I smiled back and had to fight to keep from kissing him. "We're getting married," I told him, making an instant decision. "That's the solution to what I call you."

His expression turned to annoyance. "Marriage is a mortal convention that dragons do not hold with, and if it was, now would not be the time to propose to me."

"I'm not going to spend my life introducing you to people as my mate," I said, and turned back to Hunter. "As I was saying before I got distracted by Archer—"

"I did nothing!"

"No one messes with my fiancé."

"He started it." Hunter slapped a second black binding symbol on Archer.

Archer glared at his brother. "The fact remains that you stole my mate."

"Yes, but she agreed to translate a manuscript for me."

"*My* manuscript!" Archer roared, his fire riding high in him.

Hunter waved that away. "It concerns both of us. You should share."

I suspected that if Archer could have shot lasers out of his eyeballs at that moment, Hunter would have been nothing but a smoking mass of charred man.

I mused for a few seconds over the fact that he was so furious with Hunter, but wasn't even giving Miles an occasional glare. One of the pieces of the mental puzzle that had been confusing me slid into place with an almost satisfying click.

"We have strayed from the topic of me opening a can of whoop-ass," I said, feeling there was no benefit to continuing the argument about the manuscript. I wanted badly to get out of there so I could explain to Archer the third epiphany that had struck me.

Both men looked at me like I was crazy.

"And you can just stop drawing whatever spell you're trying to draw, Hunter," I added. "Because I see you, and that is *so* not happening."

"It's not a spell," he said. "It takes a learned magister to be able to draw a spell."

"I know how to do it," I said with narrowed eyes. "Bree?"

"On it," she said, taking Ioan by the hand. "Come on, Ioan. We need to get earth and water and sky. You can help me gather it."

Hunter narrowed his eyes at Bree as she hauled Ioan out after her, but I guessed he didn't feel threatened by either of them, for he let them pass by him, confining himself to a derisive snort in my direction. "I highly doubt that you can do any such thing. You do not have the skills for such an act. For your information, this is a ward, a particularly powerful binding ward that I am using to try to control your deranged master."

"You guys so need to get a better name for leader of your tribes. What do those other dragons call themselves? The ones with all the pure colors?"

"Wyverns," they both answered at the same time.

"Oy. We'll think of something else. Well, time is wasting. Let's get to the banishment of your brother, shall we?" I rubbed my hands together. "Have you ever heard of the *Demonitica*, Hunter? No? Well, they have a very interesting section on dragons."

Hunter heaved a dramatic sigh when Archer struggled to re-free the foot that Hunter had bound a second time to the rug. He strolled over to the light switches. "Have you ever heard of a trapdoor, Thaisa? No? Well, I have one."

And before we could so much as blink, he flipped a switch and the floor literally gave way beneath us, sending Archer and me plummeting down into a dark, inky pit.

CHAPTER FOURTEEN

ARCHER GRABBED THAISA AS THEY FELL, TWISTING himself around so that it was he who hit the floor, pain exploding through his head and sending him into a well of insensibility.

It was her voice that drifted through the pain, pulling him back from the darkness to the soft glow of sunshine that was his mate.

"—and I swear to God, if you hurt yourself seriously, I will geld your brother. Slowly. With a table knife. No, that's too sharp. A spoon. I will geld him with a spoon. Archer?"

Soft hands caressed his cheeks, and softer lips kissed his face. He lay still for a moment, weaving in and out of consciousness, his body and mind drifting comfortably.

"You're moaning, my love, so I know you're alive. Are you there?"

Light pierced his brain. He rolled an eye down to see her peering at him, so close her eyes were almost crossed. "Flower," he said.

"That's right, I'm your flower." Relief filled her face. She released the eyelid that she'd peeled back, kissing his brow, his cheeks, the tip of his nose, and finally his mouth. He managed to get his arms working, pulling her down onto his body while he sent out little queries to see if he'd been injured. It was just his head that had a dull throb. "Thank God for that rug that was under us. You could have been seriously hurt. As it was, you were out for a good five minutes. How do you feel?"

He kissed her soundly, then kissed her a second time, at a more leisurely pace, enjoying the sweetness of her, his tongue making sure that nothing in her mouth was out of place. His flower, his glorious mate, the woman who brought him to such highs of ecstasy and such rages of frustration. He reveled in every inch of her.

Until memory returned.

"What the hell do you think you were doing?" He pushed himself up, unable to let her go, but needing to vent a much abused spleen. He shook her gently. "You ignored my commands and could have been seriously hurt."

"Commands?" she asked, pulling back and bristling. "You must have hit your head harder than I thought if you honestly believe you can give me commands."

Even as muzzy as his head was, he saw at once that was the wrong tack to take with her. "I tell you and I tell you of the dangers that are out there, waiting to beset you, and yet, you ignore me, ignore my requests to keep yourself safe. You can't blame me for being incensed when I see you put yourself in danger that is not at all necessary."

She took a deep breath but did not continue to rage at him, as he thought she would. Once again, he felt a little lost by the unexpectedness of her. Would the day ever come when he knew what she would say or do? "I'm going to give you extra bonus gold stars because I know behind all that bossiness is a man who feels the need to protect, but I can't urge you enough to remove the word *command* from your vocabulary when speaking to me. I am not your tribespeople, Archer."

"Dragons, not people."

"Don't split hairs," she said with a thinning of her lips. "If we're going to make this mate thing work, we must have a partnership. I don't want to be treated like a fragile china doll—either we're full partners, or . . . well . . ."

"You'll leave me?" His heart threatened to stop dead in his chest at that thought. Panic unlike anything he'd ever felt gripped him, bringing with it a hundred memories, starting when he was a child, one whom no one gave a second thought, just another mongrel running wild in whatever keep strangers had tossed him. Instinctively, he tried to separate his emotions from her, just as he'd done with those who had never given him the love he had so desperately sought.

Warmth flooded him, lighting the dark places in his soul with heat and fire, his fire and her heat. She wrapped her arms around him, her mouth pressed to his neck, her lips brushing him with soft fluttering kisses, gently biting the same spot that made her giddy. "Never, Archer. I made the decision to spend my life with you, and nothing will change that. I can't change it even if I want to because I'm so in love with you. Despite your handsome face, and your hair that I want to rub all over my breasts, and your thighs, and your chest that makes me want to weep with joy, I am yours. You're stuck with me now, dragon boy."

"Dragon master," he murmured, pulling her tight to his chest, breathing deeply of the scent of her. She smelled wild and untamed and warm all at the same time. She smelled like his flower, the one woman who fate had decreed he must wait long centuries for, and he closed his eyes for a moment against the knowledge that love had finally come to his life. "You are my breath in my lungs, Thaisa. You are the beat of my heart, the heat in my dragon fire. You are life, *my* life, and I will spend the rest of my days making you happy."

"Oh, Archer," she said, blinking back tears that swam in her intriguing eyes. "That was the most romantic thing you've said to me."

He pinched her behind and moved out from under her. "But if you ever put yourself at risk like that again, I will show you that there is a reason I am master of the storm dragons."

"And there you went and ruined the moment by giving me what sounds very much like a command," she said, but a smile curved her sweet lips, and her eyes were still soft and filled with love.

He got to his feet, glancing around at their surroundings. They appeared to be in a basement storeroom, mostly empty but for a few wooden packing cases tipped over on their sides; a long, low, blue-striped Regency-era sofa; two rose-pink wingback chairs; and a waist-high ebony statue of an elephant. On one side of the room, a dim bulb hung drunkenly from the ceiling, the glow from it a sickly yellow. "Did you try the door?"

"Yes. It's locked. Oh, I moved your things to the side. They fell off you when we dropped through the floor." She watched him gather up the bow and sword. "While we're talking about that, who has a trapdoor, an actual working trapdoor, just like in some James Bond movie?"

"My brother, the villain." Archer tried the door, but it was heavy oak, banded in iron. He wondered if he could burn it down but suspected if Hunter used this room as a form of cell, it had probably been fireproofed. There were no windows, no other doors, just a few dusty pieces of furniture, and his flower, now watching him with a thoughtful look on her lovely face.

She pulled the two chairs closer to the door, sitting

on one before she slanted a glance up at him. "What do you know about star charts?"

"The night sky? I can navigate by the stars, if that's what you're asking."

"I wasn't, but that's interesting to know. Is that something you had to learn in a sailing class?"

"You could say that," he answered, putting his shoulder to the door and leaning into it to see if it budged at all. It didn't. "I learned to use a sextant when I sailed around the world in the mid-eighteenth century. I think that bastard warded this door for strength. It's not so much as creaking."

He almost missed the look on Thaisa's face, but caught the expression of rapt amazement as she swallowed hard a couple of times. "You..." She had to stop and clear her throat. "You sailed around the world. In the seventeen hundreds. On a sailing ship."

"It was the only way to get across the oceans then."

She took a deep breath, her eyes closed, a little tremor shaking her. He eyed her, wondering if she was angry or suffering some sort of an attack.

"You," she said slowly, breathing loudly through her nose, "traveled around the world at the same time as explorers? Famous explorers? Like James Cook?"

"He was a hat of many asses," Archer said, relieved she wasn't having an attack. He breathed fire on the door just in case it hadn't been fireproofed.

It had.

A strangled noise came from Thaisa. "You *knew* him?"

"Yes. He was stubborn. Not an easy man to be with, although he knew a great number of ribald anecdotes."

"God's gonads, the man sailed with Cook, and all he can say is that he was stubborn and liked a dirty joke." Thaisa looked like she might swoon. "What about…uh…da Vinci? Did you know him?"

"No."

She slumped in relief. "Thank God. I might have had a small brain spasm if you had known him. Wait— what about Galileo?"

He squinted out of the corner of his eyes at the door. "No. I bedded his daughter, though, before she became a nun. She had several moles that she was quite proud of. Does this door look warded to you?"

"Moles like the hairy growths?" She looked both horrified and awed.

"The rodents. She used to dress them up and make them dance. She had odd tastes." He thought for a moment. "Inventive in bed for a woman who ended up in a convent, though. She particularly liked a position where I stood in front of her, and she put her hands on the floor while I held up her legs by the ankle, and—"

"Right," Thaisa snapped, jumping to her feet, her eyes all but shooting sparks at him. "I think that's about enough of historical memories time."

"Even you can't be jealous of a woman who has been dead for more than four hundred years," he told her, amused by the looks of mingled ire and desire she was throwing his way.

"Oh, I can. It might not be easy, and certainly

doesn't make sense, but I can. Her hands on the floor, Archer? Really? Did you enjoy that position?" she said, her little chin rising.

Gods, he loved that chin.

"If I say yes, will you put your hands on my chest and demand I show it to you?" he asked.

"Certainly not. I'm too top-heavy for that sort of a move." She thought about it for a minute, her eyes on his chest and thighs and groin. He reacted, as he always did, as if she were stroking him, and he made a mental note to hurry his tailor along with trousers that were Thaisa-proof. "Maybe. Well, all right, but only if I see a picture drawn first, because I get a headache easily if I stand on my head. It's why I failed the yoga class my friend Laura dragged me to."

"I would like to oblige, little flower, but this is hardly the place to make love to you."

"I'm not asking you to—" she started to say, but he, despite his words, cast an eye around the room and considered the blue Regency sofa.

She looked at it as well, giving it a good long look before turning a speculative gaze to him. "Was it a sort of scissors position or more of a wheelbarrow?"

"Scissors," he said, dragging the chairs over to block the door. Not that he expected anyone would let them out any time soon, but it was better to be safe than sorry.

"Reeeally," she drawled, giving the sofa another look.

He had his clothes off by the time she turned back to

him, her eyes widening at the sight of his arousal. He had gone from pleasantly aware of his cock, as he always was when Thaisa was near, to full-fledged marble effigy. "We will start with an easier managed position, one that is a little less reliant upon balance, flower, and work up to the more complicated ones."

"Oh no," she said, backing up when he reached for her.

He froze for a moment, unsure of why she wasn't throwing herself on him. She loved him naked. Her breath caught in her throat when he so much as took his shirt off, but when he disrobed in entirety, her eyes went round, and her fingers twitched a little, as if she wanted to be touching him.

He wanted her touching him.

"You do not wish me to love you now?" he asked, watching as she picked up his clothing, shook them out, and spread them onto the surface of the sofa.

"No. That is, yes, I do want you to, quite badly as a matter of fact, but no to you picking the position. It's my turn to pick."

"We are taking turns?" he asked, not sure how he felt about this strange new dominance in his little flower.

"We are. Partners, remember?"

"Very well," he said, deciding to be magnanimous. It intrigued him, the way her petals unfurled, revealing new elements to her personality. He didn't for the world want to undermine her newfound confidence. "But I will warn you that I do not have a submissive nature. Just as you say you do not respond to commands, I do not respond to being dominated."

She smiled and gestured to the sofa. "I promise I won't dominate you. Well, I will, but just a very little, and if it makes you uncomfortable, I'll stop, all right?"

"Hrmph," he said, but lay down on his back and watched her with some doubt. "Do you think to perform a striptease for me? You do not need to perform in order to stir my passions." He grasped his rod and shook it at her. "I am hard enough to take down a few redwoods."

"Oooh," she said, pausing for a moment in the act of unbuttoning the front of her dress. "A striptease! I haven't ever done one, but I did take a few belly dancing classes online. Let's see if I can remember some of that."

He watched her shimmy out of her dress, her hips moving to a tune that only she could hear, the sight of which made him want to claim her, to cover her body with his and make her understand just how strong the mating bond was between them, but he had given her permission to torment him, and by the gods, he would lie there and let her torture him if it killed him.

Which it may well do if she kept doing that roll of her belly, her body undulating in a way that made him a flaming brand of sexual frustration.

"Do you like this?" she asked as she pushed her dress down over her hips, the material falling to the floor with a soft whoosh.

"No," he said, his voice filled with gravel.

She paused, blinked, then smiled a slow, wicked smile. One he was shocked she knew. She wiggled her way out of her underwear and bra, revealing herself to his gaze at last. He damn near licked his lips as his gaze ran over her body even as she pushed one of his feet off the sofa, making room between his thighs so she could kneel.

If she did what he thought she was going to do, then he might very well die of sheer, unadulterated pleasure.

"Archer?" she asked, bending down over his thighs, her hair sweeping across it like little whips of fire. Her breath was soft, her mouth warm, but it wasn't comfort she provided as she nipped the flesh of his inner thigh, the top of her head brushing against his bollocks. "You're not talking." She glanced over his groin to where he was frozen in anticipation. "Or breathing. My love, take a breath. This will go much better if you don't pass out again."

He took a long, shuddering breath, his hands clenching and releasing convulsively. He wanted badly to grab her, to impale her on him, to feel her sweet heat join with the inferno that raged within him, but at that moment, he was incapable of words, let alone actual movement. "Nrng," he said.

"I know just how you feel," she said, her voice brushing across his flesh like the softest velvet. "You make me nrng every time you touch me. Let's see if we can't get a *whoa, Nelly* out of you with this." She kissed a steamy path up his thighs to his bollocks, one hand gently pulling and rolling them around in her hand. "I love your balls. I know that's an odd thing to say, because they normally are anything but attractive. They always look angry to me, darker than the rest of you, and just...well, annoyed with life. Maybe it's because they're always stuffed into your pants. Maybe it's because they don't get the attention that your dick does. Either way, I like yours."

"Thaisa," a voice said. He was amazed to realize it was his, since he hadn't thought it possible to think of actual words, let alone speak them. "If you do not stop toying with my stones and mount yourself upon me in the next two seconds, I will die. And then you will have to get yourself out of here, which I have no doubt you will do, but you will have no one to protect you from the evil that lurks without. I will be forced to haunt you. Do you understand?"

She giggled and gave his stones another little squeeze. "And I thought you couldn't even manage a *whoa, Nelly*. All right. You ready for this? I'm going in."

For one startling moment he thought she was speaking the literal truth and was about to inform her that although he knew his cousin enjoyed those sorts of things with his lovers—both male and female—he was not of the same mind, but to his immense relief—and enjoyment, rapture, ecstasy, and a number of other words that he couldn't at that moment pull to mind—she took him into her mouth.

"Whoa, Nelly," he said, his hips arching up as she swirled her tongue along the underside, making him see stars.

She giggled, the sensation of that while she tormented him with her mouth one that almost made him lose control. "You taste...it's hard to describe...you taste like the sea when a storm is rolling onto the shore. You make me feel wild, Archer. Wild and untamed, like I can do anything, but at the same time, connected to you so tightly that I don't think I'll ever be able to separate myself."

"You won't," he said, knowing he had to stop her. He pulled her up despite the frown she gave him, shifting his hips so that she had room to straddle him. "You are part of me just as I am part of you, and if you don't cowgirl me right now, I will spill my seed and you won't make that hum you make when you climax."

"Cowgirl?" she asked, leaning down to press a fleeting kiss to his lips. He took his rod and tapped her pointedly. "What do you, a man who has lived for seven hundred years, know about cowgirl position?"

"We had cowgirl then. We just called it St. George." He gave up trying to be subtle and tried to place himself at her woman's parts, but she leaned down, taking one of his nipples into her mouth.

"St. George riding the dragon," she said when he gasped in a good half of the available air in the room, his rod twitching of its own accord, desperate to bury itself in her heat. "Archer?"

"You're going to kill me," he groaned, his hips bucking in an attempt to join with her.

"I know. But it's going to be such a good death," she said, reaching between them and positioning him, slowly sinking down in a way that was certain to drive him insane. "I love you. I don't know how it happened so fast, but you fill my heart, and I will love you from this moment until the time when I draw my last breath."

He froze for a moment in time so exquisitely sweet, he thought he might just cry. And then he gave in to the need that had been riding him since she had started the torment, his body twisting until she was underneath him, and he was bucking wildly, touching her, tasting her, doing everything he could to make her as close to exploding as he was. She tensed, her legs tight around his waist, her head thrown back as a sexual flush washed upward, her eyes huge when the climax took her. The tightening of her inner muscles pushed him past all bearing, and he gave in to it knowing without a single shred of doubt that she truly did love him.

He'd just have to make sure that she stayed that way.

CHAPTER FIFTEEN

IT TOOK A LONG, LONG TIME FOR ME TO RECOVER FROM the lovemaking in the room where we'd been dumped.

Since there wasn't enough space for both of us to lie together, Archer insisted that he lie on the couch and I lie on him. As I was at that moment a boneless, incoherent puddle of goo that had been pleasured almost to the bounds of human bearing, I made no objection and lay quivering with little orgasmic aftershocks on him, his chest damp, his body solid beneath me.

"You're sweaty," I said, apropos to nothing. I trailed a finger around a pert little nipple that poked out of a curl of chest hair made dark with his sweat.

"It is honest sweat. You rode me hard."

I propped my chin on my hands and looked at his face. His eyes were closed, the thick black lashes making little crescents against his skin. He looked so beautiful it almost hurt, and I saw, with clarity that almost scared me, the long years of our life in which women would be attracted to him. Some would no doubt just admire from afar, as I had initially done, but others would not hesitate to try to take him away from me.

They could try, I thought to myself, my gaze caressing his face. I had been misled by Archer's beauty just like all those women would be—they'd think he was as shallow as I had first thought him to be, so secure in his appearance that he thought of no one else. But I knew better. Beneath that gorgeous surface, a warm, loving man resided, one who put the welfare of others before himself.

No, not man, dragon.

And he was mine.

I smiled. He was such an interesting mix of modern intelligence and medieval morals. "I like when you get aroused. You lose some of your modern words. I don't think any modern man calls his balls *stones* and his dick a *rod*."

He cracked one eye open to look at me. "Are you calling me old?"

"No, although we are *so* going to sit down and go over each and every year of your life, so you can tell me everything you've seen and heard and experienced. Then I'll write it all down, and we'll astound the world with our new insights into history."

He closed the eye. "I am master of the storm drag-ons. I have no time for such trivialities."

"Mmm-hmm." I pinched his side. "You're still go-ing to make time for it because it will make me happy."

His hands, which had been drawing little patterns on my back, slid around and under me, causing me to arch my back so the strumpets that were my breasts could have access to his hands. "Possibly."

I pushed myself off him and reluctantly gathered up my things, shaking the dust from them before I put them on. "I think I know where the pieces of the medallion are."

Archer watched me silently for the count of eight. "It was written on the leaf?"

"No. Yes. Kind of." I finished dressing and sat down when Archer began to pull on his clothing. I watched him, but for once, my gaze was directed inward as I tried to make the puzzle pieces that had slid together earlier make sense. Somehow, there were more pieces now.

I looked at him and decided to tackle the most recent of things that confused me. "You're not mad at Miles."

He pulled out his phone, shaking it as if it might have been damaged by the fall before tucking it away. "You heard me name him betrayer and cast him from the tribe. I do not do so lightly."

"No, you don't. But..." I shook my head as one of the pieces of the puzzle twisted and turned but would not fit. "But your fire wasn't filling you. Or me. It was there, simmering away, but you weren't truly angry. Nor, for that matter, were you with your brother. And that makes me wonder why. That makes me really wonder why, Archer."

He didn't look at me, just considered the door again.

"And then there's this," I said, waving my hand around the room.

"Being here was not my choice, in case you were going to accuse me of that."

"No, I don't think it was your choice," I said slowly, eyeing the couch. "But neither were you raging with desperation to get out of your brother's grip. I can't think of any other place where you'd let yourself make love if there was any danger. Except we did that in the forest..." Two pieces of the puzzle clicked into place. "But it was your brother who was supposed to be looking for me then. Which means that for some reason I can't figure out, you are not afraid of your brother."

"I am not afraid of anyone," he said, still not looking at me.

And that fact told me a lot.

"Right, but all this business about the shadow dragons attacking the storm dragons and vice versa...a show, Bree said." I stared at him with dawning awareness. "It's all a show! But why?"

"What did you learn from the leaf?" he asked, ignoring my question.

I had my own idea of what was going on with Hunter but decided to circle back to that. First, I needed to tell him what I'd found on the manuscript. "The cipher on the leaf wasn't that sophisticated. It looked like a variation of a Marseilles cipher used by alchemists in the fifteenth century, and that ties in with the Latin note at the top."

He was silent, sitting down next to me, obviously giving me time to tell him what I had found in my own way. His hand was warm on my back, his leg pressed against mine while I picked out the words. "The ciphered part of the leaf told a short tale about the birth of constellations. There's nothing familiar about that at all?"

He shook his head, looking thoughtful. "What I know is what was passed down orally, and in that, I have never heard a mention of the night sky or stars."

"The cipher said that the mother had broken the medallion and they became two constellations."

"That makes no sense," he said, frowning.

"I would have expected that one of the constellations was Gemini, because you are a twin, but it wasn't that. I double-checked. The two mentioned were Sagittarius and Orion. Do you know anything about the history of the constellations?"

"Other than most of them have origins in Greek myth, no."

"Sagittarius is Latin." My gaze met his. His eyes were beautiful pale blue, like a rain-washed spring sky. "It means *archer*."

He raised his brows. "And Orion?"

"Orion fought the scorpion that Scorpio is named for." I gave him a long look, wondering how he'd take the news. "He was a hunter, Archer."

He chewed that over. "I admit the coincidence, if it is one, is colossal, but I can assure you that I do not have either piece of the Raisa Medallion. If one was placed with me when I was a babe, newly abandoned and taken in temporarily by a mortal whose barren wife enjoyed babies, it has long since been lost."

"Let's put a bookmark in your foster mom, because I want to come back to that sometime, but the leaf was pretty clear: the mother was divided, and from her were created the two constellations. I didn't pull it together until it struck me that Bree is always calling you Archer Dragon. Not Archer, or Archer the dragon, but *the* archer dragon. She knew, dammit. She knew and she didn't say anything to me."

"If the leaf is correct, then it is worthless. The two parts of the medallion are lost to time." His lips twisted in a wry grimace. "It is nothing but a fairy story, as I have said all along."

"You don't understand," I said, taking his hand. "I don't think you have the piece of the Raisa Medallion."

"Good. Because I would know if I possessed such a thing."

I leaned forward to kiss one corner of his mouth. "My love, I think you *are* the part of the medallion."

He gawked at me until he realized what he was doing, and evidently decided that men who lead a tribe of rogue dragons shouldn't gawk so outright. "I would say you've had too much sun, but clearly, that isn't so, thus I must conclude your mind is still muddled by my lovemaking skill. Since this is right and proper in a mate, I will not chastise you for allowing your imagination to get the better of you, and instead urge you to put it to better uses, like ways you can torment and torture me with your hands and mouth and breasts and hips. And all your other bits."

"Stop distracting me with smutty thoughts," I told him, my fingers unable to keep from stroking down his arm to where his nearest hand sat relaxed on his knee. I was distracted for a moment by the knowledge that I could touch him whenever I wanted. I could just walk up to him and put my hands on him, and he would accept my right to do so. Or would he? A worry struck me. He obviously enjoyed me touching him when we were in private, but had he done so while we were around other people? I couldn't think of any show of affection that he had conducted while others were present. Perhaps he didn't care to have me touching him outside of sex. "If you were standing in that bar where I saw you with Sparkle Bosom Catriona, wearing that same silk shirt that you wore that night, surrounded by all the beautiful people who are always found there mingling and chatting and being gorgeous, and I came up to you and put my hand on your chest, what would you do?"

"Are you likely to do that?" he asked, making the little morsel of worry in my stomach grow.

"I...I might," I said slowly, wondering if I had made a colossal mistake. Had I misjudged Archer's personality so greatly? He professed what amounted to love for me, and Lord knew I was now so madly in love with him that being near him made my brain go all squirrely, but had I underestimated just what his appearance had done to his ego for all those centuries?

"Then I would most likely take you by the hips that you deliberately use to taunt me, and kiss you until your fingertips lit on fire."

I looked at him, searching his lovely, pale eyes.

"Flower," he said, putting an arm around me and pulling me up against his side, "I will be glad when the day arrives that you finally get over my face."

"Oh, that day will never come," I told him, leaning into his chest, the worry in my gut dissolving as his heat soaked into my soul. "I just wondered if you minded if I touch you when we're around other people."

"I am doing something wrong if you do not know that I encourage you to touch me when and where you desire. Go to the far end of the room."

He stood up, gesturing toward the corner.

I looked in confusion at him, startled by the abrupt change in conversation. "What? Why?"

"Because you are not yet a member of the storm tribe. Your recognition by the tribe as such was supposed to happen an hour ago, but we will reschedule, and then you will be safe. Until that time, stand in the corner. Take the rug with you, and use it as a blanket."

"Okay, see, this is the sort of command situation I mentioned."

"Thaisa." The look he bent on me was one that warned he would tolerate no bandying of wits. Since he stood before the door, I assumed he was going to attempt to open it and decided that I would be stupid to not heed his warning. Accordingly, I dragged the heavy rug over to the far corner and hoisted it up protectively as a barrier.

"Are you going to try to burn it down?"

"No." He strapped the back scabbard on, slid the sword into place, and after a moment's thought, slung a quiver over his arm, as well as the bow. He held his hands out, palms facing the door. "The only reason I am not outright dismissing your deduction that I am myself part of the Raisa Medallion is because of this."

"Because of wha—" I started to ask, then gasped when there was a sensation of the air drawing in on itself, just like it was pulling to one point. The hairs on my arms stood on end, the room suddenly becoming charged with static. Archer stood facing the door, his head bowed, his hands held out in front of him, palms toward the door. I could feel his fire from where I stood across the room, but there was something else present, a prickly feeling that wasn't fire. To my amazement, Archer didn't blast the door with fire; instead, static started to form on his arms, rolling down them to his hands, little tendrils of electricity twisting and snapping off his flesh. It was like he was in the middle of a Van de Graaff generator, the white-blue tendrils charging the air until it left me wanting to scream.

"Cover your ears," Archer yelled, gathering the electricity into his hands. A scant second after I complied, he released the power, the sound of it slamming into the door, obliterating it with an explosion that knocked me off my feet against the wall. I saw stars, actual pinpricks of light dancing before my bedazzled eyes while I slumped groggily, but then Archer was there, pulling me to his chest, his mouth warm on me as he murmured love words in Magyar.

"What…God's groin, Archer! What the hell was that?"

"I am a dragon," he said, scooping me up in his arms and carrying me out of the room just like that was perfectly natural. I gave him full marks for being able to lift me from the ground without so much as one little grunt, but was too stunned to do more than protest feebly that I could walk.

"I may not know a lot about dragons, but I'm willing to bet that is more than normal for you guys," I said, another piece of the puzzle sliding into place. "But it would fall in line with someone who was part of a mythical relic of immense power. Archer, you know what this means, don't you?"

His jaw tightened. "I know it means that you think this is proof that my brother bears the other piece."

"He has dark powers," I pointed out, smoothing my hand along his collarbone. My fingernails were on fire, but I paid them no mind. "That's also not normal. You two are clearly some sort of superdragon, and I think that it would be a good idea to bring you together to see what happens."

"Whereas I think Hunter needs to be taught a lesson

for locking us away," Archer answered, an inflexible note to his voice.

"I suspected that was going to be your attitude," I said, kissing his jaw before demanding he put me down when he came to a staircase that led upward. "Did he do it to irritate you, or protect us?"

"The latter."

"Wow. Okay. That fits, too."

He shot me an unreadable look. "Do not talk to anyone about your insights into the shadow tribe, Thaisa."

"But—"

"No. It is not safe."

I bit back my objections, trusting that he had a reason for putting on the show he had clearly been manipulating for a long time. "All right. But I have a better idea than giving your brother hell for dumping us in that room. Although I have to ask—have you always been able to do electricity thing?"

"Yes," he said, pulling out the sword as we emerged at the top of the stairs. "Stay behind me, flower. That blast was loud enough to bring all of my brother's tribe running."

"They aren't in on it?" I asked, moving around the puzzle until it made me dizzy.

"No."

"Well, that's good, because they aren't here."

He stopped and glanced back at me. "They aren't?"

"Nope. Hunter sent them out to guard his land when he dragged Bree and me inside. He said you were going to be sure to attack, so all his people went out to guard their land. Now I realize it was a way to get them out of the way."

"He always did feel like he could do this on his own," Archer muttered, stalking forward.

I tried to take his hand, but he gave me a stern look, and more or less walked directly in front of me. I smiled at his back, appreciating that he wanted to keep me safe, but more, my inner voice squealed at just how dashing Archer looked holding the sword. It was like having my own medieval knight come to life.

"Were you ever knighted?" I couldn't help but ask. My mouth fairly watered at all the knowledge and experience that was stuffed inside that insanely gorgeous head.

"Several times," he answered, pausing where a hall crossed our passageway. He listened for a moment, then gestured toward the left.

"Really? I didn't think that was common. I thought you swore fealty to an overlord when you are knighted, and you can't foreswear that without some pretty nasty repercussions, can you?"

"No, but when you live over the course of several centuries, you end up swearing more than one oath of fealty."

"I suppose that makes sense," I said, considering that, one hand holding on to the back of his shirt. "Your overlords must have died at some point, and since you probably didn't want anyone to know that you were a dragon, I imagine you had to go to different places and find new overlords. Were you always Sir Archer, or did you have other names?"

"What the hell do you think you're doing?"

The words were bellowed down the hallway to our right. Archer spun around, whipping me behind him while raising the sword in a manner that once again made Inner Thaisa squeal with delight.

"Did you blast another wall? Bloody hell, brother! Do you know how much it costs to have these custom walls made?" Hunter appeared at the far hallway, stomping toward us with an annoyed look, his hands moving in the air as he started sketching symbols.

"This ends now," Archer snarled, his body tense, his dragon fire roaring to life in him. I felt a familiar tingle on my arms that meant he was starting to draw in electricity as well. "You will stop trying to do this without me!"

"I am the master of the dark power, not you!" Hunter spat back, his expression black. "This falls to me!"

"We do this together. There is no other way." Archer's voice was filled with anger and no little amount of threat.

I narrowed my gaze on Hunter even as I heard Bree's voice behind me.

"Hey, we heard a big explosion. Did Archer lose his temper, or did you guys just have really good sex?"

I glanced behind me to see Ioan and Bree racing to us, Ioan holding a sword.

I had many things to say to them, but no time to do

it. I had to stop Archer and Hunter from whatever pissing match they were engaged in.

"Right. Insensibility spell time," I said, pulling from my memory the sigils that went along with the spells found in the *Demonitica*. I didn't have anything to draw with but decided what was good enough for Hunter might work for me. I traced the symbols in the air.

Nothing happened.

"Thaisa, I want you to leave. Now." Archer shot me a glare when Ioan stopped next to him, panting slightly.

"Oh, we are so going to have a talk about what *partners* means," I told Archer, running over in my mind what I'd done wrong with the spells that Bree and I had researched that afternoon. Everything seemed right. Maybe it was the sigil?

"Mate," he said in a warning tone, but the brief glance he cast me was filled with fear and dread, and I realized with a pain to my heart it was fear for me, not himself. He wasn't just posturing; he really was afraid something would happen to me.

If I hadn't been wholly in love with him by that point, that would have pushed me over the edge. The fact that no one had loved him, the most gorgeous of men, the most protective and warmhearted and caring man who ever lived, made me want to cry at the injustice of it all. I wanted to scream at the people who should have been there for him and who weren't and to make him understand just how vital he was to my life.

I leaned into him, saying softly so only he heard,

"I'm not going anywhere, Archer. We're in this to-gether, you and I, and no one is going to separate us. Ever. But I agree that this does need to end now…just not by beating up Hunter."

"You can't deny that he deserves it."

"Really?" I kissed his adorable jaw. "I think he's just off balance, as you are."

The look he shot me was one of outrage.

"But we can fix it," I continued. "We can fix Hunter. We can end whatever is going on between you two and bring the balance that your parents wanted."

I could sense that he wanted to argue, but with Hunter stalking toward us trailing black symbols that I knew he was using to weave some spell, Archer dragged his attention from me to that of his brother.

"Trying this insensibility spell again." I bit my lip as I sketched the symbols in the air.

"I am done with this," Hunter said, stopping ten feet before us, his hands still moving. His eyes had gone dark green, and for a moment, I had a weird sensa-tion looking at the strange eyes in Archer's face. Even his voice had gone rough, making it almost identical to Archer's. "You will not leave us be, will you? All we want is to be left alone in peace, but you won't rest un-til we're destroyed. And they call me the demon. You, brother, are more like our father than I could ever be."

I looked from him to Archer, not understanding. Archer had all but admitted that the war between them was all a show. He didn't fear his brother, didn't really want him dead, and yet now Hunter was speaking as if they really were the bitterest of enemies? Maybe he'd gone mad.

"Do not attempt to distract us with lies," Archer said, his voice low and deep and ugly, but once again, there was no sense of his dragon fire. It was a show. It had to be a show. But why? For who?

There were only the two brothers and Bree and me...My gaze swiveled over to where Ioan stood.

"It is you who will not let the storm dragons live in peace. You spread death and destruction wherever you go, and I will not suffer your presence on this earth any longer. My tribe will be safe at long last."

"Bree," I whispered.

"Hmm? Wow, is Hunter drawing the spell I think he's drawing? That's going to punch a hell of a hole through Archer if he actually casts it. I'm not absolutely sure if Archer can come back from that one."

"What is this madness?" Hunter stopped casting his spell in order to look scornfully at his brother. "Why do you deny what you truly are? Is it because you do not wish for your woman to know the true depths of your darkness?"

"Two things. First, why is my spell not working? Second, what's it going to take to stop this?" I asked Bree out of the side of my mouth.

"My mate knows what is in my heart," Archer said quietly, and I knew I had about ten seconds before things came to a head.

Bree glanced at my wrist. "The answer to both is that you are not Saule."

"Saul? Who…" It took me a moment to realize that she meant *saule*, the Proto-Baltic word for the sun. I shook my head, wondering if she'd gone loopy again. "Of course I'm not the sun."

Miles dashed around the corner behind Hunter, skidding to a stop when he saw us standing in the intersection of hallways.

"I can't help you any more than I have," Bree said, shaking her head and stepping back. "I broke the rules as it is."

"What rules? What help?" I asked when Archer snarled a few choice words at the sight of Miles. Ioan raised his sword, like he was readying himself for an attack.

I thought furiously, feeling there was something just beyond my understanding, some clue that was dangling out of my reach.

Archer was Sagittarius. Hunter was Orion. The leaf said the two must be brought together to rebalance the world, but they were here, together, ten feet apart, and the only thing that was going to happen was making Ioan think they wanted each other dead.

The sun… I dug out of my memory a star chart and realized with dawning enlightenment that Orion and Sagittarius were roughly on the opposite side of the chart, with the sun in the center.

"Saule!" I shouted, and scrabbled in the bag that was strapped across my torso, digging through it wildly so that things spilled out onto the floor. "Archer, don't you dare kill your brother! I think I figured it out…Damn, I have a lot of crap in my purse…Hang on, don't you two do anything more. Miles, don't let Hunter finish drawing that sigil. Really? I bought those cough drops two winters ago…I have *got* to clean out my purse more often…Aha!" I pulled from the remains of the items in my purse a tattered woven friendship bracelet, the one with the thin disc with the sun scratched on it. "Saule!"

"Thaisa, stay back," Archer snarled. "You cannot bring us together no matter what the leaf said."

"I can! That's just it. Listen to me, both of you." I shot Hunter a look as I slipped the bracelet onto my wrist. He ignored me and drew another symbol.

"Oh, you did not just do that. Hairy wart fingers!" I yelled, drawing the three symbols that Bree had taught me.

Hunter yelped and shook his hand as if it had been stung. He stared first at his fingers, then at me. "Stop it! That hurt!"

I wanted to move between Archer and Hunter but suspected Archer would have a hissy fit over that, so instead I moved in front of him, my body turned to the side so I could see the others but still keep my hands on his chest. Archer growled and tried to move me, but I clutched his shirt and refused to budge. "I know how to fix the broken medallion."

"Did you see what she did?" Hunter showed his hand to Miles. "That was my spell hand, too. Does that look like a wart growing? Now what the hell am I going to do?"

Miles made a face. "Maybe stop pissing her off?"

"Mate—" Archer tried to move me to his side again.

"I think maybe Ioan should take Bree out," Miles said, looking meaningfully at Archer.

Ioan looked disappointed.

Archer's jaw tightened. "I think the time for that is past."

Miles cast a worried look at Hunter but said nothing more.

I looked at Archer. "It is time."

He frowned. "Not for that."

"Please, let me do this," I said, sliding my hands up to his face, my eyes on his as I spoke against his lips. "Let me do what I am best at."

"I'm not going to stand for this," Hunter said in an injured voice. "I will simply draw my spells with my left hand. Let's see...it goes this way first...No, I have to reverse that because now it's widdershins... and a curl there...Dammit, that's not right. Starting over."

Archer looked deep into my eyes, his gaze piercing and full of doubt, but I let him see my confidence, both in him and in my own ability. "I love you, Archer. I love you so much that I'm not going to let this go on any longer. Too many of your dragons have died because of this, because of what you and your brother are. I want to live in peace with you forever, and we can't do that until we restore the medallion. Until we fulfill your parents' wish for you and your brother. Until we bring balance."

His jaw worked. I knew he was going to reject what I said and continue on the path that he thought was inevitable, one cast in stone since his birth and that would end in more deaths. But he surprised me, this dragon of mine who could hold the power of a storm in the palm of his hand. "You are that certain?"

"Yes. I think we can do this."

He looked at me, just looked at me, then did something I thought he'd never do. He took a step backward and gestured toward Hunter. "Do it."

I looked to Miles and Hunter. The latter was still muttering to himself as he attempted to draw spells in the air, but the symbols didn't hang in the air as they did when drawn with his right hand. Miles stood beside him, his eyes on Archer. I recognized the look I saw in them.

"You love Archer, don't you?" I asked Miles.

His face twisted in a grimace. "He is family. The bond between dragons with family is ever strong."

"You're not first cousins, are you?" I asked, distracted for a moment by Hunter, who was glaring at his left hand as he drew a symbol that knotted up on itself and poofed into nothing with inky black residue that drifted down to the floor.

"No." It was Archer who answered, and I saw to my relief that amusement glinted in his eyes. "Our great-grandmothers were sisters. Twins, as a matter of fact."

"So you're second cousins. That's better." I felt like a shadow had passed by.

"Well, it's not like they're going to have babies," Bree murmured in my ear.

"Damned straight. If Archer has babies with anyone, it'll be me," I answered.

She gave me a look and nodded toward Hunter.

"You're kidding," I said, startled. "You mean Miles is in—er..." I eyed Miles.

Bree grinned.

Miles looked embarrassed. "Can we change the subject back to how I betrayed Archer, please?"

"You gave him the wrong transcription, but you didn't betray him. I'm sorry I was wrong about you. I thought you were hiding something. I just didn't realize it was..." I stopped, not sure if I should go on.

Miles pinned me back with a look of belligerence. "As you said, I did not betray him. I brought Hunter the inaccurate copy of your notes."

I gawked at him. "How did you know I made a copy?"

He rolled his eyes. "I'm not a fool, no matter what you think of me."

"Oh. Sorry."

Hunter transferred his glare from his hand to his cousin. "You did *what*?"

Miles shrugged. "It seemed best. I knew you'd want to go off on your own if you had the correct copy. So I gave you the false one."

"So you don't know what the leaf says? Not really?" I asked Miles.

He shook his head. "I didn't look for the one you must have hidden away."

Archer stood with his arms crossed, the sword back

in its scabbard. His face expressed no emotion, but his eyes...oh, his eyes were warm with love.

"The manuscript tells the tale not of the Raisa Medallion but of the sun goddess named Saule, who was shattered when her two sons, two constellations, were born imperfect, together a whole, but separate... unfinished. She gave her life so that her sons Sagittarius and Orion could find their balance."

"The Archer and the Hunter," Archer said, his voice a low rumble that I felt thrum deep in my bones.

"But the constellations were separated by a great gulf—Sagittarius rises in December, I believe, while Orion is in July—at one end, the remnants of the mother, the sun, and at the other the father, the moon. Each morning, the sun mother rose to give life to her sons."

I had Hunter's attention now. He stood, his hands at his side, his eyes sliding past me to look at his twin. "You are part of the Raisa Medallion," I told Hunter. "Just as Archer is. The medallion is made up of the two of you. Separate, there is no balance. You both wield great power, but neither of you have peace."

"You're saying we, what, need to kiss and hold hands?" Hunter asked with something that very much looked like horror. "No. I am willing to put up with a lot, but I cannot live with him. He's impossible."

"I don't relish the idea of being bound to you any more than you do," Archer snarled, taking a couple of steps forward.

Hunter glowered and took a step forward as well, until the two men were separated by a few feet.

"Right. Let's hope this works, because otherwise, Archer is going to let me hear about it for a very long time." I took a deep breath and put my left hand on Hunter's chest and my right on Archer's. Nothing happened. The world continued to turn; Archer's chest rose and fell under my hand with the warmth of his dragon fire simmering softly within him. Hunter shifted, obviously impatient and just as doubtful as his brother.

I looked at Bree. "What am I doing wrong?"

"Saule," was all she said.

I thought about that. The leaf said the sun had given birth to the two constellations, but it was an allegory for Raisa, the mother of twin sons that she loved so much, she gave her life to bring them balance.

Love. She loved her sons. The connection, the bond between the three of them was love. I kept my hand on Hunter's chest while I turned to Archer, my hand over his heart, leaning into him to press a kiss to his lips, one that said better than words just how much I loved him. His mouth curved under mine, and just as his hands reached for me, the world shifted into a moment where everything went out of focus, then sharpened again with a percussive blast that sent us all flying, bringing the house down around and on top of us.

CHAPTER SIXTEEN

"MATE, IF YOU TRY TO GET UP ONE MORE TIME, I will tie you down." Archer shot Thaisa a look that by rights should have scared a good five years off her life, but she wouldn't be the exasperating, maddening, wonderful woman she was if she didn't disregard even the most reasonable of his commands.

"I don't know how many times I have to tell you that I'm fine, you annoyingly adorable man." She teetered when she stood up from the sofa that had been blown upward when the house exploded, stepping over various bits of debris, broken furniture, glass, trees, shrubs, and shattered wooden walls, while soft bits of down and thread from the destroyed upholstery drifted lazily on the night air. "Bree, is he coming around?"

"Not yet, but he's moaning, so he's still alive," Bree answered from where she sat on a big flat piece of wall that now lay in Hunter's front garden, Miles lying on his back next to her.

Archer grunted as he hauled more downed walls off the spot where Hunter had stood before Thaisa had blown the house up around them. "Anything?" he asked Ioan quietly. He didn't want Thaisa upset in case his brother had been destroyed as a result of her attempt to bring them together.

"No." Ioan shifted a solid oak chair frame, digging through the rubble with hands that were red with blood from the flying glass. Archer noticed that most of Ioan's wounds were healing, as were his. His gaze strayed to his flower. The front of her dress was splattered with blood, but since he'd managed to grab her right as the house came down, she had been sheltered by his body.

"Archer, I insist you rest for a little bit. Your back is a mess. *Again.*"

Beyond them, the shadow dragons who had heard the blast were working to dig out the remains, hoping to find their master. The looks they gave Archer were pure venom, but he ignored them, taking charge of the dragons as naturally as if they had been his tribe. He issued orders, setting teams of two to work together to clear sections around the spot where he'd clawed himself and Thaisa from the rubble. The shadow dragons didn't want to heed his instructions, but with sullen looks and suspicious eyes, they gave way before him.

He had to find Hunter. He couldn't do what needed to be done by himself.

"Hunter was standing right in front of us," Thaisa said, her hands on her hips as she looked around the crater that was the remains of the house. "Maybe if he got blown back that way?" She pointed just as one of the shadow dragons gave a cry.

Archer leaped across fallen concrete beams, scrambling down into an inky crevasse, his body protesting when he swung himself into the jagged hole.

On the ground, a female shadow dragon knelt over a black figure.

"Does he live?" Archer asked the dragon at the same time Thaisa called the same question above him.

"Yes," the dragon answered, looking indecisive. "I don't know if we should move him or not. He might have internal damage."

"He will heal," Archer said, but his hands were gentle as he turned his brother over.

"Archer?"

"He's alive," he yelled up to Thaisa. Ioan stood close to her, clearly taking up a protective position in case any of the shadow dragons should think to attack his mate. Archer made a mental note to make sure the man was promoted to his personal guard, then turned his full attention to his brother.

There was blood on Hunter's head and neck, a jagged gash that had bled copiously but that was even now sluggishly slowing while the flesh mended itself. Judging by the odd angle of Hunter's right arm, it was likely broken, as was a foot that twisted the wrong way. "Get the door open. Is there a stretcher?" he asked the shadow dragon.

"I'll check," she said, scrambling over the broken furniture and walls that had collapsed down into a basement room. Archer rose with his brother in his arms, moving slowly so as not to trip over any of the sharp fingers of twisted wood and metal that reached up to grab him. By the time he made it up the miraculously still-standing stone stairs, the shadow dragons had cobbled together a makeshift stretcher made out of a bit of bedsheet.

"Where is the healer?" Archer asked, watching when his brother was laid on the slab where Miles was now sitting upright, his hands on his head.

"On his way," the nearest shadow dragon answered, his eyes flicking between Archer and Thaisa. "Why did you remain after you set the bomb?"

"It wasn't a bomb," Archer said.

"It was magic," Thaisa said at the same time. "Very old magic, and although I'm pleased I was right about it, I'm very sorry that this happened. I had no idea the balancing would cause such a reaction."

"It's not your fault, mate." Archer straightened up, the muscles and tendons and bones in his back screaming. He'd taken the full brunt of a wall that collapsed on top of Thaisa and him, and although he healed just as fast as the other dragons, he suspected that it would take more than a few hours to repair the damage done to his spine.

Warmth flooded him, flowing along his back, causing his fire to answer. Thaisa pressed herself into his side, one hand gently rubbing his back. "Come on, my superhero. Let's get you sat down with Miles and Hunter so we can talk."

"I have no need to sit," he objected, leaning into her despite the words. He breathed deeply, capturing her scent and holding it inside him, where it glowed around the knowledge that she loved him.

"Well, I do. And I have a hundred questions that I very badly want Hunter to answer." She slid a glance up to him. "And you, too."

He raised his eyebrows, wondering what her analytical mind was busy with now. It fascinated him, that mind, and he felt a certain amount of pride that of all the people who had sought to find the Raisa Medallion over the course of six centuries, it was his Thaisa who had put it all together.

"Why did you pretend to be upset that Miles betrayed you?" she asked him.

He sighed. He had a feeling she'd seen through it. With his mouth next to her ear, he said softly, "Ioan was there."

"But he's your tribe member," she whispered.

"Yes, but he's only been so for a short time. Although I have no reason to believe he is anything but what he says he is, Hunter, Miles, and I trust no one else. Not even tribe members."

"I suppose I can understand that, although it seems like a lot of extra work."

The shadow dragons continued in a desultory manner to stack up bits of the wreckage, looking for anything they could salvage. Two of his brother's tribe sat next to Hunter, their eyes wary, but at least they stopped looking daggers at Archer.

"All's well that ends well, don't you think?" Bree hopped onto a bit of fallen masonry and peered out into the night. Archer tried to get Thaisa to sit on a stone garden bench that had survived the destruction, but she pushed him down onto it and then kept him there by sitting on his lap.

He wrapped his arms around her, her delightful round, warm breasts right there at mouth level. He eyed them, wondering just how long it would take his back to heal so he could give those breasts the attention they were due.

"I don't know that I'd quite go for that cliché, but I suppose as long as Hunter isn't seriously injured, it is apropos," Thaisa commented before making an annoyed tsk. "What are you doing, Bree?"

"Looking for my sister."

"You have a sister?" Thaisa sounded surprised.

"I have two, actually. Sasha is the eldest, and Clover is the youngest. I told Clover she needed to be here tonight, since she's looking for work, but I don't see her."

Thaisa looked like she was going to ask more questions of the sprite, but Archer, wanting to get Thaisa home and to his bed, tried to herd her to the discussion he knew she was determined to conduct. "What other questions do you have, flower?"

"Hmm? Oh, well…" She paused and looked at

Miles, who had gotten to his feet, having to hold on to a bit of tree trunk in order to keep upright. "Am I right in saying that you have a—for lack of a better word— passion for Hunter?"

Miles looked startled, then pugnacious. "I've told you before that family is valued in dragonkin."

"Even a family member you thought was killing all your members?" Thaisa asked.

He was silent.

Archer watched his cousin. He'd known that for almost as long as he'd known Miles that the younger man harbored romantic feelings for him, but since Miles knew he didn't reciprocate them, they had an easy relationship. He had no idea that affection had turned to Hunter.

Thaisa glanced at Archer, clearly asking if she could speak freely in front of the others. He gave her a little nod. "I believe the time for our deception is over."

"Good. That's going to make things a lot less confusing." Thaisa kissed Archer's ear.

"Simplification is welcome. So is a morphine drip," Miles said.

"You're a part of the whole thing, so you have no right to act like you didn't intend on pulling the wool over everyone's eyes," Thaisa pointed out. "That's what confused me. You and Archer were so adamant that the shadow dragons were killing off the storm dragons, and yet, I see now that you really did nothing about it. You didn't attack them. You didn't wipe them out. I know how Archer feels about his tribe, and I know he'd move heaven and earth to keep them safe, and yet..." She gave first him, then the prone form of Hunter a long look. "And yet, what was tantamount to a war went on and on and on."

Archer shifted to a more comfortable position, his hands on Thaisa's thighs. She really was far more prescient than he'd given her credit.

"And then there was Hunter. He said almost the same things that Archer did—that the shadow dragons were persecuted by his brother's tribe, that they just wanted to live in peace, all while they, too, did nothing to stop the war. They didn't wipe out Archer's remaining members. They didn't harm me, which I gather would have been a big deal."

He squeezed her leg and bit her shoulder. "It would have destroyed me."

"I love you, too, my darling," she said, kissing the tip of his nose.

Hunter moaned and tried to sit up, rubbing first his head, then his neck. Archer noted that the jagged wound was now nothing but an angry red welt about six inches long. "Am I dead? Is this the Underworld? Who are you?"

"My name is Sasha," said a woman who appeared out of the forest. She bore a close resemblance to Bree, clad as she was in a pink ballerina's tutu, white-and-black-striped thigh-high stockings, and a man's embroidered vest. Her hair matched the color of the tutu and looked like it was tied in a knot on the top of her head, with bits of it poking out in all directions.

"Hey, Sash," Bree said, giving her sister an odd look. "I thought Clover was coming?"

"She is. I figured you'd want everything official and stuff, so I popped along." She looked around at the remains of the house. "Cheese and crows, that was one hell of a curse being lifted."

"Curse?" Thaisa frowned. "It was a curse? I thought it was just bringing the two brothers together. Did you know it was a curse?" she asked Archer.

He hugged her tighter to him, drinking in the scent and feel of her. "It's not a curse in the traditional sense of the word, but yes, I suspected that if the medallion existed, then something like that had kept it hidden for so many centuries."

"Of course it was a curse," Hunter said, still rubbing his forehead. "What are you all doing sitting here? Why aren't any of you trying to put my beautiful house back together? What? Oh, thank you." He took the offered bottle of water from one of the shadow dragons.

The others had gathered at the sound of their master's voice, taking up a position in a semicircle behind him. Archer counted twenty-two dragons. He wondered if it would be enough. It had to be. He couldn't risk Thaisa's welfare.

"We're playing twenty questions," Miles explained, taking another bottle of water. "Thaisa is leading the production, but I'd be grateful if she could hurry it up, because I think my head is going to explode."

"Sorry, I'll try to make this as quick as I can. Archer needs to go to bed."

"Mate," he said in a long-suffering voice. "You do not say things like that in front of other dragons."

She giggled, kissed his forehead, then leaned back against him, her breast pressed into him in a manner that guaranteed walking would be painful. "Back to Miles."

"Ugh. Why me?" he asked.

"Because you were the key to it all. I just couldn't get over the fact that neither of you were trying to eliminate Hunter. How could you not want your most hated enemy dead? Ergo, he wasn't the enemy. And if he wasn't, it meant he couldn't be responsible for attacks on the storm dragons. Since I know Archer isn't the sort of man who would attack anyone unless he was defending himself or those he loves, that meant the whole thing was bunkum."

Hunter made a face at Archer. "She's smart."

"Yes. And she's mine, so you can stop kidnapping her away from me."

Thaisa stiffened in outrage as Hunter grinned at them. He was missing two teeth. "I figured you'd have my head after I saw you all but claim her in T and G."

Archer grunted a noncommittal reply.

"So then, I started wondering why you guys were making this big show of being mortal enemies," Thaisa continued.

"And?" Archer prompted when she stopped.

She shot him an odd look. "I couldn't figure out why you were doing it. Until I deciphered the leaf."

"The leaf," he said, nodding to himself. "I should have known you wouldn't miss anything on it."

"That is my job," she said with gentle chastisement.

"I don't understand," Ioan said, glancing from Archer to Thaisa. "Was there something on the manuscript that you didn't mention?"

"No," she said, and he could feel the sadness in her. "It's all there. The sun, the twin constellations who were off balance and needed to be brought together...and the moon."

Bree smiled and clapped her hands. "You got there in the end! I'm so pleased. She had to have a few hints," she told her sister, who was sitting next to her.

"You're not supposed to do that," Sasha replied.

"I know, but sometimes you gotta break the rules."

"True dat," Sasha said.

"Separate, Hunter and you were unbalanced. Dangers on your own, but not a force to be reckoned with. But by joining together—the hunter, the archer, both bound by the sun—you became what you couldn't be on your own: the first dragon hunters, able to wipe out demonic threats from the world."

"That is the result of the Raisa Medallion? It has made them dragon hunters? That's all it does?" Ioan asked, looking unimpressed.

"It has made them a whole lot more powerful, yes," Thaisa answered.

Sasha tipped her head at Archer. "Did you tell her about the moon?"

He was surprised she knew about that. "Who exactly are you?" he asked instead of answering her question.

She grinned. "You know the Court of Divine Blood?"

He nodded.

"I run it."

That explains much, Archer mused to himself.

"Go right ahead and assume I don't know what she's talking about, because I don't," Thaisa whispered into his ear.

He answered just as softly, "She runs what mortals think of as heaven."

Thaisa's eyes widened but she said nothing. She shot Sasha and Bree several startled glances, however.

"What is there to tell about the moon?" Ioan asked, looking mildly confused. "It has nothing to do with the medallion, surely."

"Actually, it does." Thaisa gave Archer a smile he felt down to the depths of his soul. "The sun is the mother—their mother, Raisa. The moon is the father."

"The blue dragon who went ouroboros and was cursed? The one who created the Raisa Medallion?" one of Hunter's tribe asked, looking perplexed.

"It didn't occur to me until I finished deciphering the leaf that no one ever mentioned the father after the medallion was created. It seemed odd, and odder still was the fact that I found no mention of his name. I still don't know what it is," Thaisa told Archer.

"It is Xavier."

Archer froze at the voice that came from behind him, but only for the time it took his heart to beat once. Then he was up, Thaisa pushed behind him, his sword in hand, and pointed at the shadow that detached itself from the inky night, strolling forward.

"Great. He would pick now. Couldn't have waited until we'd gotten patched up," Hunter grumbled, but got to his feet, looking around for a weapon.

"I take it's that Daddy?" Thaisa asked, peering around Archer's arm.

"Yes. Stay back."

Ioan slid to the side, clearly looking for a weapon but having to content himself with a tree branch.

"So you did it," the man said, looking from Archer to Hunter. He had their same high cheekbones, the same glossy black hair, the same chin, but his eyes were cold, impersonal, completely black and devoid of any color. They were the eyes of a snake considering its dinner. "You fools. Do you really think you can defeat me? I am the original dragon hunter."

"Welp, showtime, I think," Bree said, standing up and dusting off her miniskirt. She handed her oversized bag to her sister.

"Come back for my birthday," Sasha said, getting to her feet as well. "I'm going to have a chocolate fountain with sexy men holding strawberries. We get to lick the chocolate off their fingers."

"Oooh, I'm so there," Bree said, then marched over to stand next to Archer.

"Right, now I have no idea what's going on," Thaisa said to him. "What is Bree doing?"

"I don't even have a sword," Hunter complained, stumbling forward. "How'm I supposed to be heroic without an *élan vital*?"

"Oh, I found one on the drive," Sasha said, pulling

the black sword out of Bree's bag, just as if she were Mary Poppins.

"That is impossible," Thaisa said, pressing herself into Archer's side. "Someone please clue me in to how she did that."

Sasha shrugged. "Smoke and mirrors?"

"You ready?" Bree asked Archer. He looked at her for a few minutes, understanding at last why she had chosen Thaisa to help.

"Are you sure?" he asked politely.

"Yup." She gave him one of her brilliant grins and patted his cheek. "Make me proud, Archer Dragon."

He bowed. Her form shimmered, glowing like the light of the sun was within her; then her form compacted down to a little ball of golden light that bobbed along his sword until it settled in the empty socket. Thaisa gasped just as the runes along the sword lit up, glowing with the grace of the sun and moon.

"Sorry, am I late?" A girl who looked remarkably like Bree burst into their midst, panting as she looked around at them all. "Sasha, you here to give your blessing?"

"It's my job," her sister said. "Clover, meet Hunter. He'll be your dragon for the evening."

"And many more, I hope," Hunter said, giving the girl a bow.

"What is going on?" Thaisa asked in a whisper. "Why did Bree turn into a ball of light and plop herself onto your sword?"

"Such pretty manners," Clover said, giggling; then,

with a glance at him and beyond, to where the sire stood, looking bored, she, too, became a ball of glowing light that settled onto Hunter's sword.

"Now, that's what I'm talking about," Hunter said, limping forward to stand next to Archer.

Xavier applauded politely. "Is this little show over? I had expected better from you both."

"Flower," Archer said in warning.

"Yup," she said, moving back to stand with Sasha and Ioan. "You go and take care of the big bad scary man."

"Dragon hunter," Xavier corrected, and with a considering look first at Archer and then Hunter, he said, "You think to challenge me? You have in the past, and you've failed. Are you so anxious to pay the price for that failure again?"

"No more dragons will die simply because you wish to wipe us from the earth," Archer said, gripping his sword tightly. He prayed that Thaisa was correct in assuming that with the balance restored to Hunter and him, together they would be able to do what they could not do before.

"The medallion has been restored," Hunter added. "The sun has returned balance to us."

Xavier's gaze slid behind Archer to rest briefly on Thaisa. "So I see. It matters not, however." He lifted his sword. "I am not the fool you think me. Ioan?"

To Archer's horror, a horror that would, he knew, remain with him for many centuries, Ioan grabbed Thaisa, swinging her over his shoulder as he shoved aside the nearest shadow dragons and ran for the sire.

Archer roared, the night air filled with the sound of his fury, his body elongating and shifting as he leaped after his tribesman, electricity skimming his body, gathering in his hands. He wanted to hurl it at Ioan, at the traitor who dared touch his mate, but Thaisa wasn't yet fully a storm dragon. He couldn't risk harming her.

Thaisa screamed and pounded on Ioan's back, struggling for a few seconds before suddenly rising up, grabbing Ioan's hair with both hands, and flinging herself to the side, off his shoulder, effectively throwing him off balance.

Hunter and his tribe lunged forward at the sire even as Archer threw himself on Ioan, slamming the power of the storm into the man, making his back arch as it racked his body. He screamed, twitching, his body contorting horribly, unable to handle the amount of electricity that was pouring into it. Only when he was dead did Archer leash his storm.

He pulled Thaisa to her feet, the warmth of her body against his reassuring him that she hadn't been taken away from him. "Mate, are you hurt? Did he harm you?"

"No," she said, once again surprising him when she shoved him toward Hunter and the other dragons, who had attacked Xavier. "Go help your brother! I'm fine!"

Archer threw himself at the sire, his sword swinging in the night air, the glow from the espirit making the runes shine brightly.

"This is not over," the sire snarled, backing up and drawing symbols in the air. "What you have done here will be undone. I will see to it that you both right the wrong that you have done this night. I did not create the race of dragon hunters to be the saviors you imagine yourselves to be—you will be remade in my image, or you will be destroyed as will all your tribes."

Hunter's and Archer's swords sang on either side of the sire, but the song was short-lived. He was gone, having retreated into the shadow world.

"Balance," Thaisa said, moving over to Archer, her eyes alight with love and pride. He wanted to shout with joy. He wanted to embrace everyone there, right down to the last shadow dragon. He wanted to take his flower to bed and not leave until they had wrung themselves dry. "You have balance now, you and Hunter. It really does make you both more powerful. You scared your dad, you know."

Archer was silent for a moment, thinking that over. "No. He does not fear us...but he hates what we have become. He hates the fact that rather than becoming forces of evil, our dragon selves master our darkness."

Thaisa leaned into him, her touch as warm as the sun she represented. "I hope your mom knows what happened tonight."

"She knows," Archer told her, and kissed her until she couldn't ask any more questions.

CHAPTER SEVENTEEN

"Storm dragons."

Archer's voice was deep and rich with the rough edges that I loved so much. But this time, there was also a sense of satisfaction as he stood next to me on the lawn of his house, the breeze from the ocean ruffling his silky hair. Just the sight of that hair had me wanting to do any number of things to him, all of which consisted of me applying my body parts to his.

"Before you stands Thaisa, who I name as mate."

To the left of us, a table had been set with a laptop. I knew from examining the setup that Archer was streaming the binding ceremony to those storm dragons who were not local to us. In a semicircle before us, the forty-some-odd tribe members who had been able to reach us in time for the ceremony—men, women, and even a few children—stood silent.

I was very aware of Archer next to me. His dragon fire hummed in my blood, making me feel restless and itchy, like my clothing was a few sizes too small.

"From this day henceforth, she is known to be blood of my blood, a dragon of the storm tribe."

I smoothed down the dress that I'd picked to wear for this ceremony, a black sheath cocktail dress reminiscent of the 1950s, with little crystal beads sewn onto it that made me think of the stars glittering in the night sky. I wished it was Archer touching me instead and wondered how long the ceremony was going to last. If I could just get him into the bedroom, I could peel off the navy blue heavy silk tunic that all the men wore. I badly wanted to get Archer out of that tunic, naked and ready to teach me about this scissor position that he evidently had enjoyed so much.

"To her, we pledge our protection, our honor, and our respect."

A rustling was the only sound to be heard as all of the dragons present—Archer excepted—knelt and bowed their heads.

Tears pricked the backs of my eyes as I looked at him. His eyes glittered with a brilliant blue topaz light, but I didn't need the rich eye color to tell me that he, too, was thinking about the after-ceremony celebrations. He'd been too busy after we returned home from Hunter's now-destroyed base to do more than tumble into bed into an exhausted sleep, and since I knew his body had spent a tremendous amount of energy healing his hurts, I had been content to lie next to him, stroking his head and listening to his breathing as he slept.

"Mate?"

I stepped forward, lifting my voice to speak the formal acceptance of my new role. "Storm dragons, I name you kin, honored and respected in kind."

The dragons rose, watching us silently.

I turned to Archer, asking softly, "Did I forget part of my lines? They look like they are waiting for something."

"They are." His hands were warm on my hips when he pulled me into an embrace, his eyes shimmering with heat and passion and love as his mouth claimed mine. I slid my hands up his chest to his shoulders, my fingers trailing fire up the thick muscles. His hold moved around to my butt, hoisting me up until I was off the ground, kissing him with every morsel of love I held.

A cheer broke out behind us, followed by laughter and several comments of a mildly ribald nature. Someone turned on the stereo, allowing music to waft over patio, pool, and lawn.

"That was a blatant show of possession," I said, retrieving my tongue from where Archer had sucked it into his mouth. He let me slide down his body until I was standing again, but I made sure I wiggled against him in an invitation that would be impossible to mistake. "You know how I dislike it when you get all bossy on me."

"I'm about to get very bossy on you," he growled in my ear, then turned with an arm around me to greet each member of the storm dragons as they came up to be formally introduced to me.

It took almost an hour before we could escape upstairs, and a half hour after that, using a few sheets of paper to diagram the positions, Archer and I managed the Galileo scissor move, as we decided it should be so named.

"Right, time for some explanations," I said, lying on his naked body, our respective heart rates slowed to the point where I thought we might just survive.

He had his hands on my ass, giving both cheeks a little squeeze before saying, "I'm tired. You've worn me out with your lustful demands for multiple-scissoring. I will sleep now."

"I like that! You're the one who wanted to try the reverse scissor." I thought for a moment of just how fulfilling that position had been, little quivers of remembered ecstasy making me feel like I was standing in the middle of Archer's storm. "And you're going to answer some questions that have been driving me nuts for the last day. About that deception that Hunter and Miles and you kept going on about the shadow dragons being responsible for the deaths…why, exactly, did you keep it going for so long?"

He opened his eyes for a moment, the clear frosted blue making me squirm with happiness. "We really were at war for many centuries. Hunter's tribe attacked mine. We attacked his. It was our life."

"What happened to make you guys stop actually fighting and just pretend?"

His eyes closed again, his face relaxed, without the lines of pain that had resulted from his injuries at Hunter's. "After a few centuries, when my brother got his dark power under control, we assumed the deaths would stop. They did not. We knew someone else had to be attacking us, trying to eliminate both tribes."

"Xavier." I thought about that, thought about how a man could be so cruel to his own children. "It was he who abandoned you and Hunter after your mom died, wasn't it?"

"Yes. He was cursed, the demon in him strong. That's why he created dragon hunters—he wanted the dragon side to give power to the demon. But the result was the opposite: the dragon controlled the demon, a fact that clearly still enrages him."

"Enter Edgar and that manuscript leaf. Speaking of Edgar, are you sure he's not going to give us any more trouble?"

"Yes. I made it clear to your ex-employer that if he thought of revenging himself against your grandmother or you, I would finish the job."

"The nursing home called to ask me if I authorized two men they caught lurking around the outside. I assume those are your dragons?"

"They are. Even though Edgar knows he will die should he harm your grandmother, I thought it best that she be guarded at all times. Unless you wish for her to move in with us?"

I hesitated, but shook my head. "She truly is happy where she's at. I will bring her here if she gets so far in the illness that she no longer enjoys the people at the home, but since she still takes so much pleasure with everyone there, and the awesome programs they have for the residents, I'd prefer for her to be stay where she's happiest. I do appreciate you keeping the guards, though. They earn you serious brownie points when it comes to you having your wicked way with me."

"She is now my family," he said matter-of-factly, but the sentiment behind it melted me into a puddle of goo. "Her welfare is now as vital to me as it is to you. The guards will remain until such time as you desire her to live with us."

"If I weren't so worn out by your fabulous self, I'd lick every inch of you in reward for caring so much. I do have another question, though. Why was Ioan pretending to be your trusty tribe member? Just to spy on you?"

"I suspect he reported to Xavier about me. Hunter said one of his dragons was missing as well. No doubt Xavier planted spies in our tribes in order to keep track of us."

"That bastard. He really chafes my chimes. Back to the manuscript leaf…"

His lips curved. I tipped my head and nipped his chin. "I thought the tales of the Raisa Medallion were nothing more than that—just tales. Imagine my surprise when it turned up, and you deciphered it."

"Will we see Bree again, or will she stay a sword spirit? And can I say just how devious she was?"

"Doing what?" he asked, his voice rumbling around in his gorgeous chest.

"You said she was hanging around just to see if you were worthy of her help. That's devious. Although I do have to admit, she was pretty helpful. Why did her sister Sasha have to be there when she sworded herself, though? Bree, that is, not Sasha."

"I imagine part of her job is to oversee spirits binding themselves to dragon hunters and their *élan vitals*."

"Huh. Okay, next question: now that you're a dragon hunter, you must have demon in you, too, right? What does that feel like? Does it hurt? Or is it not really an issue because you're a superhero dragon who can call up lightning? I know if I were a demon, I'd be a bit wary of you."

"Hunter and I are balanced, yes. By bringing us together, I lost some of my dragon self, but I gained some of his darkness."

"A demon?" I asked, horrified and thrilled at the same time.

"Not really, no." He looked thoughtful for a minute. "Just a form of dark power. I feel it, but it does not control me. It is just...there."

"I'm glad to know I won't have to buy stock in a holy water company," I said, relieved despite my irreverent words. "Although I could have sworn that Miles said dragon hunters are half demon."

"They are. But they are not the children of the sire, as Hunter and I are."

"Oooh, gotcha. You guys are the superhero version.

That makes sense. So, what are you and Hunter going to do about your father? What did he mean about unmaking what you did?"

He sighed, rolling us over so I was underneath him, his hands immediately possessing themselves of my breasts. "I have answered countless questions, flower, and will answer no more but one."

"Really? What question?" I asked, my toes curling at the steamy look he was giving me.

He nuzzled the spot behind my ear that made my legs turn to wet noodles. "Do you want to be on top, or should I?"

"Oooh," I said, his heat flashing through me as I moved against him in provocative anticipation. "You're ready to go again? Really, Archer, I'm not going to be able to walk if you keep this up... Wait, I think it's my turn on top. Prepare to be pleasured as you've never been pleasured. Although don't think I'm going to forget my questions when we're done, because I have a lot more, a whole lot more."

He let me push him onto his back, the sound of his laughter rolling around the room, filling me with utter joy. I was confident that Archer would make all right with the world.

He certainly rocked mine.

ABOUT THE AUTHOR

For as long as she can remember, **Katie MacAlister** has loved reading, and she grew up with her nose buried in a book. It wasn't until many years later that she thought about writing her own books, and once she had a taste of the fun to be had building worlds, tormenting characters, and falling madly in love with all her heroes, she was hooked.

With more than fifty books under her belt, Katie has written novels that have been translated into numerous languages, been recorded as audiobooks, received several awards, and are regulars on the *New York Times*, *USA Today*, and *Publishers Weekly* bestseller lists. A self-proclaimed gamer girl, she lives in the Pacific Northwest with her dogs and frequently can be found hanging around online.

You can learn more at:
KatieMacAlister.com
Twitter @KatieMacAlister
Facebook.com/Katie.Mac.Minions

WOLF'S MATE

CELIA KYLE

When cougar shifter Abby Carter uncovers the shady dealings of an anti-shifter organization, she'll have to trust the too-sexy-for-her-peace-of-mind werewolf Declan Reed... or end up six feet under.

FOREVER

NEW YORK   BOSTON

*To my husband, for believing in me when
I wasn't ready to believe in myself.*

Wolf's Mate

CHAPTER ONE

A few minutes past eight and Declan Reed couldn't take his eyes off the windows in the building across the street.

"You remember our shift ended two hours ago, right?" Cole drawled. The pain-in-the-ass tiger shifter was his partner for this operation. Eh, the dick was his partner in most operations. Declan ignored the man.

Their shift had ended at six, and the other men on Shifter Operations Command Team One, Ethan and Grant, had taken over, but Declan couldn't force himself to leave. He couldn't force his *wolf* to leave.

Not while *she* still occupied the building.

Abby Marie Carter. Twenty-eight years old and five feet eight inches of tempting cougar shifter. She had long golden hair with a hint of a curl at the ends, bright blue eyes, and curves that made his palms tingle with the need to stroke every one of them.

"Not that I'm against keeping my eyes on a nice ass," Cole continued. "But since neither of us is getting in her panties, I don't see the point."

The tiger was a good ally in a tight spot and handy with a block of explosives. Declan would trust him at his back on any assignment. But having faith in the man didn't mean his wolf was okay with Cole thinking about Abby *or* her panties.

"Fuck off, Cole."

"We've been watching this place for four days and you've barely slept. Do you want to go through another psych evaluation? Because 'obsessive behavior'"—Cole formed air quotes with his fingers—"is a sure-as-shit way to end up on the doc's couch."

"Do you feel like being thrown out a window?" Declan pulled his attention from the building across the street and leveled a glare on the tiger shifter. "Because 'dickish behavior'"—he formed air quotes, mimicking Cole—"is a sure-as-shit way to end up hitting the pavement headfirst."

"Play nice, kids." A third voice joined their conversation— their team alpha—his order transmitted through the com device each member of the team wore in their ear. "Tighten up."

Declan glowered at Cole and his partner did the same to him, but they kept their mouths shut. Birch was a hard-ass bear shifter, and when he spoke, they all did their damnedest to listen. Sometimes it happened. Sometimes it didn't.

The men of SHOC Team One weren't known for their respect for authority, and they sure as hell hadn't been recruited because they played well with others.

"Aw, Birch. He started it…" Cole whined in his best impression of a five-year-old. Declan rolled his eyes, tuning out his partner's voice while he refocused on Abby.

Technically, their target was FosCo, the multinational company headquartered across the street. Except from the moment Abby walked into FosCo's lobby four days ago, he'd had a hard time tearing his attention from her. Staring at the cougar shifter was a lot more fun than watching the other staffers.

No one else popped in earbuds while they worked. They didn't get up from their chairs to stretch and add a little shake of their ass. They definitely didn't kick off their shoes and dance when the building emptied and no one was watching.

Abby did. She appeared professional when she walked into the office building every morning. Her blond hair was usually twisted in some girly knot that he wanted to run his claws through, and she wore a tight skirt suit with a pair of low heels. She fit right in with all the others in FosCo's headquarters.

Even if she wasn't a FosCo employee...or even human.

According to the file they'd compiled, she'd been employed by the accounting firm Ogilve, Piers, and Patterson for six years, landing the job straight out of college after earning her bachelor's degree. She still worked toward her master's as she studied for the CPA exam. Smart. Dedicated. A hard worker if her schedule was anything to go by. In at seven thirty every morning and out at nine thirty every night. In bed by eleven. His knowledge of her sleeping habits wasn't something he shared with the others.

"Obsessive behavior" and all that shit.

The team still wasn't sure what she was doing at FosCo, but Declan found he cared less and less about the reason as each hour passed. He just liked looking at her.

"Declan, you listening?" Cole's deep growl pulled his attention from Abby *again*.

The asshole wanted to lose his tongue before Declan threw him out the window.

"What?" he snapped.

"Guys." Cole groaned. "He's already pussy whipped even though he's never gonna get any."

Declan would tell the man to fuck off—again—but he

figured more was called for at this point. He didn't let his attention stray as he reached to his left and wrapped his fingers around an unopened can of soda. His next action was a blur—a single fluid move—as he whipped it at Cole's head.

Unfortunately, Cole's reflexes rivaled Declan's, and he snatched the can from the air. The tiger popped the top and guzzled the soda down in a couple swallows before crushing the container in one hand and tossing it over his shoulder.

"Thanks, man. I was thirsty." Cole grinned, but there was something else in the tiger's gaze. The man's body language said he was at ease, but the flicker of yellow in Cole's eyes revealed the feral beast just under the surface.

"Cole…" Birch growled over the com.

"I'd like the record to show that Cole is the one causing shit today." Grant, the other werewolf on the team, broke in. "It ain't me."

The crunch of chips and the smack of Grant's lips followed his words. The wolf was eating *again*. The man's stomach was a bottomless pit. Grant claimed junk food kept his mind sharp, which was a necessity as the team's tech operative.

"Or me." Ethan, lion shifter and genius with transportation, spoke up as well. Then he popped his gum, which had Birch growling some more. Ethan had what the doc called an "oral fixation." Declan knew better. Ethan just liked annoying Birch, and someone popping his gum while talking over the com pissed him off.

The alpha bear liked them to at least pretend to be professional like the goody-goody council Trackers, but that wasn't SHOC Team One. Declan wasn't sure why the bear shifter even bothered. Their backgrounds were varied, but they all shared a few traits—they were loners, reveled in pissing people off, and had a penchant for breaking the law.

All right, *laws*.

Violate enough of 'em and the council would send their Trackers after a shifter. Break those guys *well* enough and a shifter was given the choice between council punishment or "using their evil powers for good" with SHOC.

Declan's team was the best of the bad.

"Can someone remind me when I get to shoot someone?" Declan broke into their bickering.

"Or blow something up?" Cole added hopefully.

Birch sighed, and Declan pictured the big bear shifter closing his eyes and pinching the bridge of his nose in frustration. "Does no one remember the mission objective?"

Declan grunted and repeated the words from memory. "Observe. Confirm rumors. Eliminate the threat."

They were supposed to report in to SHOC headquarters, too, but in their tight group, they tended to get things done first and tell higher-ups about it later.

Right now Declan was ready to skip to the elimination step. After he got Abby out of there, of course. His wolf bristled at the idea of anything happening to the little she-cat.

"Get paid," Ethan tacked on. "I've gotta pay for that new Porsche in the garage."

"Exactly," Birch reminded them. "Right now we're still observing."

Cole grunted. "Observing is boring as fuck."

"We can't go in there and shoot everything to shit until we can definitely tie FosCo to Unified Humanity," Birch reminded them.

Unified Humanity was the oldest, largest anti-shifter organization in existence, bent on seeing shifters destroyed, even though the general population didn't know of their kind. Declan couldn't remember the whole story of its formation. It had something to do with a shifter wanting to mate a human woman back in the 1700s. Her transition had gone sideways, and when the dust had settled, she was dead and her family was out for blood. That one event was the catalyst for Unified Humanity's existence and the destruction they constantly wrought on his people.

"We could sneak in there and pop off a few rounds…" Declan's wolf yipped at the possibility. It'd been a while since they'd gotten to enjoy some large-scale destruction.

"No." Birch's voice was hard and deep, the bear's presence pushing forward to make its wishes known. "Quit whining like a bunch of teenagers and—"

"Looks like our kitty is about to get up and shake her tail." Grant sounded way too excited about Abby's nightly office-dancing habits.

Declan pushed to his feet, giving his left ear a double tap to shut off the com and silence the chatter of his team. He didn't want their voices filling his head. He was off duty.

"I'll see you later," he murmured to Cole, and ignored the tiger's cackling laughter.

Declan strode from the room, steps silent on the worn hallway carpet. They'd set up in an empty building across from FosCo. It'd been repossessed by the bank and sat empty for months. He and Cole watched from the top floor while Grant and Ethan had settled in on the seventh. Ethan had a thing about the number seven. Declan had a thing about being on top.

This time of night he liked the roof—cool air, soft breeze, and a better view of Abby.

He pushed open the exit door at the end of the hall, tromped into the stairwell, and took the concrete steps two at a time until he reached the door to the roof. He nudged the security door, broken panel swinging out, and trod onto the graveled surface. His boots crunched over the small rocks and debris, leaves and sticks dropped by birds snapping beneath his feet.

The night air rushed forward, the chilled breeze bathing him in the briny scent of the nearby ocean. He'd been locked up in that room for more than fourteen hours and it felt good to be outside.

And a little closer to Abby.

Declan followed the same path as he had the four nights prior, moving carefully over the flat roof to the brick railing. He threw one leg over the side, straddling the twelve-inch-wide concrete, and settled in to watch the one bit of brightness in his life.

Abby.

She kicked off her shoes, black pumps tumbling across the worn carpet and into the darkness beneath the desk. Then she pushed to her feet and nudged the office chair away. Her hair was next—she tugged on whatever held that uptight knot in place. Golden strands tumbled down her back, a little bounce now that they were freed. She shrugged, and her midnight jacket slipped down her arms to reveal the pale, snug blouse underneath.

All those curves...

Curves he dreamed about when he managed to convince himself he wasn't a violent piece of shit who didn't deserve to even think about her.

CHAPTER TWO

*A*bby's cougar tolerated being stationary during working hours—cats were nocturnal creatures, after all. At night her cat was ready to play, hunt, chase...basically, anything *but* sit on her ass and stare at numbers.

Which was why she had her evening playlist that included "O.P.P." by Naughty by Nature as well as "Stayin' Alive" by the Bee Gees. She popped in her Bluetooth earbuds and snatched her smartphone. A few button presses and the opening beats of one of her favorite songs filled her ears.

Then came a shake of her hips, a little *jiggle, jiggle, jiggle* of her ass, and she belted out the opening lines of "Wannabe" by the Spice Girls. She sang about friends, a lover, and *zigazig ah*...There were also a couple lines about lovers and *giving*, and she decided she'd like to have someone giving her something...

Something naughty and dirty and—and Abby's cat swatted at her, the inner animal hissing long and loud. Her cat didn't want Abby's mind to stray to sex if she refused to do anything about their dry spell. The feline knew her human half wouldn't leave work for at least another hour.

The cougar didn't project any other thoughts or emotions. She merely rose to her feet, presented her back to Abby, and then plopped back down on her ass. Natural house cats knew how to ignore their owners, but those kitties had *nothing* on a shifter's inner animal.

Nothing.

Abby ignored the animal and shook her ass a little more. *Shake, shake, wiggle, wiggle, jiggle, jiggle*... She even did a little "raising the roof," followed by a spin just before she stumbled and finally collapsed in the nearby office chair.

"Whew." She panted out a quick breath and then another before drawing air deep into her lungs and releasing it slowly. She slumped in her seat and nudged the ground, pushing and jerking until she was back in place in front of her laptop.

"It's Friday. You just have to make it through tonight," she murmured to her cougar, and it replied with a low grumble. "I'll let you play a little on Palm Island this weekend and then Monday it's back to regular hours at O.P.P."

Not to be confused with one of her favorite songs. This O.P.P. referred to the accounting firm—and her employer—Ogilve, Piers, and Patterson.

The cougar huffed, still a hint annoyed, but Abby also sensed the little flick of the cat's tail and the tremor of excitement that flowed through her furred body. The small island just off the coast of Port St. James, South Carolina, was a nature preserve—no humans allowed and nothing but natural animals running wild. Abby's cougar could safely stretch her legs, take a swim, and chase the island residents.

She leaned forward in the chair and grasped the edge of the desk, pulling herself back into place in front of her laptop. She popped out her earbuds, tossed them into the bottomless pit of her purse, and turned off her music, ready to focus on her job once more.

A job she loved…most of the time. While her cat reveled in the hunt for live prey, Abby's human half enjoyed the puzzles that came with accounting. She checked and cross-checked transactions, hunted for unbalanced entries, and scoured records for improperly supported payments.

Accounting was Abby's kung fu, and it was strong.

The cougar snorted at her butchered movie quote.

Brushing off the cougar's flare of anger, she snatched her pencil and the stacks of printouts she'd gathered, diving back into her audit. Her—not *their*—audit. A company the size of FosCo needed a double-digit team, not one woman, but apparently a surface audit was enough to appease the private shareholders. It wasn't her place to ask. It was her place to work and get paid. Abby ran her finger down the nearest page, comparing it to the spreadsheet displayed on her monitor.

That's there. And that's there. And that's…

She stopped and stared at the printout—a copy of a recent bank statement—and swallowed hard while she replayed conversations she'd had with the FosCo president recently.

"It's nothing but a small account we haven't taken the time to close," Eric Foster had said. "Don't even bother with it. It's nothing."

Abby gulped and kept her eyes on the account's activity.

In Abby's world, two plus two equaled four. Adding, subtracting, multiplying, and dividing…there were *rules* in numbers. As an accountant, she lived and died by them. Mainly because if she didn't do her job right, she didn't get paid, which meant she couldn't eat. It was amazing how things strung together like that.

Two plus two did not equal five hundred million dollars.

Five. Hundred. Million. Dollars.

Poof. Gone.

She stared at the screen, the digits swimming before her eyes.

It would have been fine if she'd found any type of notation in the client's files, but there was nothing. When money shuffled through accounts with nary a mention *anywhere*...

This was bad. So very, very bad. So many bads in so many languages, and it made her wish she'd taken a few foreign language classes in high school just so she could use them now.

Abby's fingers flew over the laptop's keyboard, entering the password that granted her access to her accounting firm's server. She navigated the file structure with ease, digging deeper into the electronic system. After each audit, every piece of paper the staff scribbled on was scanned and uploaded. Ten years from now the partners at Ogilve, Piers, and Patterson did *not* want to have to question an employee and hear the words "I wrote it on this yellow sticky..."

Apparently, yes, that'd happened. Coincidentally, it'd been Abby's predecessor, who was now retired and sunning herself in lovely South Florida. *But* the moral of the story was...

"Martha, where the hell did you save your notes?" Abby murmured, hunting through folder after folder until, "*Bingo.*" She'd found Martha's chicken-scratch scrawl— on a scanned yellow sticky, of course—listing every password the president of FosCo used, both personal and professional. The money had to be sitting somewhere, right? "You are a goddess among women, lady."

It didn't take long to bring up Gold Key Bank's website and even less time to log in and find...

Her missing five hundred million dollars. And then some.

She also saw where other large amounts came in and went out to...She clicked on the details for one of the most recent wire transfers—the name of the destination account holder was required when performing wires—and discovered...

She read the words. Then read them again. She skimmed them a third time and still couldn't wrap her mind around what she saw.

The cougar did, though. At least enough to push its way forward and fight for control.

Goose bumps rose along Abby's arms, and her cheeks stung while her fingertips throbbed with pain. To a casual observer she was immobile, but her inner cougar was going batshit. It paced in her mind and snarled, urging her to get the hell out of the high-rise office building.

The beast recognized something was *wrong* and they needed to *go*. Now. They needed to flee before *they* became prey.

Which was a possibility considering the information displayed on the screen.

The shifter world had their suspicions about FosCo. When conversations surrounding *that organization* came up, there were also murmurings about where *that organization* got their funding.

FosCo was one of the names bandied about—a supporter of *that organization*.

She shook her head and scrambled to find some sense of calm. This wasn't a kid's book about wizards, and *that organization* wouldn't suddenly appear if she thought of its name.

Eric Foster, holder of the controlling interest in FosCo, was funding Unified Humanity, the organization that had a hate-boner for all shifters. Abby was the first to admit that everyone could rock on with their own inner ball of loathing—Abby wasn't a huge fan of the president of her homeowners' association, after all—but Unified Humanity was bad.

No, *bad* didn't quite cover UH's actions. They killed pups and cubs without hesitation, entire families gone with a single bomb. Death and destruction to shifters were their modus operandi. And when the smoke cleared, shifters couldn't exactly call on human authorities, or the rest of the world would know about their existence. Their secret would be out.

Abby's breath rushed in and out of her lungs, her heart racing and threatening to burst from her chest. The cougar yowled and scratched, demanding she run.

But...

The cat didn't want to hear anything about "but" or "first they should" or "it would be a good idea to..."

It. Wanted. To. Run.

Abby assured the cat they would absolutely race from the building, *but* first... She shoved at the cougar, pushed it to the back of her mind and built a mental wall between her and the beast. The feline would break through at some point and overpower her human half, but the barrier would delay the animal's possession.

Delay it enough to give her time to dig deeper, find more, and make copies of everything she unearthed.

Unified Humanity had destroyed her life twenty years ago. Now she'd take every snippet of data she could so the shifter council could destroy them.

CHAPTER THREE

Something was wrong with Abby. Declan felt that certainty down to the center of his black heart. Still sitting on the brick railing, he kept his gaze focused on her. He skimmed her body with his eyes, noting the tension she now carried and her rapid-fire typing. She'd been a diligent worker from the moment she entered FosCo, but this was...different.

Methodical yet hurried.

Her pencil skated over pages, fingers dancing over the keyboard faster than Grant when he'd decided to try to hack the FBI. Her stare intent on the computer screen, she continued typing with her left hand, reached for her laptop bag with her right, and withdrew a cord. Abby diverted her attention just long enough to plug the computer into her nearby tablet.

Declan narrowed his eyes and let his wolf pull forward to assist his vision. The details of Abby's features—body—came into focus with the animal's help. The sharper vision allowed him to see the determined expression on her face and the panic lurking in her eyes.

Further proof something had gone sideways in her world. Whether it was personal or professional, he wasn't sure. He simply knew that his wolf demanded he go to her. The beast didn't know how to calm a woman or soothe her, but the asshole wanted to do *something* for her. Yes, the wolf reveled in the fear of others, enjoyed the scent of panic from their prey, but it hated *this*. Whatever had caused Abby's terror needed to die. Now.

A soft tone filled Declan's ear, his com reactivating— probably at Birch's order. The rest of the men had to see the change in Abby, too. That was the only reason the assholes would turn the device on after he'd gone off duty.

"Guys," he murmured to the team before anyone else could speak. His wolf's howl consumed his mind. "There's—"

Grant didn't let him finish. He released a harsh cough and cleared his throat. "Uh, remember how I didn't have approval to bug any FosCo offices and/or vehicles because we didn't want to risk the devices being found?" Grant chuckled. "And then remember how I did it anyway?"

"Grant…" Birch's growl rolled through the com, the rumble accompanied by the bear's heavy stomps and a hollow echo.

The team alpha was in the stairwell. Coming up to Declan or down to kick Grant's ass?

"Yo, Birch, it'd save you a lot of frustration if you didn't issue orders you know he's gonna break. You stopped telling me I couldn't bring experimental, untested explosives on ops. You're a lot happier now, am I right?" Declan could imagine the feral smile Cole wore.

"The point is…" Grant added his own snarl to the mix. "There's movement. Eric Foster leaves the office every day at five—"

"In his slow-ass SUV," Ethan muttered. "More money

than God and he drives a vehicle fresh off the assembly line with no modifications."

"—goes home and stays there." Grant continued talking as if Ethan hadn't interrupted. "Except right now he's in his SUV with four other men and they're headed back to the office."

Declan didn't like the sound of that. "Can you hear what they're—"

"Hold." The other wolf's voice snapped through the com, and they all fell silent. Tension vibrated in the air, the change in pattern putting them all on edge.

Declan's wolf leaped forward. His skin stretched and stung, the beast aching to push through.

Abby's tension...Eric's return...

The wolf wanted her out of there. Now. He tried to remind the bastard about their mission, but it just told him to fuck off. Something was *wrong*, and they needed to kill whoever needed killing to set things *right*.

And for the first time Declan realized he'd come to the roof without a weapon.

His wolf told him he was an idiot.

Declan couldn't really deny the accusation.

Grant spoke again. "They're coming for Abby."

Declan's gut clenched, and his wolf howled its objection. Adrenaline flooded his body, pumping through his veins and suffusing his muscles. The animal slipped its chain and shoved forward, wrenching enough control to change his body. Not fully, but enough to appease the anxious beast. His hands became claws, blunt human fingertips darkening and sharpening to deadly points. His gums burned, fangs straining against the flesh in his mouth until the razor-sharp points broke free.

As for the rest of his body, his muscles swelled, strength

from the wolf encompassing him from head to toe. He was power and strength personified.

Grant's words replayed in his mind, his thoughts alternating between his logical human half and the crazed wolf that fought for dominance. *They're coming for Abby.*

"No," Declan snarled, the word more growl than human speech.

"She stumbled onto something, and Foster must have gotten an alert." Grant ignored Declan.

"Hold your positions." Three words from Birch. Three words that had Declan's beast frothing at the mouth.

The wolf growled and barked at Declan, shoving at his mind while it issued its feral demands. *Go to her. Save her. Kill them all.* Declan probably should have let the animal hunt before this op. It was more bloodthirsty than usual.

"Birch…" He swung his other leg over the edge of the railing, both feet dangling above the sidewalk.

"I said hold."

Grant kept reporting on what he heard from the SUV. The joking wolf was gone, replaced by the no-nonsense SHOC agent. "Two blocks out. Weapons confirmed. Intent to use unknown."

The mere presence of the weapons was enough for Declan and his wolf. Five humans were returning to the FosCo building, armed and prepared to confront Abby. Unacceptable.

Declan planted his palms on the wide rail and pushed off, letting gravity yank him toward the ground. He twisted in midair, moving like a cat rather than a wolf.

Now he could dig into the small cracks of the building's facade and grasp window frames while he climbed down the side.

"Declan, what are you doing?" The team alpha's words

were followed by a harsh snarl over the com, and Declan couldn't help but grin.

"Out for a climb." He grunted and pushed off from the wall, allowing himself to drop a few feet before grabbing hold once again. He jumped and swung from handhold to handhold, his grip sure and firm with every flex of muscle.

"You're killing this op."

"But she'll still be breathing." Declan leaped, but his nails didn't get deep enough into the crack he'd aimed for, and he slid two feet before finding another hold. Man, he loved the rush—the danger—of free climbing.

"Declan," Birch growled again. The other guys might be afraid of a grizzly bear shifter, but Declan wasn't. He'd experienced a lot worse than a beatdown from an overgrown teddy bear. "Are you kidding me with this shit?"

"Nope." Declan didn't joke. Didn't Birch know that by now? Fight. Kill. Never joke. Hell, most times he didn't smile...unless he was about to go into a fight or kill someone.

Psychopath thy name is Declan.

Nah, one of those SHOC psychs said he was as normal as a twisted ass like him could be.

Declan made it down another ten feet, not bothering to look beneath him. He'd scouted the building before the op began. He was an experienced climber and knew what his body could take before it collapsed. Even then the wolf would help him, get him on the move within minutes. Minutes that had saved his life more than once.

He'd been grateful for the wolf *that* day. Five body shots had sent him down, but not dead thanks to his shifter nature. When he'd regained his feet, he'd hunted and taken out his own client. The bastard had sent two guys after the same target, and the other assassin had decided getting rid of the competition—Declan—was a good idea.

Declan had decided taking out the client and other assassin was a *better* idea.

He released the wall and fell the last ten feet, thumping to the ground in a crouch. He stayed in the building's shadow and scanned his surroundings. A pair of headlights came from his right, high off the ground. The wolf's hearing picked up the rumble of the approaching engine—Eric's SUV.

They were closer than he liked and that fact spurred him into action. He bolted across Broad Street and slipped into the alley between two buildings, the blackness swallowing him whole. His inner beast lent its assistance, allowing him to see in the dark.

"Grant, disarm the alarm." Declan ran down that narrow corridor and didn't stop until he reached the building's emergency exit.

"Done." Grant's confirmation came a split second before Declan punched through the solid metal barrier between him and Abby.

"Stand down, Agent." The team alpha tried, he really did, but Declan's wolf was too far gone. He took the stairs two at a time, racing past floor after floor in his bid to get to Abby before Eric and his men reached her.

"They left the SUV running at the curb. They're in the elevator." Cole joined the conversation.

"They know she's a shifter. They've got a hard-on for the kitten, Declan. Get moving." Grant's voice buzzed with agitation.

"Fuck," Declan spat, and pushed his body harder. His human mind cursed him for not having a weapon, but the wolf assured him a gun wasn't needed. They had claws. It would be enough.

"Did you bug the damned building?" Birch roared, but

Declan wasn't sure why the bear sounded so surprised. "God dammit. Declan, if you get your ass captured—"

"You'll let them turn me into a stuffed toy." He grunted and snared the door to the tenth floor. He yanked it open.

A long, dark hallway stretched before him, the soft glow of safety lights barely illuminating his path. A bright light fifty feet away beckoned him—Abby's office.

Unfortunately, a group of five human men—guns out and the thirst for violence on their faces—was bathed in that glow.

CHAPTER FOUR

A rap of knuckles on wood—two quick knocks that shattered the silence—announced Abby's visitor. Adrenaline surged and yanked the cat even further forward. It wasn't a single visitor, but *visitors*.

With Eric Foster front and center. Four others filed into the space behind him, forming a half circle of overgrown thugs at his back. Each man wore a tailored, midnight suit, but something told her the men were anything *but* mere business associates of Eric's.

Abby licked her lips and left her mouth slightly open, just enough to draw in air and sample the flavors now consuming the room. Human. Anticipation. Unease. A fury that had to come from the man in the middle, and the heavy scent of metal, an aroma her mind connected to guns. Normally that meant police officers were near, but these guys didn't look like humans intent on protecting and serving.

They seemed like the "killing and burying" type, with torture tossed in for good measure.

"Ms. Carter." A sharp voice wrenched her attention to Eric.

"Mr. Foster." She drew her lips into a gently curved smile, one that didn't expose her rapidly growing fangs. The cat was prepared to act, ready to do whatever had to be done to protect them. "How are you?"

Abby was thankful her voice didn't waver. Much.

He smiled at her, and yet it wasn't a smile. It was a violent promise. He knew something. Knew that *she* knew something. Or he'd discovered the truth about her cougar and no longer wanted a furry in his building.

That was what Unified Humanity called shifters— *furries*.

When they weren't being called dead.

"Better now that I'm here," he purred. Or rather, he tried to. She'd had a lion purr to her before, all sensual and sweet. That was not what filled her ears, but there were bigger problems than whether the human man could purr like a cat shifter.

The scent of his anger and the sticky sweetness of suppressed violence surrounded him in a whirling cloud. She knew those aromas, the hint of impending pain. Abby swallowed hard and pushed those distant memories aside. Now wasn't the time to let the past intrude on the present.

"Is there something I can do for you, Mr. Foster?"

Eric clicked his tongue. "Such formality. Call me Eric."

Abby forced her fangs to retract. No sense in revealing her inner cat and poking the crazy person.

"Is there something I can do for you, Eric?"

Other than die, of course. She smiled wide and tried to portray the innocence and sweetness everyone told her she possessed.

Her cougar snorted.

I am sweetness and light. Sugar wouldn't melt in my mouth, and you don't need to throw me out the window.

"Actually...you can." Eric moved around the desk, his

footfalls slow and easy as he neared. When he drew to a stop, he was in the perfect position to see her screen.

Her fingers tingled, desperate to hide what she'd discovered.

"You were instructed to ignore a specific account, Ms. Carter." He lifted his hip and sat on the edge of the desk. "And yet I was informed you disobeyed that simple directive."

"Eric, I..." Abby swallowed hard—she was doing that a lot lately—and fought back the rising bile in her throat. She wasn't going to puke all over the desk. For one thing, *ew*. For the other, it'd slow her down when she finally grew a set of brass ovaries and ran.

Because she was *so* running. The second she had the chance. At five eight and more curvy than lean, she had her bulk and her cougar's strength behind her, which meant she'd be a match for him. Maybe.

She licked her lips, mouth dry. "I didn't get a chance to look things over. I just opened the site and logged in. I didn't realize I was in the wrong account." She chuckled and tapped her forehead. She kept her eyes on Eric and reached for her mouse, intent on closing the Internet browser. "Sometimes I should be called a dumb blonde. I haven't really—"

"Do you know what else I learned?" A crazed light filled his eyes, a sharp edge of madness. Another wave of panic and adrenaline entered her blood. "I learned your secret."

"I—I—I don't have a secret." She shook her head and battled to suppress the trembles attempting to shake her from the inside out.

"Liar." He hissed the word. Again with the animal references.

"I just…" *Discovered your company funds an organization intent on exterminating my kind. That's all.*

"You're a shapeshifter." He spat the word.

Abby kept shaking her head. "I don't know what
you're talking about. You mean, like werewolves? Mr.
Foster, I'm hu—"

"Human?" He snatched her wrist in a punishing grip,
squeezing muscle and bone. "You're still lying, but I know
that pain breaks your kind."

Agony could shatter a shifter's control. Hell, it often did
snap her kind's restraint and release the animal.

The cat thought freedom was a wonderful idea. She'd
bust out with fur and claws, take a few bites out of the men
in the office, and then run for safety.

"Eric…" She pushed the two syllables past gritted teeth,
hissing as the pain grew. It spread from her wrist, tendrils
of pain crawling through her veins and scraping her nerves.
"I'm not a—"

"It took one phone call and now I know what you are."
He bared blunted human teeth, as if the expression would
frighten her.

The guns the others carried? Yes, they were scary. His
sneer? Not so much.

He grasped her throat with her other hand, fingers curling around her neck as if they were claws. He'd accused her
of being a shifter, but he couldn't be sure, right? She had
to cling to her skin. It was illegal to reveal herself to humans. His hold tightened, gradually cutting off her air, and
she fought to draw oxygen into her lungs.

"You're a furry who poked her nose where it doesn't
belong. Now you're going to pay." Menace filled his every word, hatred evident in his voice. "But first we'll have
some fun."

Abby didn't want to have any kind of fun with Eric Foster *or* his minions. Her cougar yowled, the cry consuming Abby's mind. It surged, giving her strength—enough that she should be able to overpower a single human man. At least enough for her to break free. Except the longer he kept hold of her throat—cutting off her air—the weaker she grew.

The beast's horror joined the terror consuming her human body. It blanketed her in a layer of blind alarm until she was hardly more than an animal driven to live. The cougar's emergence began with her whiskers, the flick of one thick strand after another pushing past the skin on her cheeks. *Pop. Pop. Pop.*

Her inner animal knew it'd fucked up by pushing free, but the deed was done and she hadn't finished. Fur came next, a golden layer of short strands that slid along her forearms. It led to her hands, fingers coated in her cat's coloring. Her fingertips burned, and she knew that her human nails were giving way to off-white claws.

"Boss, she's got claws." A deep murmur from one of the thugs, and Eric's attention flicked to her hands before returning to her face once more.

"You still want to tell me you're not a furry?" More disgust on Eric's features, and the stench of his hatred filled her nose. He shoved her away and rose from the desk. He stepped back, putting space between them before he spoke once more. "Tie her up. We'll transport her to—"

"Unfortunately"—another man rounded the corner, dressed in black from head to toe; he looked just as deadly as the others, pure danger etched into every line of his body, but something told her he wasn't part of this shifter-hating group—"Ms. Carter is otherwise engaged."

Then he became a blur of motion, whipping into action

before the goons could draw a weapon. The newcomer struck first, punching one attacker before kicking another. Each assault was quicker than her eyes could track and all followed by the snap of bone. She'd heard her own bones break each time she shape-shifted. There was no mistaking that sound for any other.

Grunts and groans filled the air, warring with the *thud*s of flesh striking flesh.

The newcomer caught someone's fist mid-punch and twisted his grip, turning until the human's forearm hung loosely at his side. He followed the action with an elbow to the face that sent his opponent stumbling back into the wall.

"Who the—shoot him!" Eric's voice joined the sickening echoes of the fight.

One of the remaining three reached into his jacket and withdrew a handgun, pointing it at Abby's savior.

Abby swept her gaze over the desk, searching for something to . . . Her eyes landed on the ancient ten-key calculator to the left of her laptop. Five pounds of plastic and metal that had to be more than ten years old.

She wrapped her hands around the device, yanked it until the cord ripped free of the wall, and launched it at the gun-holding goon. The calculator flew, a trail of calculator paper streaming in its wake, and slammed into the side of the human's head. The adding machine sliced into his flesh and tumbled to the ground, and her target swayed in place. He turned slowly, his dazed eyes locking on to hers for a split second before he collapsed.

Two bad guys down; three to go.

Assuming her savior didn't want to hurt her after he defeated the others.

"You bitch!" A fist collided with her cheek, knuckles

striking flesh with a solid punch that had her head whipping around.

She fell forward and caught her weight on the desk, slumping over the furniture. Pain blossomed in her face and quickly spread, expanding until the ache throbbed through her head. The room spun, reality swaying with a wave of dizziness that had her stomach lurching.

The punch was followed by a kick, Eric's designer shoe slamming into her leg, and another splash of agony filled her. "You *fucking—*"

"I'm not a fan of men who hit women." That dark voice slithered over her, almost emotionless except she thought she heard a soft thread of rage in the syllables.

Abby shoved the pain away and regained control of herself. Yes, she was grateful for this stranger's interference, but did she want to be around when he had no men left to fight?

She drew air into her lungs, moving beyond the dizziness and pulsating aches, so she could focus on escaping. Her plan hadn't changed—it had merely been delayed.

She pushed herself upright and swung her gaze to her computer and the tablet still connected to the device. The fight continued behind her, and she spared a quick glance for the battling men. The stranger split his attention between the three remaining humans, aiming more painful blows at Eric than the other two.

The stranger *really* wasn't a fan of men who hit women.

That didn't mean he wouldn't pick up with Abby where Eric had left off.

Abby snatched the tablet and yanked it free. She crawled over the desk and slipped off the other side, stumbling over the human she'd knocked out. She snapped her gaze to him and met his glassy stare, pupils wide and gaze unfocused.

Mostly.

He recognized her. He narrowed his eyes, hatred surging in his stare, and went into motion. He extended his arm, hand seeking his weapon, and she decided waiting around for him to find it wasn't the best idea.

She scrambled to her feet, tablet still clutched in one hand, and ran for the door. She gripped the doorjamb and used the hold to swing into the hallway.

But not before the loud *pop* of a gunshot reached her ears.

CHAPTER FIVE

*T*he shot didn't stop Declan's attack. Nah, it was the scent of Abby's blood followed by a sharp cry that was a mixture between cat and woman.

Abby had been shot.

"You about done playing with the humans?" Birch's drawl reached him through the com in his ear. "Because the cat is escaping."

Escaping and hurt.

Which meant Declan didn't have time to play with his opponents any longer. He didn't have time to kill them either. When these five died, it would be slowly, painfully. He'd settle for broken bones and blood for now. The wolf wanted Declan's promise that they could hunt them later. They'd scared Abby—*hurt* her. The beast decided they deserved to die.

Declan allowed the wolf to strengthen him, giving him the power to end the battle with a few more punches. Though he did make sure he broke noses while he was at it.

He finally turned to the office door and laid eyes on the shooter, the human slumped in the doorway, gun still in hand. This was the one who'd attempted to shoot Declan—stopped by Abby's insane intervention.

He leaped over the prone body at his feet, eyes not straying from his target. He couldn't eliminate them all, but he figured this enemy was on his way out the door anyway.

The human turned his gun on Declan, but a quick grab and twist ended with the weapon in Declan's palm. He quickly tossed it out of reach and continued his forward momentum. His speed didn't falter as he bent and wrapped his hands around the human's head. A harsh yank was followed by a ripple of bones snapping in rapid succession, and then he was in the hallway, racing down the long stretch of darkness and back toward the stairwell.

Drops of blood—Abby's blood—stained the ground, and his wolf urged him to go faster, push harder. She was bleeding and they weren't with her. The scent of her pain filled the air, and it pushed his wolf to the edge of savagery.

He burst into the stairwell, and the beast lent its assistance once again. He leaped down the steps, following the trail of Abby's blood. With each new drop, the beast became even more enraged, and it was torn between the chase and returning to finish the human males.

"She's on the ground. Heading east," Cole murmured.

"Declan, stand down. We'll—"

"Mine."

"*Declan.*" Birch's growl was filled with every ounce of dominance the man could exert, and Declan's wolf...

Didn't give a fuck. It didn't encourage him to at least stop and listen to the bear. No, it pushed him onward. He hit the bottom stair and emerged into the cool night. Abby's scent still filled his nose, and he let his inner animal direct him. Cole said go east, but she wouldn't remain visible to his team for long.

Declan rounded the corner of the building and took off

after Abby, his fury growing with every droplet of blood on the ground. His feet pounded on the concrete, boots thumping in time with his heartbeat. "Cole. Her status."

"Gunshot wound to the side. Slight limp. Not wearing shoes, so her feet will be torn to hell if her cat doesn't help."

"Her cat will help." Declan didn't doubt the she-cat's desire to survive.

"Break it off, Agent." Birch tried again.

"*Fuck off*, Agent." He wasn't stopping.

"North on Bay Street." Cole again.

"I've got eyes on her—tracking her with street cameras." Grant annoyed the hell out of him, but it was good to have the rule-breaking asshole on his side.

"Got the van purring and ready to go," Ethan drawled, the lion looking for any excuse to get behind the wheel.

"I didn't authorize—"

"Birch, give up. I'm taking her." Declan couldn't stop the wolf now. Not after it'd been teased with her scent, the flavors of her fear and blood.

The team alpha just sighed, and Declan could imagine the big bear dropping his head forward with resignation. "Grant, keep eyes on her. Cole, monitor the shit-storm across the street. When the live ones are out of that office, take care of cleanup."

"I've got these new guns I designed that alternate C-4 pellets and detonators that have a timing trigger, so—"

"Cole," Birch growled, and they all knew what that particular grumble meant. *I don't care. Just get shit done already.*

"Yes!" Cole shouted, and he imagined the tiger punching his fist in the air before he bolted.

Birch just sighed. "Ethan and I will rendezvous for a pickup once Declan has her in hand."

Declan grinned and took a sharp left onto Bay Street, still following the bloody trail. "See how easy that was?"

Birch grunted. "Move out."

The sounds of his team bursting into action filled his ear, but he focused on one single voice—Grant. The other wolf fed him directions, giving him a play-by-play of Abby's movements.

"Heading for the pier, Declan."

The fucking pier. A bullshit tourist attraction and family-friendly hot spot. Crowds filled the area every night, and their stench would overlay Abby's.

"Crowd won't hide her," Declan muttered, and increased his speed. Or rather, the crowd wouldn't hide her *for long*. Short-term, though, it could make tracking difficult.

Then she came into sight, those golden curls streaming out behind her and that ass he liked so much jiggling with every pounding step. It was fucked up that he was turned on by her while she ran for her life, but he couldn't stop himself.

"I have eyes on her," he told Grant. He'd been distracted when she'd bolted—trying to save his own life tended to do that—but now he noticed she clung to a tablet, grip so tight as if it held the secrets of life. What was so damned important that—

She reached the very end of the pier, bypassing the families and teens who lined the railing. She shoved them aside and climbed the safety rail.

That was when it hit him like a baseball bat to the kneecap: she was pulling a jumper.

Nah, no way. She couldn't be *that* dumb. She wasn't going to jump. More than one stupid-ass kid had lost his life against the maze of a pier's support beams. Good place to hide a body or two, perhaps, but that wasn't currently on the agenda.

She balanced atop the eight-inch-wide slab of wood. The one that was supposed to keep people safe, not act as a diving platform. She placed the edge of the tablet in her mouth.

"Abby!" He shouted her name without thought, the word erupting from his lips in a roar. His beast aided him, made his voice boom through the air, and it silenced everyone.

She glanced over her shoulder at him, reflective golden eyes—cougar's eyes—meeting his as they widened in surprise only to be replaced by fear. Why the hell was she afraid of him, dammit? He'd saved her. After beating a few others to shit, sure, but still...

"Abby." He took another step forward, hand outstretched. "Wait." Then she was gone. She spun in place and leaped over the side. He stood there a moment, immobile, and tried to get a handle on his riotous emotions. "I lost her," he rasped. "She went wet."

"What the—"

"Say again."

"You're joking."

The men on the team mirrored his thoughts, and he didn't reply. Not until he knew more. He raced to the edge and searched the sea for her just like everyone else on the pier. He ignored the humans' cries for help while he plunged through the crowd. It wasn't until he reached the spot where she'd stood only moments ago that he knew she'd be okay.

Abby delved beneath the surface of the black water, the darkness swallowing her whole, but not before he recognized the change that rippled over her. Skin as pale as moonlight shimmered, to be replaced by fur golden like the sun.

Slipping quietly away, far from the shouting tourists, he ducked into the shadows and made his way back to solid land. Chatter from the others filled his ears, invading his mind. He kept his voice low but firm when he cut through them all. "Ethan?"

"One block south of your location."

Declan increased his speed when he hit the sidewalk and turned left. He wove through the crowd and broke into a jog when he spied the van. The side door slid open, Birch holding it wide, and the moment Declan was inside, the vehicle went into motion.

He glanced at the team alpha, noting the man's black eyes and the layer of dark brown fur on his cheeks. Birch's bear was right at the surface, just shy of busting free and tearing them all to pieces.

"Declan?"

"You can kick my ass later." He turned his attention to Ethan. "Get us to her place. Grant, what else do we know about her?" Yeah, she'd escaped, but why would a *cat* take a swim in the sea? He thought maybe desperate times called for desperate measures, but there'd been so many other ways to escape that wouldn't have gone so completely against her natural instincts.

"You read the history. My shit is thorough," Grant snarled at him, and Declan's own beast growled back.

"Hit him for me, will ya, Cole?" Declan's question was followed by a *thump* and a grumbled *ow* from Grant. "We know she's an orphan. Where'd she end up when her parents died?"

A silent pause, and then Grant spoke again. "Seals up in Alaska from eight to eighteen."

"Okay." That gave him the explanation he needed. Sure, Abby was a cougar, but she'd been raised by seal shifters. Her inner animal did okay with water and her foster family taught her familiarity with the ocean. "She'll use the water to travel. Won't come to shore until she's forced to. Grant, keep an eye out for her on the cams. Ethan, get us to her ASAP."

"You think I could lead the fucking team?" Birch's glare slammed onto Declan's shoulders, and he turned his attention to the bear. "What makes you think we're gonna keep chasing her?" Birch raised a single brow, black-eyed stare boring into him.

Because Declan couldn't *not* go after her. He couldn't exactly say that to Birch though.

"When shit went sideways, she stopped long enough to grab that tablet," he pointed out. "It's got something on there worth risking her life over. We want it."

Birch shook his head. "It won't last through the swim. We'll regroup at the office and try to salvage this op. Let's call in a team to tail her. You know the newbies need field time. Let them chase her down."

A flush of rage attacked Declan. The wolf didn't want anyone else near Abby.

Declan grinned. "You think her shit isn't going to be water resistant? It's gotta be instinctual by now." He shook his head. "Ten will get you twenty that our girl makes sure her gadgets will make it through a dip or two. A new toy came on the market not long ago."

"Our girl?" Now Birch raised both eyebrows.

Declan ignored the bear—*and* his knowing smirk. Asshole.

CHAPTER SIX

So. That happened.

Holy fuck a duck with a truck that happened.

Abby's heart pounded so hard it threatened to break through her rib cage, but she didn't have time to die. She was too busy trying to swim to safety. As in, somewhere very, very far from Port St. James.

Abby jerked and twisted, muscles and bone stretching and contracting. Familiar pain assaulted her, an experience she'd endured for years, as parts of the cougar overtook her human body. When she'd first shifted, her screams could be heard throughout the state. Now she reacted with no more than a small shudder. Her new shape ripped her clothes; bits of thread and cloth drifted from her body, portions of her skirt suit lost in the ocean's currents.

She pushed harder, flexed, and spun. Rather than fighting the flow, she moved with it, allowing herself to be dragged down the coast.

The tablet clenched between her teeth wiggled, and she tightened her bite. She couldn't lose it now, not after what she'd gone through to get it out of the building. The shifter council needed to see it, look over the evidence, and then send in their bogeymen to do whatever it was they did. She didn't want to think about how they did their jobs. She just wanted FosCo and Eric Foster to not exist any longer.

Buh-bye.

God, her fear was making her even more sarcastic than usual.

Fear of being caught. Fear of being killed. Fear of the tablet not getting into the right hands.

Fear of that blue-eyed stranger who'd saved her. The one who'd known her name.

And if he knew her name, he had to know where she lived.

She couldn't get caught. Not with the device in her possession. She had to hide it before she ventured onto land.

Abby twisted and bolted away from the beach, racing for Palm Island. No one would think to look there. It would be safe. It *had* to be safe.

Her destination came into sight, and she put on a last burst of speed, racing to the rocky gathering of coral and stone. Less than ten feet from the outcropping, she dove beneath the rolling waves, down and down until she reached the opening she sought.

She ducked into the pure darkness and used her claws to climb the interior walls of the small cave. Cool water enveloped her fully, the black encroaching on her like a monster from her nightmares. Her cougar pushed the panic aside, reminding her this was a safe place, a welcome place. Her cat loved the cave or running on four paws across the island—a place closed to humans.

Abby burst past the surface of the water, sucking in a breath of air. She placed her palms on the stone edge surrounding the cave opening and heaved herself onto a small ledge. She rolled to her back, laid one arm across her eyes, and pulled the tablet from her mouth with her free hand.

She fought to recover from the mile-long swim to the middle of the bay, preparing her body to do it all over again and get her home. Her cougar wanted to wait for a little while. It wasn't ready to venture back into a world of being chased.

They didn't have a choice. The tablet was safe. Now she had to nut up or shut up. It was one of her foster father's favorite sayings and one he'd often repeated when she'd hesitated to dive into the frigid waters off the coast of Alaska. "I don't have a thick layer of fat like the rest of the family" was not a good excuse for avoiding swims with the other seals. Neither were the polar bears that had tried to eat her. Or the killer whales. Or the bull moose. Those suckers didn't play.

Abby squared her shoulders and huffed, taking a deep breath before diving headfirst back into the inky sea.

Now she needed to swim home, get clothes, and disappear. Go somewhere and call someone, and when things weren't so hot, she'd come back and—

Look at her, sounding all gangster and like a criminal. *When things weren't so hot...*

Some of her fear floated away with her swim back to shore, exhaustion replacing the rapid race of panic and terror. The adrenaline that'd powered her every move no longer filled her veins, and her heart gradually slowed to a regular beat. Which, yay for calming down, but she needed the panic to keep her going. Abby dug deep, refusing to let the adrenaline crash sap all her strength. She'd do this. Home. Run. Call.

Abby lifted her head and scanned the beach, searching for landmarks, and sighed in relief. She was home. Or as close as she could get with the hundred yards of sand separating the waves and her building.

The hundred yards she'd have to walk half naked.

Great.

The night was just fan-fucking-tasmagorical.

Abby gulped and breathed deep, preparing herself for her cat's retreat. It was bad enough she'd come limping out of the ocean. She couldn't sport claws, fangs, and fur as she emerged. Then she repeated the slow, deep breathing for good measure, bracing herself as best she could.

Right. No screaming.

Her fur retreated first, her bones snapping and reshaping at the same time. The claws retracted and fangs receded. Her muzzle and whiskers were last, gold and dark brown replaced by her pale skin.

She was back to her human form, and she reached for her side, hand slapped over her wound. It hurt like a killer-whale bite—firsthand experience at sixteen, don't ask—but a quick glance told her it wasn't all that bad.

The cougar disagreed. Between the bullet wound, her black eye, and her limp, it believed it was dying—*dying*.

Chest deep in the water, she eyed the shore once more, searching for any hint of someone watching her. She stared into the shadows, trying to see past the darkness that filled the corners. She didn't see anything, but...

Abby had no time for "but." She had to get her ass moving.

She trudged through the water, feet sucked down by the sand, as if the ocean was trying to keep her. Like it knew what stupidity she was walking into and wanted to save her from herself.

With the water at her knees, she stumbled forward, fall-ing to the sand and catching herself with her free hand. She shoved herself to her feet once again, strength all but gone. When she looked down at her injury, she was kinda thankful for the sea water. The blood didn't stand a chance against the waves, brushed away before she could realize the wound was a little worse than she'd originally decided.

The ocean lapped at her feet, and then she stood on dry land, the sand shifting beneath her soles. She was close now. The glowing lights of her building loomed, and she forced herself forward. Her body tightened and jerked with each step, muscles and skin around her injury pulling with her movements.

Thanks to the awesomeness of spandex, at least her bra and panties had survived the impromptu swim.

It hurt to breathe, to think, to do anything but hopefully trudge in the right direction. She knew her cougar worked to heal the damage, but she'd been logging long hours at the office—leaving early and coming home late—and hadn't been eating properly. Her body was tired before she even got out of bed in the morning, and with the injury...

The cat was doing the best it could, but it couldn't do much.

The entry to her building came into sight, the glowing door a beacon to her exhausted body. She pushed herself, determined to do this.

She could.

She would.

Suddenly fabric enveloped her head and wrapped around her body, swallowing her in darkness. Strong arms kept her in place, holding her immobile. A large body aligned with hers, her captor's front against her back.

"Got you."

CHAPTER SEVEN

*A*bby was dead. Done. Ex-living, un-living, once upon a living, and now heaven and hell fought over her soaking-wet, shivering, miserable corpse. Apparently, her soul wasn't worth having because she still seemed to have *that* along with parts of her deluded mind.

Wait. It wasn't heaven and hell fighting over her wretched body. It was a couple of men. Maybe three? It could be a hundred for all she knew. The scent of the sea, briny and tinged with a hint of *eau de fish*, filled her nose. It obscured the different flavors in the air, and she couldn't figure out who—what—surrounded her. She could only go by voices and sounds coming from her captors. The baritones, scratchy rasps, and deep breathing echoed around her, bouncing off the metal walls.

She frowned and tilted her head, urging her cougar to come forward and give her a hand, er, paw. The persnickety feline hissed at her, reminding Abby *she* was the reason they were in this mess and *she* could be the one to get them out.

As if they weren't one and the same. She mentally groaned. Stupid, *stupid* cat.

Giving up on her cougar, she focused on the world

around her. Her vision was masked by the thick blanket over her head, but she could tell she was in a vehicle, large and heavy. She sniffled, but only inhaled seawater.

The cat released a wheezing chuckle.

Bitch. Just see if she ever bought catnip at the pet store. *Just see.*

That assumed she made it out of the hot mess alive so she could go to the pet store. If she had a Magic 8-Ball, her fortune would be "outlook not so good."

The voices echoed in the space, muffled by the blanket and too low for her to figure out what they said. So she focused on the tones, the tiny variances in speech patterns and pitch.

And heat. There was one man close to her, utterly silent but warm. A warmth that chased away the cold and made her forget about the bullet hole in her side. The vehicle swayed, tires rumbling over uneven ground, and she used the rocking motion as an excuse to ease closer to him.

The van rocked hard to the left and then right. The sudden movement threw her forward and then back, slamming her head against the unpadded wall of the vehicle. A soft whine escaped her.

A low rumble, no words, just a rolling sound, reached out to her, and a large hand cupped the back of her head. It rubbed her gently, touch easing the throbbing ache, and as quickly as the caress came, it was gone. But it reduced her panic just a little. That meant he cared, right?

Could she develop Stockholm syndrome after just five minutes?

She needed to focus on how the hell she was going to get out of this mess. Three men had kidnapped her. Oh, it'd been only one guy to toss a blanket over her head and shove her into the vehicle, but she heard two others. When she got free, they'd all go down and get carted off to jail.

When. Not if. She had to stay positive. She'd be free and they'd be gone.

More murmurs, one voice snapping, another snarling, and one that was soft and hard at the same time. One the rest listened to without question.

The van swayed, and she rocked forward with the rolling motion, losing her balance. She tensed, waiting for the inevitable pain from slamming into the floorboard. But it didn't come. A thick, strong arm wrapped around her waist, hand settling on her hip as he pulled her closer. His touch slipped from her waist to her shoulder, and a soft tug pulled her against him—Hot Guy.

"Rest." The low murmur reached out for her, and Abby was torn between doing as he said and refusing whatever comfort he provided. This had to be some sort of good cop/bad cop scenario. Except his actions had been a mix of the good cop/bad cop behavior. Maybe he didn't know how to play the game.

Regardless, resting seemed like a great idea. As adrenaline fled her body, the ache in her side grew, agony increasing with each passing second. She lowered her head to his shoulder and slumped against him, giving her captor her weight. There was no harm in relaxing and conserving her strength.

Abby beckoned the cat once more, needing its help to heal her wound. If she saw a chance to escape, she'd take it, but her bid for freedom would be hindered by the injury.

The animal grumbled but pushed forward, the beast's rapid healing swirling and surrounding her wound. It tingled, a warm rush sliding over the area, followed by the burning itch of knitting flesh.

She gritted her teeth and trembled against her captor, the pain snatching her control. He tightened his grip, tugging her even closer until their bodies were aligned. They fit together like two pieces of a puzzle sliding into place. As if they were made to complement each other.

And wasn't that a screwed-up thought? Exhaustion, pain, and fear were making her crazy.

"Six minutes out." A low murmur filled her ear—Hot Guy again. His voice was soothing, and somehow it drove away the sharp edge of pain. Her cat responded to his deep tenor, releasing a low, trilling purr of her own.

So. Fucked. Up.

Instead of replying, Abby swallowed hard and nodded. She needed to focus, dammit. These might be the last six minutes of her life.

The van slowed, rolling to a stop for a moment, and the mechanical hum of a window rolling down filled the space. A few beeps and the sound repeated, window going back up as the vehicle rocked back into motion. Then they were going around and around in what seemed like a never-ending spiral.

The squeak of tires and the roar of the engine echoed around them, and she took a little comfort in that. The space they drove through sounded empty, a large cavern that only held their vehicle. Maybe she'd only have to face the guys that currently held her and not some big team of baddies.

The van took one last sharp turn and rocked to a stop, gears thumping when the driver put the vehicle in park before he turned the key and cut the engine. It dropped them into silence for one beat and then two before her captors burst into action. Metal grinded against metal, someone yanking open the side door. That was followed by the heavy *thud* of boots on a hard surface. Concrete?

Metal clanged, cloth rustling but not cotton—something else. Nylon? The rasp of Velcro and then a heavy weight *thump*ed beside her. She squeaked and jolted with the sudden sound, and followed that up with a moan. Her wound pulled, what little healing she'd managed now undone by her thoughtless movement.

Everyone fell silent with her groan, and the heavy weight of their gazes settled on her shoulders. She didn't know how she knew that they stared; she just *knew*.

And didn't like it one bit.

Abby bit her lower lip and swallowed any other whimpers and moans that threatened to break free. Being the center of her captors' attention could never be a good thing.

Soon their movements picked up again, the jangle of buckles and the metallic rasp of zippers with the occasional grunt and low whispers. They spoke, they moved around, and they left her alone.

Which was great as far as Abby was concerned.

Then a large, strong hand wrapped around her biceps, holding her in a punishing grip, and yanked her to the left. She scrambled to gain her feet, silently cursing when her captor jerked and she scraped her knee on the sand-covered, uneven van floor. Now her knee throbbed in time with the pulsing ache in her side.

Her captor pulled her out of the van, further tearing her wound, and blood flowed free of the cut. What little clothing she wore had dried during the ride and was now soaked in blood.

"Careful, asshole!" The deep, chocolatey baritone boomed through the cavernous space. It was tinged in rough fury that felt more like a caress to her cat. And hell, she wasn't sure how a voice could sound like chocolate, but his *did*.

All chocolate and smooth and sweet with a hint of hot and...*Ahem*.

The tight grip on her arm eased a little. She'd be bruised by the rough handling, but if she had bruises to bitch about, it meant she was alive to do the bitching.

She'd take it.

She listened for everything, counted every step as they led her to what felt like a smaller area. Their footsteps were now muffled—by carpet? The buzz of lights—fluorescent—reached her as well. An office of some sort? With an attached parking garage?

The three men remained silent during their trek down hallway after hallway. They turned left, then right, then left and two rights? Why did she have to be a number person and not some amazing Tracker chick?

Soon their pace slowed before they stopped altogether. At least for a moment. Just long enough for one of her captors to...unlock a door? And if it was *un*locked, it could then be *re*locked.

She might be blind, hurt, and exhausted, but she wasn't stupid. Okay, maybe a little stupid because she'd already let them take her to a secondary location. Statistically, that meant she was *for sure* going to be killed.

Abby was taking a hard pass on going into that room though.

The man holding her tugged and she tugged back, leaning away and digging her bare heels into the carpet. She shook her head, the blanket still blinding her, and it swung with the rapid movement. A whimper escaped her lips, terror stealing her ability to speak.

Had she mentioned hard pass?

The grip on her arm tightened, a growl following the squeeze, but she was already too scared to be even *more* frightened by the man. "Move."

She moaned, fear still forcing her to be silent.

"Let her go." The voice was louder, but familiar—Hot Guy. That order was followed by the disappearance of the other man and a deep grunt. Then she found herself lifted from the ground and cradled high against the stranger's chest. "Got you."

The first time he'd said those words, a wave of panic had overtaken her. This time a blanket of something else drifted over her body—calmness. A calmness she didn't expect to experience again manifested with his touch and murmured words. There was something wrong with her.

The cat snorted and wondered if her human half had always been so slow.

Hot Guy took two steps into the room and paused; then a hard *thud* was followed by the squeak of hinges.

"Dec—" The man's voice was cut off by the slam of the door.

There was the familiar scrape of a lock, and her captor growled low, "Keep out!"

When no one opened the door once more, he seemed to relax, shoulders dropping though he still held her securely. He carried her across the space, five long strides, and then he slowly bent, placing her on a hard surface before withdrawing.

Abby stayed in place, huddled beneath her blanket— cold, bleeding, and in pain—while she waited for whatever happened next. Questioning? Torture? A game of Uno?

The blanket was swept away, exposing her to the room's bright light, and she blinked against the harsh glow. Bright splotches filled her vision, and she squinted while she fought to bring the room into focus.

A man towered over her—dark hair, blue eyes, heavily muscled body, and black clothing.

"You," she whispered. He'd saved her once, but was it only to kill her now?

CHAPTER EIGHT

*M*e," Declan grunted, and stopped himself from saying anything else. She feared him—face pale, eyes wide, and the stench of her fear nearly overwhelming the coppery tang of her blood.

Blood that soaked into her clothing and turned her pale top a deep red. A fact that enraged his wolf. The beast paced in the back of his mind, snarling and growling with every step. For an animal who normally enjoyed the scents of fear and blood, it was pretty pissed about both coming from Abby. And Declan wasn't going to question why. At least, not yet.

He couldn't help her fear of him, but he could handle tending her wound. He'd patched up himself—his team—enough over the years.

Declan dropped to a crouch and slipped his knife from the sheath strapped to his side. He tugged on her shirt with his other hand, lifting the bottom edge to expose her side. "Take this off."

He expected her to listen.

He *didn't* expect her to shove him away with flailing hands.

"No." Abby even went so far as to push the fabric back into place. "I'm fine. Thank you for your concern."

"You're fine?" He moved her shirt out of his way *again*, pointed the tip of his knife at her seeping wound, and then met her stare. "That's a bullet hole in your side."

"I have no idea what you're talking about." More tugging down while he wanted the cloth *up*. "I'm perfectly fine."

More like perfectly delusional. Declan didn't remember chicks being so difficult, but it'd been a while.

He closed his eyes and sighed while he prayed for patience. "Lift your shirt."

"No."

"You know, most people would try to be accommodating after they've been kidnapped," he drawled.

"Why should I make killing me easy on you?" She clenched her jaw and tipped her chin up, a stubborn gleam in her eyes.

Her arguing made his dick hard. Her words made his wolf growl all the louder.

"I didn't save your ass to kill you." He yanked her shirt up and held it in place, ignoring her when she tried to wrench it free again. "I rescued your ass..."

Because the wolf hadn't let him stay on that damned rooftop, and he still wasn't ready to examine why his beast had been so determined. It hadn't cared about orders from the team alpha and his responsibilities to SHOC. It'd needed to keep Abby from harm. Period.

He changed tactics. "You've been working for FosCo all week, but something changed tonight. What was it?"

"Who are you?" she countered.

"A concerned citizen." He rolled his eyes and placed his knife between his teeth. He used his free hand to press on her side. The bullet had entered her back but hadn't popped out the front. Which meant he had to dig it out before her cat got too far in her healing.

Extracting a bullet after the wound closed was a pain in the ass.

He felt along her waist, fingers pressing her soft flesh, and he pretended not to notice the silken feel of her skin beneath his hand. He'd spent days fantasizing about Abby, but none of his imaginings included her bleeding all over him.

Declan ignored her harsh inhale, the way she stiffened, or the fact that she'd stopped breathing altogether. He knew he hurt her—he'd been shot more than a few times, and that shit never got easy—but it couldn't be helped.

He finally worked around to her front, still searching for that bullet, and...He withdrew his touch and pulled his knife from between his teeth. He gestured at the vague shadow beneath her milky skin.

"There it is. Hold your shirt for me and don't move." He released the cloth, and it fell back into place. Declan closed his eyes and begged for patience. Again. "Do you know how to follow directions? Or do you ignore hired killers for shits and giggles when they give you an order?"

Abby's swallow was audible, and a new wave of her fear slipped into the air. He could scent her sweat, the flood of adrenaline that filled her body, and the stark panic that followed in its wake. He hated that he could sense the changes in her—that she even experienced the riot of emotions—but he had to admit it was useful.

She surged, throwing her weight forward while she struggled to gain her feet. Struggled because he easily reached across her, his hand finding the curve of her hip, and pushed her back into the chair. She flopped against the seat, and a long, low groan eased past her lips.

The wolf snapped at him for causing her pain. Apparently, it thought he could have been gentler. Declan was getting real damn tired of the animal. If it wasn't demand-

ing he jolt into action no matter the consequences, it was
bitching at him.

"You done?" he drawled, and she glared at him. At
least she still clung to her spunk despite the pain. "Because this is happening. You can sit still, let me take care
of this, and get your inner cat working on healing you,
or you can fight me."

"Inner cat?" She licked her lips, small pink tongue darting out. "I have no idea what you're talking about. Who
are you? Are you crazy? They have hospitals for that. And
drugs."

He snorted. "Abby, you're a cougar shifter. You know
that, I know that, and the guys outside that door know that.
I'm gonna tell you again—sit still and let me treat you.
Then you're gonna answer some questions."

"Then you'll kill me?"

"For the love of…" He growled, and his vision wavered, the wolf snatching control for a split second before
Declan managed to wrestle the beast back.

Abby gasped, eyes widening with her shock. "You're
a…"

"Wolf," he snapped. "A very pissed-off, annoyed wolf."
He waved his knife, drawing her gaze. "One who's trying
real hard to do this the easy way, but I'm losing my patience."

His beast told him he'd cling to his patience and his
human half would be happy about it, dammit. For some reason, the animal bounced between the need to take over and
dominate the curvy cougar and the desire to give her the
time and space she needed.

Contrary wolf.

Voices outside snared his attention, and he split his focus
between Abby and the world just outside that door. His

team—Birch and the others—was near, but too far away for him to make out their words. His animal told him they weren't important. Nothing was more important than taking care of Abby.

Declan sighed. "What do you need to hear so that I can do this already?"

"Who are you?"

"Declan Reed." He bit off the words and reached for her for what seemed like the thousandth time.

She leaned away. "I wasn't done."

"Of course you're not," he grumbled.

"Why did you help me at FosCo? Why did you chase me? Why did you kidnap me? Who—"

"I should have just gagged you and tied you down. It would have been easier." The wolf told him he would have *tried*, but the beast wouldn't tolerate restraining her... unless she asked nicely. "I'm with Shifter Operations Command and we're on assignment."

"To rescue me from Eric Foster?"

"Sweetheart, while your death would have been a devastating loss to the hot-blooded men of the world, you aren't the reason for this op."

She shook her head. "I don't understand. Then why...?"

Declan didn't understand either. As for the why... he shrugged. "Felt like it."

He also felt like he was done with their back-and-forth. Pain etched Abby's features, and the scent of her blood made his stomach churn.

Deciding to act without her help, he kept her shirt raised with one hand and pricked her stomach with the other, not giving her a chance to object. She screamed. Just a quick shout followed by a deep inhale, which she held in her lungs.

Blood welled at the new wound, and he placed his knife between his teeth once more before pinching the flesh around her cut. He rubbed back and forth, encouraging the ball of metal to rise. It moved up, up, up, and then popped through the slice. He caught it with ease, the silver slug coated in her fresh blood.

The moment he released her she gripped her side, but she didn't make a sound. Not a single breath passed her lips.

But she didn't need to yell or cry out for him to know she was in pain. The woman who'd chattered and questioned him was pale and trembling, giant tears pooling in her eyes—silent tears.

A twinge of regret needled his heart. "Sorry," he mumbled, and focused on the tip of his blade. He wiped the flat of the knife on his pants, cleaning it of her blood, and then slid it back into its sheath. Declan pushed to his feet. "I'll get you some protein so your cougar can heal you, and I'll see what kind of clothing we've got around here."

Clothing? A whole lot of nothing, probably. An abandoned office building wasn't exactly a place that had an overflowing lost and found.

My clothes…

Nah. They'd be too big and might give his team the wrong impression. Like he claimed her or something. Which he wasn't. Even if he'd already disobeyed orders for her. Probably would again before the night was through. Not much to be done about it though.

"You could let me go home." Her voice was tiny, more a rasp than anything.

"Abby," he huffed, ignoring how good it felt to say her name. Damned good. "You think you can just walk away now? After that mess?" He shook his head. "FosCo—their *associates*—aren't going to let that happen."

Golden eyes zeroed in on him, the woman's cougar staring out. "You mean Unified Humanity."

He narrowed his eyes. "What do you know about it? Them?"

"I—"

Two heavy thumps, the door shaking in its frame, cut her off, and Birch's shout came through the thick wood panel. "Declan. Get out here."

The wolf bristled, snarling and growling while it shoved forward. It recognized Birch as its alpha—of a sort—but it didn't like taking orders when they clashed with the animal's desires.

Birch's tone had an edge that usually came when the man was getting ready to tell the team something they wouldn't want to hear. Which was why he didn't want to leave Abby even if she needed food and clothing.

"Declan!"

CHAPTER NINE

*W*hen Declan joined Shifter Operations Command there'd been some give-and-take during negotiations. Declan got a pardon for his past and future "extracurricular activities" if he limited his freelancing to humans. In exchange, he'd agreed to abide by SHOC hierarchy and commands. There'd been a big ceremony and everything.

So when Birch demanded Declan leave Abby, he did. Eventually. He made sure her cougar stopped the bleeding first. His wolf couldn't stand the idea of her waiting for him to return while blood continued to seep from her wounds.

Once the cat did its job, he pushed to his feet with a murmured, "I'll be right back."

And he would be *right back*. He'd made it only two steps toward the door before his wolf whined and pulled against Declan's mind. He wasn't going to give in to the animal's desires. Yet. He'd see what had Birch's dick in a knot first.

He tugged open the door and stepped into the wide hall. Birch stood in the center of the passageway, arms crossed over his chest and fierce glare in place. Ethan leaned against the opposite wall, legs crossed at the ankles and his attention on his cell phone. He wondered what game the lion was obsessed with now.

Declan pulled the door closed once more before he spoke. "Where are the others?"

"Cole's focused on cleanup." Translation: blowing up the offices next door. "Grant's keeping tabs on emergency services. He also said we're having difficulty contacting headquarters."

"Really?" He lifted his eyebrows. "*Grant* is having problems—"

Ethan snickered, and Birch's glare snapped to the distracted lion—waste of a scowl in Declan's opinion—before returning to Declan once more.

"Grant doesn't have tech problems." Ever. The other wolf might appear to be more obsessed with his stomach than his job, but there wasn't anything he couldn't handle.

"Yeah, well…" Birch sighed and glanced at the lion. "Ethan, keep an eye on her. She doesn't leave. Declan, you're with me."

Declan didn't want Ethan to keep an eye—or anything else—on or around Abby. So when Ethan pushed away from the wall and moved toward the door, Declan shoved him right back into place.

"You can watch the door from where you're at."

The lion pulled his lips into a knowing smile. "No need to get your tail in a twist, wolf-boy. Just thought I'd keep the kitty company."

"She doesn't need company." And she sure as hell didn't need some pretty-boy lion near her. "She prefers to be alone."

Ethan snorted in disbelief. "Uh-huh."

Yeah, Declan didn't believe himself either.

Birch spun on his heel and stomped down the hall. "Move it, wolf."

He turned to follow his team alpha, his inner animal howling, urging him to remain and guard his territory. The beast didn't get that people couldn't be territory. His wolf told him he was an ignorant idiot and to just watch how quickly Abby turned into...

Declan tugged on the wolf's mental leash. He didn't have time to deal with the whiny bastard. Not when a sense of unease permeated the air.

The set of Birch's shoulders and the tension in the bear's fingertips put Declan on edge. He wasn't gonna like what came out of his team alpha's mouth next.

Birch led him down the hallway and around the corner, not stopping until they reached the inner stairwell. Then the team alpha turned, face an expressionless mask. He tried to hide his thoughts, but Declan wasn't sure why. They'd stared down death together too many times to have many secrets.

Declan mirrored Birch's stance, an appearance of relaxation while ready to burst into action. "Just get it out."

"You blew the op."

"We got most of it done." Declan shrugged. "We confirmed FosCo's part of Unified Humanity."

"No. We verified that Eric Foster is a member of UH based on what Grant picked up on his wiretaps. We have nothing on FosCo or their dealings. Like I said"—Birch pointed at him—"you blew the op."

Declan shook his head. "Can you bitch at me later? I need to get Abby something to eat and new clothes."

The wolf's growls grew louder with each passing second, and he wasn't sure how much longer he could resist the animal's demands. There was just something about the cougar that gave the beast a strength he hadn't experienced in a long time—nearly fifteen years. Back then—on *that* day—he'd lost control and...

Yeah.

Declan huffed. "Fine. We'll get the bitching out of the way, but make it quick. Which lecture do you wanna go with? There's 'Shifter Operations Command put their faith in you and you swore to blah, blah, blah...' or would you prefer 'As your team alpha, I expect my orders to blah, blah, blah...'?"

Birch dropped his chin to his chest. "I could save myself a lot of aggravation if I just killed you now."

"True, but I'm good at what I do, so you won't."

The bear grunted and lifted his attention to Declan once more. "Not today. The director might have different ideas when he knows the details."

"He doesn't need to know everything. Just leave the worst out of the field report." It wasn't like they hadn't done it in the past.

"Not an option."

Declan jolted and furrowed his brow. "Why not? Ethan totaled a million-dollar *Lamborghini* on SHOC's dime and you conveniently 'forgot' to tell headquarters. I only killed a guy. It wasn't like he was an innocent."

It wasn't like it was the first time he'd doled out a little justice while on the job, either.

"No, they weren't, but that's not why this can't get swept away. The director already knows."

"Knows...?" He lifted his eyebrows in question.

"The director knows about the fight *and* Abby."

"How? Did fucking Grant report in while—"

"No, he didn't." Birch sliced his hand through the air,

and Declan snapped his mouth closed. "I'm not sure how they know about Abby and what went down tonight. Headquarters com'ed while we were on our way back with her. Grant got the initial orders, but our systems have been 'down' since."

"Initial orders?"

"The director is en route to the southern field office. A team has been dispatched to take custody of Abby and bring her to him for questioning. As soon as we transfer custody, we're ordered to return to headquarters for debrief."

His wolf growled, and Declan did nothing to suppress the beast. The rumble rolled through the air, his animal making its displeasure known. His fingertips burned, the wolf's claws attempting to push through his human skin. His fangs strained against his gums, the sharp points piercing his flesh and slowly dropping into place.

SHOC was taking Abby from him.

"No." He sounded more wolf than man.

"You don't have a choice." Birch pointed at him. "You created the mess. You brought her to the director's attention. She'll have to deal with the consequences."

Declan shook his head, still unwilling to accept Birch's words. "She's not involved."

Birch dropped his voice, tone grim. "That's not for us to determine." A growl slid into Birch's words. "It's our job to follow orders, Agent."

"He'll..." *Hurt her. Break her.*

Normally Declan didn't care. Whoever ended up in a room with the director deserved the punishment—usually. Not Abby though. Never her.

The SHOC director was cunning, unbending, and often

violent. And everyone was damn loyal to the asshole. Kinda made sense since he was the one who made sure agents didn't end up hunted by council Trackers. Or worse— imprisoned by the council.

Declan's skin stretched, the wolf scraping him from the inside out. It gnawed on him, punishing him for the situation.

"Yeah, he probably will." Birch's look layered a heap of guilt on his shoulders. The man's brown eyes turned black with the presence of his bear. He rolled his shoulders and cracked his neck.

"It's not happening." Declan pushed the words past his wolf's teeth.

Birch snorted. "No choice, remember? Disobeying orders brands you a rogue."

He simply shrugged. Declan had been called worse by better men.

"Bottom line, a team is inbound and you'll hand her over. Now isn't the time to enter a dick-measuring contest with the director. There are whispers coming out of headquarters—shit that doesn't make sense—and it's making me damned twitchy."

No one liked it when a grizzly with a short temper got twitchy.

"We done?" Declan was afraid to say anything else. His animal had him riding the edge of control, and now wasn't the time to shift and destroy everything within reach. They could go feral and vent their anger later.

"We're done."

Declan spun on his heel and strode down the hallway, the need to get to Abby pushing him onward. He split his attention between his path and Birch at his back. He listened to the slow, rhythmic thumps of the bear's boots on the stairs, the team alpha probably returning to Grant.

With each step closer to Abby, a plan began to form. One that'd cause a fuck-ton of trouble, but it sure as hell would be fun.

And it started with Ethan.

CHAPTER TEN

*A*bby concentrated on remaining calm. She breathed deep, meditated—complete with *ohm*—and added a prayer to any available deity for good measure. Anything to keep her body relaxed and loose while her cougar did its thing.

Declan hadn't returned with any protein to help feed her cat, so the animal made do with what little strength remained. Then again, even if he *had* brought her food, should she have eaten it? Her Stockholm syndrome–infected brain said, "*Of course I would because he would never hurt meeee.*" It even added a little trill on the end.

She was losing her mind. It was bad enough she had to balance her human mind with her cougar.

She took a deep breath and released it slowly. She emptied her mind of the cat and the part of her that decided her captor's eyes were sexy. She beckoned the animal forward, nudging it to focus on her wound. Well, *wounds*. Declan had given her another one, but at least now she was metal-free. The cougar grumbled, both appreciative and annoyed in equal measure. Now it had *double* the work with *no food*. *None*.

Food was a big thing the cat kept circling back to. It was

hungry, dammit. They'd run and swam and then there'd
been a lot of panic and…Was it too much to ask to get a
burger or something?

Focus. She spoke to the she-cat, and it hissed at her.

But at least the beast did as she demanded. The wounds
on her side burned and itched, skin and flesh drawing closer
as the animal encouraged healing. It worked from the inside
out, repairing the deepest parts of her side before moving
closer to her skin. Nerves and veins pieced back together,
muscle merging until it was once more whole.

The cougar whined and huffed, swaying on her paws due
to exhaustion. She hung her head low, spine curved and
snout nearly brushing the ground. Even the animal's tail
drooped, the tip not flicking an inch.

The holes in her side still throbbed, the healing not complete, but it was better than it'd been.

Rest.

The cougar whimpered, soulful golden eyes flashing in
the darkness of Abby's mind.

You did good. Rest now. You can try more after we eat.

If they ate. She hung her prayers on Declan—that he told
the truth—but he could have simply been telling her what
she wanted to hear.

SHOC were the good guys—ish. They were the mon-
sters in the dark who hunted and killed the bogeyman—by
any means necessary. Lying, cheating, stealing, killing…
They did it all without guilt.

At least, those were the rumors passed around.
*"SHOC keeps us safe from humans who want to harm
our kind. Just don't make them angry because they know
how to hide bodies."*

The shifter council monitored and policed shifters. They
got accolades and awards. SHOC got looks of pure fear and

a wide berth. But Declan had been nice, right? The niggling doubt nudged her once more.

The sound of someone's approach reached her, muffled by the solid wood door but still audible. She'd call on her cat for assistance, but it'd already done so much for her—them. If the newcomer was entering, she'd find out what he wanted when he appeared.

Low murmurs followed, one voice tinged with an animal's growl while the other remained slow and calm. The growl drew her attention most. She might not understand the words, but she recognized the rise and fall, the pitch and tempo.

Declan had returned. Which thrilled her cat a little too much, a delicate purr sliding through her mind. One that also gathered in her chest and threatened to break free. She wasn't going to purr for her captor—she *wasn't*.

The voices rose, Declan's snarl deepening, and then his rumbles were countered by the other man's. Their volume grew, growled words gradually becoming clearer, and then...

The voices snapped off like a switch followed by a low *thump*, a door-shaking *thud*, and the brush of fabric on wood. One of them hit the other and sent him collapsing against the door.

If one was on the floor, who was left standing?

Please be Declan. Please.

It was better to have the devil she knew-ish, right?

The knob turned, near silent until the latch fully disengaged with a soft *click*. The panel gradually swung inward, revealing the hallway as well as the man collapsed in the doorway—blond with tanned skin and deep brown eyes.

Wait, what?

Declan stepped over the fallen male and strode to her. "Time to go, Abby."

"I think you cracked a tooth when you hit me, asshole," the man on the floor growled.

Declan didn't respond. Hadn't he heard the guy snarling?

"Declan, he's awake." She pointed at the guy, who looked to be getting comfortable. He reached into his pocket and tugged a cell phone free, attention on the device rather than them.

Declan glanced at the other man and then back to her and shrugged. "I only kill other agents on Tuesdays."

Abby wasn't sure if he was joking and was too afraid to ask.

"Declan had to make it look like I tried to stop him." The man tilted his head and met her eyes. He gave her a wink and a smile. "He hits like a declawed house cat—all paws, no claws."

"Ethan, shut the fuck up," Declan snarled, but his touch was gentle as he pulled her from the chair. He wrapped his hand around her wrist and led her to the door, holding her steady while she stepped over the other man.

Ethan snorted. "You're just mad that I'm right."

"Can you run?" Declan stared at her, his gaze heavy and intent.

"I . . ." The way he stared at her, the way his wolf peeked out from behind his blue eyes, told her that her answer was very, very important. "Yes."

She didn't think she had any other choice.

"You realize that the moment you hit the garage, the alarm will sound, right?" Ethan lifted his head and quirked a brow.

"I'm aware." The heat of Declan's glare warmed the area around them.

"And that the van has a global positioning tracker? If you think stealing it will help…"

"Ethan, spit it out already."

Ethan frowned. "Cranky." The man turned his attention to her. "You really want to go with him, kitten?" He waggled his eyebrows. "Once you go lion…"

"Ethan…" Declan's grip tightened, nails digging into her flesh.

"Fine," Ethan grumbled, and dug into his pocket, yanking a set of keys free. "It's on the second level of the garage." He tossed the jangling keys at Declan, and he caught them with ease. "Be nice to her. She's a delicate piece of—"

"Machinery." Declan grunted and tugged on Abby, pulling her to the right and leading her down the hallway.

"I don't get a thank-you?" Ethan called after them, but Declan simply kept walking and Abby had to jog to keep up.

He didn't slow until they reached a solid metal door, and a peek through the small window showed a dimly lit parking garage on the other side.

He paused, his gaze on the garage while he spoke to her. "We're going out this door and down two flights. Birch is above us on seven with Grant. Ethan will take his time joining them, which will give us a few extra seconds."

Declan turned his attention to her, stare intent and unwavering. There was a tension in his jaw and determination in his eyes. As if getting her away from the building was the most important thing in his world at that moment.

"Why are you doing this?"

"I can't let you stay here." A different set of emotions flittered across his face. Something she couldn't read, but she didn't imagine it was anything good.

"I thought SHOC were the good guys. I thought…"

"'Sweetheart." The corner of his mouth quirked up in a smirk, his tone condescending. If she wasn't so exhausted, she'd kick him. "You want a good guy who'll always do the right thing? You call a council Tracker. You want a job done no matter the cost? You call SHOC. We're good if the money's right. If not…" He shrugged.

Abby licked her lips, a sliver of fear making her mouth go dry. "I can't pay you to be good."

"Yeah, well, for some reason my wolf is determined to be good for you anyway." He didn't sound happy about the situation, either. "You ready?"

No. But she didn't have a choice. She jerked her head in a brisk nod.

The scrape of metal on metal—the bar handle slamming in its casing—was followed by the clang of the panel striking the exterior wall. Before they'd even cleared the doorjamb, an alarm sounded. The high-pitched whine chased them into the stairwell and down the steps.

It spurred her to push her body harder, run faster, and match Declan's long strides step for step.

Another echoing bang reached them, the sound from above them and distant yet still too close for comfort.

As was the roar that followed. It vibrated the air around them, bouncing off the concrete walls and shaking her from inside out.

"Birch isn't a happy camper." Declan almost sounded pleased by that fact.

They finally stopped descending, and he pulled her across the near-empty garage, toward the single car that occupied the level. A sports car—low-slung and black—gleamed in the dim light.

He released her and rounded the vehicle, and she immediately reached for the door, sliding into the passenger seat and then yanking it closed. Declan slipped behind the wheel, started the engine, and threw the car into gear.

He tossed a glance her way, a smile playing on his lips. "Hold on. This is gonna get rough."

The tires squealed, echoing through the large, empty space. The car lurched forward, engine roaring. Then they were moving again. Not moving, *racing*, across the concrete parking lot. The car hit the winding exit, back bumper scraping on the ramp with a loud screech.

That was followed by a roar. Not from the car or Declan—from behind them. A beast, a shifter, and he was *pissed*.

Abby half turned in her seat and peeked out the back window in time to catch sight of someone bursting from the stairwell.

"Uh, there's a half-shifted..." She swallowed hard. She hated the surge of fear that assaulted her, but she could work past the terror. She flicked a quick glance at Declan. "Something. It's brown."

Declan changed gear. The whine of the engine altered slightly before the mechanical roar picked up again. "That's Birch. He's a grizzly."

Grizzly...Mean. Violent. Determined. Which simply freaked her out even more. "Is he gonna catch us?"

"He'll try." He snorted and then chuckled. "But we're in Ethan's baby, and we have a head start." He shook his head. "Not happening."

"But..."

"Abby." His voice was low compared to the other noises surrounding them, but it still reached out to her. It caressed her in a soft brush of invisible hands on her skin. He spared her a glance, amber eyes flashing in her direction before his gaze went back to the road. "I'm not gonna let anything happen to you."

Her cougar purred, creeping out of hiding in the back of her mind. It padded forward—curious, anxious—to be closer to Declan. And his wolf.

"You can't promise—"

His chuckle was deep and dark—threatening. She'd be afraid if every part of her didn't want to stay at his side, if every part of her didn't somehow trust him already. And wasn't that screwed up?

"No one's gonna put their paws on you." That smooth murmur reached out for her, another caress, another stroke of his voice over her skin.

They made the last turn, night sky in sight, and she could practically taste freedom.

Then she tasted her own blood as she bit her lip.

A gate, thick metal bars that'd mean more captivity if they fell into place, started to lower from the roof of the tunnel.

"Declan?" She hated the way her voice shook, the tremble in her body, and the fear that attacked her, but she couldn't suppress the sensations.

Another gear, the engine so loud she couldn't hear anything but its rumble, and the car shot forward in a last bid to escape. The gate inched closer and closer to the ground, and Abby eyed the distance between the gate and the concrete, attention not wavering for even a moment. And then . . .

Then they sped through the opening, the gate scraping the back half of the car, but they managed to burst free. The clear night sky embraced them, moon illuminating their path while the stars twinkled in welcome.

Free.

For that moment, anyway.

She peeked out of the back window once more, searching for anyone who still gave chase. She shouldn't have bothered, though. She should have just accepted that SHOC agents weren't ones to give up easily. The gate that'd nearly blocked their exit now retreated, their pursuers simply waiting for it to retract once more.

He'd said the others would never catch them, but...

"Can they track us? With GPS or something?"

"Nope." Declan whipped the car onto a one-way street, tires squealing in protest. The moment he finished the turn, he cut the lights. As in, the actual *headlights*.

"Don't you need those to drive?" Abby hated being scared. Like, a lot.

"Nope." He accelerated through the next turn.

Abby clung to the car's door, bracing herself for the crash to come. Because there would be a crash. Her cougar knew it, too and now, even though it wanted to rub all over Declan like he was catnip, it also wanted to get the hell away from the crazy wolf.

"Hold on." He jerked the wheel to the right, taking a hard turn that had her clinging to the door for dear life while he swung them through the bend.

Abby gripped the door handle with one hand and her seat belt with the other while she prayed. Hard. Not to a specific god—any would do. She merely wanted to get out of the mess alive. She'd take battered, bruised, and a little broken if she was still breathing when the car came to a stop.

Declan's next turn made her wonder if he had a death wish. Tires squealed and moonbeams revealed whirling clouds of smoke from burnt rubber, the acrid scent stinging her nose. The vehicle slid sideways across the asphalt. Declan just laughed, a chuckle full of crazed joy filling the car.

He changed gears again, dropping low as he pulled out

of the skid, and they shot forward, up an on-ramp and right into late-night traffic. The highway wasn't filled by cars and SUVs, but it wasn't empty either. A nice middle ground that allowed Declan to zip through the other travelers.

"You're enjoying this." She shook her head. "Like, *really* enjoying this."

"Hell yeah, baby. It's been a while since I had a good high-speed run." He jerked the wheel to the left and then right, sliding through a space that looked hardly big enough to fit her, never mind a car. But he did it, moved through the traffic like a river of water—slick, raging, unstoppable. And elated. Until he glanced at her and his smile turned into a frown. His nostrils flared, chest expanding for a moment, and then he huffed out a quick exhale. "You're scared."

"Yeah." She nodded to reiterate. "Eric and those men. Then the fight. Then the running." She skipped over the tablet part because...because her cat had lovely thoughts about Declan, but her human mind still wasn't quite sure what to make of him. "Then the kidnapping and then the re-kidnapping and then..."

And she was using "and" and "then" a lot, but damned if she could figure out how to talk like a normal person. Normal people didn't hop in sports cars with potential lunatics.

"Okay." Declan reached between them, grabbed the emergency brake, and gave it a fierce yank. They slid sideways again, the move followed by blaring honks from other drivers while they slammed on their own brakes.

The car drifted down an exit, and a flash of white filled the interior of the car for a split second. "What...?"

"Automated toll booth." They ran a red light, shooting beyond oncoming cars. "Means we'll have to ditch this one."

The smiles were completely gone, replaced with the grim, furious shifter who'd dragged her from the building.

"I'm sorry. I didn't mean to cause all this—"

"Abby." Declan reached for her, and she didn't feel the urge to flinch or cower. Not from him. Even though she'd experienced pain at the hands of SHOC members, and what she'd seen him do to the massive tiger, she didn't fear him. "No reason to apologize. I'm gonna get you safe and keep you safe. Not letting anything happen to you."

CHAPTER ELEVEN

Declan whipped the car down another side street, working to get lost in the network of the small downtown roads. It was a convoluted maze of turns and one-way streets he'd memorized a long time ago.

He knew most of the team hunted them—Birch, Cole, and Ethan racing through the city while directed by Grant. The technological eye in the sky. Declan just had to get them hidden—lost in a part of town that didn't have cameras and streetlights at every corner.

Ethan had helped them escape. Would he drag his feet giving Grant any information he had about the Porsche? Probably. Ethan enjoyed annoying the hell out of the other wolf, and Declan was thankful for once for the lion's dickish behavior.

Another two turns and he followed those with a sharp third. It brought him into a tight alley, space hardly wide enough for Ethan's car. No way the SHOC van would fit down the narrow alleyway even if they caught up. Less than an inch on each side? Nah, they were gone.

Didn't mean Declan would slow down, though.

The front quarter panel scraped the brick wall to his left, and he grimaced. Ethan would be one pissed-off pussy at the damage to his car.

He whipped the wheel around, swinging them onto the next road with a loud squeal of tires. The second he joined the traffic, he brought their speed down to match the surrounding cars. A shot down the interstate for another few miles, then a handful more turns and they'd reach their destination—food, water, and a soft bed. Somewhere he could take care of Abby while he figured out how to fix this mess without them both ending up dead.

"Where...? Where are we going?" The wolf didn't like the way her voice trembled.

"We need to lie low and figure out what to do next. Get you cleaned up." He glanced at her, hating that she still wore rags that stank of the sea and were stained red with blood. "New clothes. Food. Weapons. New car."

"How far—"

"Close. About ten miles outside of Port St. James." He reached into his pocket and tugged out his cell phone. A swipe unlocked the device, and it took him no time to fire off a text.

"Texting? Seriously?" she screeched, and he winced with the high-pitched scream. "I can see my headstone now. 'Here lies Abby. Death by emoji at eighty miles an hour.' There will even be a colon and parenthesis to make a cute smiley."

Declan rolled his eyes. "I'm a master of multitasking and I'm only doing seventy-five, baby." He smirked when her growl filled the interior. "I was just contacting a friend."

Of sorts.

He flicked his attention to the rearview mirror—searching for the rest of his team—and a little of his tension eased when he didn't see them. The traffic had a nice, easy flow. Not too many cars on the highway—just enough to hide them, but still leaving them space to dart past other vehicles if he had to hit the gas. Thankfully, that room wasn't necessary. He glided across the lanes, the Porsche's ride smooth as they took the next exit.

Declan slowly rolled down a long, two-lane road past a handful of houses—his neighbors. They had no idea that the guy down the street was a werewolf who stored enough explosives in his basement to blow up the whole block. He hoped they'd never discover the truth. He liked the house. He *really* didn't want to have to blow it up.

"We're here." He turned down his driveway, manicured bushes and trimmed trees bracketing the long concrete lane. His headlights flashed over the swath of green grass that covered his front yard before settling on the ranch-style home set back from the road. It looked like everyone else's on the street—nothing special as far as the casual observer was concerned.

His neighbors didn't need to know that the walls were lined with steel and his windows were bullet resistant. They didn't need to know about the special surprises he put into place for anyone who thought it'd be a good idea to break into his home, either.

He followed the driveway around to the back of the house and rolled to a stop in front of the garage.

He shifted into park and cut the engine. "C'mon."

He climbed out and headed toward the back door, stopping only when he realized Abby hadn't moved. Trying to tamp down his annoyance, he went to the passenger door and tugged it open, lowering to a squat once he had enough room. His irritation vanished when her fear-filled eyes met his.

Scared. Hurt. Tired. It brought out some hidden caring he didn't know he possessed.

"Hey, let's go inside." He kept his voice low and tried to be as reassuring as he was capable of.

Abby's lower lip trembled, drawing his gaze. Declan wanted to nibble on that plump lip, take her mouth and kiss her so hard and deep she forgot her own name.

Instead, he reached across her to the seat belt buckle. His chest brushed hers, full breasts flush with his body. He was a piece of shit for liking it, but he did.

"We'll get you fed and clean."

Her breath fanned his cheek, and the beast howled with its sweetness. The briny tang of the sea couldn't hide her flavors when they were so close—all sex and honey with a hint of natural musk. It solidified his beast's assurance that they weren't letting anything happen to Abby. The wolf wanted to go on, to explain exactly what it desired from her, but Declan cut the beast off.

The wolf told him he was a delusional idiot if he thought he could just ignore her—and it.

Well, when the wolf was its own separate being and could talk in complete sentences, its ass could take a chance on Abby.

"C'mon." He disengaged the seat belt and retreated, letting the restraint roll back up on its own. "We don't want to be out here any longer than we have to."

"Is...Is SHOC going to find us here?"

Blue eyes met his, fear and something else battling it out across her features. He wasn't sure what was on her mind, but he could figure it out in a little while. Like, when they were in the safety of the house.

"No. This place isn't registered to me. It's hidden behind shell corporations and fake names. No one knows I own it." Or any of his other properties across the world. There was only one other person who knew where he was, and he trusted that person with his life.

Declan pushed to his feet and held out his hand, waiting for her to show a little trust in him—which she did.

Abby nodded and placed her palm on his, their fingers curling together while he helped her from the low-slung car. He wanted to keep holding her hand, but he forced himself to release her and take a step back, put a little space between them.

Otherwise he'd throw her over his shoulder and carry her off. And then she'd really have reason to be afraid.

"This way." Declan strode away. His wolf calmed a little when he heard the soft patter of her bare feet on the concrete.

He paused at the back door, just long enough to rub the thumb pad clean and press his thumb to the smooth surface. A green light flashed and the door's lock disengaged, granting them entrance to the home's mudroom. He pulled the door open and stepped back, waiting for her to enter the house before him.

Except she didn't budge. Her eyes focused on the blackness beyond them before she tipped her head back and met his stare with her cougar's eyes. The color as pale as sandy beaches caught a hint of moonlight. His own wolf inched forward, wanting a better look at the she-cat, and he didn't want to bother pushing it back. Not when fighting the animal meant taking his gaze from Abby.

He was losing his mind, allowing himself to be distracted by a *woman*, when he should focus on getting behind a secure door.

"Go inside. I can't disengage the other locks until this door is closed." Abby jerked with the harshness of his voice, but he'd be damned if he'd apologize. That didn't mean he wouldn't make sure she got the first hot shower.

She shuffled past him, and he stepped into the mud-room, tugging the door shut behind him—shutting out whatever light came from the moon. It snatched his sight, but Declan didn't need his eyes to see. He had a nose, hands, feet, and a damned good memory. He also had a trembling she-cat whose scent clouded the air with her panic.

"Abby," he murmured. "You're fine. I'm right here."

"Dark." She whimpered, and his wolf snarled, furious that she was so scared even when she was in their presence. The wolf didn't like that. At all.

Declan listened to the rasp of her breathing, the thump of her heart, and the shuffle of her feet on the tile. He didn't need to see to find her. Not when his body was drawn to her in a way that scared the shit out of him. He wanted—*needed*—Abby too much.

He reached out, arm circling her waist, and pulled her close while he sought to disengage the other security measures.

A thumbprint got them through the first door, but there was still more. He placed his palm on the plate set into the wall to the left of the door. The wolf focused and moved forward to change the temperature of his human hand until he matched his wolf form. That change was enough to trigger the next security protocol. From there it was another few tests—blood and both retinas.

"So much security."

Declan shrugged. "I don't plan on dying today. This'll keep us safe for tonight."

"Only tonight?"

Declan rubbed his thumb over her cheekbone. "Tomorrow will take care of tomorrow."

Tomorrow Declan would put a bullet in anyone who even looked at Abby, but he didn't think she'd appreciate the sentiment.

CHAPTER TWELVE

Tomorrow will take care of tomorrow. It should have comforted her, Abby supposed, but it didn't. Not when her hands still shook. Not when the pure adrenaline and terror that'd plagued her through their mad dash to safety still flowed heavily in her veins. Her knees threatened to go out from under her at any moment.

More whirring and clicking as the second door's lock disengaged and Declan withdrew. His retreat pulled a whimper from her throat, fear forcing the sound past her lips.

"Hold on to me. I'll lead you to the living room." His fingers wrapped around hers, and she clutched him with both her hands, unwilling to release him anytime soon. He didn't complain about her tight grip and merely gave her a gentle tightening in return. "Ready?"

No.

Instead, Abby whispered, "Yeah. Sure." She couldn't see him, but she could *feel* him. "I'm fine. Let's go."

Declan huffed but didn't argue with her. His boots thumped on the hard ground—tile?—and she kept pace. She shuffled along, farther and farther into the blackness before finally...

Click.

Low lighting flooded the area, bathing the home in a soft white glow and revealing their temporary sanctuary—pale walls, beige carpet, and large, plush furniture.

A tug from Declan reminded her she still clutched his hand, still clung to him for support even though she could see with ease now. She should let him go. She could walk on her own. And yet...she didn't want to release him. They were behind locked doors inside a place Declan considered safe, but she still couldn't shake her unease.

When he pulled again, she forced her fingers to uncurl and release him—let him go when all she wanted to do was pull him closer.

Abby's cougar purred. *Not* that *close.*

She remained in place while Declan flicked on other lights. More and more of the home was revealed to her— the great room, small dining area, large kitchen, and a dim hallway to Abby's left.

So *normal*-looking, but she knew Declan was anything but normal. Guns, pain, and blood were an everyday occurrence in his world. A man like him...

She shook her head and shivered, memories of Eric's attack churning in her mind. A man like Declan had been comfortable punching people out. He didn't look like the kind of guy who found happiness in the rural hills.

She shivered again—this time from cold—and rubbed her arms.

He didn't spare her a glance as he padded back across the room, heading toward an open door, and she spied a large bed. The master bedroom?

He disappeared through the doorway and still Abby remained in place, not sure what—

Declan's head poked out of the doorway. "You coming?"

She jerked and nodded. "Yeah, sorry."

"Don't apologize. Just c'mon." He vanished again.

She shuffled forward on the thick carpet. The deep pile caressed her soles, and the thumping pain in her feet lessened. What she wouldn't give for a bed just as squishy.

"Abby?" His voice was like chocolate, silk and smooth and very, very bad for her.

"Coming," she whispered. She wasn't sure why, but she always whispered in the dark. Even with so many lights on, deep shadows remained inside the house. She always kept her voice low. If she talked too loud, she'd be found, and then her parents' death would have—

She cut off that line of thinking, destroyed the path her mind wanted to travel. It'd only lead to heartache and pain, to memories that'd bury her in agony and tears.

Abby stepped into a large bedroom, with its massive king-sized bed. But then her attention immediately went to the adjoining bathroom, as she heard the shower.

Her cougar surged, anxious to scrub the sea from her skin. She tried to remind the beast that they didn't know Declan. Did the cat really think getting naked around some violent stranger was a good idea? The animal snorted, and Abby wasn't sure why she'd even bothered asking. When it came to a cat and getting clean, her feline would always vote for a shower.

Logic had no place in a battle between scrubbed skin and the stench of the sea. They'd spent too many days—and nights—stinking of the ocean when they were younger.

Never again.

She padded across the room, past a large dresser and the expansive bed and further until she stood within the bathroom's doorway.

Her breath caught and eyes widened at what she found.

While the rest of the house had been a study in neutral tones and bland decorations, the bathroom was...glorious. A shower with at least a dozen showerheads, a massive jetted soaking tub, and a double vanity. Shades of silver accented with hints of bronze were threaded throughout the room, the space bright and airy without appearing feminine.

Declan leaned into the shower, his back to her, and the position drew his pants snug against his body. The dark fabric clung to his thick thighs and cupped his ass. As for his shirt...it was gone, tossed aside to leave him bare. The muscles of his back clenched and flexed as he reached into the shower, and her fingers tingled with the itch to trace every rise and fall of his body. Then she'd follow that path with her tongue and...*No*.

She could fantasize about him later. Specifically, when she was safe.

Declan withdrew from the shower and turned to face her and she really wished he had remained in place. Not two seconds ago she'd told herself that licking Declan was a bad idea, and now he'd had to show her the deep carving of his abdomen all the way to the lines at his hips.

"A. Hem." He coughed, and heat surged in her cheeks.

She wrenched her attention from those lovely lines and refocused on his face. She ignored the smile that teased his lips *and* the sensual heat in his eyes.

"You can take the first shower." He moved aside, striding to the counter and taking a seat on the gleaming granite surface.

Abby stared at him and he stared at her and she stared at him staring at her staring at *him* and...

"Privacy?" She lifted her eyebrows in question.

"Shifters aren't modest." He waved at the shower, water still pattering against the tile. "Get going."

She narrowed her eyes, attention pulled from the hot water calling her name to the annoying male who thought privacy didn't exist. "Shifters aren't modest during a run, but I'm not used to wandering around with my ass hanging out around strangers."

His lips no longer twitched, instead pulling back into a wide, sizzling smile. "That's one fine ass."

"I'm not stripping—"

The wolf moved fast. Not just fast, but *fast*. One moment he relaxed on the counter and the next less than an inch separated their bodies. He towered over her, more than six feet of muscular shifter male. His scent filled her nose.

"I worked too hard to get you here. I'm not ready to let you out of my sight yet," he murmured, his voice soft yet still somehow loud enough for her to hear over the running water.

Except when he said "yet," he made her think he meant "ever." Her cat was warming to the idea of "ever."

Abby shivered. From cold? From fear? From...desire?

"Declan..." she whispered, not sure what else she meant to say. She just...she liked the feel of his name on her lips. And how screwed up was that?

Very. The answer was very.

He reached for her. His large, scarred hands brushed her hair aside, tucking a few strands behind her ear before he ran a single finger down her cheek. "You're tired, hurt, and dirty. We'll start with getting you clean and move on from there." His finger traveled along her cheek to her chin, and then he brushed the pad of his finger over her lower lip. "I saved you. I need to take care of you."

"I understand." Abby nodded and forced herself to remember their situation. She wasn't his girlfriend, lover, or mate. She was a woman he'd saved and needed to keep healthy until things were resolved.

"No." He shook his head. "I don't think you do." She opened her mouth to question him, but he quickly withdrew his hand and cupped her shoulder. He nudged her toward the shower. "Get clean. I'll be here."

Those few words soothed her, calmed her in a way she couldn't explain. The night had been hectic—bloody—but she found comfort in a violent stranger. So very, very odd.

Abby stepped into the shower and sighed as the wet heat enveloped her in a welcoming embrace.

She tugged at the tattered remains of her clothes, panties practically disintegrating in her hands. A pull on her top had the fabric falling away with ease, and another yank snapped the elastic of her bra. She closed her eyes with a deep sigh and let the water's heat sink into her bones, drive away the chill that'd consumed her, from the moment she'd leaped into the sea.

One more step and she was fully beneath—

A wave of dizziness had her listing to the left, and her arm shot out to catch herself before she tumbled. A combination of exhaustion, blood loss, and the disappearance of adrenaline sapped her strength.

Note to self: closing my eyes is a bad idea.

A cry escaped her lips, the sound followed by Declan's hissed "dammit," and then two large hands gripped her biceps. His hold was firm yet gentle as he supported her until she regained her balance.

"Lean against me. I won't let you fall," he murmured, and she was too tired to argue. She'd take his support for a second while she fought to banish the wooziness. Except when she gave him her weight and experienced the feel of his unwavering strength, she decided she'd take more than a second. Maybe two.

"You're gonna get all wet." Though, in one corner of her

mind, she recognized that she should be more upset with him for invading her shower. She'd get all indignant and scandalized after she had a nap.

"I think I'll survive a little water." He moved, stretching and reaching for items in the shower while remaining a steady presence at her back. "I can't say the same if you fall and hit your head." He nudged her. "Bend forward a little and wet your hair."

Abby stared at the cascade of water. "I don't think I can do that without toppling over."

Did he groan? She was sure he groaned. Maybe. But he didn't say a word, otherwise. He simply slipped one arm around her waist, his bare skin sliding along her slick flesh, and she shuddered with the contact. A tendril of awareness flooded her blood, and her cougar purred, reveling in Declan's closeness. She shoved at the beast, reminding the cat that they'd just met the wolf.

The animal reminded Abby that *she* was the one taking a shower with the near stranger. The wet nakedness was all on Abby's human shoulders. The cat was just along for the enjoyable ride.

She hated when the cat was right. Hated. It.

"I've got you." Yeah, Declan had her in several ways. "Go ahead."

She kept her mouth shut and did as he asked, fighting the vertigo when it threatened to swamp her. She lifted her arms, ruffling her hair and letting the clean water rinse away the worst of the salt water. She nearly lost her footing as she leaned into him once more, but he kept his promise and didn't let her fall.

She rested her head on his chest, sending water down his upper body, but he didn't seem to care. No, he ignored the soaking and reached for something else. The snap of a cap and then the squirt of a bottle was followed by the warm scent of sandalwood.

Declan released her waist, removing his touch for a bare moment, and then his hands were back. They sank into her hair, fingers massaging her scalp, and she moaned deep and long. His hands were gentle yet firm at the same time. When he reached the base of her skull, she dropped her head forward with a groan she felt all the way to her toes.

This time it was his breath that caught. He was the one who froze for a split second—just long enough to snare her attention. She focused on Declan, on the tenseness in his muscles and...

It wasn't just his muscles that'd grown hard. His stiff cock settled between her ass cheeks, nothing but soaked fabric separating their bodies. A jolt of unease snaked down her spine, the comfort she'd taken in his presence gone with the rise of his desire.

Abby stiffened and reached for the wall, intent on putting distance between them.

"Stop." His voice was firm but not harsh. A simple command he expected her to obey without question.

Abby was a questioning sort of girl. An accountant—auditor—had to be a person who always asked "what the hell?" "Declan, I appreciate what you've done." She ignored his snort. "But the dizziness is fading." She ignored the chuckle laced with disbelief. "I'm fine."

"Abby, here are a couple truths." One arm returned to her waist and the other hand nudged her shoulder, pushing her to stick her head back under the water. "Beautiful women make a man's dick hard. Period. Even stinking of fear, blood, and the ocean, you're a beautiful woman. You've got a body that makes men ache, *and* I'm holding you in my arms while you're all wet and naked."

She disagreed with his assessment of her beauty. She would have told him so if it weren't for the fact that the longer he talked, the rougher his voice grew. As if the wolf crept forward to override the man.

"So, yeah, you're gonna make me want, but that doesn't mean I'll take what's not freely given. I'm an asshole and a killer, but I don't hurt women."

She didn't struggle or argue when he helped her upright once more, and she *definitely* didn't whimper in disappointment when he removed his arm from around her waist. She didn't miss the feel of his callused palm on her skin *at all*. Or the heat of his palm, which felt more like a caress than firm support.

He remained a solid presence at her back as he shifted his weight and snatched something else—two somethings. In one hand he held a washcloth, a bar of soap in the other, and she grasped both. Which left him free to rest one hand on her hip while the other brushed her hair aside and bared her neck to him.

He lowered his head, lips grazing the shell of her ear while he whispered, "That doesn't mean I won't if they ask very, *very* nicely."

CHAPTER THIRTEEN

*I*f Abby shivered or moaned *one more time*, he wasn't sure he could control himself. Not that he'd pounce on her—he hadn't been lying when he said he didn't hurt women. He wasn't an adolescent kid who'd just discovered his cock. He was a hardened killer. A mercenary. A heartless bastard.

Not someone who should even think of caressing Abby, touching her until she came and screamed his name before sliding inside her wet heat.

Nope. Not him.

Which was why he steadied her and stepped back, letting her support herself. The moment she stood firm, he put even more distance between them. He left the shower, not trusting himself so close to her any longer, and sought towels in the linen closet. He grabbed a few white fluffy bath towels and snared the robe that hung on a hook just to the closet's left. He'd still need to get clothes for her, but the sooner she covered those curves, the better.

What the fuck was wrong with him? Lusting after some stranger...

But was she really? She knew nothing about him, sure, but he'd been watching her for days. He'd read her file and kept tabs on her even when she wasn't at FosCo.

He'd…creepily stalked her. He admitted the truth. Hell, he embraced it. There was just something about Abby Carter that grabbed his attention and wouldn't let go.

The water shut off, and he imagined beads of liquid clinging to Abby's skin, sliding down her curves. God help him, he was jealous of *water*.

"Declan?" Her soft voice reached out to him and he tensed, fighting the shudder that threatened. "Can I have a towel?"

He swallowed hard and opened his eyes. Abby moved, the subtle change of her position grabbing his attention, and he met her stare in the mirror. The frosted glass shielded most of her body, but he could still see the outline of her breasts, the dip of her waist and the flare of her hips.

He was going to hell, and Abby was sending him there.

"Yeah," he rasped. Or growled. A bit of both. The fucking wolf fought him with every breath, and it was determined to be present while in Abby's company.

He snatched the towel and turned to face her, forcing himself to keep his attention above her neck. If only he didn't think her eyes were gorgeous and her lips sexy as hell.

Declan only allowed himself to get within arm's reach, and he held the towel out to her, releasing it the moment he could. Then, like a coward, he retreated to the counter.

Because he didn't hurt women.

I sure as fuck seduce them, though. Can Abby be seduced?

He'd heard her moan, the hitch in her breath when she said his name…Yeah, she could be seduced. That didn't mean he should. Abby wasn't the kind of woman a man like him touched.

"I'm done. Are there any—"

This time he didn't even turn his head in her direction. He grabbed the robe and shoved it at her. "Put this on for now. I'll get you something else after I shower."

And it'd be a *cold* shower. He could let his fantasies run wild after she was safe. Then he'd think of her on her knees, his cock between those pink lips and—

"Thank you."

He rolled his shoulders and cracked his neck, moving uneasily while he tried to banish those thoughts. Now. Wasn't. The. Time.

"No problem," he grunted, and turned to face her, keeping his eyes on the shower as he took her place within the tiled area. "Just sit on the counter while I shower. I won't take long."

"I could go to the kitchen and—"

Declan froze in place. "No. You'll sit on the counter and wait." He tormented himself and glanced over his shoulder, gaze taking in her appearance in a single, sweeping look. She shouldn't look sexy in his oversized robe, but she did. "I can't keep you safe if you're not with me."

He returned his attention to the shower and focused on his next steps. Strip. Get clean. Dress so there was fucking clothing between him and Abby. Feed her. Sleep.

The wolf reminded him that he should sleep *with* her.

He shoved the animal away once more and worked on getting clean. He made sure the water was ice cold. His beast snarled at the frigid temperatures.

Then it suddenly decided frozen was okay because maybe Abby could warm them.

Horny little shit.

Declan took half as much time as Abby, efficiently ridding himself of sweat and grime before joining the little cougar. She handed him a towel, her gaze on his face and cheeks flushed pink. Then the tiniest slip of her feminine musk reached his nose, the scent of her attraction taunting his wolf.

"Like what you see, baby?" He tipped up the right side of his mouth in a smirk. Words and an expression meant to annoy her. If she was pissed, he couldn't seduce her. It was one more wall to put between them.

She pressed her lips together so tightly they formed a white slash beneath her nose and she wrenched her gaze from him to focus on the bedroom—bed—twenty feet away. He'd think she was pissed if he didn't notice the deepening of her blush and the increasing heaviness of her desire.

His cock stirred back to life and he swallowed his groan. Flirting needed to wait. "Let's get some food in you."

Declan strode past her and listened to make sure she followed. The patter of her small feet on the tile transitioned to soft padding when she moved to the carpet.

He paused beside the dresser to the right of the door just long enough to drop his towel and pull on a pair of cotton shorts. He didn't miss the small catch of her breath when the terry cloth thumped to the ground.

Shirtless, he strode through the home's main area and slowed, nudging her toward the couch.

"Go sit and rest. I'll whip up something real quick." He didn't know how to make too many things, but he could feed her.

"I thought we had to stay together." She gave a token protest, but swayed on her feet at the same time.

"I can see you from the kitchen." He nudged again. "Go."

She hesitated only a split second more before finally nodding and shuffling toward the seat. She flopped onto the worn leather and curled up into the bathrobe until all he saw was the top of Abby's head.

And those sand-hued eyes—cougar's eyes.

Declan's wolf pawed him, gently scraping his nerves to remind him that they had to feed the cougar. She'd been hurt and needed protein. Protein that only they could provide, so he needed to get his ass in gear.

He did. He turned away from Abby and strode into the kitchen. He focused on cooking—defrosting a steak in the microwave while he heated a pan so he could give it a nice sear. Shifters didn't like much more than a hint of char before they dug in, and right now he had to appeal to Abby's cougar. She needed the cat to heal her human body.

He split his attention between the stove and her unmoving form. He counted her breaths, watching as her chest rose and fell, and tried to forget what that robe hid from view.

He slipped her steak onto a plate and snared a knife and fork, quickly cutting the meat into bite-sized pieces. He snagged a bottle of water from the fridge—thankful he'd had the place stocked before the team had been dispatched to Port St. James—and went to Abby.

He placed the plate and bottle within reach on the coffee table and then knelt at her side. He took a moment to stare. Her dark lashes rested on her cheeks, the deep brown a stark contrast to her pale skin. Purple smudges marred the area beneath her eyes, proof of her exhaustion, and he hated that he had to wake her.

"Abby." He kept his voice low so he wouldn't startle her. She didn't stir. "Abby." He tried again, slightly louder. She frowned, a small crease forming between her eyebrows. He attempted to convince himself the move wasn't cute. Or sexy. *"Abby."*

Abby drew in a deep breath and released it with a low moan. Her eyelashes fluttered, gradually parting to reveal her cougar's eyes once more. Damn but he wanted her. "Declan?"

"You need to eat," he practically snarled at her, and he ignored her flinch. It wasn't her fault he had a hard time controlling his own body.

She drew in another deep breath, attention snapping from him to the plate on the nearby table. "Steak?"

He couldn't miss the yearning in her voice, and part of him was inordinately pleased that they were giving her something she wanted. Instead of answering her, he snared the plate and speared a hunk of meat. He held it carefully in front of her mouth and waited for her to take the bite.

And waited some more.

Feline eyes flicked from the meat to his face and back again, as if the cougar couldn't decide if she trusted him. *Finally,* the cat seemed to be showing some sense.

"I didn't save you to poison you, Abby." He moved closer and rubbed the steak over her lower lip. He brushed it back and forth, painting the plump bit of flesh with the meat. Her nostrils flared, and she took in a lungful of air. He knew what she scented—pure, unseasoned meat. Shifters didn't need—or want—a whole lot of seasoning. Or any seasoning, really.

Abby's tongue darted out and lapped at the bite, wiping away the pink juices that'd covered her lower lip. His cock surged with her action, hardening as if she'd licked *him* instead of a piece of beef.

When she did it again, her gaze never leaving his, he shuddered and pushed back the moan that threatened to break free. Her pupils dilated until the blackness swallowed nearly all her eye color. The musky scent of her desire tickled his nose, the aroma growing with each passing moment.

"You need to eat so you can heal." He added a growl to his voice, hoping to intimidate her at least a little. Instead, her gaze flared with a new wave of heat.

"I feel good." Dear God that sounded like a purr.

He shook his head and nudged her lips. "Open. I can't risk you not keeping up when it counts."

She didn't say anything else then. Simply parted her lips, and he placed the morsel in her mouth. She wrapped her lips around the fork tongs and slowly withdrew. The sensual slide of her lips over metal made him think of what else he could place in that perfect little mouth.

A shudder attempted to overtake him, but he pushed it back. Once again he reminded himself now wasn't the time *or* the place. Maybe once she was safe…

No.

He kept repeating that single word, making sure it echoed through his mind and slammed into his wolf with every beat of his heart. She wasn't for him.

She didn't say another word as he took care of feeding her. The quiet should have been strained, uncomfortable, or…something. But it wasn't.

He wondered if she'd hit her head and that was why she was so easygoing at the moment.

Declan placed the last bite in her mouth and then laid the empty plate and fork on the table along with a now half-empty water bottle. "Want me to cook another, or was that enough?"

"I'm full. It was delicious. Thank you." She had that sated, sleepy smile he'd seen on others in the past. The one that said she'd happily pass out once more if he let her.

Which he would. For self-preservation if nothing else.

"You're welcome." He was sure he was supposed to do something then, but Abby...

She licked her lips, and he swallowed his moan. "Thank you for everything else, too."

He hated the reminder of all the other bullshit they had to handle. "Don't thank me until you're safe."

"You mean *we're* safe."

He shot her a half grin. One he'd perfected over the years. A bit of patronizing with a dash of doubt. He'd never be safe, not truly. "Until we're safe."

She narrowed her eyes, the cougar and her human half peering at him. "Do you think you won't make it through this? That you'll..."

The scent of her worry overrode the delicious aroma of her arousal, and the wolf didn't like that *at all*.

"Sweetheart." He cupped one cheek, unable to keep his hands to himself. "You'll come out the other side of this whole. As for me, I wake up every day wondering if I'll make it past breakfast."

"But..." She shook her head. "You got me out of there, got us here like it was nothing."

"Training." He leaned over and pressed a soft kiss to her forehead before he moved away. "I've been destroying, hurting, and killing for a long time."

She snorted. "Long? You can't be that old."

Memories crept up on him, his past threatening to intrude on his present. He fought them off, but some things couldn't be banished entirely.

Declan placed the plate in the sink before he gave Abby his attention. "Baby"—he hated the way she flinched with that endearment, but it was another way for him to keep distance between them—"I was fifteen the first time I killed a man."

Abby pushed herself upright, opened her mouth and then snapped it closed. "I didn't realize SHOC recruited so young."

"They don't. I didn't join SHOC until..." His voice trailed off. Declan tilted back his head and stared at the ceiling with narrowed eyes. He tried to remember back to the first time he'd met Birch. He ran his hand along his jaw, the rough scrape of his shadow scratching his palm. "It's been about two years, now. They'd gotten word of my, uh, talents."

"You killed people," she whispered, and he didn't like the look in her eyes. Nothing good came from a woman with that sad, curious, and worried expression. Ever. "Why?"

He shook his head and got back to cleaning up after himself. Just because he'd left home at fifteen didn't mean he'd forgotten everything his mother taught him. "It was a job."

"A job? People hired you to..."

He placed the empty plate in the sink before turning to face her. He propped his hands on the counter and braced his weight on the polished stone. "People hired me to fix their problems. Permanently. Sometimes quickly and other times painfully, but it'd be done."

"And you got paid."

"Well. I got paid *well*." He didn't try to hide the pride in his voice. It'd been hard in the beginning, but he and Pike had figured things out eventually.

Abby shook her head, brow furrowed. "I don't understand. Today you rescued me."

"The wolf didn't give me a choice today, just like it didn't give me a choice when I was fifteen. It wanted, it took. A person, a life, it wants what it wants. When I worked freelance, it enjoyed the chase and the kill." He sighed and ran a hand through his short, dark locks. "I took advantage of that."

"What kind of people did you kill?" Why did she keep asking questions? Questions he wasn't sure he wanted to answer. The only positive note to her line of questioning was that it did a good job of squashing his arousal.

"The kind I was paid to kill," he drawled.

"Bad men? Good? Women? Kids?"

The wolf surged for an entirely different reason, the beast snapping and snarling at Abby's question. His eyesight flickered, colors dancing in and out of his vision while he stared at the woman huddled on the couch. His skin burned, the beast's fur attempting to burst free. His arms and hands ached, paws pushing to be freed.

"Never pups. *Never*."

"But what about their parents? Did you kill their parents?" Still Abby pushed. Still Abby taunted his wolf. He relished her voice, but not her words.

"Dammit, Abby." His gums burned, and he resisted the urge to bare his fangs at her. "I took the jobs. I took them, I eliminated the target, and I put money in my offshore accounts."

In *their* offshore accounts, but she didn't know about Pike. She wouldn't ever know about Pike as far as Declan was concerned. The less she knew about him—his life—the better.

With a shake of his head, he got back to kitchen cleanup. He'd make something for himself later. When Abby was sleeping and not badgering him with questions that made his stomach churn.

"How did you kill them?" Why couldn't she just stop pushing? *Why?*

"Does it really matter?" Because his mind didn't want to remember that part of his past.

"Yes." Of course it did. Of course it'd matter to her. Sweet, sinfully sexy Abby with a soft heart and gentle words for everyone.

He didn't turn back to her while he tried to figure out what to say. Then he wondered why he bothered. He'd given her brutal honesty up to that point. There was no reason to stop now. "It depended on what the job needed. Whether they wanted an accident or to send a message. Guns. Hands. Poison."

"Bombs?"

Declan pushed away from the counter and returned to her, his gaze on her eyes as he approached. Her eyes widened, pupils dilated, and her breath caught as she watched him move closer. Her lips parted, tongue darting out to wet them as if she prepared for his kiss, and then her natural scent teased his nose.

She didn't like him—what he did—but he knew she wanted him.

He didn't stop until his knees touched the couch and he leaned over her, one hand on the back while the other rested on the furniture's arm. He leaned down, closing the distance between their mouths until his lips nearly brushed hers. It'd be so easy to capture her lips with his own, to snatch a kiss and drug her with passion. So easy...

"I'm not a good man, Abby," he whispered, and she swallowed hard. "I killed because I'm a selfish asshole. I saved you for the same reason."

Liar. The wolf's growl consumed his mind, rolling over every other sound.

"You didn't answer my question."

"Which one?"

"Did you kill parents?" The question seemed torn from within her soul, and he hated the truth he'd have to give her. He knew her past—knew how she'd feel about his answer—and decided it was for the best. Pushing her away was a good idea.

Finally, Declan answered. "Yes."

CHAPTER FOURTEEN

*D*eclan's stark declaration sent Abby's mind tumbling into the past. To a time when she'd been a carefree child with a sassy cougar shifter mother and a grumbling werewolf father. They'd been a study in contrasts until their last breath. Her dad snarled at anyone who got too close to his family while her mother rolled her eyes and ignored his growling. A cat and a wolf who had so much love...

Was that why she was so drawn to Declan? Because he was a ferocious wolf who threatened her in one breath and then protected her in the next?

Abby wasn't sure. She also wasn't sure if she wanted to examine her feelings for the SHOC agent any further. He'd answered her questions, stabbing her in the heart with his truth, and there was nowhere for her to run. He was the embodiment of everything she despised, and she couldn't leave him.

Shifter Operations Command wanted her—alive, at least for a little while and then who knew. Unified Humanity wanted her—probably dead.

And Declan...what did he want?

Bile churned in her stomach, the scents of smoke and burned flesh searing her nose while the memories attempted to overtake her: their small family sitting down for dinner, her father carefully helping her mother into her chair. They'd tried to hide it, but Abby had already recognized the changes in her mother's scent. Abby was going to have a little brother or sister—wolf or cougar, she hadn't cared.

Then came a knock on the front door. Her mother's smile as she rose to go answer and her father's growl because he didn't want her doing anything but sitting. When Abby tried to follow them both, her dad told her to stay put. If Mom ignored Dad she got a glare that lasted two seconds before he sighed with frustration. If Abby ignored Dad she didn't get dessert for a *week*.

So she remained in her seat and waited for them to return because there was a chocolate cake on the counter in the kitchen.

She also ignored the manners her parents drilled into her. She was *supposed* to wait for everyone to be seated before eating. She figured that since they *had* been sitting together before her parents left it was okay to eat some macaroni and cheese.

Abby had a mouthful of mac and cheese when her mother's first cry reached her. She swallowed it right before her father's roar shook the house. Her feet had just touched the floor when his yell echoed off the walls.

"Run!"

Then a deafening boom. The crackle of fire. The suffocating smoke. The darkness of the hidden closet. It'd kept her safe—protected—while destruction consumed their small house.

Then it was done and she was alone.

Unified Humanity had rid the world of two shifters whose only crime was love and creating a family.

With a bomb.

"Do you want details?" Declan's question snapped her thoughts from the past. "I can—"

"No." She shook her head to make sure he understood. "You've said enough."

More than enough.

Declan pushed away from the couch and stepped back, his intense gaze a heavy weight on her shoulders. She looked anywhere but at him. The past still intruded, the events of those first few days after her parents' deaths fighting for release. Mourning. Healing. Being sent to a godmother—a total stranger and seal shifter.

"Then I'll get you some clothes and you can rest." He turned and moved to the bedroom.

The bed in there was so large and covered in pillows and blankets, tempting her to form a squishy nest just perfect for hiding—safe and warm.

Then Declan reappeared, standing in the doorway with his amber eyes locked on her. "I laid out clothes. They'll be big, but they'll cover you. Get changed and crawl into bed. I'll be there in a minute."

"We're sharing a bed?" Was that excitement or worry churning in her gut? Maybe a bit of both.

The color of his eyes deepened, looking more like his inner wolf. "I told you I'm not letting you out of my sight."

"But…" She licked her lips, mouth dry while her tumultuous emotions continued to beat at her. She didn't feel any hint of anticipation about sharing a bed with Declan. At All.

The cougar told her she was a big fat liar from Liarton smack-dab in the middle of the great state of Liar-isiana living on Lying Avenue.

"Remember what I said, Abby." Heat lingered in his gaze, and the spicy scent of desire drifted through the room.

He was hot as hell and he wanted her, but she *did* remember what he'd told her.

He would only take what was freely given, and even then, she'd have to ask very, *very* nicely. Abby wasn't ready to ask, so she kept her mouth shut and rose, padding toward Declan. He remained in place, amber eyes stroking her from head to toe like a physical caress, and she couldn't suppress the shudder that slid down her spine.

He didn't step aside when she reached him, not at first. He simply stared, feral eyes missing nothing. He took a deep breath, eyelids fluttering closed, and then released it just as slowly. A rumbling growl followed, but it didn't hold a hint of threat. No, it was a different kind of growl entirely.

A sexy one. One that made her nipples harder and her pussy grow heavy with a desperate ache. *Stupid wolf*, she mentally grumbled. What right did he have to be all sexy and hot and fuckable and *bad*?

Finally, Declan turned to the side to let her pass. Mostly. She had to wiggle past him, going into the room sideways, and...she sorta paused when she was halfway through. Mainly because their fronts brushed. Abby's nipples hardened further, her clit twitched, and a knee-weakening wave of desire rolled over her. And she wasn't the only one affected. Declan was just as aroused, his hard cock nudging her middle as she inched into the room.

The moment she got past him, she strode to the bed and snatched the clothes he'd left out. Clothes that still had that stiffness from being new and carried the chemical scent of its originating factory. There was something else, too. Just a hint of...Declan.

A baggy shirt and cotton pants waited for her—her bra and panties probably tossed in the bathroom garbage. Ugh, she was going to have slightly saggy, free-swinging boobs in front of God's gift to vaginas everywhere. *Gravity how I hate thee!*

She reached for the knot of her robe, fingers plucking at the tied fabric, and glanced over her shoulder at Declan. "Can I have a little privacy now?"

He snorted and crossed his arms, feet braced shoulder-width apart. Right. He wasn't leaving her. Why was she being all shy, anyway? She'd already been naked in front of him. What did it matter? Her cougar also reminded her she was a shifter. Nudity wasn't a thing to get bent out of shape about.

Then again, Abby wasn't getting bent out of shape. She was just thinking about her *actual* shape and the cellulite on her legs.

She huffed and focused on her next task. Declan's robe was big—oversized—and she kept it on while she dressed underneath. She tugged on the sweatpants. Bottom half covered, she let the robe fall from her shoulders while she reached for the shirt. She wiggled into the top, squirming as she tugged it over her head.

When she finally turned back to the big, bad, super-deadly wolf...all hints of teasing sensuality were gone.

"What happened?" Dark gray fur slipped from his pores, sliding down his arms in a river of near-black strands.

"Happened?" She frowned. "I..."

"Your back." He bit off the words, syllables muffled by the fangs now crowding his mouth.

"Oh." She grimaced. *My back.* She twisted her lips in a rueful smile. *"That."* She shook her head. "It was a long time ago."

"How long?"

Abby ran her palm down her face. "It doesn't matter."

"What happened?"

"It doesn't matter."

"Why didn't you heal properly?"

"It doesn't matter." Really, how long did it take a guy to get a clue?

"It does fucking matter!" The whole house shook with the strength of his yell, the ground trembling as the echoes filled the air. His face flushed red beneath the peppering of dark fur. His muscles tensed and veins bulged beneath his taut skin.

Okay, maybe it didn't matter to her—the cougar called her a liar—but it obviously bothered Declan. Since she really didn't feel like dealing with a feral wolf, she went to him, steps slow and careful. She moved as if she approached a natural predator—an animal rather than a shifter male. She reached for him, palm gently coming to rest on his bare chest.

Short strands of midnight fur tickled her fingertips, proof of his tenuous control of the animal inside him. "Declan," she murmured. "I'm fine."

"Who did it?" The words were a garbled mess, his inner wolf making it difficult for him to speak.

"Unified Humanity." That old pain struck her heart, but she pushed it back. "They blew up my home."

"Bombs." Hardly more than a mumble. A question and statement in one.

"Yes." She pushed the word past the strangling knot in her throat.

"Wanna see." The wolf still had control as he forced her to turn, amber eyes brighter than ever.

"Declan…"

He grunted and simply tugged on her shirt while he encouraged her to turn. He pulled it up to reveal her back. She sighed and helped, drawing it higher to show him everything. Claw-tipped fingers ghosted over her skin, the sharp tips teasing her scarred flesh while he explored her back.

He said nothing while he looked her over—traced each twisted knot with his fingertips. Then his touch disappeared, and she bit back the whimper that threatened to escape. She missed the feel of his skin on hers.

There was definitely something wrong with her. One hundred percent. She wondered if they made pills for Stockholm syndrome.

Moist, warm breath bathed her back, and Abby froze, not moving a muscle while Declan... His lips brushed her back, low and just above the edge of her sweatpants. It was the worst scar out of them all. Being confined in such a tight space while her cougar had fought to heal the damage had resulted in some ugly, twisted scar tissue.

He moved on, teasing another spot just above her hip on her left side. The kiss wasn't meant to incite passion. It was almost reverent.

The werewolf who proclaimed to be so deadly, dangerous, and unfeeling now gently touched her as if she'd shatter at any moment. Another kiss, this one to the right, a long, thick line that still gleamed shiny white even after so many years. He continued, and she closed her eyes, imagining more than six feet of violent male kneeling behind her—comforting her?

He didn't caress her. He kept his hands from her body, only his mouth learning the uneven plane of her back. Warm lips. Moist breath. The scent of the clean forest at dawn. It called to her cougar, luring it forward while lulling it into a restful calm.

His travels continued higher, not stopping until his lips finally rested at the base of her neck. She didn't have any scarring there—her cougar had been able to heal that part of her. But it was like he sensed the damage had extended beyond that twisted part of her.

Because it had.

Declan's careful handling brought tears to her eyes and she blinked them away, unwilling to break down. She hadn't cried when she'd been *shot*. She wasn't about to start now over mere memories.

Declan murmured against her unblemished skin. "I'll kill them."

Abby shook her head. "It was a long time ago. I don't even know who it was exactly. I just know it was them."

"I'm a very good hunter, sweetheart. Unified Humanity gave the order. I'll find the ones who carried it out." He still had his lips on her. As if he couldn't force himself away.

"It doesn't matter anymore."

"I can smell your pain." Now a growl traveled from Declan to her. It slithered down her spine, and she fought the oncoming tremble. "You're lying to yourself."

Abby chuckled and shook her head. "Maybe I am." She shrugged. "But we don't have time for me to burst into tears over something that happened when I was eight."

Eight years old and untouched by violence until that day.

He stood, his heat moving along her back as he changed position. He tugged her shirt back down, and then two thick arms wrapped around her. He cradled her in his strength, almost like a living, breathing wall of protection. "Why didn't your cougar heal everything properly?"

"Because after I was hurt, I hid like I'd been taught." She closed her eyes. Those stupid tears were really determined now. "I stayed curled up in a cupboard for two days. My cougar healed what it could as it could, but the position and tight quarters..."

Declan rested his cheek on top of her head. "Every time you healed, you'd twist and hurt yourself again."

Abby nodded. "And I was so weak that—"

"You were *eight*. The fact that you survived..." He sighed. "I'm going to find them."

"It doesn't—"

"It does," he snarled, but his hold remained soft and gentle. Then he withdrew, hands releasing her and arms slipping away while his warmth vanished. "Let's get you to bed."

"Yeah," she whispered, "okay." She took one step and then two, fighting her body to put distance between them. Her cougar wanted to turn and rub all over him, but... but her human mind needed space.

She crawled into bed, wiggling beneath the covers and claiming one of the pillows. On the other side, Declan did the same, settling into place with a deep sigh. Silence descended then, the sound of their breathing the only thing that broke the quiet.

Until Declan grunted and moved. In a whirl of sheets and flex of muscle Abby found herself plastered to his side. Their bodies aligned, her curves molding to his hard frame. His arms were like steel bands, hands putting her in place before he held her immobile. He pressed her ear to his chest, arm curled around her shoulders. He rubbed her shoulder, fingers dancing over her side. He traveled up and down the length of her back, shoulder to hip.

"I'm going to kill them, Abby."

Part of her wanted that. She wanted them hunted and punished for what they'd done to her life, but she didn't want that blood on her hands. "I know what you want to do, but—"

"*Will* do."

"But can you hurt them for doing the same thing you've done countless times?"

He flinched, just the tiniest twitch, before he answered. "One, I know how to count. It's not countless. Two"—he nudged her, forcing her to tip her head back and meet his stare—"never women. Never children. I told you that already. I'm not a good man, but I have limits." He lifted his free hand, callused fingertips tracing the slope of her nose, the curve of her jaw, and on to her lips. "I'll tell you something else. I haven't taken a contract in two years. Not since I joined Shifter Operations Command. I've done things I regret, but that isn't who I am anymore."

"Then who are you?"

"The wolf who isn't going to let anything—anyone—hurt you."

CHAPTER FIFTEEN

*D*eclan didn't sleep. The shit-storm had begun around eight thirty and now the clock was ticking past midnight. His mind remained alert, wolf constantly listening for intruders while his human thoughts focused on the woman in his arms—Abby.

Abby who'd been through hell—and not just what had occurred in the last few hours. Reading her file had given him bare-bones details. Seeing her back... It stabbed him with the truth and damned if it didn't *hurt*. What the fuck?

It explained her anger, though—the scent of her emotional agony that'd assaulted him with every question about his past.

He hadn't been lying when he'd assured her he didn't touch women and children. Not after what he'd seen.

Abby sighed in her sleep and rubbed her cheek on his chest. She nuzzled him, her lush body sliding against his, and he cursed the clothing that separated them. Oh, he knew it was necessary—her naked body was too damned tempting—but he hated its presence.

Damn, then she went and moaned and wiggled her hips and *like that* he was harder than nails. He rubbed his free hand over his face and pinched the bridge of his nose. She'd kill him if she kept it up. All those curves, her fresh scent and sweet little sounds.

His wolf nudged him, urging him to explore the pretty little cougar, but he shoved the animal away. They hadn't saved her to fuck her. They'd saved her...Shit, he wasn't sure why anymore. He only knew he'd been driven to shield her from harm and wouldn't let anything stand in his way.

Abby took a deep breath and released it with a soft sigh, but this time she didn't settle back into sleep. She moaned—she *really* needed to stop—and tensed.

"Declan?"

"Go back to sleep, Abby." His wolf lined each word with a growl.

She stiffened and edged away, as if she wanted to move out of his embrace. "Sorry. I didn't mean to crawl all over you. I..."

He tightened his hold, not letting her budge. She drove him crazy with her closeness, but he couldn't let her go. "Don't be sorry." He wasn't gonna tell her how much he liked having her in his arms. "Just sleep. You can rest for a while yet. We won't leave until tonight."

"How long have we been here?" she whispered, and even that aroused him.

He was such a twisted fuck. "Not too long. Not long enough."

She fell silent for a moment, but he knew it wouldn't last. He could practically hear her thinking. "What happens next?"

Declan grunted. "You're not going back to sleep, are you?" Abby shook her head, and he figured he'd have to content himself with the short time he'd held her. "Eat. Coffee. Plan our next move." Then the one after that and then the one after that. So much bullshit. He turned his gaze to her and tried to ignore her sleep-tousled hair and bedroom eyes. "You don't deserve this. Any of it."

"It's my own fault in a way." She grinned, even though she didn't have much to smile about. "Curiosity killed the cat, right? I'm too curious for my own good. I found a loose thread and pulled. When it all unraveled..."

"Curiosity isn't killing this cat. You're not gonna die." He snarled.

"You can't guarantee that."

"The fuck I can't." His pulse increased, the wolf's anger surging with the mere thought of something happening to Abby. "I didn't turn rogue just to lose you. It won't happen."

"Taking me out of there branded you a rogue?" She shuddered.

"According to SHOC—the director." He shrugged. The director was an asshole. "I'd do it again though."

"Why? I'm nobody."

He snorted. "You're Abby Carter. Survivor. Smart as hell. Hard worker. Determined. Stupid because you jumped off that pier." He pressed his lips to her temple, reminding himself that she'd lived through that dumb stunt. "*Brave* because you jumped off that pier."

"I don't feel very brave."

He shook his head. "I've met cowards." Killed more than a few. "You're not one."

"I ran."

"After you knocked one of the humans out with a calculator." He grinned. She'd been a fierce little she-cat. "Then you grabbed that tablet and bolted. You gonna tell me what's on there now? Maybe where it's hidden?"

She tensed, and he wondered if she'd trust him enough to tell him. He could guess, but he'd rather get the truth from her.

"I was auditing FosCo." She turned in his embrace, moving to her stomach and propping herself on her elbows. "I logged into one of their bank accounts and discovered they're funding Unified Humanity."

"That's why Eric Foster showed up with those other men." She nodded even though he hadn't asked a question.

"I didn't realize he got notifications when certain accounts were accessed. I don't know how he knew I was a shifter, but he did. He said it took only one phone call." A tremble shook her. "Before he got there, I downloaded every screenshot and record I could find. I figured I'd hand it over to the council. Let them see if they could piece things together and find anyone else—any other companies—that are connected to Unified Humanity."

"See?" He grinned and twined an errant lock of her hair around one finger. "I told you. Brave."

She rolled her eyes. "We'll agree to disagree."

"Uh-huh." He tucked the strands behind her ear.

"How did you know I needed help?"

Declan winced. "The team's on assignment. We were ordered to observe and see if there was any connection between FosCo and Unified Humanity."

"There is. I have the proof."

"And we have audio recordings and video of Eric's attack." He paused and figured he'd tell her the rest. "We've been watching the building for almost a week. Twenty-four hours a day."

Abby groaned and turned her head, hiding her face against his biceps. Her cheeks heated, her warmth transferring to his arm. "Oh God. You saw me..."

Declan chuckled, recalling the sway of her hips and her little shimmy. "Yeah, we did. I watched you shake your ass every night. I watched you work all day, too."

"That's a little creepy."

He just shrugged. Probably. "You should get some more sleep if you can. I'm not sure how much you'll get over the next few days. With luck, we can get your tablet and wrap this up quickly, but I doubt it."

She shook her head. "I can't sleep anymore."

Which meant he had to let her go. His wolf whined and grumbled, not wanting to release her just yet. He reminded the animal she'd probably think that was creepy, too. The animal reminded *him* that creepy or not, she'd still be in their arms.

Ignoring the beast, he lifted the blankets and rolled away from Abby before the wolf won their battle of wills. "Let's get up, then. The quicker we get this done, the quicker you can go back to your life." He didn't look at her as he strode to the bathroom. If he did, he'd pounce. "Give me a second and then the room's all yours."

"I thought you weren't going to let me out of your sight?"

Yeah, that was what he'd said. But that was before she'd slept in his arms and been all sensual and sweet as she woke.

He paused in the doorway, one foot on the cold tile. The chill chased away some of his need for her, but not nearly enough. "I'll just be gathering supplies in the living room."

It'd let him put space between them—physical, but more importantly, emotional.

He was in and out of the bathroom in moments, striding across the bedroom and out the door without a word. His wolf remained focused on Abby—the sounds of her moving around his home—while his human half moved on autopilot. He had preparations to make, supplies to gather.

Declan strode to the entertainment center and tapped

on drawers and doors. They opened on silent hinges and quiet drawer rails. Overhead lights illuminated each tray, the light glinting off his babies. Hand guns. Rifles. Knives.

He ran his fingers over the array of deadly metal, stopping when he reached a nine-millimeter handgun. He wrapped his fingers around the grip and lifted it from the tray, adjusting to the weight. He released the magazine and counted the bullets before he pushed it back into place.

The soft rustle of clothes drew his attention, and he looked to his right. Abby stood nearby, gaze trained on his hands—the gun—before she turned her stare to the others, and he couldn't miss the question in those eyes.

How many people had he killed with these guns?

"None." He didn't look at her, choosing instead to concentrate on his task. He returned the nine-millimeter to its home and moved on to the next handgun. "I haven't killed anyone with these. Practice only so I knew how they shoot, but that's it."

"How...?"

Abby's voice stroked him, and his body reacted. A reminder that he needed to put space between them.

Declan smirked. "Baby," he murmured. Condescending. Cocky. Asshole. "You wanna talk about my longest shot or how hard I can make you come?"

"Neither." She licked her lips, wetting her mouth. "What's the plan today?"

"Coward." He sniggered.

And I'm an asshole.

"Are we taking all of those with us? Do we need them all?"

"Tell me something." He turned his head and met Abby's stare. She kept her mouth shut and raised her eyebrows in question. "After having guns pointed at you, getting shot, jumping off a pier to hide something in the fuck-ing sea so it won't be found, and being picked up by SHOC. When I get your ass outta there, the rest of my team is drooling over the idea of catching you and you know we're still being hunted. Now, all that"—he whirled his finger in the air—"and you ask me if we need all these guns?"

Abby's eye flashed, cougar now staring out. "Fuck you very much."

He grinned. Damn but he liked that fire. "Well, baby, if you want it that bad—"

"Enough." She snarled at him, even going so far as to bare a fang at him. "You're having a lot of fun at my ex-pense. It was a stupid question—I get it—but you don't have to be an asshole just because you have one."

"You're gonna be okay." Declan released a low chuckle. "If I can keep you alive." He sighed. "Speaking of… You're going to walk me through what happened—what you did—again. You're not gonna stop until I'm ready to slit your throat if I hear your voice again and then you'll say it once more."

Abby jerked back, his words piercing her as if they were bullets—sharp, hard, unavoidable. "Okay."

He huffed and ran a hand through his hair. "Sorry. Just tired." He pinched the bridge of his nose, eyes closed. "'Knowledge is Power' isn't some motivational poster. It's the truth. In my line of work, knowledge is life. I've known a lot of people who died because of ignorance. Not gonna have you be one of 'em."

CHAPTER SIXTEEN

*A*bby blindly stared out at Declan's backyard—one he'd turned into a lush oasis. Also known as a space with enough trees and foliage to make the area as private as possible without turning into a wild jungle. Because a wild jungle would result in notices from the HOA. Abby knew all about HOA notices, though hers were usually noise complaints because *someone's* cat liked snarling at seagulls at two in the morning.

And the cougar never apologized. *Never*.

New sounds within the home drew her attention. Ones that were different from the click and clack of Declan's fingers on a keyboard or the scrape of metal as he disassembled and reassembled one of his guns *again*. She'd been listening to that for what seemed like forever while he made sure they had what they needed to survive.

Knowledge was power, all right. But guns were power, too.

The slam of wood on wood—cupboard banging closed—was followed by the gurgle of running water. Then glass clicking against...stone? Declan was in the kitchen, then. She wondered how long it'd take him to hunt her down again. It'd been a while since that steak, and her stomach grumbled—empty.

With a sigh, Abby turned on the window seat and swung her legs over the edge. She straightened her back and tilted her head from side to side, then twisted at the waist and stretched her arms over her head. No tenderness or pain that would slow her down. Every hint of her wounds and exhaustion now gone after some good sleep and food.

The cougar purred, and Abby mentally stroked her inner feline, praising the she-cat for a healing job well done. It spun and flicked its tail, a hint of cockiness easing through her mind. Yeah, the cat had done good, but could it get her through what was to come?

The beast sniffed and then hissed, offended that Abby even had to ask. She ignored her inner animal and pushed to her feet, taking a moment for one last stretch before she sought out Declan with her gaze.

Declan...She practically purred his name. Muscular. Sexy. Tempting. Declan.

Declan who wasn't in sight. He'd claimed he wouldn't let her leave him, but maybe it was okay if he was doing the leaving?

She padded across the floor—away from the window seat tucked into the dining area—and toward the center of the great room. Her feet sank into soft carpet. It was a sumptuous temptation her cat had difficulty resisting. It wanted to shift and roll around on the cushioned surface, coat it in her scent so other females would know Declan was taken.

Abby thumped the cat on its nose. *No time*. Plus, he wasn't taken.

The animal disagreed. It definitely wanted to *take* Declan.

"Hungry?" Declan spoke from her right, and she drifted in that direction. He stood on the other side of the bar, empty glass resting on the counter. "You need to keep up your strength before we play the rest of this game."

"Yeah. I could eat." She nodded and headed in his direction. "But you don't have to make me anything. I can..." Amber eyes met hers, the wolf giving her a glare that had her voice trailing off. "Or not."

Declan grunted and pushed away from the counter, his movements fluid and easy. A grace she normally attributed to a cat, but he was all wolf. All dominance, aggression, and possessiveness.

Well, if he wasn't going to let her cook for herself, she could at least enjoy the view. His worn jeans—frayed at the hems and other areas whitened—hung low enough to expose the V on his hips. She let her gaze wander over his chest, caress each of those thickly carved muscles and honed body with her eyes. His stomach was flat, ridges of his abs exposed and begging for her touch—her mouth? She let her attention drift farther up his body, to his strong pecs and broad shoulders. Then to his thick biceps. Arms that had cradled her close when he'd rescued her.

He put on a show just for her. There was nothing sexier than a man—half naked and sexy as hell—in the kitchen. He opened an upper cabinet and grabbed a pan, stretching to reach the handle. The move made his jeans drop just a hint, exposing more of those muscles she wanted to lick and nibble.

Her center clenched, clit throbbing with a surge of desire, and she bit her lip to keep her whimper in check. Then...then he made it so much worse—better? He set the pan on the stove and went to the fridge, tugging on the door so it swung open. It gave her a clear view of his back, of the play of muscles while he moved, the way they slid beneath his skin. That was when he made it all worse. He leaned down to peer into the space, attention firmly on the fridge's interior.

Meanwhile, her attention was firmly on his ass. She wanted to bite and nibble him there, too. Okay, she wanted him everywhere, all of him. Oh, she wouldn't destroy herself in that way—Declan was dangerous, heartless—but that didn't mean she couldn't ogle. A lot.

"You done staring yet?" Laughter tinged his words, and she wrenched her attention from his ass. He remained bent over and peeked at her from beneath his arm. She met his teasing gaze for a split second, his twitching lips enough to make her face flush, and then shot her stare to the ground. "Or should I go ahead and strip for you?"

"I don't know what you're talking about," she mumbled.

"Liar." His chuckle turned deep and dark, like smooth chocolate that lured her forward a step before she realized she'd moved. He straightened and turned away from the fridge, nudging the door closed with his foot.

His bare foot.

Could feet be sexy?

Abby's cougar purred. Apparently.

"Come eat." He placed a carton of eggs and a bag of shredded cheese on the counter.

"You keep trying to feed me." She steeled herself for the impending encounter, prepared herself for being so close to Declan without touching him.

"Because you need to eat." He didn't give her a spare glance, just cracked an egg on the edge of the pan, a nice sizzle following the move. He tossed the empty shell in the sink and then focused on her, blue eyes intent. "We need to be ready for what's coming."

"Coming?" Her heartbeat stuttered, and fear threatened to take over.

Declan's eyes bled amber for a moment, flickering between man and wolf, and he refocused on the stove. "A team is hunting you on behalf of the director." He flipped the egg and then waved the spatula toward the corner—his computer system. "They've already hacked the traffic cams, and I have no doubt they're routing everything through facial recognition."

"I don't know what that means." Or rather, she didn't *want* to know.

He was quiet then, attention wholly on the frying pan, as if his cooking decided the fate of the world. The longer he ignored her, the more nervous she became, until she simply couldn't take it anymore.

"Declan?" He didn't make a sound, just flipped the second egg onto the plate and slid it across the counter. Declan was fast, but so was she, thanks to her cat. She reached for him, fingers wrapped around his wrist before he could fully retreat. "Declan, what does that mean?"

He stared at her hand, eyes no longer holding even a hint of his human half—the wolf was in residence. "The director wants you—what you know. Badly. Which means that team wants you even more." He turned his wrist, shifting position until he held her hand in his. And he was so gentle, so careful with her. "Bad enough to do what it takes to get it."

"Would it be wrong to give—"

"Sweetheart," he murmured, blue eyes black and staring deep into her soul. "Shifter Operations Command is a pretty name for men who do bad things. You can't imagine that the director is better than any of his agents. Regardless, Birch is feeling twitchy, and that's never a good thing. Until we know more, you're with me. Once we're holding all the cards, we'll figure out our play. For now it's just us." He pointed at the plate with his free hand. "Eat."

Abby squeezed her thighs together, core tightening and aching with a jolt of desire. He'd aroused her with a single word and a dark look, and she called herself an idiot for getting hot and bothered over the wolf because he'd told her to *eat*.

There was something very, very wrong with her. Very.

She fed herself with her free hand, the other captive in Declan's gentle grip. He traced her wrist with his thumb. So calm, so gentle. The assassin who touched her as if she'd shatter at any moment.

Maybe she would because that thought was enough of a reminder for her. Declan wasn't simply a man seducing a woman. He was a killer—cold and merciless.

She tried to withdraw from his hold, but he merely tightened his grip, keeping her captive. "You didn't tell me why."

Declan increased the pressure of his thumb on her wrist. "Your heart's racing."

"Tell me what's going on."

"Is it racing because you want me, baby?" His deep voice was a seductive caress until he got to *baby*. That was enough to drown her desire.

Abby whipped her head up, eyes snapping open, and she glared at him. "No," she snapped. "It's racing because an asshole won't let me go and won't tell me what the hell is going on."

The corner of his mouth curled up in a seductive smirk. "You keep lying to yourself if you want, but, baby"—she internally flinched—"I can smell your need. I can practically taste it on my tongue. I may be an asshole, but you like it."

She did like it, but she wasn't going to say the words aloud. "Tell me."

"You want the truth." He shook his head. "That's what you'll get."

Declan released her, and she snatched her hand from his, rubbing her wrist and trying to wash away the feel of his skin on hers.

"You need to eat because everything up to this moment has been a cakewalk and you're gonna need all the strength you can get just to survive what's coming."

CHAPTER SEVENTEEN

*T*he beast scraped Declan from the inside out, determined to gain its freedom so it could soothe the damage he'd done. But he didn't want the wolf smoothing things over. He—they—needed the distance. The thing inside him, his feral half, had one too many long-term ideas about Abby. It didn't care that Declan wasn't a long-term guy. He was the go-to guy if a woman needed an itch scratched and didn't care if he'd blown up a yacht five minutes before he walked through her door.

Abby would care. A lot.

"What do you mean? What's coming?"

Sweet naive Abby with her pale sparkling blue eyes and golden hair. God, he wanted to taste her. Wanted to take her and keep her safe from all the bullshit that was about to go down.

"Gimme this." He pulled her plate away and placed it in the sink. "We can go over to the desk."

He pretended his dick wasn't rock hard and he rounded the counter. Not looking at her, he strode to the computer station, intent on getting the dangerous explanation done and over with before he did something stupid. Like bend her over the couch and...

And she wasn't following. He paused and turned back to her. "Abby?"

Her face flushed red, all pink and sexy, and his cock throbbed. Hell, it'd been hard from the moment he'd first heard her wake. He needed to get rid of her and get into some other woman's bed. Soon. Before the wolf convinced him to take her.

Abby's attention drifted down his body, and he had to admit he was fucking pleased that she liked what she saw. She licked those plump lips, her breathing speeding up while the delicious scent of her arousal filled the air.

"Still don't want me, baby?" He smirked because it pissed her off. Called her *baby* for the same reason. It was fun, ruffling her fur and being the recipient of fiery glares.

"No," she snapped, but her darkening blush told him she lied. Eh, he'd let her keep lying to herself. It'd make his life easier when it was time to walk away. If she kept giving him those "fuck me" looks, he was bound to have her. The only question was whether it'd be hard and fast or gentle and slow.

"All right, then." He returned to his path, not stopping until he got to his desk. Entering his password took less than two seconds and then they were in his system.

"These guys"—he waved his hand toward the left screen—"are the team hunting you. Decent enough. Not as seasoned as my own, but they do what they're told for the 'greater good' or some shit." He flicked her a glance and caught her confused expression. "They joined SHOC voluntarily."

"You didn't?"

He had to open his fucking mouth, didn't he?

"Let's say that I was *encouraged* to put my skills to use in an alternative capacity."

Abby grinned and he sure as hell wasn't pleased about it. "Really? Kill the wrong guy?"

Declan shrugged. "*Didn't* kill the guy."

At least, that was what'd originally put him on the council's radar. Then he'd gotten out of the game and Birch showed up and... Two years of bullshit he didn't like thinking about.

"Most teams are made up of men who've found that SHOC is a nice alternative."

"To what?"

"Death," he drawled. "We do the dirty work that needs to be done. SHOC has an accord with the council that gives us diplomatic immunity when it comes to freelance work." He shrugged. "We can't turn into serial killers or start slaughtering humans left and right, but we don't have to keep looking over our shoulders when we take on a little action on the side."

She swallowed hard, and he could practically read her thoughts. She wanted to know about his past—whom he'd killed—but on the other hand, she didn't. "And that team?"

"Like I said, they're puppies. Their team is made up of ex-Trackers turned agents who were born and bred to appease their superiors. That used to be the council." He glared at the screen displaying the team moving around their safe house. "They just want to please the director. No matter the cost."

"I'm a shifter," she said. "Isn't SHOC supposed to help and protect...?"

Declan pitied her. He really did.

"Sweetheart," he murmured, liking the way the endearment rolled off his tongue a little too much. He reached for her hand, and when she didn't pull away, he tugged her all the way onto his lap—one arm around her waist and the other still holding that delicate hand. He liked having her close, touching her and holding her. He'd hate himself for it later, hate himself for staining her with the darkness that clung to his skin. For now he'd enjoy her nearness.

"We're not dealing with the council here. The SHOC director is a lot like the rest of my team—dirty and not giving a damn about anything but completing a job."

Her lower lip trembled, and he felt like the asshole who told a bunch of kids that Santa wasn't real. "But we could call the council, right? They could..."

"When it comes to intense shit like this? I don't trust anyone."

"Not even your team?"

Declan's wolf sneered at him, the animal's general "you're an idiot" attitude more than clear. "I would trust my team," he allowed slowly. "But I won't call them in for this. Not when it means going against SHOC. I don't want them to be branded rogue for something I did alone."

He leaned forward and tapped a few keys, then grabbed his mouse, sliding the cursor from screen to screen.

Declan clicked another corner of the screen, bringing it into focus. "The team tasked with retrieving you are into traffic cams and some of the big-boy security systems for the buildings surrounding your home."

Abby jolted, and he stroked her back, palm sliding up and down her spine. "They'd know if we were coming."

"Yes." No sense in lying. He gestured at a different set of images. "On this side is Eric Foster—FosCo—and by extension, Unified Humanity. His guys tapped in, too, but their tech is slower. As soon as we pass a traffic cam, we'll end up with SHOC on us before UH gets their thumbs out of their asses."

"You hacked into UH *and* SHOC? How?"

Declan snorted. "Baby"—he hated the way she flinched, but it was for the best. She was sweetness and light and he...wasn't—"I didn't live this long by being stupid. My eyes are everywhere."

He pulled up footage from the previous night, the recordings he'd pieced together to make a mini-movie of her dash to freedom. It showed Abby racing away from FosCo right until she reached the edge of the pier. He paused the recording there—an ethereal image of her standing on the precipice and prepared to jump.

"I *don't* have eyes in the ocean. Where did you hide the tablet?"

Abby hesitated, lower lip caught between her teeth and indecision plain on her face.

He squeezed her hip. "I can't protect you if you don't give me a little trust."

Abby sighed, and her shoulders slumped. "Can you pull up a map of the coast? There's a little island—Palm Island."

"You hid the tablet on an island?" He raised a single brow. "You *swam* to an island, hid the tablet, and then swam to shore? That's some stamina."

Stamina he wouldn't mind enjoying. How long could they fuck before she got tired?

"*After* I got shot."

"Yeah, I remember." Hated that he remembered, but he did. "So we'll have to steal a boat." He brought up the map she'd requested and scanned the coastal marinas. "How long will it take you to find the tablet once we hit the island?"

"Not long. I know exactly where I left it."

"Five minutes? Fifteen? I need numbers, ba—" He snapped his mouth closed and tried again. "I can't plan without numbers."

"Five, then." She jerked her head in a stiff nod. "I can get it in five."

"Good. The less time we're exposed, the lower the risk."

"I don't want you hurt because of me, Declan. You can hand me over to the director."

"No, I really can't." Because fuck all, it would be a lot easier to wash his hands of everything. Except...except something deep twisted at the mere idea of letting her get more than ten feet from him.

She didn't say anything for a moment, and he waited, tensed and ready to snap at her if she started in with that "hand me over" bullshit again.

"Okay," she whispered. "We'll avoid SHOC and UH, but what about your own team? Where are they?"

Declan shook his head, hating the answer. "I have no idea, but we'll worry about that later."

For now they were going over the plan. And once this shit was sorted, he was gone. She'd go back to her number-crunching life and he'd...force himself to be anywhere but with her.

CHAPTER EIGHTEEN

COLE

*C*ole figured he should probably listen to Director Quade's bitching. *Should*, but wasn't. It was one of those "same shit, different day" things. It all boiled down to the same message: the team fucked up, so they'd better fix it, dammit. They might.

And then they might not.

It depended on whether he—*they*—felt like it. Right then Cole was trying to juggle six balls of C-4 while sitting in a chair balanced on two legs. His record was five.

"One girl. How fucking hard is it to hold on to one fucking girl?" The head of SHOC snarled—his inner snake baring its poisonous fangs. Yeah, the director of Shifter Operations Command was a snake. Literally.

Waves of the man's fury darted through the room. The asshole who was *supposed* to have gone to the southern field office had decided to head on over and supervise Abby's retrieval instead. Lucky them.

"Apparently," Cole drawled, and slowly turned his attention to the raging bear, focus split between the C-4 and the director, "very."

The snake shifter's gaze seared him, but Cole couldn't find an ounce of fear. His tiger obeyed orders by choice, not some knee-knocking terror. Right now it wanted to *choose* to lift his tail and spray the asshole with piss for shits and giggles.

"You." The director pointed and glared at Cole.

Cole lifted one corner of his mouth in a smirk. "Me."

"You knew about this." He stomped closer to Cole. "He's your partner, and you—"

The nearer Director Quade drew, the more agitated his tiger became. The striped cat rose within Cole's mind with a low, rumbling snarl. He caught each tumbling ball of C-4 in his hands, one after another until he held all six.

"*I* have a name." He adjusted his weight, and the other two legs of the chair *thump*ed to the ground. "*I* am part of a team." He placed the balls on the table that separated him from the director. "*I* don't like your fucking tone."

Quade leaned across the table, midnight eyes boring into his own. The bastard's snake was on the rise, and Cole let his own beast edge closer.

"You joined SHOC and agreed to do as ordered." The deadly black mamba curled his lip. "You were *ordered* to secure the prisoner and turn her over so she could be interrogated."

"Interrogated?" Ethan came into the room, the lion's walk smooth and slow, as if he were relaxed, but Cole knew better. The lion shifter hated Quade just as much as anyone. "I was under the impression you had a few questions for her. A couple of finer points to discuss before you patted her on the head and sent her on her way."

The director spun. "What I do with a prisoner—"

"Aw, she's a prisoner?" Grant whined around a mouthful of sandwich. His boots thumped heavily on the thin carpet. "When did that happen?"

"After your communications *mysteriously*"—the director's heavy glare landed on Grant—"went down."

"I know, right?" Grant's eyes were wide. "What's up with that?" He shook his head and took another bite of his sub. "Funny how shit randomly breaks. Know what I mean?"

Cole snorted and rolled his eyes.

"You, Mr. Shaw"—the director's midnight eyes narrowed on Grant—"were hired—"

"Drafted," Cole coughed, but the director ignored him.

"For a specific purpose." Quade continued as if Cole hadn't interrupted. "If you cannot meet the requirements of your job, you will find yourself in a council prison."

Ethan strolled deeper into the room, eyes on his cell phone until he came to a stop at Cole's side. He tucked his phone away and crossed his arms over his chest. "Then the council will find its newest prisoner missing within twenty-four hours of him walking through the front door." The lion tipped his head to the side. "Or did you forget who I am?"

Ethan wasn't just a pretty boy with pretty cars. He was a ghost—in and out of any situation before anyone registered his presence.

Grant joined them as well, hopping onto the table, legs swinging.

"I want her." The snake followed the words with a long hiss.

Cole tipped his head to the side. "How's it feel to want?"

"You will locate and secure her." The threat was obvious in Director Quade's voice.

"Or what?" Cole growled. His tiger didn't take threats

well. "Why do you have such a hard-on for her?" He crossed his arms over his chest and matched Ethan's stance. "She's cute, sure, but what about her had you hauling ass and stumbling into the middle of our op?"

"She might have information on Unified Humanity. She could be an excellent source."

"I think he saw a video of Abby shaking her ass and wants to tap that," Grant murmured not so quietly.

Cole reached over and whacked the wolf in the head. "Shut the fuck up."

"I'd tap that." The wolf shrugged and then shook his shoulders. "She did that little shimmy when—"

"I will drop you where you stand if you keep talking." He pointed a claw-tipped finger at Grant.

Grant just took another bite of his sandwich and spoke around the mouthful. "I'm sitting."

Cole ignored the wolf. Declan could kick Grant's ass for being disrespectful of Abby when they finally found the fucker. Instead, he spoke to Ethan. "Ethan, tell me something. You've been with SHOC for a while, right?"

"Going on ten years," Ethan said, and then grinned wide, exposing his elongated fangs. "They said I was a troubled teen. I like to think of myself as a prodigy."

"You jacking cars is a thing of beauty. And your driving? *God damn.*" Cole nodded, and he could practically see the steam coming out of the director's ears. "But when was the last time the director of Shifter Operations Command entered the field to apprehend an everyday shifter?"

Ethan grunted. "Never."

"Huh. Makes you wonder what his game is."

"This is insubordination." The director truly did hiss then. "Abby Carter is—"

"A nobody accountant who was in the wrong place at

the wrong time." Birch strolled in, limbs loose and relaxed. At least that was how he appeared to the casual observer— to the people who didn't know the grizzly better. The team alpha didn't stop until he stood between the team and the director. "Nothing more. Nothing less."

"An accountant that your weapons specialist decided to kidnap for no reason?" Quade's voice was deceptively calm. Cole saw the menace in his eyes.

"You saw her ass. He *definitely* had a reason," Grant said, and Cole resisted the urge to whack the werewolf again.

The director was quiet for a moment and then two. "I expect all of you to stand aside for the secondary team. If you impede this search, I will see all of you in a council prison."

Quade didn't say anything after that. He spun on his heel and stomped from the room, leaving the stench of fury in his wake.

But Cole wondered if he caught the slightest touch of fear. His tiger liked to think so, but Cole wasn't sure. Now he understood why Birch was twitchy about the director's behavior. Quade had been too enraged, too determined to have Abby.

The moment Quade disappeared, their tight cluster relaxed. Ethan retreated to lean against the wall. The lion hated leaving his back vulnerable. Birch took his normal position at the front of the room—facing their band of psychotic mongrels. Cole flopped into his seat and tipped his chair back until he balanced on two legs once more.

Quiet reigned for a little while, each of them focused on their own bullshit, and finally Cole decided to get the conversation going. "Anyone wanna address the missing werewolf in the room?"

Ethan grunted, gaze on his cell phone. The lion was

obsessed with some crop-growing, money-sucking game. Grant echoed the sound, his mouth full.

And Birch...He got a text message. A low *ding* shot through the room and drew their attention. Birch didn't give his cell phone number out, which meant he sure as hell didn't get text messages. Except, apparently, he did.

"Ooh, Birch has a girlfriend..." Grant singsonged, then chuckled.

Cole just shook his head. "Birch is gonna rip your head off your neck if you make fun of his girlfriend."

"Children. You're all fucking children." Birch rolled his eyes and tapped on his phone's screen.

"Yo, Grant." Ethan looked up from his game. "How come you didn't know Birch had a girl? You can't find Declan or his kitty. Now you didn't know about Birch's piece on the side. What the fuck good are you?"

"Asshole." Grant put his sandwich aside, which meant the wolf was *pissed*. "I wasn't the one who let Declan wander off with my untagged car."

Cole grinned. It was always fun to watch the puppy and kitty go at it, and he had a front-row seat.

Until Birch sighed and stomped between the two men. "Can we *not*?" The team alpha pushed against Ethan's chest and then Grant's. "We got shit to do. Like find Declan."

"Grant tried. He failed," Cole called out, all helpful and shit.

Birch's phone *ding*ed again, but the bear's dark gaze didn't turn to the device. It settled heavily on Cole. "Fortunately, I have my own resources."

CHAPTER NINETEEN

*W*atching Declan pack supplies, his mood darkening with his every movement, Abby decided their plan was bad. Perhaps the worst plan ever known to plandom.

A *better* plan was to remain in Declan's hidey-hole and come up with a new one. One that didn't involve leaving said hidey-hole.

Ever.

Not because she wanted to be locked up with Declan—that'd just be a bonus—but because she was pretty done with risking her life.

"Abby?" His voice wasn't loud, but she felt it all the way to her toes. It danced along her nerves and plucked each one, making her even more aware of Declan as a man—as a prospective *something*.

The cougar thought that *something* might start with the letter "m" and possibly end with "ate." The cat didn't care about his past.

"You ready?" His steps were silent, but she could almost *feel* him moving, sense when he drew closer. Then he stood in front of her, six feet of muscular male dressed in black from head to toe. Dark. Foreboding. Dangerous. Deadly. She had to remember he was very, very deadly.

"Yeah. Sorry I didn't answer right away. I'm ready."

"Something wrong?" He stepped closer, his large presence overwhelming her. He drew even nearer and lifted his hands, cupping her cheeks in his scarred palms. Amber eyes stared into hers, searching her gaze for something. What?

"I'd tell you we can wait," he murmured.

"But we can't." Abby pulled away and turned her attention to finishing her preparations. She snatched the jacket he'd given her and kept her gaze down while she tugged on the black coat. "It's fine." She straightened the fabric, smoothing out the wrinkles. She did anything to avoid looking at him. Anything to avoid getting caught by his intense gaze once more. "I'm ready. Let's go."

Declan tilted his head to the side, eyes narrowed, and she forced herself to remain immobile. She wasn't going to squirm beneath his gaze. She wasn't going to give him any other hint of emotion.

He grunted and stepped back. "All right, then." He turned and strode back the way he'd come, his long strides putting space between them, and she did her best to keep up. "Let's do this."

Declan didn't stop until he'd reached the home's exit, two duffels bracketing the hallway while a gun rested on a nearby end table. When she joined him, she reached for one of the bags only to have him wrap his hand around her wrist—stopping her.

"I'm carrying these. The gun's for you." He tipped his chin toward the weapon.

"I don't know what I'm doing with guns."

"This"—he picked up the gun, snapped the magazine into place, and wracked the slide—"has a grip safety. If you're holding it and pull the trigger, it'll fire." His lips twitched. "Try not to hit me."

She gave him a tight-lipped smile and drawled, "Aw, you've ruined my fun already."

Declan snorted and grabbed the two bags in one hand. "Uh-huh. Just focus on shooting back at anyone who shoots at us." He glanced at her over his shoulder. "Can you do that?"

"I'm an accountant, Declan. You want me to count the number of bullets in a magazine, I will. You want me to count them as *you* shoot at people, I'll do that, too. The actual shooting and killing..." She swallowed hard and pressed a hand—her *empty* hand—to her stomach and prayed she wouldn't lose her lunch everywhere. Memories flashed; images of broken bodies and bright red blood filled her mind. So much blood. "That's not something I can handle." .

He took a deep breath and tipped his head back, releasing it slowly. "If we don't get that tablet and turn it over to the SHOC director, you'll be running for the rest of your life. You'll be hunted to the four corners of the Earth, Abby. Is that how you want to live?"

She wasn't going to cry—she wasn't. The only way to avoid crying was to laugh. Even if the laughter was fake.

"Declan?"

"Yes?" He released a long, heavy sigh.

"The Earth is round."

Utter. Silence. It was as if even the house held its breath and fell quiet after her attempt at a joke. It wasn't a very funny joke in all honesty, but it should have broken some of the tension. Even a tiny bit.

But Declan remained in place, hands on his hips and face turned up to the ceiling for another dozen heartbeats before he gave her his attention once more. "Abby?"

She nibbled her lower lip for a minute and then realized

it betrayed her nervousness so she stopped. Of course, that was before she remembered he could scent her unease, but it wasn't like she could tell the cat to stop smelling up the joint.

"Yeah?"

"You're not funny." The words were flat, but the corner of his mouth had the tiniest hint of a curl.

"You think I'm hilarious," she countered, and she had no idea where the urge to tease came from. Possibly because if she wasn't laughing, she'd be crying, and wasn't that just another reason to cry?

"I think—" A low tone, the beeping soft, interrupted him, and Declan glanced at his watch. He tapped a small button and lowered his wrist, any hints of his smile gone in that instant.

"It's time." She said the words even though they both knew what would happen next.

"It's time." He nodded. "Don't shoot me, don't shoot yourself, and don't get shot."

"It sounds so easy." She fake chuckled.

He didn't respond. It was now or never, and never wasn't an option.

The door slid aside, letting the cool night air into the home. The air and something else. Something small and metal that bounced off the door's steel frame. It *ping*ed— *several* things *ping*ed—one after another and another, and it took Abby a moment to register what was happening.

And then she did. The bad guys who were supposed to shoot at them as they were *chased* through the streets decided to cut out the chasing aspect.

They were right outside, and they'd skipped straight to the shooting.

CHAPTER TWENTY

*F*uck him sideways with a barbed-wire-wrapped baseball bat. Shit was hitting the fan *now*. Not later.

Another bullet slammed into the door's frame, then ricocheted and embedded itself in the drywall-covered concrete of the home's entryway. That was followed by another and another, the attackers doing their best to hit him and Abby.

Declan's wolf howled and barked, its fury palpable. The beast pushed and shoved at Declan's mind, demanding to be released. It wanted to hunt, kill, the ones who dared attack. Not because it was worried about its own ass. No, the beast was furious about the threat the attackers posed to Abby.

Unacceptable.

The stink of gunpowder filled the air, his animal picking out the scent. He drew in a deep breath, sorted through the wispy smoke and dust, and tried to identify their attackers.

The beast helped, adding its abilities to his human nose, and then the truth hit him.

"It's UH," he snarled, fangs pushing free of his gums with a renewed wave of rage and fury.

"Unified Humanity?" Abby's voice trembled, and he spared her a glance. He didn't spy any wounds, which meant the shaking came from fear, not pain.

"Yes." Declan grabbed the nearest bag and withdrew several guns, laying them out carefully on the floor. He checked the magazines and chambered a bullet in each one.

"How did they find us? I thought you said no one knows about this house."

Yeah, he knew what he'd said, and he was going to make sure he left one of the fuckers out there alive long enough to get the truth out of him. Then he'd put a bullet right between the asshole's eyes.

"I did. They don't."

"So how—"

Declan took a deep breath and swallowed the snarl that threatened to break free. It wasn't Abby's fault. "I don't know, but I will. Just as soon as I get my paws on one of them."

He holstered his weapons, sliding them into place with practiced ease, but they were all backup to his preferred method—claws. He formed tight fists with his hands and then relaxed the fierce grip. Fingertips blackened, the wolf's claws in place while the beast also altered their shape. Bones cracked and muscles stretched, rearranging so they'd become the perfect hand-to-hand killing machines.

Fur slid over skin, dark gray with shots of silver. The transition was so fast the sting of the change didn't register before it was complete. Now his two-legged form would fully blend with the night, black clothes and the animal's hues making him disappear in the shadows.

His shoulders broadened, the fabric of his shirt stretching to accommodate the increased breadth. That was followed by a bump of strength to the rest of his body, the beast adding its power. It was anxious to have their attackers' blood on its paws and flowing down its throat.

The wolf hungered for death, for destruction, for the

cries of his prey and the sound of their begging in his ears. Their fear already teased his nose, the delicate hints of terror drifting to him on the gentle winds that passed through the open door. They attacked, but were afraid.

They should be.

Another wave of fear assaulted him, the stench greater than the others, more concentrated and piercing and... coated in a blanket of near-panicked feline.

The beast happily took joy in the terror of others, but not Abby. Never Abby.

Small changes complete, Declan turned his focus to her. She cowered on the opposite side of the doorway, back pressed to the wall and the nine-millimeter handgun clutched between her breasts. She was shaking with terror.

He wanted to go to her, reassure her, but that would have to come after this was done. He waited for a lull in the shooting and whispered to her, "Abby." Once he had her undivided attention, he issued orders. He was asking a lot of her, but there wasn't anyone else around. "I'm going out there."

She shook her head, her hair whipping through the air with her speed. He countered that with a sharp nod. "Yes, I am. And you're going to lay cover fire." He tipped his head toward the gun in her arms. "You don't have to aim. Just make sure you don't hit me."

"No." She mouthed the word, any sound lost to the renewed flurry of shots.

"Yes. Nonnegotiable. You're going to lay cover." He cracked his neck and rolled his shoulders, loosening up before he got to what he did best—killing. "I'm going to slip outside. I'll let you know when it's safe to come out."

"What if they catch you and force you to yell for me and then—"

Declan's lips twitched, and he managed to swallow the laugh threatening to break free. "Not happening."

"They could—"

"Sweetheart," he murmured, liking the way some of her fear bled away just a little too much. "There's no killing me. I've been hunted, battled, and bled almost dry and I'm still here. They're nothing."

Her lower lip trembled. "Is that like the old 'I had to walk to school in the snow uphill both ways' thing?"

"No." He shook his head. He had to give it to her. Scared out of her mind and she still tried for a joke. "It's the 'when I was fifteen I killed my alpha' thing."

Not exactly the way he'd wanted to reveal all that—fuck it, he hadn't wanted to talk about it at all—but the shit was there.

He tipped his head toward their attackers. "Empty the magazine and then hide in here. I'll be back in a few minutes."

Her face paled, eyes widening. Fuck, he hated seeing her scared. "A few..."

"Shoot, Abby." He growled the words, adding a curl to his lip to expose a single fang. The threat was clear, the push one that she needed no matter how much he disliked the action.

She straightened away from the wall and rose to her knees. She changed her hold on the weapon, carefully wrapping her hands around the grip before she gave him a firm nod. "Okay."

Declan grunted. "Good girl."

He focused on the exterior, his wolf's vision making it easy to pick out the location of their attackers. They hid within the brush, trees acting like cover for them. They didn't realize the cover was for *him*. Each bush and tree was positioned exactly as he desired so that attack—retribution—was easy.

"Go." He bit off the word and she reacted, peeking around the edge of the door and squeezing the trigger.

Pop. Pop. Pop. He counted each of her bullets, timing his actions based on how many she had left. Even with an extended magazine, he had only sixteen rounds—fifteen in the mag and one in the chamber—to get the job done.

The first was easy, a duck and then roll followed by a leap that put him behind attacker one. A snap of his neck and Declan slowly lowered the body to the ground.

Second required a little climbing, a shimmy up a tree—each movement precise and perfectly balanced so he didn't upset the massive pine. That man ended up with a broken neck as well, a sharp twist doing the job.

Pop. Pop.

Abby still shot into the dark, and Declan moved to the next target. He swung to the ground and landed in a low crouch. He crept through the blackness, his beast allowing him to see and sense the ones who meant Abby harm. Sure, they probably wanted to kill him, too, but he wasn't concerned about himself. Whatever happened, he'd live. He was too evil to die since the devil would just kick his ass back when he appeared in hell.

A soft crackle, the spit of a radio, came from his right, and he changed course. Low whispers drew him forward, two men arguing over something. It didn't matter. Only their deaths mattered.

He moved until he stood no less than three feet from the two men, a whispered exchange joining the sounds of Abby's shots.

Declan took advantage of their distraction. He darted forward, his movements quick and fluid. His wolf howled in excitement, the beast already prepared to revel in what was to come. He reached for the man on his left, half-shifted fingers curled and nails ready to pierce flesh. His claws sank deep into his opponent's throat.

With his right, he grasped the back of the male's neck and held him captive for a moment. Only long enough to finish killing his friend. Then he snapped the second man's neck with a quick wrench.

Two more down, four total.

Not enough.

He tipped his head back and scented the breeze, the animal searching beyond the scents of death that surrounded him. The wolf identified two others. It'd been a six-man team sent after them.

He ducked through the brush, tasting the air and following the low sounds that came from the shadows. The rustle and snap of twigs and leaves acted like a beacon for his wolf.

He remained silent, letting Abby's shots mask his movements and taking advantage of the men's inattention. They worried about getting shot. Declan worried about how long it'd take him to kill the last two. He wasn't sure how UH had found him, but if those idiots had figured out his location, SHOC wasn't far behind. If they were behind at all. Were they just waiting to see if UH would do the job for them?

The snap of a branch cut through a lull in the fight and he turned left, heading back toward the entrance to the bunker. To his left and then a hint right. Clouds parted to reveal the moon, and he spied his quarry. He wasn't carrying a handgun like the others. No, he had a rifle, one braced and ready to be fired—at Abby.

One hand went to the barrel, and Declan yanked the gun

out of the man's grip while his other hand...He reached around his neck, sank his claws in deep, and jerked, filling his palm with flesh and blood once more.

Which left him with one target—one last human intent on getting to Abby.

Declan focused on the sounds surrounding him, the ones that slipped through his body and reverberated in his bones. Except he didn't have to be careful or cautious. Not when Abby's shots came one after another, hardly a pause in between. Not when her piercing scream accompanied the sounds. Another weapon fired just as quickly, the source of the shots moving through the forest.

"Declan!" Pure panic that was more than just fear or terror. It delved into his soul and nearly wrenched him inside out with the unending need to be with Abby.

He didn't think about himself or the dangers he faced by revealing his position. He broke into a dead run, dodging and ducking trees and branches, leaping over low bushes and sliding across the leaf-strewn ground. He didn't slow and his steps didn't falter when he burst past the tree line. In fact, he doubled his speed, the scene before him spurring his wolf to move faster, run harder.

A human male stood above Abby, dressed in black and with weapons strapped to his body. Declan didn't care about what he wore, only about what he held.

A gun.

Pointed at Abby.

And then it fired.

CHAPTER TWENTY-ONE

*B*eing shot *sucked*. It sucked more than being chased by a killer whale, and Abby actually *had* been chased by a killer whale, followed by a polar bear and *then* a bull moose once. That had been a bad day.

Plus, she hadn't even been allowed to hurt the guy who'd shot her, dammit. The least Declan could have done was leave the guy breathing long enough for her to shoot him back. Or kick him in the balls. Or even better, *both*.

Both sounded good.

"You'll have to get over it. He's already dead." A tug and tear of cloth followed Declan's words, and she turned her attention to the partially shifted wolf doing his best to do...something.

"Huh?"

"You can't shoot him or kick him in the balls." He paused and shrugged. "Well, you could, but he wouldn't feel anything."

"What are we talking about?" She frowned and squinted, trying to follow the conversation, but things weren't going that well. Stuff looked very fuzzy.

"Abby, focus on me, okay?" Another tear of cloth and he jiggled her leg.

"I am focusing— *Holy fuck what are you doing?*"

Now she remembered. Before she'd gone off with her violent thoughts, she'd been shot. It seemed Declan's method of fixing her was to cut her fucking leg off.

"I'm not cutting your leg off," he growled, the deep rumbling more calming than threatening. Even his amber-hued glare soothed her ragged nerves. "I'm making sure you don't die."

"Dying would be bad," she murmured. "This hurts really bad. More than the other time I got shot."

Hurt didn't describe the burning sensation, the fire in her blood, and the scrape of nails inside her skull. She'd bitch about her cat attacking her, but the feline was in just as bad a shape as her human side.

"Well, yeah. Poison bullets will do that," he drawled.

"I don't like that you're not more upset about this." And no, she couldn't keep the grumbling growl out of her voice.

"Sweetheart." A single finger beneath her chin lifted her head. When had it fallen forward? "I wish I could bring them all back so I could kill them again. Slowly. Painfully. They hurt you, and my wolf is fucking pissed that I can't return the favor." His eyes were all wolf—no hint of his human mind lurking in the background. "I'm very, *very* upset."

"That's nice." She liked that he cared. Liked it more than she should since as hot as Declan might be, he wasn't for her. No matter how loud the she-cat yowled.

"Yeah," he drawled. "Nice."

He pushed to his feet and she just sat there, staring up at six feet of hunky werewolf. So much power, so much dominance. She wanted to lick him all over.

"Baby, you can do whatever you want to me once I get you patched up and safe."

Ugh. *Baby*. And apparently, she'd said that aloud. Nice. "I don't want to do anything to you."

Liar.

"Liar." Declan echoed her thoughts. He had to be some kind of voodoo magician to read her mind that way. He sighed and shook his head. "Let's go."

"Go where?"

He ran a hand down his face and sifted his fingers through his hair. "You need medical attention."

He tipped his head toward her leg, and she turned her attention there as well.

"Huh. There's a hole in my leg." She looked to the large werewolf. "Did we know there's a hole in my leg?"

"Yes, we did."

"Oh." When had that happened? She glanced at her surroundings. Oh. Right. Dead people. Guns. *Pop*. "Are we going to fix it?"

"Does it hurt?" Declan answered her question with a question.

"No." She shook her head, and he groaned.

"The poison is making it hard for your cat to do its job, and shock is settling in. We need to get you out of here. Lift your arms. I'm going to pick you up and you need to hold on."

"I don't think—"

Declan didn't let her think. He only let her feel. As in, feel his arm sliding beneath her legs while the other went around her back. Then there was the feel of being lifted. And the feel of his tightening grip. And the feel of his fingers very, very close to the *hole in her leg*.

A scream rocketed up her throat, threatening to break free and dive right past her lips, but her cougar snarled at her to be quiet. Abby would show the cougar being fucking quiet, the little she-bitch.

But she understood the point the animal tried to make, which was why she didn't scream. Instead, she turned her head and sank her teeth into Declan's shoulder. Fabric filled her mouth, his scent filled her nose, and his taste crept past the cloth to dance over her taste buds.

Declan grunted but didn't say a word. He simply turned and strode off into the dark with her cradled in his arms. Each jarring step sent a jolt of pain along her spine, but it disappeared as quickly as it arrived.

Shock was a beautiful, beautiful thing.

"It's not beautiful," he growled.

"Makes it not hurt," she mumbled, and leaned her head against his shoulder.

"Hurting reminds you that you're alive."

Abby snorted. "I don't need the reminder."

She'd never forget that she lived while others had died.

"Who died?"

Okay, she *didn't* like that shock made her say all her thoughts out loud. "No one."

Everyone.

"Abby—"

"How come I didn't go into shock the first time I got shot? Would have made the swim easier." By, like, a lot.

Declan shrugged in answer. "Who died?"

Abby shrugged. If it worked for him, it could work for her. She didn't want to answer his question. "What kind of poison is in me?"

"We're coming back to who died." His glare came to rest on her shoulders, heavy and determined.

They'd never get back to it if she had her way. "I can't go to the hospital."

He snorted. "I didn't survive this long by making stupid decisions."

"That house was stupid." She closed her eyes and groaned, burying her face against his shoulder. "I'm sorry. That was mean."

"I don't know how they found us, but I will find out before this is over. I'm also going to get a whole new set of fucking safe houses after I blow up the current ones." The growl in his voice told her he wasn't joking. "And it isn't mean if it's the truth." Something soft and sweet brushed her temple. Declan's lips? Nah. "The answer to your question—we're going to see a dead man."

For some reason that tickled her. It made her smile and giggle. She released his shoulder and waved at the darkness behind them. "There's a dead man back there."

"Six."

"Six what?"

"There are *six dead men* back there."

"Oh." She stared at his profile, the strong length of his nose and the small bump. She kept her eyes on the carved edge of his strong jaw. She also observed the tension in his muscles when he clenched his teeth. "You killed six?"

He shrugged. "More like five and a half. You got a few shots into the sixth. He would have bled out. I just nudged things along."

Abby's stomach lurched and she swallowed hard, fighting to keep her nausea at bay. "I killed..."

"Would have killed, but didn't." His steps slowed, and he nudged her forehead with his chin. "Hey." She tipped her head back and met his intent stare. "None of that blood back there is on your hands. It's all me, understand? This is my world and those stains are on my soul, not yours."

Her chin wobbled and tears stung her eyes, tears wholly unrelated to the hole in her leg and tied to the one in her heart.

"You hear me?" His yellow eyes were intent, the moon's dim glow reflecting off the beast's gaze.

"I..." she whispered, and he glared at her, the wolf's anger prodding at her while he waited for her agreement. "I hear you."

Declan grunted. "Good."

He returned to his trudge through the woods, his pace even and measured as he traveled the randomly winding path.

"Declan? Where are we going?"

"Can you just go back to quietly dying for a little while?" he snapped at her, and she met his annoyed stare with a glare of her own.

"Well, excuse me for breathing, asshole."

He continued stomping through the underbrush until they came to a long stretch of barren road. Lights shined in the distance, a low glow that acted like a beacon—luring them onward.

Curiosity got the better of her and she spoke. "Is that where we're going?"

"That's where we're stealing a car."

"A nice car?" She raised her eyebrows. "Like a luxury car or something?"

"Want to ride in stolen class, baby?"

She didn't even flinch at the endearment anymore. Her heart simply turned in on itself, shrinking smaller and smaller each time. "No. It's just...If someone has an older car that needs to be fixed up, then maybe that's all they can afford. If the person has a super-expensive, fancy ride, they might have better insurance or more disposable income."

"A thief with a conscience?"

"Stop laughing at me and let's steal a car already," she snapped.

He chuckled. "Yes, ma'am."

Declan carried her closer and closer to the distant light. His breathing remained even, and there was no hint that he grew tired. Soon they reached the source of the lights and he lowered her to the ground in a shadowed corner of the parking lot.

"You good?"

Abby nodded even though she was very, very not good. The shock had worn off and the pain returned, the pounding of her heart a physical throb in her thigh.

"Good. Stay put. I'll be right back with a *fancy* car."

"And the owner doesn't have kids," she rushed out. "Or anyone ill in their family." She nibbled her lower lip. "And they can't be ill either because—"

Rough fingers came to rest against her lips. "I'll get a car from someone who will be mildly annoyed by the inconvenience but it won't cause a major disruption in their lives, okay?"

Abby nodded once more, lips sliding over his scratchy skin.

"Good. Give me five minutes."

Five minutes to steal a car. She wondered how long it'd be before they met with the man who was supposed to be dead. Then she wondered if maybe Declan had been shot and he was caught in the grasp of shock and poison, too. Maybe he thought they were going to see a zombie?

No. She mentally shook her head. She hadn't scented his blood—only her own. She was the one off her rocker.

Headlights nearly blinded her, wrenching her from her thoughts, and she focused on the world around her once more. The world that included a vehicle slowly approaching. One with Declan behind the wheel.

And—once he had her settled in the passenger seat—

a deep breath told her it wasn't owned by a parent, the owner didn't have an ill relative, *and* the owner was in good health.

Once she was done sorting through the scents in the small space, she turned a wide smile on Declan. That wide smile even remained in place for a little while.

At least until he spoke. "I even checked his insurance card. We can total it and he'll be fine."

CHAPTER TWENTY-TWO

Stealing a car from a gas station wasn't the smartest move, but it was the quickest way to get them from *Point A* to *Point Kicking in Pike's Door*. One quick car ride later and they'd traveled from Declan's safe house to the center of Port St. James.

He cradled Abby in his arms, her breasts pressed to his chest, and he pretended not to notice how good it felt to hold her close.

The wolf noticed. The wolf liked it—*a lot*—even if she was a feline and their pups might spit up the occasional hairball.

Fuck that. There wouldn't be hairballs because there wouldn't be pups.

The wolf wanted to know how it felt to be delusional.

Declan nudged the wolf back and returned his attention to caring for Abby. He'd only been half joking when he'd mentioned totaling the car, but he'd settled for abandoning it a few blocks from Pike's place. Shitty part of town filled with shady people who wouldn't report anything to the cops. Or at least wouldn't make a call until they'd stolen what they wanted from the vehicle.

They wouldn't mention a man all in black carrying a

giggling woman down the street, either. And how Abby managed to laugh with a bullet embedded in her thigh he would never know. It did beat tears, though. Man, he couldn't take a woman's tears.

Declan strode up Pike's crumbling sidewalk—cracked, coated in black mold, and overtaken by weeds. He didn't slow his approach when he reached the two low stairs that led to Pike's poor excuse for a front porch. He skipped both, placed his right foot on the edge of the concrete slab and his left…well, it came up and he drove the heel of his boot into the steel-coated panel, just to the right of the knob, and the door jolted inward with a resounding *crack*.

Declan stepped back and ducked, waiting for what was to come next. Two low *pop*s and *thud*s immediately followed, bullets striking the doorframe where he'd stood only moments before.

"Anybody dead?" Pike called out, and Declan rolled his eyes.

"If I were dead, could I tell you?" he drawled, and stepped into sight, ducking once more when the other man took another shot. "Dammit, Pike."

Abby decided it was a good time to laugh and released a tinkling series of chuckles. "He shot at you."

Declan turned his attention to the woman in his arms, her glazed eyes and flushed face pointed in his direction. "Yes, he did, but it's not funny."

She snuggled close, rubbing her cheek on his chest, and released a soft sigh. "Okay."

Damn she wasn't doing good. Her quick agreement and the sensuous way she lay against him made him wonder just what kind of shit was in that bullet.

"Declan?" That familiar deep rasp came from within the run-down house.

"Who else has the balls to break down your fucking door, asshole?" he snarled, and stepped into the dark home. "Turn on a fucking light."

Pike just snorted and hit a switch, a soft *snick* preceding a flare of brightness. A gold glow fell across the space, illuminating Pike's living room.

"Cleaner than I expected," Declan murmured.

No pizza boxes or take-out containers. Then he turned his attention to the other man. Declan expected to see long hair, scruffy bristles on Pike's face, and his ever-present bottle of beer in hand. Even if shifters had a helluva time getting drunk, it didn't mean Pike didn't try. Hard.

Except this version of Pike was clean-cut, freshly shaved, and clutching a soda instead of alcohol.

"What happened to you?"

Pike lifted a single brow. "What happened to you?" He waved a hand toward Abby. "And who's that?"

Right. He wasn't there to check in on Pike. He had a different—more important—purpose.

"I've been shot at a lot, and this…" He tipped his head toward the woman in his arms.

"I'm Abby." She breathed deep and huffed out the breath, her breathing growing more difficult the longer that bullet stayed inside her. "I actually got shot. Twice."

Fur, shades of gray that ranged from near black to the lightest brush, slid forward to replace Pike's skin, while his eyes flashed bright amber, and Declan wondered if he'd end up fighting someone else instead of helping Abby.

Except as quickly as the man's beast had rushed forward, it withdrew, retreating into Pike's human shape. "Sorry." He cracked his neck. "I'm good."

"He's not a fish." The softly whispered words drifted through the room. "He should be a fish."

Pike's anger over Abby's injury vanished, replaced by a dark glare. One she didn't see because she'd closed her eyes, more of her weight resting against him.

"I'm tired, Declan."

He ignored Pike and focused on Abby, pressing his lips to the crown of her head. He drew in her scent—not because he needed her flavors to fill him more than he needed air. No, he needed to know how far the poison traveled, how firm a hold it had on her body.

Too hard. Too much.

"I know, sweetheart. Let's get you patched up, and then you can sleep."

"But not in the water? Don't wanna sleep in the water."

"Not in the water." He had no idea where she'd come up with that, but he'd promise her the world to keep her happy.

"Because that's where fish sleep."

"And Pike's not a fish." He refused to look at Pike, but there was no way he could suppress the smile that leaped to his lips.

A rolling growl slid through the room, Pike's annoyance a physical thing within the space. Declan opened his mouth, ready to counter the growl with a snarl, but Abby beat him to it in her own way.

"Shhh, Mr. Not-Fishy. Good puppies don't growl." She even lifted her hand and petted the air as if a dog were within reach.

"Declan…" Pike's annoyance slammed into him, but Declan didn't have the strength to censure Abby. Not when her face paled even more and her breathing transitioned from slow and easy to rapid and uneven.

"Need a room and your kit, Pike. She's got a poisoned bullet in her thigh that needs to come out."

Pike glared at him, then her, and then Declan once more. "I'm not a fucking hospital."

"Like I could take a damned cougar to a hospital?" Declan strode deeper into the room. "Tell me where I'm going or I'll lay her on the first bed I find." He let his wolf come forward. "Then I'll tear you—and this place—apart until I find what I need."

Pike rolled his eyes. "When'd you become such a bitch over a woman?"

"About twenty-four hours ago." Really, four days ago. The first time he'd watched her shake her ass.

Pike shook his head. "This way."

He led Declan down a nearby hall, the narrow space dark and crowded. Nice area to draw opponents and pick 'em off easy with—he lifted his attention and located the hole in the ceiling at the end of the hall—a sniper rifle. Dead before they knew Pike was near.

Pike nudged open a door. "Put her there. I'll get the supplies."

Declan strode into the room and lowered her to the narrow bed. "Abby?" He gently called her name and gave her shoulder a soft shake. "Abby, I'm going to have to cut your pants off."

"Have a headache, Declan. Maybe later," she mumbled, and patted his hand.

He just chuckled and shook his head. "Abby . . ."

"I have to wash my hair."

"Abby," he murmured.

"I'm not in the mood to get jiggy with it." She glared at him, the cougar staring out through Abby's eyes. "Can't you find porn like a normal guy?"

A snort came from behind him, and he glanced over his shoulder. Pike stood in the doorway, bag in hand

and smirk on his lips. "Yeah, Dec, can't you watch porn?"

"Shut up, asshole, and give me the bag." He curled his lip—exposing a fang—and held out his hand. The moment the handle rested on his palm, he drew it close and laid it beside her. "And, Abby, I don't wanna fuck"—right that second—"I need to get that bullet out."

"Later though?" Glassy eyes met his, her smile so soft and sweet and tempting as hell.

"Later." His wolf howled, fucking thrilled with the idea. Horny asshole.

The beast still wasn't disagreeing.

"Okay." She turned her head and nuzzled the pillow, giving a little wiggle before she sighed and relaxed into the mattress. "Wake me when it's over."

Pike snorted. "She serious?"

Declan clenched his hand into a tight fist and resisted the urge to punch the man in the face for laughing at Abby. *Shit*. He had it bad.

"Pike?" He was determined to remain calm until he got through this shit with Abby. Then he'd gut Pike like he *was* a fish and Declan was a bear in fucking salmon-spawning season. "Shut up and come hold her down."

Pike grunted and strolled forward, moving slow as molasses. If Declan didn't need the other wolf so much, he'd kill him.

Pike knelt on the other side of the bed and leaned forward, arms hovering above Abby's unconscious body. "Chest and knees?"

"Yeah." Guilt churned in Declan's gut. He hated what was about to happen, but it had to be done. "Hopefully I won't have to search long."

"Mind telling me why you aren't taking her to one

of your Shit Dick docs? Or why Team Fuckhole isn't here?"

Yes, Declan was going to tear Pike into tiny pieces when this was through. "It's SHOC—"

"Not Shit Dick."

"And my team will tear a hole in your ass—"

"So big and all that bullshit." Pike snorted. "You're still so easy to rile up. Didn't answer my question, though."

"We caught her. I took her." Declan shrugged. He left out the part about rescuing her from Unified Humanity first.

"Why?" Pike raised his eyebrows, and he shrugged again.

"Seemed like the thing to do at the time."

Declan decided the conversation was done and reached for Abby's pants. Instead of pulling them from her body, he simply enlarged the hole around her wound. He wasn't about to let Pike get too good of a look at what belonged to *him*. He still wasn't addressing the "belonged to him" portion of his thoughts, either.

"You ready?" He shot Pike a questioning look and waited for his nod. "Then hold her still and pray she stays out."

The first cut into her skin told him God wasn't answering their prayers. In fact, God gave him a big old "fuck off" in the shape of feline claws, pointed fangs, and long hisses that made his blood run cold.

CHAPTER TWENTY-THREE

*C*onsciousness returned slowly, Abby's mind easing awake in gradual increments. An ache encompassed her from head to toe, and the throbbing pain attempted to lure her back to sleep. But for some reason, she couldn't. There was a reason she had to open her eyes. Right?

Abby furrowed her brow, mind muddling through her body's aches on a hunt for why she couldn't just stay on the comfortable bed and hide from reality.

Reality... The word was no more than a whisper. There was a reason she still lived—a reason she hadn't died and was instead saved by a...

She furrowed her brow and murmured, "Saved by a fish?"

A low, masculine chuckle came from her left, and the gentle caress of a large hand soon followed. "Not a fish. Wolf."

Declan. She sighed in relief and something else. Something that felt like pleasure, but she'd never say that aloud. Fingers sifted through her hair, brushing strands away from her face. She turned her head and nuzzled his palm, breathing in his natural, woodsy scent. A scent that soothed the restless animal inside her.

More than restless—near panicked. The beast alternated between snarls at Abby and purrs directed at Declan with bouts of weak chuffing in between. The cat had been frightened—more than frightened—by her injury.

Injury?

"I was..." With those two words, Declan pulled away from her, his touch retreating, and she whined. *She*—Abby—not the cougar. Her body cried out for him. Even weakened by her wound, she wanted Declan close—touching her, surrounding her. "No." She lifted her arms—or tried to. Fabric held her captive, her body so weak she could hardly toss off a sheet. "Don't go."

She didn't care if she sounded needy, like a child desperate for comfort. His scent, his presence, soothed whatever invisible rough edges continued to cut into her body and soul.

"Easy," he soothed, palm returning, fingers rubbing small circles on her skin. "I'm right here."

Abby purred—*purred*—and nuzzled him. She rubbed her cheek on his rough palm and fought against the sheet until she could half roll toward him. An ache bloomed in her thigh, but it was nothing compared to the pain she'd experienced shortly after being...

"I was shot." She breathed deep and released the air with a soft sigh. "You killed everyone?" She kept her eyes closed, but raised her brows with the question. Declan grunted, and she took that as his agreement. "Then you stole a car?"

He snorted. "An expensive car that didn't belong to a single parent or a person who had someone ill in their life. You were also happy that they had good insurance."

She quirked her lip in a half smile at his annoyance. It sounded like her. Even shot, she worried about others. "It's fuzzy after that."

She ceased nuzzling Declan but kept her cheek rested on his hand. But just because she stopped moving didn't mean he did. His thumb traced circles on her cheekbone, the touch gentle and sweet, even though she knew how quickly his hands could kill.

"I'm surprised you remember that much." His words were soft. "More surprised that you're awake."

"Take a licking and keep on swimming." Old wounds, old emotional pain and agony, pushed forward with that memory. "'Cause if you're not the winner, you might be dinner."

He stiffened. *"What?"*

Abby pried one eye open and considered that a victory. She'd worry about the other one in a minute. Specifically, after she'd stopped Declan from wolfing out. She got one arm free and reached for him. Weakness dragged her down, and the farthest she got was his forearm. She'd aimed for his face, but any amount of skin would work.

"Shhh...It's a herd joke."

"A *what* joke?" She felt—rather than heard—his growl. It vibrated through him, encompassing his body, and soon the tremble filled her as well.

"Seal shifter herd. Did SHOC do any research on me?"

He slowly nodded. "Yeah, but—"

She shrugged. "The alpha didn't have the patience to deal with a cougar in his seal herd, but if I was going to be part of the herd, I'd be *part of the herd*."

"What the hell does that mean?"

He seemed to get angrier with her every word, and the more upset he got, the more fur appeared. Dark gray fur slid free of his pores, gradually overtaking his cheeks before heading south and stretching across his shoulders.

She quirked her lips in a teasing smile. "You're sexy when you're all mad. Did you know that?"

"Abby," he snapped at her, but she didn't have the energy to be annoyed. Or afraid. She should probably fear a large wolf shifter that'd managed to kill so many men so quickly, but she didn't. Maybe tomorrow.

"Wild animals don't care if you're a shifter. Swims took us into predator territory more than once."

"I'll kill him."

"It's over." She shuddered, a hint of that old fear surging inside her. "It's over." She whispered the words to herself more than to Declan.

"Is it?" So soft, so caring. Surprising considering his past.

"Yeah." She kept her voice low. "I left and I've never been back." She had no reason to return. No family, no friends...nothing.

"Did you find a pride? Isn't that what cats do?"

"Lions do that. The rest of us are pretty solitary."

"So you've been alone."

"I've been me." She shrugged. "I've been happy."

"Liar."

She chuckled. "Maybe. But I don't have to evade killer whales."

"Just SHOC and UH," he drawled.

"But not whales." She wiggled in place and tugged on the sheets shielding her body. She got her other arm free, and the room's cool air slipped beneath the soft fabric. That was about the time she realized—"I'm naked."

"Yeah." Declan's attention pulled from her and he focused on the wall, a hint of pink staining his cheeks.

"And you're blushing?"

That earned her a glare. "You were shot and covered in blood."

Oh, right. Shot. Now she remembered. She'd let him divert her for a little while, but reality intruded once again. "Where are we? And the fish? It's dead, right? I think I remember that."

Declan shook his head. "Not a fish, a wolf. His name is Pike, and he's alive."

"That's a shitty name for a wolf."

He sighed and pinched the bridge of his nose with his free hand. "Your filter still hasn't returned." He shook his head. "He's only pretending to be dead, and his name is what he wants it to be."

"Is he on the run from the mob? Is it like witness protection?"

"Abby." He growled low. He probably wouldn't make the sound if he knew she didn't find it the least bit threatening. He'd just saved her life. He wasn't going to kill her now.

"If it's not the mob, what is it?"

"Complicated." That growl continued, his expression grim.

"Try me."

Declan ran his palm over his face and released a heavy sigh. "If I don't, will you stop asking?"

She shook her head. "No."

"It's an old story, and you need to rest." The pressure on her cheek lessened—Declan pulling away—and her cougar whined with the impending loss.

She placed her hand over his and...and did something she hadn't done for a very long time. She begged. Heartfelt, bone-deep, soul-touching begged. "Please don't leave me."

Declan's breath caught, and he froze, his blue eyes bleeding amber before turning blue once more. "I'm just going outside—"

"Please," she rasped. The last time he'd left her… "Just…talk to me. Tell me something, anything. I don't…"

I don't want to be alone.

"You don't understand how dangerous you are, do you?" He went from caressing her cheek to tracing her lower lip.

"I'm not," she whispered, the words barely audible.

"Oh, you are." He gave her a rueful grin. "You make me do things I shouldn't. Make me feel."

"There's nothing wrong with feelings." Except when she didn't want to face them. Except when she took her heartache and pain and shoved it so deep it could no longer touch her.

"Sweetheart." The startling blue of his eyes remained in place, his human half in full control. "My feelings died the day I discovered my alpha with…"

CHAPTER TWENTY-FOUR

*D*eclan had been relieved when Abby opened her eyes five hours after he'd dug the poisoned bullet out of her body. Now he wished she'd go back to sleep. If only to avoid the conversation he'd found himself dragged into.

"I discovered my alpha with..." The words were there, suppressed for so long. But releasing them meant experiencing the agony and betrayal all over again. It meant feeling claws ripping through his flesh once more.

He should keep the memories all bottled up. Should tuck them away like he'd promised and never let them see the light of day. But this was Abby, and she had him doing everything he shouldn't do. She gave him impossible thoughts and pointless dreams that didn't seem quite so pointless anymore. Maybe starting at the end was the problem. Maybe he had to go back—closer to the beginning.

"When I turned two, it became obvious I was an alpha pup." He grinned, earlier memories driving out some of the darkness that lingered. "I began organizing raiding parties for cookies and, if we got caught, jail breaks."

"You terrorized your parents."

"I terrorized every parent in the *pack*." He paused, small

smile still in place. "And when Jacob was old enough, it was the two of us causing trouble."

"Jacob?"

"My brother. He's two years younger. Not quite as strong, but smart as hell."

Annoying and bothersome with a penchant for shooting at brothers who kick down their doors.

Declan kept his hand in place, thumb brushing Abby's lower lip. He used the touch to anchor him in the present while he let his mind drift to the past.

"When I turned twelve, I started training with the alpha. I was the oldest alpha pup, and he named me as the next in line. I felt so important. Being the alpha." He shook his head. "It's supposed to be about caring for the pack. *Everything* he does is for the betterment of everyone. When he takes the oath and forms that bond with his wolves, he's driven by instinct to protect and never harm without cause."

"But?"

There was a "but" in every story. More than one in Declan's.

He released a rueful chuckle, lips quirked in a half smile. "But after three years in training I discovered that what's written in books—the stories passed from elders to pups—isn't always true for everyone."

Delicate fingers slipped through his hair, and he realized she'd changed position. She'd eased closer, pulled that sheet taut across her plump breasts, and stroked him as if he were a child in need of comfort. He didn't need comfort. He hadn't then, and he didn't now.

But maybe she needed to give it, which was why he remained still and let her brush his hair aside, sift her fingers through his strands, and caress the side of his neck.

She needed it, not him.

Right.

"I trained six days a week with the alpha. I went to school during the day, and then I went to the pack house for training—Saturday through Thursday with only Friday night to myself." He snorted, remembering the alpha's order to go out and have a little fun. *Good alphas can't lead without letting the animal have a little fun.*

His stomach clenched as he recalled how the alpha liked to have a "little fun." He breathed deep and pushed away the nausea that bubbled inside him. He had to get through the telling. She needed to understand the kind of man she touched, the kind of man she spent time with.

"I broke the rules. A girl stood me up and I was pissed, so I went to the pack house to work out. I thought I'd see if any of the guards wanted to spar to burn off my anger." He could still hear the screams. The begging and pleading.

She cupped the back of his skull and pulled, but he remained in place. "No, I need—"

"You can explain it next to me just as well as you can kneeling beside the bed. Now, c'mere."

She was right. More than being right, he simply wanted her touch. He wanted more of her and—if his wolf got its way—all of her. Even if he didn't deserve one of her smiles. He'd always taken what he wanted. He'd take her.

"Move over." The wolf filled those two words, beast rejoicing at their impending closeness.

Abby wiggled and shifted, moving until she balanced on the edge of the mattress. Before he could talk himself out of it, he crawled in beside her. But that wasn't all. He pulled her close, naked curves flush with the hard planes of his side. He wore nothing but a pair of worn jeans, which meant he could rejoice in the feel of her warmth meshing with his chest.

She rested her cheek on his chest, her warm, moist breath fanning his heated skin, and he breathed deep, drawing in her natural flavors. She was more than a naked body. More than a pain in the ass. More than... simply more than anything—anyone—he'd ever known.

Scared the shit outta him.

Pleased the fuck outta him, too.

Declan let his hands wander, fingers ghosting over silken flesh, and he allowed himself to *feel* her body. It'd been different when she'd needed care. Now he wouldn't hate himself for exploring her.

"Tell me." It was a soft whisper, moist air caressing his chest. She lifted her hand and laid it over his heart, her soft palm covering the most broken part of him. "Tell me."

Two words. If only it were that easy.

He closed his eyes and let his touch wander, let himself trace her spine and revel in the feel of her hair sliding through his fingers. "That pack was fucked. Top down, it was fucked up." He sighed, his mind leading him back to that time. "I just never saw it because I was an alpha pup. Weaker wolves..." He shook his head and swallowed hard. His throat wasn't clogging up. It wasn't. His eyes sure as hell weren't burning, either. "They suffered and I had no idea."

"But you did something about it." Her words were filled with unbreakable conviction. Not a hint of doubt.

"How do you know I did anything? I'm not some kind of hero who—"

She lifted her head and pressed a single finger to his lips. "We'll agree to disagree on this one."

Declan rolled his eyes and grunted, not speaking again until she was back in place. Her presence was the only thing keeping him sane while he told the screwed-up story.

"I didn't knock on the front door—just walked right on in as if I lived at the pack house already. The alpha told me to treat it like home, and I did."

He fought for air, his throat threatening to snap closed and never open again. His throat felt tight. Maybe he was getting sick. Shifters didn't catch diseases, but there was a first time for everything.

"I heard…" Declan cleared his throat. "I heard her whining before I even made it up the porch steps. I knew." He licked his lips. "I knew what that cry meant. I knew the sounds wolves made when they were scared—hurt." Could Abby hear him anymore? He could hardly hear himself talk. "I heard her, and I leaped up those steps. I rushed through that door and hunted her through the massive place."

Opulence. Marble. Hardwood floors. More than a pack needed, but the alpha had always wanted to flaunt his status.

"I found her." Declan's cheeks were wet. He'd have to tell Pike that his fucking roof leaked because he sure as hell wasn't crying. "I found her with the alpha. She hadn't stood me up. I found the strongest wolf in our pack—the alpha—*abusing* my girlfriend."

He couldn't say the words. Not the real ones.

"I died that day, Abby. Alphas are meant to…" Fuck if he was crying over this bullshit. Pike's roof leak was bad. "She was broken, bloody. He took that spark out of her eyes."

"What did you take?"

He'd never said the words. Hell, he'd never told anyone about this. He shifted their positions—Abby on her back while he lay on his side next to her. He met her stare, gaze intent.

"I took his life." Four words. He couldn't look at her while he explained the rest. Not while the wounds from that time were so fresh. "I didn't have a plan. I simply acted. The alpha tried to talk. Maybe. But I wasn't listening. He hadn't listened to her. I wouldn't listen to him. I don't even remember half of what I did."

Which was a lie. He remembered it all. Painfully. Clearly. Eternally.

"When I was done, I left that room—the pack—and never looked back." He forced himself to look at her, to meet her stare even though the wolf wanted to tuck tail and run. "Do you understand now? I don't have a heart. I don't do feelings. That part of me died all those years ago, and smiles or laughter aren't gonna bring it back."

"I don't believe that."

He snorted. "Why?"

She tucked his hair behind his ear, fingers stroking his jaw. "You protected your girlfriend. You protected me."

"I've killed people for money," he snapped. "Don't paint me with a brush coated in sunshine, Abby. I'm heartless, I don't have a conscience, and I'll happily put a bullet through someone's head for the right price."

She shook her head and lifted her other arm, her hands wreaking havoc on his senses. "You may be a killer, but that's not all you are, Declan."

"What am I? Tell me since you seem to know so much about me."

"You're mine."

CHAPTER TWENTY-FIVE

*A*bby tried not to be hurt by his snort or the derisive twist of his lips. She tried not to let his impending denial jab her in the heart. Because it was coming. She could see the shift of emotions in his features, the change in his eyes. He'd deny her, and maybe that was for the best.

His first killing...after what the girl had been through...was justified. More than justified in her opinion. But the deaths since then. They tore at her, grabbed her arms and pulled her in two.

"Yours? You think—"

"Why'd you join SHOC? For the money?" She pushed on, not letting him respond. "The prestige?"

That mocking smile widened. "I didn't have a choice, remember? Besides, it's a tax write-off. My little bit of charity work to offset my freelance income."

"You're trying to push me away."

"You pushed yourself away," he countered. "You asked me if I killed parents. Asked if I left orphans scattered around the world. I did. I do. That hasn't changed." He chuckled and shook his head, but she kept her hands in place, fingers caressing his skin and his soft hair. "That'll never change. I freelance when I'm not busy with SHOC.

Sometimes I manage to sneak in a job or two while we're on a mission."

She *had* pulled away from him. She'd built up a nice brick wall between them, but her cougar...her cougar wanted it gone. The animal saw the heart of Declan's beast and judged him as worthy. Worthy of what, she wasn't sure and wasn't ready to know. Not...not yet.

"How do you pick them?" She stroked his jaw, rough scrape of his scruff replaced by his wolf's soft fur.

"Huh?"

"How do you pick your jobs? How do you decide who you'll kill and who you won't? Do you accept every assignment tossed your way?"

"What does it matter?" He shot the words at her, harsh and fast.

"Tell me." She pleaded with him with her eyes, silently begging him to answer. In her heart, she knew what he'd say, but she needed the words. "Disgruntled housewives? Angry business partners? Scorned lovers? Who do you choose? How do you choose?"

With each question, his breathing increased, his lungs heaving. He collapsed forward, forehead resting on hers, his eyes closed. She shut hers as well, simply *being* with him in that moment.

Abby wrapped her arms around him, crossing them behind his neck and holding him tightly. He wouldn't escape her, not until he lanced the wound and let it out.

"Tell me." Her lips gently brushed his as she released the words.

"Evil. I go after evil." A drop of wetness fell to her cheek, a single bead that hit her skin and slid down her face. A tear—Declan's tear. "I attack and destroy it until nothing is left. That means that sometimes kids suffer. Sometimes they lose parents they might have loved in their own way, but those people..." He shuddered, and she tightened her hold. "They needed killing."

His lashes brushed her eyelids as he opened his eyes, and she did the same, meeting his intent blue stare. "Do you understand now?"

So many questions in his gaze. So many emotions that flickered through eyes the color of the sky. This wasn't the wolf's pain, but the man's, and she understood.

"Yes," she whispered, and arched her back, straining upward until her lips caressed his. Just a hint of a touch, a barely there stroke that she felt all the way to her core.

"Abby," he murmured against her mouth, and a new tension overcame his body. "We can't. You were just—"

"Kiss me, Declan. Just kiss me." She'd start with a simple kiss.

She sensed his indecision, a struggle inside that made him tremble. A tiny, nearly imperceptible shake, but one she felt nonetheless. She practically shouted in triumph, but swallowed the yell. Instead, she stretched her neck and pulled on his once again, bringing their mouths back together.

He slipped his tongue into her mouth, delving deep and exploring her with a single sweep. Their tongues twined, strokes and caresses mimicking what they desired most.

And they both desired.

Her pussy ached, growing hot and slick with every beat of her heart. He surrounded her and filled her, his scent and taste enveloping her in an arousing cloud of need.

Declan's cock hardened against her hip. His thick length settled snuggly to her curves. His warmth passed through the layers of fabric separating them, the sheet and his boxer briefs shielding the proof of his desire. He rocked his hips and she shifted hers, giving him a hint of friction, and he moaned into her mouth.

Abby wanted to give him pleasure, to give him everything. She wanted that thick hardness between her thighs, sliding against her moist slit and then sinking deep inside her. She wanted his passion. She wanted it all.

Her thighs parted slightly as her body silently pleaded for more. She ran her hands over Declan's back, stroking his skin, touching every part of him she could reach. But it wasn't enough. It'd never be enough.

Abby pulled away from his mouth, separating their lips just long enough to...

"Declan." She breathed his name against his lips, forming the word before delving into their kiss once more.

What they'd shared before had been heated passion, but this went so much deeper. This was simply *more*.

She tugged on him. Craving more contact, she ignored the twinge in her leg. "Declan, please."

"Abby," he rasped, and she met his now-amber eyes. "We can't. I want..." He shuddered, a ripple of gray dancing over his shoulders. "But I'm not that big of an asshole."

Abby slipped her hand between them, smoothed it down the flat planes of his stomach and didn't stop until she reached the proof of his desire.

"Fuck." He shuddered so hard the bed shook and his length twitched against her palm.

"Please," she murmured against his lips. "Just this. I need..." So bad, so much, she thought she'd lose her mind.

"You're gonna kill me." The words were rough, almost angry, but his touch was gentle and slow.

Careful.

The sheet was pulled aside, and suddenly Declan was above her. His hands explored her body, his legs twined with hers, and she gave him the same treatment. She traced every inch she could reach, learned the rises and falls of his carved body—the way it fit perfectly against hers.

Their mouths continued their erotic dance while they studied each other with their hands.

Still it wasn't enough. Her nipples pebbled to hard points and her core was slick and prepared for his possession—but it wasn't enough to push her over the edge.

She reached into his boxer briefs, inching beneath the taut fabric until her fingers brushed what she sought. She wrapped her fingers around his thickness and gave him the gentlest of squeezes. This moment was for her, a chance to simply feel evidence of his desire for her. And then...

Then she tightened her hold ever so slightly, a squeeze that drew a deep moan from Declan. From there, she stroked his thick length, gliding up and down. He groaned and growled, his hips flexing with her every movement.

At the same time, his hands drifted on, one large palm sliding down her stomach and farther south to cup her mound. He pressed, putting pressure against her folds, and she cried out for him. "Declan!"

She arched her back and rolled her hips, searching for more.

"Right here," he murmured against her shoulder, lips drifting over her skin.

She shuddered, her body moving in time with his. They both rocked their hips in a matching rhythm while they took—and gave—pleasure.

Declan slid a finger between her folds, sliding easily through her wetness until he teased her very center.

"Yes." She hissed the word.

"Abby," he rasped, the word both a question and a plea. She knew his thoughts since she had no doubt they mirrored her own.

What are you doing to me?

Please don't stop.

She didn't. He didn't. They made love—*fucked*—and yet didn't.

Whatever they did, whatever anyone wanted to call it, it still made her pant and moan with the growing ecstasy.

He circled her clit, and she let herself be swept away with the sensations. She imagined it was his mouth on her pussy, his cock sliding in and out of her sheath. Her mind drew out the fantasy, an image of her straddling Declan, his hardness stretching her core. She'd ride him, cry for him, beg him...come for him.

"Declan..." A shudder overtook her, one that didn't end when it reached her toes. No, it retraced its path, dancing along her veins and easing back up her legs. The pleasure plucked her nerves, bringing them to life with each flex and twist of muscle. She mewled and whined, needing more, but already it felt like too much.

Too much but not enough and still too much and...And her body was being torn apart by the bliss, pulled in a thousand directions while Declan tortured her.

And she tortured him.

She gave as good as she got, drawing and pushing them both to the precipice. It was near, just out of reach, but soon she'd jump and embrace that ultimate joy. She'd...

"Declan..." Her muscles tensed, body curling upward with the overwhelming wave of deliciousness.

"Here," he growled low, beast not man. "Give it to me."

A scream. Long and loud. It came from her very soul, the source of life and love and everything that made her Abby. Her pussy clenched around Declan's finger. And Declan...Declan stiffened and released his own sounds, a wolf's howl while he came. A wet warmth bathed her hand, proof he'd reached the pinnacle along with her.

Part of her didn't want the orgasm to end. It was too delicious, too perfect. She wanted to hold on to it—him—forever.

That single thought was followed by her cougar's purr, the cat thrilled with the idea of...keeping Declan.

Keeping Declan?

No.

But...

He...

"Abby." Two syllables. Just two syllables left his mouth, but there were so many other words hidden in his voice, hidden within his tone, in the way he said her name and the hitch in his speech. She knew what he meant because she knew *him*.

And it scared her. Down to her toes, down to her *soul*, the idea scared her.

"Perfect," he murmured, and nuzzled her neck, his damp, warm breath bathing her skin. "So perfect."

"Declan." She released his softening length and withdrew her hand. "I—"

He groaned and growled, rolling away from her in a blur of movement. She nearly whined at the loss of his touch. He returned almost as quickly as he'd left, now nude and beneath the covers at her side. The jeans were turned into a makeshift cloth to wipe away their passion before they were tossed away.

Then it was just them. In the dark together, and yet she somehow felt a little alone.

Until he pulled her into his arms. Until the deadly assassin tugged her close and gave her a gentle kiss on the forehead.

"Sleep."

CHAPTER TWENTY-SIX

*T*his time he'd kill Pike for real. He'd disembowel the asshole and leave him for the vultures.

The pounding—Pike banging on the bedroom door—came again. It'd already woken Declan, and if it pulled Abby from sleep...

Dead.

He slid from beneath Abby, stomped to the door, and wrenched it open. He didn't care about his nudity. Let the man see his dick swinging. It was what the ass got for interrupting.

Pike stood just on the other side, fist raised as if he was about to bang once more.

He glared at the other man and dropped his voice to a low growl. "Don't you fucking dare."

Pike smirked, his glance taking in Declan before flicking over his shoulder and focusing on Abby. Declan followed the other man's line of sight and spied Abby, all right. *All* of Abby.

"Nice," Pike murmured, and it was too much for Declan's wolf to tolerate. Another male looking at her? Wanting her when Declan hadn't claimed her? Not happening.

His hand transformed to wolf-like paw in an instant. He

grabbed the male's throat and pushed him back, not stopping until the other wolf struck the hallway wall with a deep *thud*.

He leaned in close, crowded Pike until hardly any space separated their bodies. His gums stung for a split second, and then he had the wolf's fangs at his disposal—long, pale, and deadly.

"You don't look at her. You understand?" Declan whispered the words, growl in his voice but still low so he wouldn't wake Abby. "You don't even think about her."

"Dec…" Pike tried to speak, but Declan tightened his hold.

"She's mine, Pike. You think of her like a brother would. You *don't* look at her like you wanna fuck her. Do you get that?" Something else stirred in Declan's blood, that midnight darkness that craved death, the bits and pieces of evil that still plagued him. It told him to finish Pike—eliminate the threat—permanently. It didn't care about their connection—their history.

Pike opened his mouth and wheezed.

"Just nod. You don't need to speak to nod."

The wolf nodded, a barely perceptible jerk of his chin.

"Declan?" Soft. Sleepy. Feminine. His. Then came the delicate patter of her feet as she left the bed and drew nearer.

Declan cracked his neck and rolled his shoulders, wolf disappearing in a rush of fur and claws.

"What's wrong? Why are you…naked?" Her husky voice rolled over him in a soothing caress, calming the animal further.

In some ways, anyway. There was a specific part of him that perked up and wanted nothing to do with calm.

Wolf gone, he released Pike and turned to face Abby.

"Pike was knocking and I didn't want him to wake you. You need more sleep. Go on back to bed." He padded forward until he filled the doorway, blocking her from Pike's view. No one got to see her like that, all sleep tussled and covered in nothing but a sheet. The white swath of fabric caressed her curves, hinting at what the cloth hid from others.

"I'll be there in a minute." Less if he just flat-out killed Pike. Which was an option if Declan could close the door. He didn't think breaking a neck in front of her would put her in the mood, and he *needed* her in the mood.

"But…" Drowsy blue eyes blinked up at him, golden tendrils of her hair falling across her face, and he tucked the strands behind her ear. "But don't we need to…"

Declan put a crooked finger beneath her chin and encouraged her to tip her head back a little more. He lowered his mouth and brushed her lips with his. It was supposed to end there, but she had to go and sigh. He tugged her closer, ready to steal a little more. He'd just—

"Ahem." A low cough followed.

Declan pulled his lips from hers and released a growl, long and low. "Mother. Fucker." He set Abby away from him and spun, facing Pike once more. "I'm gonna kill you."

The rustle of cloth told him Abby moved, repositioned herself to his right, and he eased in that direction. He didn't want Pike's last sight to be of her. Then she had to be a pain in his ass and move left.

He glanced over his shoulder at her, and his anger surged. She didn't have that sleepy, sexy look anymore. "Who's this?"

Declan sighed and ran a hand down his face. Snippets of the night, pre-orgasm, flickered through his mind. "This is Pike. You were out of it when we got here. This is his place, and he"—he shot Pike a glare that'd kill a weaker man—"is gonna leave us the fuck alone now."

"He..." Abby squinted, her gaze bouncing between them. "The dead man?"

"Yes." He kept his narrow-eyed stare on Pike.

"He looks alive." She pointed at Pike. "And a lot like you. Like you two could be..."

"Brothers," Pike purred, and Declan clenched his fist. He hadn't hauled his brother's ass around for the last fifteen years just to send his fist through the wolf's head. "Didn't Declan tell you?"

Abby's attention settled on Declan. "I thought you said his name was Jacob?"

Declan ignored Pike and turned to face Abby. "It's complicated."

"Not that complicated," Pike grumbled. "A guy fakes his own death and you act like—"

"You wouldn't have *had* to fake your own death if you'd fucking listen and stay out of shit you know nothing about, but *nooo*, you just have to—"

"Kiss my ass, Declan. You wouldn't have made it out of the last contract if I hadn't—"

"Are you fucking *kidding me*?"

"I came to tell you that Team Fuckhole is having coffee in the kitchen." Pike's attention flicked to Declan's dick and back to his face. "Put your cock away before you come out."

"You called them?" Declan snarled. "What the fuck?"

Pike shook his head and snorted. "You think they didn't know you'd end up here? They're assholes, not idiots."

"They're not taking her." He'd go through them all if they tried.

"Like I said, not idiots." With that, he turned and left,

striding down the hall as if Declan hadn't threatened to kill him, which meant that now he was alone. With Abby. Who was *naked* under that sheet.

His wolf liked the way his thoughts were headed and gave an approving chuff, wanting to cover her in his scent. But looking at her, the wide eyes, parted lips, and shock written all over her features…Nah, naked time wasn't in the immediate future.

"We need to get dressed," he said, and backed her into the room once again. The moment he had space, he nudged the door shut, putting that barrier between them and a bunch of bullshit he wasn't ready to deal with quite yet. "There are some clothes here. They'll be big, but at least you'll be covered."

And not prancing around in a sheet. Sun shone through the window, rays dancing over her body and revealing even more of her. The brightness made the fabric nearly invisible—the dark pink of her nipples, the dip of her waist, and those curls at the juncture of her thighs.

The rustle of fabric, a small hand on his arm…He'd killed men last night without a thought—he was a tough asshole—but apparently he was nothing when it came to Abby.

"Pike is your brother, Jacob, and he faked his own death?" When she said it that way, it did sound a little odd, but he didn't have time to explain. "And when he said Team Fuckhole, did he mean your SHOC team?"

"Yes to both. Put this stuff on and meet me in the kitchen."

"But will they…?" She pressed a hand to her throat.

"It looks like the team is going to help deal with this." He gave her one last hard kiss. Just in case Ethan knew what'd happened to his sports car and managed to land a punch. Hurt like hell to kiss with a busted lip. "Get dressed. I'll see you in the kitchen."

Declan smacked her ass, flat of his palm curving to rub away any sting, and he couldn't help but smile at her squeak and growled "Declan."

Yeah, he smiled then, but as soon as he stepped into the kitchen and faced his team, it turned into a glare. "You assholes are gonna be fucking polite and fucking apologetic, or I'll fucking kill your fucking asses right now."

"That's a whole lot of fucking." Birch raised a single brow.

Of course Pike couldn't keep his mouth shut and snorted. "'Cause he didn't get any fucking last night."

"You piece of shit." He snarled the words and leaped. Not because he spoke the truth, but because Declan needed to work off some of his sexual frustration and Pike was closest.

CHAPTER TWENTY-SEVEN

*W*hen Abby walked into the room five minutes later no one noticed her standing just inside the long hallway, beneath the arch that separated the great room from the bedrooms. They were all too focused on Pike—Jacob, though she wasn't sure if the others knew of the brother/death fakeage going on there—and Declan rolling around on the ground. They traded punches and bites, claws occasionally flashing.

Pike delivered a hard punch with a fast right, nailing Declan's cheek, and Declan returned it with a head butt. The crunch told her he'd broken Pike's nose. She winced. That had to hurt.

Then thoughts of hurting vanished. She'd been such an idiot—so intent on following the growls and snarls—she hadn't realized what she'd be rushing *into*.

Like, a great room filled with men who she assumed were Declan's SHOC team. And her arrival? That wince? It had drawn attention.

Not from all of them. Three remained focused on the brothers trading blows, but one of them... *He* sat at a dining table, his chair kicked back as he balanced his weight on two chair legs. His feet rested on the table's smooth top, and he had his hands linked behind his head.

A hat shielded half his face from view, but she didn't need to see all of him to *know* his gaze was on her. Dark. Intent. Heavy. A tremor slid down her spine, and she swallowed hard and took a step back into the shadows. She wished the dark would swallow her whole and hide her from his view, but it didn't.

His eyes flared brightly, a gold that remained focused on her, his stare unwavering. Cold. She shivered. Like ice—barren and emotionless. He didn't flinch when Pike and Declan crashed into the wall, sending pictures tumbling from their nails.

Everyone was at ease. *He* was not.

Everyone cheered and laughed. *He* did not.

Everyone ignored Abby. *He. Did. Not.*

Abby took a step back, and he let his weight bring the chair back to four feet.

Another step. Would any of the doors in the house hold back...? She wasn't sure exactly *what* kind of animal he was on the inside. Not a wolf—the eye color wasn't right. A big cat, then. Lion? No, the jawline and coloring didn't match one of those felines. Tiger?

Her heart raced, and adrenaline flooded her veins. She didn't know—didn't *need* to know—his species. Danger surrounded him in an invisible cloak, and her pulse doubled.

Yeah. Tiger. A tiger who was all about *her*.

The tiger rose from his chair and took a step, pausing only to speak to one of the other shifters for a split second before he was intent on her again. Intent. Determined.

"Declan?" Her voice—her whole body—trembled, but she remained stuck in place. Terror gripped her tighter and tighter as the stranger neared.

That quickly, the fight between Pike and Declan ended

and she faced two broad backs pressed shoulder to shoulder—twin wolf growls directed away from her.

"Back the fuck off, Cole." It was Declan's voice, but the growl that followed was unfamiliar, a rumbling roll so like Declan's yet not.

It was Pike. Pike threatening a tiger on her behalf—defending her just like Declan said he would.

"Aw, c'mon, Dec," the tiger mumbled, and Abby pressed up to her tiptoes to peek over the brothers' shoulders. The tiger—Cole—stood halfway between his seat and their small trio, but instead of staring at her like she was dinner…he suddenly looked anywhere *but* at her. "Just gonna talk to her a little."

Gone was the feral intensity, and in its place was over six feet of slightly embarrassed badass. The "badass" was assumed since he was one of Declan's team members, but the pink tinge to his cheeks was unmistakable.

"No, you're not," Declan countered. "Your ass is staying over there and your mouth is staying shut." She'd seen him coldly angry, deadly, but this was different. Harsher. Wilder, which made him even more dangerous. "No one's talking to her. No one's even *looking* at her. As far as the team is concerned, she doesn't exist."

Declan stepped forward, his skin now sporting more than a little gray fur and his fingers turned claw. She didn't have time to think or question what she did next. She simply went into action.

With that single step, she had enough room to slip between the brothers and move in front of the furious wolf. She blocked his path and eased closer, resting her cheek on his chest while she wrapped her arms around his waist.

"Declan. Stop." Hardly more than a whisper, but it was enough. Her presence, her voice, halted his approach. The tension remained, his body prepared to launch at Cole, but he didn't shove her aside and go after the tiger. He simply stayed in place, let her hold him captive while his beast drove him to take on the other shifter.

"Well, damn. She's like a dick whisperer or something. Stopped his cock with one word." Ethan's voice was filled with awe, his words low, but it did the job.

It broke the rising tension, popped the growing bubble of violence and deflated it with a handful of words. Declan shuddered, his muscles relaxing. His shoulders curled forward while he slipped his arms around her as well.

"Abby." His voice still held the wolf.

"I'm right here. I'm fine. I was just..." *Scared. Terrified. Petrified.* Any one of those would work. The sudden scrutiny, the intense stare... "Surprised. I was just surprised for a minute."

Declan snorted, and Pike chuckled, but Pike had to take it a step further and comment. "Your girl's not a good liar."

"Aw, man..." Grant—werewolf, if she remembered Declan's description correctly—stomped into view, whining like a five-year-old. "You already called dibs? Figures," he grumbled. "I'm stuck behind the computer and that asshole gets the girl."

Abby turned just in time to see Ethan chuck something across the room at Grant.

Grant jumped up and caught it with his mouth, then chewed. He looked toward Abby, wide grin on his lips while he chomped his food, and gave her a wink.

"Grant, you're a wolf, not a fucking dog." Yet another man eased into sight.

Grant shrugged. "I'm a man, I'm hungry, and that was food." Grant jerked his chin toward their small group and spoke to Pike. "Puppy, what else ya got? Dinner rolls ain't gonna cut it if we've got to go balls to the wall tonight."

"You guys aren't doing anything." Declan's growl was back, and she shushed him, rubbing his arm gently. "That's not working twice, Abby," he drawled. "I'm determined, not preparing to take Cole down."

It was worth a shot.

"Take *me* down?" Cole chuckled. "You're deluded if you think your scrawny, flea-bitten ass can do anything other than bark at my cat."

Declan tensed and pushed against her. "Motherfu—"

Declan wasn't "scorched earth" angry, but he *was* "annoyed seal pup who'd had his first cod snatched by his older brother" angry. And that was something Abby was qualified to handle.

"*Hey!*" she yelled. Tried to. Mostly raised her voice a little bit because in all honesty, every single shifter in the house towered over her. Declan pushed against her, his superior strength forcing her feet to slide over the carpet. Abby shoved back, but he just kept on coming. "I mean it. Stop."

Declan wasn't listening, and when she glanced over her shoulder, she spied Cole bouncing on his toes and shaking his arms, like a boxer loosening up for a fight.

"That isn't helping." She grunted and pushed against him a little harder.

"Twenty on Cole," Grant called out.

"I'll take that bet, but you're just throwing away money. Declan's got sexual frustration on his side," Ethan added.

"Forty that Declan is the first to end up with a broken bone." Even Pike joined in.

The only one who hadn't hopped into the betting game was the last stranger. He simply roared. That was it. He opened his mouth, drew in a heaving breath, and released a roar so loud it shook the house down to its foundation.

That had to be Birch, the team alpha.

The deafening sound continued, Birch's face flushed with the strength it took to silence the men with a single bellow.

Fur sprouted along his cheekbones, eyes bleeding black while his mouth cracked and reshaped to mimic his inner animal's maw. Birch bowed his back, mouth to the ceiling, and the last echoes of his roar escaped him with a final push of air from his lungs.

And then it was over...

Silence. Utter silence.

It wasn't Birch's volume or his roar—she'd grown up with wild polar bears always on the hunt for the herd—that surprised Abby. It was the reaction of the men. All of them—even Pike, and he wasn't a member of SHOC—fell quiet. More than quiet.

Her attention drifted from one agent to another, eyes touching each one and finding them all holding a similar pose—head bent, eyes down. Not so much in a show of submissiveness, but like rowdy children who'd been caught doing something they shouldn't.

Grant went so far as to kick the carpet as if he was scuffing the dirt. "Sorry, Birch."

"Sorry." Then Ethan.

Cole simply grunted, while Declan huffed. She figured that was probably the most Birch would get out of those two.

Pike snorted as if he didn't care and padded toward the kitchen. "Whatever. I'm hungry."

Yeah, he acted like he didn't care, but she saw him pause beside Birch, murmur a word or two, and then the bear slammed his hand on the wolf's shoulder.

"You got any steaks?" Grant jogged after Pike.

"You've got paws; go chase something down." Pike sounded annoyed and yet not, as if it was an old argument, a normal routine the wolves went through.

"We're going to eat and then we're going to plan," Birch stated, soft, unassuming. No growls or snarls, a simple statement that somehow got everyone moving and working toward their goals.

Food.

Then they'd hunt … for information.

CHAPTER TWENTY-EIGHT

COLE

*C*ole didn't do jealousy. If he wanted what someone else had, well, he'd take it. Or buy it.

Except staring at Abby snuggled in Declan's arms and seeing that possessive glint in his teammate's eyes...he wasn't sure the taking would be easy. As for buying... Abby wasn't the kind of chick to tuck a few hundred dollar bills in her bra and crawl onto his lap. She was sweetness and light with sharp claws and a backbone of steel.

Which made him want her even more. Dammit.

He tore his attention from the couple and refocused on whatever the hell Birch was bitching about *now*. The team plus Pike and Abby sat around Pike's scarred dining room table, arguing over who went where and did what. He hadn't exactly been paying attention. Staring at Abby's blushing cheeks was more fun than listening to growls.

"Someone remind me when I can blow shit up?" He tipped his chair back and twined his fingers behind his head. "Or at least shoot someone? I know guns are Declan's game, but I'm getting desperate for a little blood."

Birch glared at him, Ethan snickered, and Grant ignored him in favor of a steak he'd gotten *somewhere*. Declan's attention was all on Abby, and then she had to go and *giggle*. Pike's focus remained on the map spread across the table.

Cole narrowed his eyes, staring at the little puppy while he studied the map. The kid hadn't joined SHOC with his brother, Declan—at Declan's insistence—so he wasn't sure why the puppy was included in the planning session.

But he was. He stood over the city's plans, fingers tracing the shoreline.

Sure, Cole could understand why the director made Birch twitchy. He simply wondered why Pike *didn't* have the grizzly shifter on edge. Because Pike sent his tiger's senses tingling, and the cat remained uneasy the longer Pike stared at that map.

Cole turned his attention to Birch. He ignored the bear's grumbles and caught his team alpha's eyes. He flicked his focus to Pike and back to Birch, then lifted his eyebrows in question.

The grizzly pressed his lips together and shook his head, remaining silent.

Ethan snorted and leaned close. "Subtle."

He elbowed the lion. "Fuck off."

"Focus, assholes." Birch's voice cut through their joking. He didn't yell, but shouting wasn't necessary. They knew their jobs—when to settle in and when to dare Grant to shotgun a case of beer.

Birch snatched the map from Pike and leaned over the large diagram. He pointed at a small island just off the coast. "The tablet we need is hidden here on Palm Island, right, Abby?"

Abby's face paled, and she nodded like a bobblehead toy. Aw, poor kitty was afraid of the bear.

Sure, Declan tried to calm her, but Cole's tiger assured him they could do a better job. She seemed fine getting up close and personal with a psychopath. He and Abby would get along well. He simply had to get rid of Declan first. Cole's tiger purred at the idea, saliva flooding his mouth, and he kicked the cat's ass to the back of his mind.

They were brothers—not by blood, but by choice.

Fuck. He needed to get laid. He had to be able to find a nice little piece who looked all sweet and innocent like Abby. *Had to*.

Birch tapped on another area of the map. "This is the accounting firm—Ogilve, Piers, and Patterson."

"You mean O.P.P.," Ethan murmured.

"Yeah, you know me." Declan tipped his chin toward Ethan.

Grant snickered. "It'd be wrong to whip up a mix tape for the mission that began with 'O.P.P.' by Naughty by Nature, right?"

"Yes." Birch's voice was flat, face expressionless.

"Awesome." Grant snapped and then made finger guns at their team alpha. "I'll work on that once you're done ordering us to break into O.P.P. and download their servers."

Birch ignored Grant and got back to plans.

Cole decided to ignore Birch in favor of staring at Abby on the down low. Oh, he listened—mostly—so he knew he'd have to gear up and haul out around ten, but he left the other details to Grant and Ethan. Ethan did the driving and Grant handled the tech. He was only muscle and guns for this little trip.

"Everyone know what the hell they're doing?" Birch's voice rose, snaring Cole's attention once more.

"Your decision is final. You're not letting me take part in this op?" Pike's voice dropped to a low growl, the words rumbling through the room.

"Pike..." Declan matched his younger brother's growl, but the pup kept talking as if he didn't hear the wolf.

Pike stood and squared off against Birch. "Declan came to me for help. You can't—"

Well, maybe Cole would get a chance to work off his excess energy before they had to leave. There was a lot his tiger would tolerate. Like the Energizer Bunny, he'd keep going and going and going...until someone fucked with what belonged to him.

Cole didn't have a family—he had the four men around the table.

"Puppy." He rolled to his feet, his movement smooth courtesy of his cat. He placed his palms on the worn table-top and leaned forward. "You need to think real hard before you finish that thought, 'cause it sounds like you're giving my team alpha an order. But you know better than to do that, don't you?"

Amber eyes met Cole's, Pike's wolf riding the edge of the other man's control. He was a big wolf—rivaling Declan in size and strength—but Cole had the man in height and pure bulk. He didn't want to get into a fight with Pike, but he would. The team could give Birch shit, but no one else. Not unless they wanted to meet Cole's claws up close and personal.

Pike clenched his teeth, jaw flexing, and a vein throbbed in his temple, but he remained silent.

"Puppy?" Cole quirked a brow. "You weren't demanding anything from Birch, were you?"

"Pike," Declan snapped.

"No." Pike ripped his gaze from Cole and turned his stare to the map.

"All right, then." Cole eased back into his seat. The moment he relaxed into the chair, conversation returned, the others murmuring, plotting, and planning.

It didn't take long for Birch to finish issuing orders and end their little meeting. They had their assignments. Now it was a matter of execute and regroup. Each member of the team peeled away. They all had their own prep rituals— including Cole.

Which was how he ended up outside, sitting on the edge of Pike's back porch, and...listening in on Pike's phone call. A call that included statements like, "on my way" and "Palm Island."

Cole strode after the pup, his anger rising hot and fast as he realized Pike was telling *someone* about their plans. Only to have a large presence block his path.

A wave of strength—dominance—crashed over him just as a single order sank into his mind. "Stay."

CHAPTER TWENTY-NINE

*A*bby wouldn't look at him. *Hadn't* looked at him from the moment they climbed into the car. It'd been just north of forty-eight hours since Declan had wrenched Abby from SHOC custody, and hopefully the ordeal would be over soon.

The three of them—him, Birch, and Abby—had left Pike's tasked with retrieving the tablet.

Declan talked to Birch and Birch talked back.

Birch talked to Abby and Abby murmured back.

But when Declan tried to hold a damn conversation with her, he got half-stuttered answers and her flat-out refusal to even look his way.

Abby was hiding something. Declan knew it just like he knew how to assemble a Glock blindfolded while parajumping. He knew it just like he knew how to kill a man with one finger. And he knew it like he knew the curves of her body and the moans she made just before she came.

What he *didn't* know was what she was lying *about*. But he would soon. She couldn't keep up her game of pretend forever.

Cole, Ethan, and Grant were off breaking into Ogilve, Piers, and Patterson in search of any additional data on

FosCo, along with information on the accounting firm's other clients. Clients that might have deep, long-standing ties to Unified Humanity as well.

Pike hadn't been included in their plans. He was a "civilian" despite his past association with SHOC.

Which left Declan with Birch at his back and Abby... lying to him.

Birch piloted the small boat they'd "borrowed." A quick little thing that would get them from the shore to Pine Island and back again. They didn't need fancy, just fast.

Abby sat near the bow, clinging to the side of the craft. The vessel sped across the black waters, wind tugging at her blond hair. He wanted to be back at Pike's, wrapped around her, his face buried in that hair. Instead they were on a damned boat and hunting for a tablet that hopefully held proof of FosCo's activities and a ticket to safety for Abby.

Declan eased forward, carefully making his way to Abby, and he slid onto the bench seat behind her. Even with the sticky, briny scent of the sea surrounding them, he could still capture her natural smell. Crisp air. Dew-touched trees. Sweet like flowers. And so fucking sexy. His cock was hard just thinking about her, smelling her, and when he let his mind wander toward imagining her naked...

He dropped his head forward and leaned into Abby, resting his forehead on her shoulder. He managed to swallow his groan—barely. She tilted her head to the side, rubbing her cheek on his skull.

Because she was driven to by her cat? Or was it a feline apology for lying?

Probably a little of both.

He turned his head so his lips brushed her ear. "Abby," he murmured. "Wanna tell me why you're—"

But she cut him off. Not letting him finish the question. "We're close. Birch should slow down."

Declan sighed. "When we beach, you're going to tell me why you're lying."

She blinked at him, eyes wide, guileless. He could practically read her mind. *I don't know what you're talking about.*

"I..." She grimaced, a hint of guilt fluttering across her features. "We're not beaching. He should stop about twenty feet from the south end."

"He—"

"Go tell him before he gets too close and can't stop before he comes up against the rocks." Abby nudged him with her shoulder, and he gave her a glare. One that would have frightened the average person. Apparently making her come ruined his ability to intimidate her.

Declan half turned and held his hand out to Birch, hand flat and palm facing his team alpha. Then he brought it to his forehead, palm down as if he saluted Birch when he was telling the bear to keep an eye out.

The engine dropped to a low idle, momentum and the current carrying the vessel forward. The small waves rocked the boat, and his wolf's hearing picked up the low whoosh of water lapping at the island's shore.

"We're here," Abby whispered, and Declan formed a fist, silently instructing Birch to cut the engine entirely.

Once silence surrounded them, Birch moved close. Even with the boat swaying, the bear shifter looked damned intimidating when he crossed his arms over his chest. "Someone wanna tell me why we're stopping so far out?"

Declan turned his attention to the woman who'd dragged their asses to some nothing of an island. "Abby?"

She kept quiet and turned her gaze to the bottom of

the boat, but that didn't mean she was motionless. Nah, he couldn't get that lucky. Because as he and Birch watched, she snared the hem of her shirt and pulled it upward.

Declan reached for her, snatching the fabric and tugging it back down. "What are you doing?"

She scrunched her nose. "Can I tell you later?"

He leaned closer and drew in a deep breath. The sting of unease with a hint of worry and fear burned his nose. His wolf wanted to sneeze and banish the scent. Declan simply wanted to know what the fuck was going on. "No. You can tell me now."

Abby grimaced.

"Abby..." He added a little growl, his beast finally realizing all was not well.

"Um..." She nibbled her lower lip.

At least until Birch's feral growl vibrated the air around them. "Tell us."

"It's in an underwater cave."

Declan couldn't help it; he roared. "It's—" He cut off the rest of his question, remembering they were trying to be quiet. "This isn't something you could have revealed before we left the coast? We would have stolen a diver's boat."

Abby propped her hands on her hips, one cocked slightly to the side when she shifted her weight. "It's only mostly underwater. I don't exactly swim out here with climbing gear. I go in from the bottom."

"You're not going—" Declan started.

"She is." The bear cut him off. "She's got this. She goes down, she gets it, she comes back, and we're out. We're spending more time arguing than it'd take her to go and return."

Declan dropped his head forward and took a deep breath, fighting the urge to throw Birch overboard and then tie up

Abby so she couldn't do something stupid like jump off the boat.

Unfortunately, the idea came too late. Because Abby... jumped off the boat.

He spun in place, eyes searching the darkness, and found a pile of clothes where she should have been standing. He rushed to the side and peered over, glaring at the trail of bubbles that popped to the surface of the water. A shimmer of golden fur shined through the darkness, the moon's light caressing her partially shifted form, and then she was gone. Swallowed by the midnight waters.

"Dammit, Abby." He snarled and growled, the wolf pissed at what she'd done and even more furious that she wasn't standing in front of him so he could wring her damn neck.

"Birch." He shook his head. "If she gets hurt…"

The bear sighed and tipped his head back. "God save me from lovesick males."

Declan rolled his eyes. "God should save you from pissed-off wolves."

Because he sure as hell wasn't lovesick. Cocksick, maybe. But not lovesick.

"Look." Birch pointed at Declan. "Everyone pulls their weight on this team, and they do what they're best at." He pointed at the water. "This is what she's best at."

"She's not part of the fucking team." He snarled the words, voice low but filled with every ounce of fury his wolf could gather. "She's a civilian. She's here because the director is gunning for her and I won't turn her over to that sadistic fuck. Civilians don't do shit in the field. It's why Pike's not here or with the rest of the team."

"That's it? That's all she is? A civilian who has something that will appease the director and give us more intel on Unified Humanity. Nothing else? She's got no other connection to you?" Birch lifted a single brow, smirk on his lips, and Declan wanted to claw it right off the smug prick's face.

Was that all she was? No, but making her more meant she'd be at risk. It meant that tying her life to his could see her roped into an op. If one half of a couple was in, they were both in.

And Declan didn't want her anywhere near danger.

"Yeah, she's just a civilian," he rasped.

"Then when she gets back, we'll park her with the team and treat her as a civvy." The dick sounded so damned cocky.

"Fine," Declan growled. "But no one lays a paw on her. No one."

Because if they did, he'd rip it off.

Birch just shrugged and turned his attention to the water. They *both* turned their attention to the dark, churning water, stares unwavering as they waited. Twenty feet down, then another twenty up just to get inside. Then she'd retrace her path. Birch had said it wouldn't take her too long, but...

But she hadn't returned. Not in five minutes and not in ten.

His body vibrated with his wolf's growing frustration and anger, the animal debating between lashing out at Birch and diving into the water himself. A flurry of bubbles, a blossoming of red, and a scent that caused his hair to stand on end made the decision.

"Human," he hissed, and mixed in with the human's blood now surfacing was the scent of… "*Abby*."

CHAPTER THIRTY

Contrary to popular belief, tasting human blood didn't suddenly turn Abby into a flesh-craving beast intent on murdering all of humanity. Oh, her beast wanted to do some murdering, but not for consumption—for being pissed off. The cat hissed and snarled in the back of her mind, tail whipping and claws flexing and contracting—as if her nails were thirsty for blood as well.

And it wasn't just *any* human she wanted, either. She wanted the asshole with the tranq gun. The one who'd shot her just as she exited the cave mouth. The drug had been fast acting, dragging at her the moment the needle pierced flesh. She'd tried to resist her attackers, had even gotten her fangs and claws into one of the men, but soon lost the underwater battle.

She'd been tossed into this fully tiled room, complete with drains set into the floor. It was empty save a shiny metal table and her—shackled to a chair, wearing nothing but a bra and panties. Now she waited to see who'd walk through the door. So far no one had appeared, but she doubted they'd leave her alone forever. Not when they knew who—*what*—she was.

That was something she recalled during her partially unconscious travels. There'd been hands—rough when they hauled her around. Then voices—snickering, derisive, and taunting.

A familiar one amid them all. Dark, angry, vicious... Eric Foster. Mr. Foster hadn't been pleased about Abby's escape *or* what she'd had in her hands when she'd fled.

Which meant she was with Unified Humanity and hadn't been taken by another SHOC team. The human blood had been a clue, and this man's statement locked her guess into place.

"Can't we make her shift and skin her? She killed Roger."

Abby had mentally smiled at that one. Roger was dead because she'd torn off a good chunk of his hand and then more than a little of his throat. *She* hadn't killed him per se, but she'd nudged his life closer to its end. A lot closer. She hadn't cared for the "skin her" part of the guy's statement, though. She liked her skin exactly where it was—on her.

But back to the tiled room and the chains and the cold. Couldn't they keep her warm and kill her? Did they have to make her freeze before they got to whatever they planned on doing to her?

Abby snorted. There was something wrong with her when her first thoughts—after being kidnapped—were to complain about the temperature. Not her impending... whatever the humans planned.

It was Declan's fault. Declan's and SHOC's, and she'd blame cougars for being solitary and prideless, too. If she'd had a pride, they would have helped keep her safe. Her cougar joined in on spreading the anger around, though it did feel she was being unfair when it came to blaming cougars and their naturally solitary nature.

Traitor.

Ugh. Maybe she was losing her mind. That was as good an explanation as any. Her thoughts ran in scattered directions, mind grabbing on to one thread only to have it snap so she'd pick up another. It meant she bounced from wet to Declan to cold to Declan to...

No, her thoughts weren't scattered, not really. Her mind simply kept going back to the man—wolf—who'd gotten her into this mess. She missed that argumentative, dominating, gorgeous wolf. She wouldn't mind him kidnapping her—again.

If he could find her. She'd been hauled through the ocean, spirited away in a boat, then driven through the city in an SUV. Too many scents would overwhelm the trail.

Well, she'd get her own happy ass out of the clusterfuck she'd stumbled into. Raised voices came from outside the room, deep tenors intermixed with lighthearted laughs. She recognized one voice—that laugh. It was the asshole who'd wanted to skin her.

He drew closer by the second. Maybe she'd get lucky and the group of idiots would keep on walking and... They paused just outside the door, booming voices echoing through the solid sheet of metal that separated them.

"What are we bothering with her for? Just let me kill her and be done with it. Foster got what he wanted." One voice. It seemed familiar, but she couldn't place it.

"It's not your job to make that decision. Foster wants to know what else she has in that head of hers. Why do you think he wants you interrogating her? He said you like playing rough." Roger's friend chuckled. Did sadistic, heartless bastards like the people in UH even have friends?

"I like what I like." That familiar-ish voice again, and it

was followed by a handful of beeps, as if he typed some-thing on a keypad.

He was coming in—panic sent her heart rate soaring. She closed her eyes and dropped her head forward, feigning unconsciousness. Maybe if they thought she was out of it, they'd leave her alone. Perfect plan. Prey in the wild played dead and it worked for their stupid natural predators.

She was desperate prey. They were stupid, asshole, should-be-dead predators.

Abby forced her body to relax and concentrated on un-clenching her muscles. She slowed her breathing and begged her cougar to stay in the background. Busting out fur and fangs while out of it wouldn't exactly sell her "I'm still passed out" plan.

The door screeched as it slid open, metal on metal.

"I like getting dirty." Two heavy *thud*s, one step and then another. "I like doing what I'm told." That voice pricked at her ears, the cougar's curiosity surging, and she mentally whacked the cat on the nose. Her curiosity was go-ing to get them both killed. The little shit.

"But what I *don't* like is an audience." The masculine voice came out hard and flat, and even Abby recognized the order in his tone. No negotiation. The man wanted to be alone—with her.

So not good.

"Aw, c'mon. I heard they can take a lot before they die on you. I've never played with a shifter. Just lemme go one round." The whiny jerk. She didn't want to know what he meant about one "round," and she never wanted to find out.

"Goodbye, George." Metal scraped metal once more, the squeal and grind sending a jagged shiver down her spine. Like nails on chalkboard, a horror-movie bad guy dragging a knife along a house window, or the big bad wolf huffing and puffing at someone's front door.

Rubber squeaked on the tile, and then came the slow, rhythmic *thud* of those boots on the hard surface as he approached. Methodical. Unhurried. Heavy with foreboding. This guy wasn't in a rush. Abby wasn't going anywhere and he knew it. Each step was a taunt, a foreshadowing of what was to come. Would he hit her just as slowly? Would he take his time while he cut her? Wasn't that what UH did? She'd heard stories, whispers from the older seals in the herd.

Would he—

A wave of warmth eased around her, her captor now circling her and surrounding her with his scent. It teased her nose, a hint of something known yet not. She parted her lips just enough for her to draw in the man's scent. The cougar lent a hand, tasting his flavors and trying to put a name to the aroma. The seawater still filled her nose, masking most of the scents. All but one—fear. She mentally shook her head. As if a member of UH would be afraid of a shifter in chains—*tight* chains.

"I know you're awake." That husky voice came, his breath ghosting over her cheek, and a hint of his scruff brushed her skin. His lips feathered over her ear.

Close—so dangerously close. The cat urged her to turn her head and take a chunk out of the human.

But she didn't. She remained in place, feigning sleep, while she hoped he'd give up and leave her alone. Leave her be just long enough for Declan and SHOC to find her. Because he would. Maybe not because he cared for her— all they'd shared was passion—but at least because UH had the tablet and they'd want it back.

Abby's animal grumbled and huffed, scraped at her

mind when she thought of Declan as nothing more than a bed buddy. He was more than that, and the cat couldn't understand why Abby's human half hadn't accepted that truth yet.

If she didn't let hope grow in her heart, there was no way she could suffer the pain of disappointment.

The man ran his nose along her jaw, the warm tip sliding toward her chin and not stopping until he'd continued to her other ear. "You smell good. Even covered in sea water. Is that why he likes you? Is that why he betrayed SHOC?"

She wasn't going to react to his words. She wasn't. Unified Humanity wouldn't learn anything from her.

Not. Happening.

"The longer you pretend, the more it'll hurt, you know." His voice changed, a hint of a smile filling his words, as if he hoped she'd continue her charade so he could hurt her.

Abby clung to her relaxed state, determined to hold out against this man. But then...then a palm landed on her knee, fingers curling around the outside of her right leg. That hand traveled north along her thigh—slow, methodical, and easing closer and closer to the juncture of her thighs.

Her cougar whined and snarled, demanding she stop the coming attack. It wanted to fight. It wanted to claw and bite and bathe in the blood of their enemy.

"Open your eyes, kitty." Fingertips teased ever upward. "And maybe I'll stop. Or did the wolf not do it for you? Do you want a real man? You're pretty enough for a furry." A little farther, his first knuckle catching on the stretchy lace. "Open your eyes."

That last order did it. Not because he injured her, but because his lips brushed hers, a soft caress that made her stomach lurch and her body move without thought. She jerked her head away from him, leaning back as much as she could while she opened her eyes.

And froze.

"Pike?"

Pike. Jacob. Werewolf. Her tormentor?

"What . . . ?" Movement slowly returned to Abby, and she shook her head. "What are you doing?"

The man she'd met was gone. The man who'd stood shoulder to shoulder with Declan—to defend her—had vanished. *That* Pike wasn't in front of her. She didn't know who this was.

Malice sparkled in his blue eyes, a hint of anticipation and joy joining the emotion. He enjoyed this—taunting her, scaring her.

"Hello, pretty, pretty pussy," he murmured, and curled his fingers into the curve of her ass. He didn't break skin, merely squeezed until the pain of his hold suffused her. "Nice of you to wake up."

"What are you doing?" She repeated her question, mind unable to form any other words. That same question repeated on an unending loop, and she wanted—*needed*—an answer.

Pike didn't give her one. He released her and straightened, pulling his arm back as he rose, and then *crack*. The back of his hand collided with her temple and her head whipped right, forced aside by the strength of his slap. Skin split, the searing pain jolting through her body, and blood flowed from the wound. It slithered down her body, covering her arm.

This was why grates were set into the tile floor.

"You speak when spoken to."

Her cougar snarled and pushed forward, but she shoved it into a mental cage. She couldn't shift and attack. Maybe later, but not then. They had to be careful, smart. Didn't the she-cat remember getting cornered by a polar bear? They'd lived because they didn't panic and lash out. Abby needed *that* version of her cougar.

With the cougar's assistance, the wound on her head burned as skin sought to stitch—

"Nu-uh." Pike gripped her face, fingertips digging into the slash on her head. "Your kitty doesn't get to heal you. Not yet. I want to see you bleed for a little while."

The cat snarled and bared its fangs but ceased its attempt to fix the damage. For now.

"Much better." He smiled wide, pristine, white, *human-shaped* teeth revealed with the evil grin. "Good kitty."

He even went so far as to pat her head as if she were a pet.

"Now"—he leaned down and rested his hands on his knees—"you're going to sit there like a good little pet and tell me everything you know and everything you revealed to others."

No, she really wouldn't, and not only because she didn't know much. Because she would never betray her kind. Not to Unified Humanity. Not ever. Not like *him*.

Instead of saying the words aloud, she simply gave him two hard shakes of her head, the denial firm and unmistakable.

Pike straightened, took a step back, and then began a lazy stroll around her. "I just can't decide what to do with you. There are so many options. On one hand Foster ordered me to get you talking. On the other"—he clicked his tongue—"I just wanna play."

Another tremble, goose bumps rising on her skin. She didn't want to play with Pike. At all. Unfortunately, she didn't get a choice.

"Does that sound good to you, sweetheart?" A smirk,

one she wanted to claw off his face. "That wolfie not giving you what you need?" Pike reached down and grabbed his crotch, shaking his hand slightly. "You want a real man?"

Abby sneered, lifting her lip to bare her still human canine. "Maybe if you bring me one." She glared at him, her taunting stare sliding down his body from head to toe before she met his eyes once more. "Because all I see right now is a piece of shit." She pulled at her bindings, straining to reach him. "A weak, *insignificant* piece of shit not worthy to lick my boots."

If she'd been wearing any.

His eyes flared, a flash of amber for the barest of moments. There was something else in his eyes, too. Pain?

He leaned down, bracing his hands on the arms of the metal chair. "That's a lot of big talk for someone who's staring death in the face. Keep pulling on those chains, baby. Isn't that what he calls you?" He lowered his voice. "Keep pulling on them—try to break free. It'll give me an excuse to hurt you even more."

"Should I beg for my life and promise you my undying love, *Pike*?"

"Little bitch." He spat the words in her face, saliva splattering against her heated skin. "Don't know when to shut up, do you?"

"What the hell are you doing? You're working for UH? *Really?*" Another shake. "I never thought I'd see the day when a shif—"

His next movement was fast, a blur of his hand rising and then a shot of pain to . . . her ear? What the hell?

"Speak when spoken to." The words were a growl, and she lifted her head to meet his intense stare.

"Fuck. You." *Probably* not the best response, but the only one that came to mind.

Pike chuckled and backed away, shaking his head. "You're trying to get me to end it too soon. You don't want to give me a chance to enjoy myself."

Honestly, she'd been reacting on instinct rather than with some sort of grand plan in mind, but she wouldn't tell him that.

His lips curled into a dark smile, a smirk she swore she'd seen before... on Declan? "Are all shifters this stupid?"

No. *No.* Just... no. Tons of guys smirked. It was a thing with men. They thought they were all sexy when they quirked their lips even though half the men who tried the expression just looked like they were constipated.

Pike's smirk wasn't familiar in any way. It sure as hell didn't remind her of Declan.

She stared at the man in front of her, eyeing his nose, the angle of his jaw, and those blue eyes. *Stop it.* She wasn't following that line of thought.

"Of course we're not all dumb. I think it's just cougars." She pulled her lips back into a wide, feral smile. "And wolves."

Pike narrowed his eyes, and she felt his cold glare all the way to the marrow of her bones. "What did you tell SHOC about what you learned at FosCo?" Abby shook her head, and he lowered to her height once again. "Come on, sweetheart. Just tell me what I want to know and this won't have to hurt so much."

She snorted. "I don't know anything. How about you tell me why you're doing this, instead?"

He ignored her question. "You don't know anything? Hmmm... That's why you with one of their SHOC teams? Why you were working at FosCo? Because you don't know anything?" He poked out his lower lip, eyebrows furrowed.

"Poor baby, just happened to be in the wrong place at the wrong time, is that it?"

He tapped her cheek. "One more try, sweetheart. Tell me what you—and now the others—know, or things are going to get real."

"I don't know what you're talking about."

"I don't want to hurt you more than I have to." Another expression covered his features, one that pushed the truth to the forefront of her mind.

She didn't know why Pike had betrayed the shifters in this way, but it wasn't *only* shifters that he'd betrayed. "Why? Is it because you don't like getting blood on your hands? Or is it only 'furry' blood? Maybe you have a thing about torturing women." She captured his stare with hers, making sure her gaze didn't waver while she delivered her final guess. "Or maybe it's because you don't like betraying your *brother*."

CHAPTER THIRTY-ONE

*D*eclan now understood why zoo animals paced. They were hungry for their captors, anxious to break free and destroy whoever had them locked in a tiny cage. He wanted to be free to run and hunt, but instead he'd remained locked behind reinforced bars for the last two hours.

He hadn't stopped growling from the moment Birch restrained him. Oh, there was no arguing that the rope and chains had been necessary, but logic wasn't high on Declan's list of "shit to think about." At the top was worry about Abby, then escaping, then hunting Abby while killing anyone who stood in his way.

A new sound filtered through the walls of his prison in Pike's basement. Two of the walls were concrete, made of bricks and mortar—the house's foundation. He moved to the closest wall and rested his ear against the hard surface. His wolf was already pushed forward, straining to help Declan sort through the sounds.

Rolling tires over rocks and glass. Big tires, heavy vehicle, moving slowly through the darkness. The grating of metal on metal followed by the softest squeak of the transport's springs. Something—someone—heavy exited the vehicle.

The deep *thud* of someone's approach. No, more than one. Three large men—his team. He knew the sounds of their walks as well as they knew his. The vibrations slid through him, the feel of their boots on the walkway and then the front porch shaking his bones. Then came the squeak of the front door opening. Dirt rained down from the basement's ceiling, dust loosened as they strode through the small home's entryway.

The team was there. They'd support him in his fight with Birch. They would let him free to find Abby—to destroy whoever had taken her. They *had* to because...because he didn't have Pike to depend on. The damn wolf hadn't been home when Birch had dragged him into the house, and he still hadn't returned. Gone. Vanished. Like so many times before. The fucking kid...Declan sighed and shook his head. That fucking kid. Pike had bitched because Birch wouldn't let him participate in the op and then made like a rabbit—running and hiding.

Declan's wolf snarled, furious about Pike's abandonment, but he did his best to soothe the near-feral beast. He could be angry with Pike later. His focus had to be on Abby.

Declan pushed away from the wall and tipped his head to the side, closing his eyes as he listened for the activities above. Low murmurs, too low for him to hear. The clinks and thuds of the men removing their gear and the bouncing springs of a protesting mattress. It seemed they were dropping everything on the same bed. Good. He'd need it all when he escaped.

When. Not if. *When.*

Everyone in his way would...die. If Birch, Cole, Grant, or Ethan attempted to keep him locked away, he couldn't guarantee their safety. Right now he couldn't think beyond the blood in those churning waters, the humans who'd had their hands on his mate.

Mate.

It couldn't be…He wasn't the type of male who…He wasn't mate material, and yet his wolf howled, a hint of sadness and joy in the sound. It was overjoyed he'd finally recognized the truth—Abby belonged to them—but aching to have her at their side once more.

Now he understood the drive to steal her, to keep her safe, to touch her when he should have stayed away. She deserved more—better—than him, but her fate was sealed, and the truth expanded to fill his body. It changed from a hesitant guess to an unbreakable certainty.

Abby was *his*. And his SHOC team was keeping them apart.

Declan brought more of the animal forward, encouraged it to gift him with increased strength and larger size. His shoulders broadened, fur sliding free. His arms thickened while his fingers gradually took on the shape of paws. The animal's fury coursed through his veins, adrenaline and blood thirst pushing him to break free.

Run.

Hunt.

Find.

Not yet, he said to the wolf. He needed to know what SHOC had learned before he broke free. Did they know where she was?

"What the hell, Birch?" Ethan didn't have a ton of respect when annoyed. "We're in deep and then you're breaking into the com with some order to—"

A low murmur cut Ethan off. Declan couldn't hear the words, but he knew that tone—the timbre of that rumble. Birch spoke. The team listened.

"What?" Ethan.

"Aw, shit." Grant.

"Where is he now?" Cole's voice was flat, no-nonsense. Evaluate, plan, and execute.

Birch answered once more, the bear's voice too low...

"I looked at that before we left. Pike's cage won't hold him for long." The tiger spoke the truth. Declan had already taken the time to inspect the bars, the brackets, and bolts that secured the cage. Could it keep him captive? For a little while. He was too motivated, too determined to get free.

"Ideas, then?" Birch murmured, his voice followed by the scrape of chairs on worn linoleum in the kitchen. "You guys get the data?"

A smack of plastic on Formica. A USB on the tabletop?

"Pulled the whole server before your interruption had security on our ass." Ethan still sounded damned pissed about the disruption, too.

"Casualties?" The bear asked the question as if it didn't matter to him. Life or death, he simply had to make a report. But the team knew the truth, the team knew Birch had his own demons.

"Bumps and bruises, but I didn't kill anyone." Cole snorted. "Wouldn't have been fair. They were practically puppies." The tiger grunted. "Didn't even have guns. Just bullshit pepper spray. No fun in it." He could imagine Cole's shrug.

"Grant, you'll work on digging through the data you guys grabbed. Look to see if there are any FosCo holdings tied to Unified Humanity. Actually, I need to know about anything that's tied to UH on that USB drive."

"You think that's who took her?" Grant's dark rasp held more than a hint of the man's animal.

"Yeah." Birch sounded grim, frustrated. "I have headquarters researching known UH locations and any activity surrounding them. Initial eval is that they'll have stayed close, but there aren't any records of UH or FosCo holdings in this or surrounding towns." He sighed. "A whole lot of fucking nothing so far."

Declan didn't know anything about FosCo's real estate, but something tickled the back of his mind. Something that'd happened years ago near here and…and it danced just out of reach.

"Did we get the tablet at least?" Cole again. "Not for nothing, but if we've got what we came for, we can walk away. No one needs to know that Declan lost it. We can tell the other team that she's gone and give the director the tablet. Just sweep this shit under the rug and move the fuck on."

Declan hadn't wanted to kill his team, but Cole would die. The idea that he'd leave Abby…His wolf growled and followed it up with a howl, fury over Cole's indifference straining his control over the beast.

"No. No tablet. We need to get her—and the tablet—in our hands. At minimum, the tablet." Declan didn't like Birch quantifying who—what—was more important.

"So, what do we do?" Grant spoke up. He was a good wolf but liked having clear direction. It annoyed Declan to no end. Being an alpha meant doing what he wanted when he wanted, but packs needed betas, and their team was a pack of sorts.

"Research. Go through the data."

And while they did that, he'd do some work of his own.

Maybe what he was about to do was stupid as hell and he should just sit around with his thumb up his ass while his team did the rest.

Except he wasn't that guy.

Declan was the guy who silently worked at the boards in the far corner, the ones that once removed, would give him access to the small bedroom above. It'd taken time, time he hadn't wanted to waste, but it was worth it in the end.

He got into the bedroom with hardly a sound, nothing more than a low creak coming from one of the older boards as he pulled himself up through the hole he'd created. He scanned the space and grinned at what he found—weapons and gear galore.

Standing in the center of the room, gaze moving across the space, that niggling thought in the back of his mind pushed forward once more.

One town over, big house on a big piece of land. Tall fences that shielded the home from neighbors...He could picture it as it'd been all those years ago. But it hadn't been registered to FosCo then. Or Unified Humanity. He squeezed his eyes shut, trying to remember who'd owned the property, but the name wouldn't come to him. Dammit.

He refocused on the room. There was the predictable neat pile from Cole, the random mess from Ethan, and Grant's area was a little in between. Guns were cared for. Clothes? Not so much.

Declan remained silent while he crossed the room and tugged on a tactical vest. Then came the weapons, guns and blades strapped to his body until he figured he was as ready as he was going to be. Guns, mags, knives, a grenade or two, and a com unit settled into place.

The memory still teased him as he prepared to escape, and with each passing second, certainty grew. Liv at headquarters was a badass techno bitch. She hadn't found anything yet, and Grant was just starting his search. He could sit around and wait. Or he could do what his gut was screaming at him to do.

Rumors had led him to a building years ago, and he'd purged it of Unified Humanity to atone for the sins in his past. He had a funny feeling they'd refilled it with their crazed kind. He knew how he'd get there—a man never forgot how to steal a car. He knew exactly how many he could kill with what he wore. The wolf would take care of the rest.

He padded to the window and ran his gaze over the frame, searching for any security measure his brother might have put into place. Nothing obvious, but who knew. For now he'd go quiet rather than shatter the glass.

Declan placed his hands on the bottom edge of the window and held his breath as he tugged, lifting the panel and letting in the night air. A tendril of relief suffused his blood, and he sighed, thankful Pike was a big enough idiot to leave his home without any kind of alarm.

Then the alarm went off and Declan cursed his brother for being all prepared and shit. He threw the window up and dove through the opening, rolling as he hit the ground. He kept the tumble going until he gained his feet, and then he ran. He bolted into a ground-eating pace, leaving his team behind while he let the wolf free to do as it desired.

Hunt.

CHAPTER THIRTY-TWO

*D*eclan skirted the ragged lawn, sticking to the perimeter, staying in the shadows while he sought an entrance to the dilapidated house. If he recalled the layout correctly, a bolt-hole would get him into the winding corridors beneath the home, bypassing the guards inside. Sure, he'd have to kill the guys up top eventually, but remaining undetected for a little while would let him find Abby quicker. Then he'd fight their way out.

His beast growled, shaking Declan. It didn't like thinking about Abby being in such danger. Declan didn't either, but he had to take solace in the fact that he'd avenge his mate for every hint of pain they caused.

His mate. Each time he thought of her—said her name in his mind or whispered it beneath his breath—the certainty strengthened. He'd always sought something—something to fill the hungry beast inside him and fill the bottomless hole in his heart. It had come in the form of a cougar shifter named Abby.

Declan continued his path, steps nearly silent as he moved through the welcoming dark. He soon reached the backyard, the area just as run-down as the front half of the house. It appeared to be a forgotten place—a building filled with people who didn't care about the home.

Declan cared about it—it and what it held. Because at that moment the wind shifted and a ghost of feminine scent teased his nose. A sweetly seductive aroma his wolf knew without a doubt.

"Abby." He breathed out her name, his lips tingling as he spoke. As if she gave him a gentle kiss when he said her name aloud.

The wind changed once more, and with the subtle shift came something else, something that had the wolf leaping forward without thought, old reflexes snapping into place as if he'd never left his previous life.

The crunch of a blade of grass. Just one. Some would dismiss the soft sound, but those were the same people who'd die beneath his claws.

In one smooth move, he whipped the gun strapped to his left thigh from its holster, the glide of metal on its custom casing silent. Without diverting his attention from the house, he pointed the weapon at the intruder, arm steady and aim perfect.

No other sounds came from his left, the darkness broken only by the random echoes from inside the home.

"Easy way to get yourself killed," Declan murmured low.

"You don't have my silencer, and the muzzle flash would betray your position." Cole didn't sound the slightest bit concerned, no hint of sour fear coming from the tiger, nor a tremble in his voice. Then again, Cole was like him— tired, old, jaded.

Until Declan had met Abby and now…things were different. Good different or bad different? He wasn't sure. It depended on whether he lived through the next half hour.

"Don't think I can take down a handful of humans?" Declan snickered.

Cole grunted. "Got a plan, or are we just winging it?"

If Cole was willing to help, Declan had to toss the original plan aside. "Are the others here?"

"Heads up."

He lifted his right hand and caught the device the tiger tossed while he kept his gun trained on the male. Sure, he listened to what Cole had to say, but until he knew more, he'd keep the man at a distance.

He sure as fuck wasn't going back into some damned cage.

Declan slipped in the earpiece and turned it on. "Declan in."

"Team on deck." Birch was all business, but Declan sensed a hint of fury. "No records. Entry?"

The whole fucking team is here. There are no fucking records on file. How the fuck are we getting in there, Declan?

Birch said a lot when he was barely speaking.

"There's a storm cellar."

A low click filled his ear, a notice that someone else on the team was about to speak. "There's a ten-digit keypad," Ethan said, but Declan knew that already. "Code?"

"Known," Declan murmured. "Self-programmed."

It'd been his last task before he'd left the carnage behind. Just in case he'd needed to return, he'd wanted easy access with his personal backdoor code.

"Repeat visit?" Grant sounded surprised, but no one else said a word.

They all had secrets from the past. Declan wasn't about to have a heart-to-heart while Abby remained in the hands of Unified Humanity.

"Who's on point?" Cole asked from his left, voice filling both ears.

Declan hated giving up control, but his wolf was too close to losing it. The beast could think of nothing but its mate. Fuck battle tactics and strategy. He'd defer to his team alpha for this one. "Birch?"

Birch sounded more normal when he spoke. "Grant's up. Cole on our six. Low, tight..."

"First." They finished the order as a group.

Keep their asses low, keep a tight formation, and shoot the assholes before they got their own off.

Grant peeled away from the fence, sticking to the shadows of the few trees in the backyard. The trees were half dead and sad with drooping branches, but the gloom kept their movements hidden.

Then there was Birch, and Declan slipped into formation behind the team alpha. Ethan followed, and Cole joined them at the back. Five men in a line, ready to risk their lives for...

"She's my mate. They've touched her. They die."

The whole team froze in place—not even breathing. Finally, Birch spoke. "They die. Move out."

They moved as they'd been trained—as one. Their steps matched, their strides identical so they could walk in each other's path. Someone coming across their boot prints wouldn't know that five men attacked. They'd assume there was only one.

Until reports flooded the security station. Then it'd be too late.

They reached the deep shadow of the back of the house, the moon gifting them with cover, and they dropped into low squats. Declan's wolf's sight let him peer through the midnight black, to lay eyes on his teammates.

Each male was dressed all in black, a gun in one hand and the other in the shape of a claw. Two halves making up a whole, two parts of each man working together to save Abby.

"Code?" Grant grabbed his attention.

Declan recited the numbers from memory, the digits seared into his head for eternity. The date of his last kill—the last bullet he'd shot for money.

Grant pressed the keypad, and soon the whir of the lock disengaging sounded. They remained in place a beat longer, waiting for any alarm or sound from inside. Then they were in motion once more, through the door and trooping down a bright hall.

Declan's wolf sorted through the plethora of scents, the hints of gunpowder, sweat, and the rotten flavor of hatred.

"I scent at least twenty. One female," Declan said. No one had to question the identity of the female. Abby's terror consumed the air, filling the space with her fear, but there was another scent he recognized from yesterday. "Foster."

"One known male—friendly." Birch's words made Declan jolt. A *known* male? A friendly? "Move out." Birch gave an order, and they all complied, training overtaking Declan's curiosity.

They dealt with the first duo they came across quickly and quietly. They'd take their time, eliminate enemies as they went. They *would not* turn the op into a bloodbath.

How many times had Declan heard those instructions in the past? Too many to count. Though this time Birch hadn't drummed the words into their heads before they breached the cellar doors. So when he heard Abby's scream, he didn't feel *too* bad about breaking formation and launching into a dead run. His boots pounded on the white linoleum, the rapid, heavy thuds announcing his presence to one and all.

He didn't care, because Abby screamed. Again. His adrenaline, the beast, pushed him onward.

Curses echoed down the hall in his wake, the team damning him for busting out of line, but he couldn't find a single fuck to give about their anger. Not when a human man was in his path. Punch with his claw. A strike to the nose with the butt of his gun. Finally, a slash that sank through flesh and scraped his carotid artery.

More humans. More deaths. He hadn't come across Foster yet. He should have killed him when he had the chance.

With every fallen body, he drew closer to Abby, the stench of her pure terror growing with each step closer. The sounds of fighting, his team's struggles, reached him, and he was suddenly torn. He could run on and kill everyone in his path, mow every human down until he reached Abby. Or he could help protect his team. He'd abandoned them, broken formation for his own selfish needs, and...

Birch stopped mid-fight to meet Declan's gaze. "Go!" he roared.

Declan bolted, breaking into a ground-eating run. He hunted Abby, he hunted his *mate*, and all else could fuck off as far as he was concerned.

He turned another corner and then another, spying a set of stairs at the end of the hall. The second his feet touched the top step, he jumped, using his beast's agility to get from one floor to the next with a single leap. He went down one level and then two and then...

He stopped.

Blood. All Abby's, though there was another scent that teased his beast...No, he needed to focus on his mate. The amount of terror and the existence of the blood confused him, the past attempting to overlay the present and cloud his thoughts. He wasn't with his old pack, and he didn't smell his girlfriend's blood. He wasn't rescuing his girlfriend. He was in a UH compound, and Abby needed him.

The farther he traveled down the hall, the more concentrated the scent became.

Declan turned yet another corner, still hunting, and then there was her voice. Furious. Pained. Taunting. It came from his immediate right, a solid metal door that didn't appear to be anything special. But it was. It was the single item that stood between him and Abby.

He didn't hesitate to attack. He went at the door, a boot to the handle, which he followed up with a hard slam of his shoulder. The door wrenched from its hinges, the grinding scrape of metal piercing the air with a complaining screech as it was torn from its tracks. That was when he saw Abby—his mate—secured to a chair in the middle of the room. Half naked. Cold. Scared. Hurt. Bruises and shallow scrapes marred her body—they didn't worry him—but where had the blood come from?

A low growl—familiar? *No*—drew his gaze to the only other person in the room. To the man stained with Abby's blood.

Something new filled him. Hotter. Stronger. Fiercer.

And wholly focused on killing... his brother.

CHAPTER THIRTY-THREE

*A*bby had known he would come. She'd only hoped Pike wouldn't be in the room when he did. Because looking at her and Pike, there was no disputing the truth—the wolf had hurt her.

She still couldn't figure out why Pike didn't just pass along his own knowledge to Unified Humanity. Pike wasn't in SHOC, but he knew the answers to his questions just as well as she did. Which meant there had to be something else.

Something they'd never know if Declan killed Pike.

"Declan." Pike's voice was flat, unemotional. "Nice of you to come."

"*You*," Declan rasped, and Abby's heart ached for him.

She saw the emotions in his eyes, the way his shoulders trembled and the curve of his stomach as he lurched. His brother's betrayal speared him deep, digging into his soul, and she wanted nothing more than to go to him. She ached to pull him into her arms and pretend none of this had ever happened.

Pike smirked. "Me."

The twist of his lips was cocky bravado, but Abby spotted the fear as well. Her world, her entire life, depended on the details in the world around her. Whether it was listening for a polar bear or catching sight of another's emotional pain, her life depended on her abilities.

"Declan," she whispered. She'd lost her voice at some point. Now she could only scream, and even that nearly brought her to tears. "Declan." She tried again, tugging against her bindings. The jangle of her chains and last whispered plea got his attention. "Declan."

Those wolf eyes landed on her, his narrow-eyed stare taking in her appearance once more. She needed him to push past the pain of betrayal and think clearly. If he let his beast take too much control, the wolf would—

Pike destroyed her attempt at distracting Declan. In truth, it didn't take much—a simple shift of his weight from one foot to the other. The connection she had to Declan snapped like a dried twig.

That was the moment Declan went after his brother. He tossed aside his gun and leaped, transitioning as he flew. The wolf's maw appeared, and his other hand shifted into a claw. Fangs grew, long and sharp, descending from his gums. His shoulders broadened, and arms thickened. That increase in size continued down his body, legs stretching his pants to their limits.

Dark gray fur—nearly black—covered him from snout to tail, and his eyes glowed an eerie amber. A yellow that wasn't *quite* that of a natural wolf. It betrayed his status as something *more*, something *better*. To her anyway.

And his size...A natural wolf stood two and a half feet at the shoulders, but Declan easily hit nearly four feet, and the rest of him was just as large. The snout, the teeth, the paws and thick muscles that hid beneath his midnight fur.

Bigger than any wolf she'd ever seen.

Declan landed on Pike with a snarl, and the other wolf

grunted when his back struck the hard tile. But while Declan embraced his beast, Pike...didn't.

He took Declan's punches, one after another after another. He didn't retaliate, only defended, blocking Declan when he would have captured Pike's throat between his jaws.

They rolled, exchanging the dominant position, while Declan continued to beat on Pike—beat on his *brother*.

"Declan!" The shout was hardly more than a wheeze, her voice abandoning her. Neither wolf gave her a glance. She turned inward, sought her cougar, and beckoned her forward. They couldn't get out of this, end the battle and escape, if they remained bound.

Her cougar released a soft whine. It didn't want to come out. It didn't want to experience pain. It'd had enough over the last couple of days.

Abby talked to the cat. *And we can't mate him if he loses his mind after he kills his brother.*

The cat purred at the word "mate." Purred and rubbed and changed her tune when she realized Abby was giving in to the inevitable. Declan was hers—theirs—and their future could be over before it began if they didn't figure this mess out. Like Declan, Abby began to shift.

The bindings would still take some work, but there were differences between human-shaped Abby and cat-shaped Abby. Differences that allowed first one wrist and then the other to jerk free of her chains while Pike was distracted.

She glanced at Declan and Pike, at Pike's limp body and Declan's continued shift. It wouldn't be long before her mate was done. Then Pike would be *done*.

Her legs shifted next, making it easy to pull out of the cuffs that bound her. And the moment she had unrestricted movement, the cat withdrew, returning human feet and leaving only delicate claws at the tips of her fingers. The cat knew human was needed, but they didn't want to be unarmed.

As if Declan would ever hurt her.

But Pike would. Pike *had.*

Declan's shift was nearly complete, his exhaustion plain. He shouldn't have taken this long to change. Or he was simply giving Pike plenty of time to match him.

She tried to call Declan's name, but she had no voice.

Five feet separated her from the two men. Then four. Then three. With that next step, Declan's shift completed, his wolf fully in control and aching for blood. There was a hunger for death in his eyes, one that would be sated only by eliminating Pike.

She couldn't let that happen. Not when questions remained. Questions that could be answered only by the unconscious shifter.

Which was why, when she should have stayed out of the way, Abby fell forward. She stumbled one step and then another until her bare knees hit tile and her chest fell across Pike's. She was a battered blanket of protection. Now Declan would either recognize her presence or kill her, but it would give Pike a chance. It would give *Declan* a chance. He already carried too many kills on his conscience. She wouldn't let him add this death, too—no matter how pissed she was at Pike herself.

Hot fangs pressed tight to her neck, saliva dripping, and hot breath fanned the side of her face. She was captured, her neck vulnerable and in the place of Pike's. Her life was in his jaws. He tightened his bite, fangs digging in to her skin but not yet piercing her flesh.

Until he froze.

The wolf above her growled. It was a pure threat, the

beast's frustration voiced aloud. He could be as angry as he liked. It wouldn't change her actions. Standing between the brothers—saving Pike—seemed so *right*. Pike might be sentenced to death for his actions, but he wouldn't die at Declan's claws. It would kill her mate. Kill him.

Abby swallowed hard and licked her chapped lips, working to bring a little moisture to her mouth so she could attempt to talk once more. "Declan, stop." She winced with the effort and the rough scrape of her throat, but she pushed on. "You have to stop." His renewed growl told her he didn't agree. "Please." That growl increased in volume, and she shuddered. "Please, Declan. Please stop."

A single tear escaped her eye, trailing down her cheek and sliding through blood until it fell to the tile.

Declan whined, the wolf shuddering, and then released a whimper while he shifted his weight from foot to foot. Indecision. Worry. Finally the wolf opened his jaws. He retreated slowly, carefully, until her neck was no longer held immobile by his deadly fangs.

He moved away yet stayed close the entire time. He let her ease off Pike, and she stayed on her knees, unable to even consider pushing to her feet.

At least that'd been her plan until a new wave of threats piled into the room. One after another they rushed into the space, fangs bared, claws flexed, and guns searching for a target.

The rest of Declan's team.

CHAPTER THIRTY-FOUR

*I*f they shot Declan, she'd kill them. Kill them all. She wasn't sure how, but it'd happen. It would take time, planning, money if she had to hire someone like Declan, but by the end they'd all be buried six feet under.

"Abby, wanna tell me what I'm looking at?" Birch's gaze flicked through the room. There was so much blood, it was hard to discern hers from Pike's from Declan's.

She opened her mouth, ready to say *something*, but Declan chose that moment to move. Not toward Birch, but her. He darted across the slick tile floor until he stood in front of her. Legs braced, muscles stiff, ruff standing on end, and teeth bared—he acted as a physical shield between her and his team. A shield? Or a possessive claiming?

Regardless, Birch squeezed the trigger, and a bullet slammed into the tile where Declan once stood.

"What the hell?" She managed to shout the words, her cougar having healed enough of her vocal cords to make speech possible. At least for that one yell. She wheezed the moment her bellow left her mouth, a new wave of pain squeezing her throat.

Three other guns pointed in their direction. At Declan.

She swallowed hard once more and begged her cat for help, pleaded with her to heal her voice instead of her cuts and bruises. The feline whined, torn between listening and preparing their body for a fight. If it came to that.

Her throat tingled, followed by a healing burn and a scratchy itch as flesh knitted back together. She coughed and wheezed, then cleared her throat.

"Easy," she said in an attempt to calm the beast. "I'm right here. I'm alive. I'm okay."

The wolf snorted, and the team echoed the scoff, which only served to draw Declan's fury once more.

"Don't listen to them, Declan." She kept her voice soft and low. "They don't matter." Abby's fingers brushed fur, and she sank them into his bloody ruff. "You saved me and protected me. They just want to help."

Cole changed position, the tiniest shift of his weight from one foot to the other, and destroyed the minute progress she'd made.

"*Cole*, keep your ass still." The cougar even went so far as to add a growl to her voice. Sure, the tiger could tear her to shreds without breaking into a sweat, but the idea of losing Declan trumped any pain the other man could inflict.

Another growl from Declan, more soft shushes from Abby. "Easy, Declan."

She moved the tiniest bit closer, knees scooching across the uneven tile while she closed the distance between them. His attention remained locked on the males in front of them while she crawled nearer and nearer. So close her bare stomach brushed his side.

"I'm right here," she whispered, and leaned forward, giving him some of her weight, proving that she lived and breathed because of him. "I'm right here. You got to me. You protected me. I'm okay."

She sifted her fingers through his matted fur once more, sliding her arm around his rib cage and finally resting her head between his shoulders. She listened to his heartbeat, the pulse steady despite his obvious fury. The heart of a killer. One who stared at danger and didn't feel an ounce of fear.

But he was ready to fight—to die—for her, wasn't he?

"I'm okay." She breathed deep and exhaled slowly, sending her breath swirling around them. He needed to creep past the aromas of the blood and find hers. "I'm okay and you're going to take me home."

His growl renewed, bursting through the room like a shot. Her cougar purred, the animal able to translate his rumble. It was pure possessiveness and a soul-deep determination to keep her at his side.

"Your home, Declan. We're going together. We're going to let your team deal with Pike, huh?" The growl changed, anger creeping into the rolling rumble. "The team will handle him. They won't let him go. Shhh..." She rubbed her cheek on his back. "He'll be punished, but right now I need you, huh?"

He narrowed his eyes, attention stroking what little of her he could see, and she could pinpoint the moment he was reminded she wore very little. Possessiveness filled his wolf's gaze once more, and the growl returned, directed at the conscious males in the room.

"They don't want me, Declan," she rushed to assure him, keeping her volume low.

Grant had to talk. "Well, I mean, I'd—"

The sound of flesh striking flesh was quickly followed by a grunt, and she hoped one of the other men had hit Grant to shut him up.

"Birch, how do we get out of here?" Abby stroked the

spot behind Declan's ear, carefully petting him—even if he wasn't a dog—to calm him once more.

"Helo's inbound. Less than five, and that's about how long it'll take to get to the surface." The bear spoke, but when she glanced at him, she realized his attention was on the unconscious Pike behind them, not on her and Declan.

"Birch?" She waited until his eyes met hers. "He hurt me, but I don't think he's..." She couldn't figure out how to put it into words. "There's something off. Just...talk to him before you do anything, okay?"

Birch grunted, and she figured that was the most she'd get as far as agreements went. He brought a hand to his ear, attention split between her and Declan and whatever voice came over the com. "Let's go. They're dropping in for a landing, and I want to get to work on this place."

"Okay." She stroked Declan once again, touch gentle. "You ready, wolf?" She combed his fur with her fingers. "We're going to walk out of here. No one is going to try to take me or hurt me, huh?"

He kept up his growl but with a tiny change, a shift of the tone that told her he grumbled out of habit instead of true unease and anger.

"We'll give escort." Birch broke in once more. "Grant takes point, and for the love of fuck, Grant, keep your trap shut."

Declan huffed in annoyance, but she felt his muscles relax, some of the greatest tension bleeding away.

"Okay, we're ready." As Abby pushed to her feet, she swayed, her legs wobbly. But she could work through the lingering pain and exhaustion. If she didn't, there was no telling what Declan would do—to the others and to Pike.

She kept one hand buried in his ruff, fingers fisting the strands, and she used that grip as both a restraint and support. She didn't want him diving after anyone, but she wasn't sure she could stand on her own either.

Grant left first while the others retreated, giving them space to pass, and they trailed in the other wolf's wake.

She paused long enough to glance at Birch. "Where are we going?"

Though, did it matter? They simply needed to be *away*. Wherever they traveled it simply had to be *not there*.

"Our home base is in North Carolina. You two can recover there."

When Declan didn't growl or stiffen, she figured he was okay with being shuttled off to another state, which meant Abby was fine with it as well. In truth, she simply didn't have the energy to fight.

"What about the director?"

Birch grunted. "He'll be happy to see UH destroyed." The bear shifter waved his hand and then looked to Cole. "Find Foster, and that tablet, grab any other computers they have, and then bring the fucking thing down."

"And Pike?" Cole's voice dropped to a low murmur.

Abby strained to hear Birch's response, but Grant realized she hadn't followed. "Abby? Something wrong?"

Declan released a soft grumble and stepped forward, his head and shoulders in front of her. He held her captive once again, standing between her and any perceived threat.

"I'm fine." She stroked the uneasy wolf and spoke to him. "I'm fine, but tired. Let's go, Declan."

The tablet, the compound, *Pike*...could all be handled by someone else.

CHAPTER THIRTY-FIVE

*D*eclan's mouth remained flooded with saliva, the need for flesh still riding him hard. He wanted to tear into his enemies and bathe in their blood. He wanted to show them *all* that they shouldn't touch what belonged to him.

Abby was *his*. Her small hand knotted in his fur, her weight firm against his side. Grant led them through the halls, gun in hand and body tense. Humans littered the ground—some shot, others torn by claws.

Pride and joy twined inside him. His team had done that—his *pack* even if they weren't all wolves. Not just his pack...the closest thing he had to family now that he knew about *him*.

The wolf's feral mind pulled on him, wrenching him away from thoughts of his brother and what he'd done.

Abby gave him more and more of her weight with every step, her slow strides gradually turning into shuffles. He turned his head and gave her a low bark. He swept his gaze over her, seeing the blood and bruises.

Fury—scorching hot and lightning fast—overtook him in that instant. More adrenaline flooded his four-legged form, and the craving for blood—retribution—

doubled. He'd calmed with Abby's presence, but the reminder of what she'd endured snatched away that hint of peace.

Her fist eased, and she ran her fingers through his fur. "Shh...I'm fine."

She wasn't fine. She limped. Some of her skin was purple. *She bled.*

He ached to go back and finish what he'd started in that room.

"Declan?" Grant called out. He flicked one ear toward his teammate while his gaze remained on Abby. "Helo's landing. Let's move."

Declan grumbled and closed his eyes for a moment. His wolf resisted when he fought for calm.

"Declan! Move your furry ass."

He'd show Grant a furry ass, the asshole.

As they finally exited the building, the echoing *thump, thump, thump* of the helo's propeller reached them, overwhelming any other sounds that crept into the space.

Which was why they—*he*—didn't see their attacker until it was too late. Because one moment Abby clung to him and the next...the next she was wrenched away and into another man's arms.

Declan spun with a snarl, muscles tense and lips pulled back to expose his fangs. He growled long and low, the sound escaping before he even recognized who he faced.

Eric Foster held a gun to Abby's head.

He'd kill him. Slowly. Painfully.

"Back off!" Eric's voice wavered. The man's eyes were wide and filled with terror. The muzzle of his gun shook the tiniest bit. In this other hand, he held Abby's tablet.

"Let her go." Grant's rumble rose above the sounds from outside.

"I'm leaving and you're going to let me." A tremble of fear still lingered in Eric's words.

Declan wanted nothing more than to leap onto the human and rip out his throat.

Grant snorted. "Not happening."

Definitely not.

Eric pressed the muzzle tighter to Abby's head. "I'll kill her."

Declan flexed his claws and sank lower, muscles tense and ready to roar into action. One leap. One bite.

"And you'll die before she hits the ground." The slow drawl was followed by the familiar racking of a gun's slide. Movement behind Eric signaled another team member's presence.

"Fucking furries... You think you can just kill me?"

Declan watched the man's eyes, his gaze unwavering. He could almost read Eric's mind as his options flickered through his head. In truth, there wasn't anything he could do to get out of this situation alive. Not. A. Thing.

Declan moved his attention to the gun Eric clutched in his right hand. It let him see the minute tensing of muscles and slight movement of joints. The shot was coming, the human was a split second from putting a bullet in Abby's head.

Declan leaped. Mouth wide and fangs bared, he sliced through the air with his gaze intent on his target. He craved blood—Eric's blood—and wouldn't stop until it flowed down his throat.

Screams. Shouts. Pain. Snap. Pop. Tear.

Blood. Eric's blood. But there was something else. A metallic tang that reminded him of his own scent.

Declan's blood.

He opened his mouth and let Eric's flesh fall from his jaw to land on the once living and breathing human. The body beneath him twitched and jerked—death throes creeping in. Declan swung his head to his right, to eyes landing on Abby slumped to the ground—crying but alive. A quick glance revealed that she wasn't injured. At least, not any more than she had been already.

Tears flowed down her cheeks and he whined. His mate shouldn't cry. He'd killed the man who wanted to hurt her. She should smile.

He stepped over Eric's downed body, intent on getting to her. He'd nuzzle and nip her, show her everything was okay and...

And he found himself flopping onto the ground. Had he tripped over Eric? Sloppy of him. He normally...

Was it harder to breathe? A little. That was odd.

Abby sobbed, her body shaking with the harsh sound, and he lifted his head. He released a soft chuff and mentally growled at the wolf. They could calm their mate better if he had lips instead of wolf's jaws.

Wait, had that chuff come out as a pained whine? No. He wasn't hurt. He'd killed Eric and...

And suddenly there were hands on him. Not just Abby's, but others as well. A firm grip that held him steady when he fought against their hold. It *hurt*.

"Don't die on me," Abby pleaded with him.

Why would he die? He...

"Please, Declan. *Don't die*."

She was being ridiculous, and he'd shift and tell her so. Women were a pain in the ass. Though he also liked her ass a whole lot. He snorted—maybe. He definitely nudged his wolf to retreat so his skin could overtake the fur. But nothing happened. Or rather, *something* happened, but not what he expected.

The world—his world—went black.

CHAPTER THIRTY-SIX

*T*hey hadn't made it to the base in North Carolina. Hell, Abby wasn't sure they'd managed to cross state lines. Bullets. Blood. Death.

She shuddered, and a tear—one of many—slid its way down her cheek. She'd experienced physical pain and heartbreaking loss in her life. It was nothing compared to the agony consuming her now.

Declan had died more than once during the mad flight to…wherever the hell they were. Some kind of medical center—obviously SHOC or shifter friendly. A regular human hospital was too dangerous, their shifter blood too different from humans.

And they'd managed to keep Declan alive.

Abby hadn't taken her attention off Declan from the moment they'd wheeled him out of surgery. Even now she kept her eyes on his chest, watching the rise and fall with his every breath. He'd stopped breathing more than once—first on the helicopter and again before they'd gotten him through the doors to surgery. She was sure it'd happened while he remained under the knife as well.

But he'd survived. He'd rescued her, protected her with his body, and survived. His skin was pale from blood loss.

At least that was what the SHOC doctors told her. She wasn't sure what to believe—or who she could trust. Not really.

Not after Pike—Declan's *brother*—had...Her stomach churned, twisting and knotting with a mixture of anxiety and rage.

She drew in a deep breath, tasting Declan's scent on her tongue, and released it slowly. She pushed some of her worry out of her body with every exhale. It had no place in the room. She had to remain strong. She could shatter into a jumble of sobbing pieces once Declan woke.

And he *would* wake.

Abby gently slid her hand beneath Declan's. The heat of his palm contrasted with the cool sheets against the back of her hand. If he was warm, he was alive. She had to remember that fact.

She leaned forward and rested her head on the soft mattress. She adjusted her position until she could see his chest—count his breaths.

In. Out. He's alive. In. Out. He didn't die. In. Out.

Fear still gripped her though. The terror that if she didn't keep her eyes on him, he'd succumb to his injuries.

Yet twenty-four hours of watching and waiting, twenty-four hours of dread, took its toll. The moment she let herself relax was the moment she lost herself to what could have been.

Her eyes fluttered closed, darkness enveloping her in a midnight blanket. When she opened them once more, *they* had her.

A roar shook the air, the bellow sinking past her flesh and into her bones. Rage accompanied the sound, the scent of fire burning her nose. Beneath that aroma was another— one she identified with ease—Declan.

Declan in pain. Declan filled with fury. Declan... calling to her with every howl and snarl. Other sounds joined—rattling chains, the *drip, drip, drip* of liquid striking tile, and the squelch of cut flesh.

A dim light flickered, blink, blink, blinking until the glow turned steady and illuminated the room.

Yes, she'd been right. *They* had her. No, *they* had *them.* Her and Declan both. They were in that tiled room—Abby secured to that chair once more while Declan hung from chains.

"Declan," she whispered, and she blinked back the tears stinging her eyes. Not tears from her own pain, but from his.

He'd come for her again, except this time he'd been captured. Now she was forced to watch Pike sink his claws into Declan's flesh and—

He screamed. Or did she? She wasn't sure. The shout echoed through the room, consuming the air and surrounding her in the unending cry. She jolted and jerked against the chains, fighting to be free, and... came awake with a harsh gasp.

She sucked air into her lungs, breathing deep, and her cougar sorted through the flavors. The air wasn't filled with the coppery tang of blood but the stinging stench of the hospital.

And Declan. His scent was not quite right—he remained tainted by the poison, but his true flavors persisted. The fabric beneath her cheek was cool while his hand on hers was warm. She drew in more of his aroma, savoring the intricate fragrance.

His chest still moved. Heat still bathed her skin. Abby called to her cat and the beast altered her hearing so she could listen to the rhythmic thud of his heart.

Declan lived.

She drew air in through her nose and held the breath
while she begged her racing pulse to ease. Except that inhale brought her hints of someone else's presence. Snake—
black mamba. Strong and yet somehow weak at the same
time. Fury mixed with joy and a hint of...something.

Abby tore her attention from Declan and sought the
source of that scent. She turned her head and found her
stare captured by a stranger's. He stood on the other side
of Declan's hospital bed, an immaculately pressed suit covering his towering frame. Midnight hair and nearly black
eyes coupled with deeply tanned skin gave her a sense
of...wrongness. No, it wasn't his coloring so much as it
was his smell—the combination of both.

His eyes darkened further until she couldn't even see
the difference between his iris and pupil. She felt as if she
stared at the devil himself.

Then he smiled and shifted his weight, a dark lock of
hair falling forward to curl above his brow. A seductive
devil anyway.

"Miss Carter." He tipped his head. "I'm Harmon Quade,
the director of Shifter Operations Command."

She should be at ease in his company, right? Because he
was the director of SHOC and SHOC had helped her and...

"Mr. Quade."

"*Director*," he corrected.

"Director Quade," she whispered, and swallowed hard.
Okay, *Declan's* team had helped her. For some reason, she
felt as if this guy would have gladly left her for dead.

"Miss Carter, I—"

The room's door swung inward on silent hinges and the
hallway's glow slipped into the room. The light cast the
newcomer in a deep shadow, leaving only the newcomer's

outline visible. He took one step and then two into the room, his steps heavy and solid on the aged linoleum floor.

She couldn't see his face, but his scent... She knew who'd come to her rescue. Again? Crisp forest, fresh rain, and newly turned earth. They weren't flavors that appealed to Abby's cougar, but the cat trilled with his presence anyway.

Better the devil she knew. "Cole."

CHAPTER THIRTY-SEVEN

COLE

*U*nfortunately, Cole couldn't kill the director for scaring Abby. He didn't think Birch would let him maim the snake either, so he settled for glaring at the other male. He slowly made his way across the sterile room toward the woman huddled on the right side of Declan's bed.

Abby wasn't *theirs*, but she belonged to Declan, which meant that—in some way—she belonged to the team. Cole was part of the team, so...

So, he was trying like hell to justify his feelings toward the she-cat. The tiger rumbled a warning in his mind.

"Hey, Abby. How are you feeling?" he asked, not stopping his approach until he stood at her side. He eased close enough for his thigh to brush her shoulder in silent support.

"Tired."

"Agent Turner, your presence isn't required." Quade bit off those few words, and Abby stiffened.

A wisp of fear teased his nose, joining the other tendrils of terror and anxiety that clouded the room.

"Funny how I don't care." Cole curled the corner of his mouth up into a small smirk. Just enough to annoy the director. He wanted the asshole's attention on *him*—not the little cougar.

"Maybe you don't understand. I don't want you here." Quade's eyes darkened, his snake coming out to play.

"Uh-huh. Why are you here, Quade?" Cole balanced his weight on the balls of his feet, body ready to spring into motion in an instant. It was never a good idea to relax in the presence of another predator. If he faced off against someone like himself, brute force would get the job done. A snake shifter? He had to be quick or he'd end up with the poison of a black mamba coursing through his veins.

"I'm taking Abby—"

"Miss Carter." Cole spoke over the other man. The team could call her Abby—no one else.

Quade's expression darkened. Yeah, they were having a pissing contest, but he didn't care. The director would attack any perceived weakness. "I'm taking Miss Carter, as well as the tablet recovered at the scene, to the southern field office."

Abby tensed, and Cole reached for her, giving her shoulder a firm squeeze. "Abby remains with her mate."

"She doesn't have a mating mark."

"The lack of a mark doesn't change her status. She's Declan's mate." He gestured at the unconscious werewolf. "Declan's a little indisposed right now, but I can pry his mouth open and force him to take a hunk out of her if you'd like." Cole lifted a single brow in question.

"That won't be necessary." Quade spoke through gritted teeth, the *s* long and drawn out. "I can wait for the debrief. For now I'll take the tablet and speak with Declan and Miss Carter at another time."

"Funny thing about that tablet." Cole scratched the back of his head, playing the good old boy just to annoy the director. "It didn't exactly make it through the op."

Dark scales rippled over Quade's skin, tanned flesh disappearing beneath the black of his snake for a flash before he regained control over his beast. "Excuse me?"

"The tablet was fucked during evac."

"Then Miss Carter will accompany me *now*. I need to know everything *she* knows about FosCo and Unified Humanity."

"See, the thing about it is…" Cole shook his head. "That's not happening."

"Agent Turner—"

"Harmon." A wave of dominance rolled into the room, the newcomer's strength as overwhelming as it was gentle. Birch wasn't a flashy alpha. He didn't beat anyone with his alpha strength unless necessary. He let his mere presence do the talking. "Is there a reason you're bothering my team?"

"Nah, he's not bothering us, Birch." Cole let himself relax—just a little—and was gratified to sense Abby's tension easing. "He's just checking on Declan here. He thought about taking Abby to the field office…"

"But he knows mates don't get separated when one of them is injured. Of course, he offered to wait until Declan is fully healed." Birch took over. His tone was light, but a core of steel lingered in his words. "Though I'm not sure why you want to waste time questioning her. The tablet was destroyed, and her only knowledge is that FosCo wired money to Unified Humanity. There's nothing more she could tell you."

He could mention what they'd downloaded from the Ogilve, Piers, and Patterson servers, but the team wasn't ready for the director to have access to that information just yet. Possibly never.

"I see," Quade murmured.

"I am glad you decided to visit Declan during his time of need, though. It saves me having to e-mail you later." Birch played the good old boy just as well as Cole. "Since you'd decided to suspend us, the team is going to take some time off. Declan needs to recover, and the rest of the team needs a little breather. Plus there's the matter of Pike, as we discussed."

Quade shook his head. "Pike requires further discussion. Right now you need to focus on finding someone to replace Declan. He'll be punished for—"

Abby whimpered, and Cole growled, his tiger taking control of his voice. "Excuse me?"

Birch shot him a dark look—a silent order to shut the fuck up—and then spoke to the director. "Why?"

"He went rogue and absconded with a prisoner. A clear violation of SHOC orders."

The tension in the room doubled, the air thick with the growing need for violence. Birch locked gazes with Quade, the two men staring each other down. Abby cowered, leaning into Cole when yesterday she would have put as much distance between them as possible.

Cole snorted, rolled his eyes, and decided to channel Grant. "Yo, Birch. I know we say he's got a stick up his ass, but maybe it's a dictionary. 'Absconded.' What kind of bullshit word is that?"

Quade glared. Birch kinda glared while he fought the urge to smile. Abby released the breath she'd been holding but remained tense.

"Agent Birch, I will not stand here…"

"So leave?" Cole lifted his eyebrows, and hope sparked in his heart.

Unfortunately, Quade just went back to glaring at him and stayed put.

"As far as Team One is concerned, Declan Reed secured the cougar shifter, Abby Marie Carter, in a secondary location and awaited the team's arrival. At no time did he violate SHOC directives." Birch tipped his head toward Cole. "Agent Turner as well as Agents Grant Shaw and Ethan Cross will testify to that fact."

"Bullshit," Quade snapped. "You expect me to trust a bunch of heartless, mercenary killers?"

"You should." Cole's tiger padded forward. Even if he *was* lying, the cat didn't like being called a liar. His vision changed, altered by the presence of his inner beast. "You should believe us because we *are* a bunch of heartless, mercenary killers. It'd be better for your health."

"Are you—"

"Director Quade." Birch cut the other man off. "I think Declan needs his rest. Grant has compiled the team's field report, including Abby's statement." The team alpha's tone softened slightly while he worked to placate the director. "While her intel is minimal, he's also piecing together the tablet recovered at the scene."

Quade gestured toward Cole. "This one said the tablet was destroyed."

This one. Cole swallowed the growl that threatened to break free. This was one time he needed to step back and let Birch do the talking. He had more experience with these games.

"We don't know the extent of the damages, but you *will* be the first call I make once Grant has finished his analysis," Birch assured the director. "Miss Carter, unfortunately, was in the wrong place at the wrong time."

Quade's stare held a speculative gleam, as if he didn't quite believe Birch. Considering the grizzly was lying out of his ass—that the tablet was toast—he had a reason to be suspicious.

"Fine." Director Quade stomped from the room, bypassing Birch without another word.

Then Cole had the grizzly's attention. "Stay put. I'll send Ethan in to relieve you in a few hours."

Cole jerked his head in a brisk nod, and then he was alone with Abby once more, the curvy cougar shifter slumping against him.

"Abby? You okay?"

She snorted.

"Yeah, dumb question." He chuckled. He was so fucked up. Even Abby's snort was cute. He sighed and shook his head, stepping away from the curvy cougar. She didn't belong to him. She belonged to Declan. He had to remember that.

Cole padded to the other side of the bed, taking up the space the director had left. He snagged a nearby chair and tugged it close before flopping into the seat. He leaned back in the chair with a sigh and turned his attention to his friend's profile.

The lucky fucker. He got his ass kicked—almost died— and he still got the girl. Not that Cole wanted Abby, per se, but...He glanced at her, gaze touching on her blond hair, pink lips, upturned nose, and sparkling eyes. He wanted what she represented. Or at least, what she *could* represent someday.

"Abby?" He kept his voice low, just loud enough to draw her attention.

"Yeah?"

"Declan is your mate." She shook her head as if to deny him, and he snorted. "He's going to wake up territorial as hell. Don't let anyone else put their scent on you, okay?"

"Like you?"

He hadn't exactly touched her with the intent of pissing off his friend, but he wasn't exactly upset about it either.

"Yeah." He gave her a small smile. "As soon as he gets some protein in him, he'll want to leave. Birch is sending you two to his lake cabin. It's private and secluded—no other shifters there. He can finish recovering, and he'll have some time to figure this mate shit out."

She shook her head. "But we're not—"

"Suck it up and quit lying to yourself. He's yours just as much as you're his." And didn't *that* hurt like a bitch.

CHAPTER THIRTY-EIGHT

*D*eclan had been "healing" for two days at Birch's lakeside cabin and he was about to lose his mind. Shifter healing didn't take that long, dammit, and now he was bored as hell.

He needed someone to kill. Someone he was *allowed* to kill. He had plenty of guys he *wanted* to take out—every UH human he could find—but Birch told him he couldn't step off the property. The team had shit to do at the North Carolina SHOC base, and Papa Bear didn't want him stirring up anything new.

Birch also told Declan that if he was so fucking bored, he should quit being a pussy and claim Abby already. Declan hated to admit Birch was right, which made him hate the grizzly even more. As if it were that easy, but it fucking wasn't. Asshole.

Declan stared out the window of Birch's cabin and eyed the mountains in the distance. Normally the forest and mountain areas were for runs—alone or in groups—but maybe he could find a natural grizzly bear and take his frustrations out on one of them.

It'd get him out of the home and free of Abby's tormenting scent. They hadn't shared a bed since their time at Pike's place. It was enough to drive a wolf mad.

Which brought him back to needing to work off some of his pent-up desire.

He let himself imagine hunting a big-assed bear—just for a minute—and then sighed. It'd probably make Abby angry, and for some reason that *mattered* to him and the wolf.

He shook his head and sighed. She'd tossed his nuts in a jar and didn't even realize it.

"Declan?" Her soft voice drifted down the hallway, stroked his chest, and moved lower, giving his dick a nice squeeze.

"Yeah, I'm coming." Not really, but he'd like to—deep inside her over and over. Except that wasn't happening. Yet.

The short hallway led to the central living room, a great room that also housed an open kitchen and a space tucked in a corner with a dining room table and a couple of chairs. Solid wood floors with layer upon layer of sealant filled the area. Pretty and easy to clean. At least that's what he'd been told.

Abby had her back to him, that curved ass swaying from side to side while she danced at the kitchen stove, some random oldies song playing on the radio. The scent of frying bacon and eggs reached out for him, and his stomach growled, the wolf hungry. In truth, he was hungry for Abby, but the beast would take breakfast as a consolation prize.

"Hey," he murmured, drawing her attention, and she glanced over her shoulder. A soft smile curved her lips, blue eyes intent on his. Then they focused elsewhere, traveling down his body in a sweeping caress. "You need help with breakfast?" he asked.

She gave him another heavy-lidded look, pink tongue darting out to lick her lips. Then she had to go and nibble that plump lower lip, and all he could think about was tugging it free and giving her something else to put in her mouth.

A soft breeze drifted through the room, sliding through the kitchen window and swirling around the space. Sure, it brought in the crisp scents of the country air, but it gave him something else, too. The musky sweetness of her desire. The delicious scent of the sweet cream between her thighs, and he wondered when she'd let him get a taste.

His cock throbbed in his jeans, length hardening within the confines of the thin fabric, and that was where her eyes went next. Right to his dick, staring at him as if she was starving and the bacon in that pan wasn't going to do shit to sate her hunger.

She needed him? As much as he needed her? She'd had a great big no-trespassing sign stamped across her forehead from the moment he'd woken in the hospital. She'd kept her distance.

She'd pulled away every time he'd gotten close. It made him realize he'd obviously been good enough for some fun when they were being chased, but now that things were calm, she'd changed her mind.

The wolf kept telling him he was a dumbass and that he needed to nut up already.

"Sweetheart." He moved forward, stalking her as if *he* were the cat. Wolves knew how to hunt, though. How to watch and wait for the perfect moment to pounce. Fuck, he hoped it'd be time to pounce on Abby soon. "You keep looking at me like that, I'm going to take what you're offering."

Abby's face flushed pink and she dropped her gaze to the ground before she spun and refocused on breakfast.

Another gust of wind, another tempting wave of her desire. His threat hadn't diminished her need. Nah, it'd intensified the scent of her yearning. She wanted him—bad.

Declan kept up with his slow and steady tempo until his body was less than an inch from hers. He placed one hand on either side of her, palms resting on the front edge of the stove—away from the flames, but close enough to hold her captive.

He bent down, not touching her, but he was damned close, and murmured next to her ear, "Abby."

She shuddered, a full-body shake that he couldn't miss. "Declan. How do you want…?"

His cock throbbed, and he groaned before nuzzling the side of her neck. He breathed deep, took in the delicious scent of her skin. "Any way I can get you. Beneath me. On top of me. Clinging to me." He kissed a spot of bare skin just beneath her ear and smiled when a tremor racked her body. "While you come on my cock and scream my name."

Abby whimpered and swayed, as if her knees were no longer willing to support her. "Declan, you can't…"

"Can't what?" He could do anything he set his mind to, dammit. Right now his mind was filled with fucking Abby hard and deep.

For-fucking-ever.

"You…we…" She stuttered every other word, and he nibbled her earlobe, making her shudder once again.

"We? We can use this counter? We can use the couch? We can find a bed?" He eased forward the tiniest bit, his body brushing her sensuous curves. Curves he wanted to worship with his hands—his mouth. He wanted to drop to his knees and explore every inch of her lush body. "There are several down the hall to choose from."

Abby shook her head, her hair caressing his skin, and he

was the one who trembled. His balls drew up tight and he rushed toward the edge of release, his body ready to find that ultimate pleasure from a simple tease from her *hair*.

What the hell was wrong with him?

Abby. Abby was wrong with him. Those few moments they'd shared hadn't been enough. He'd never get enough.

"You know we can't."

"I know we *can*," he countered.

Abby sighed, and he nearly groaned aloud. He knew that sound. That was the "we need to talk" sigh.

She placed the greasy tongs on the spoon rest and turned to face him, forcing him to back up a little and give her space. He didn't want to give her space, dammit. He wanted them to occupy the same space at the same time—specifically, with his dick inside her.

"Declan." Another one of those sighs.

Fuck.

"Abby?" He quirked a brow. Maybe if he teased her, he'd get out of some emotional "express his feelings" talk. He'd done enough of that with SHOC-appointed therapists over the last two years.

Same answer, different doctor. *The subject is a sociopath who cares for nothing.*

They didn't get that he cared about something in his life. Things he refused to talk about. Like his brother. Well, before Pike facilitated Abby's kidnapping. Now he only cared about her.

"This..." Now she was on to head shaking. Not a good sign.

"This is something we should take to the bedroom. Great idea," he murmured, and curled his left arm around her back, palm flat just above the curve of her ass, tugging her closer. He'd forgotten the feeling of her lushness, the softness of her skin, and how he reacted to the points of her nipples against his chest. Another signal that she was aroused.

"No."

He hated that word. Normally he simply ignored it because it generally came with "please don't kill me."

With Abby, it was "no, we can't get horizontal."

Dammit.

He sighed and dropped his head forward, resting his forehead on her shoulder. He closed his eyes and tried to block out her scent, the sound of her heartbeat, and the way her breath fanned his shoulder and then drifted down his back. He basically ignored everything about her that made his dick hard.

She squirmed and wiggled, trying to do...something.

"Abby? Just...just sit still for a minute." Maybe a century. Or ten.

She didn't stop, though. Nah, she had to torture him further. Had to wriggle until she had her arms free and wrapped around his shoulders. One hand rested between his shoulders while the other toyed with the hair at the base of his neck. He shuddered and gritted his teeth. He wasn't going to come from a hand in his *hair*. He wasn't some adolescent pup who'd never gotten his dick wet.

"Abby." He added a growl to his voice, dropping it low in a clear threat. Not that he'd ever hurt her, but she didn't know that.

She snorted.

Okay, maybe she did know. Dammit.

"We really, really can't. Not while things are so..." She shook her head, dark strands caressing his heated skin, painting him in her scent. It soothed the wolf—a little—to have that hint of her on his skin. "So in the air."

"Birds are in the air. I'm not a bird," he grumbled.

She chuckled. Here he was, hard as a rock and desperate for her and she *chuckled*.

"No," she whispered. "No, you're not. You're a wolf. A big, bad SHOC agent and..." More sighing, more head shaking. He hated that shit. "And I'm a cougar who has a life somewhere else."

"You seriously think I'm going to let you go back to that number-crunching hellhole? So they can assign you to another company that's in bed with UH?" He pulled away from her, his rising anger doing a lot to tamp down his lust. "Or that I'll let you walk around as if UH doesn't have a target on your back?"

Her lower lip trembled, and he hated himself a little bit. Not a lot, because she needed to understand, but a little.

"Aw, shit," he grumbled, and hugged her tight. Not because he wanted to get in her pants but because she was on the verge of tears. He couldn't have that. "I'm not gonna let anything happen to you. I swear it. We'll figure something out."

"I had a life, Declan. I had a place," she whispered, pain in every syllable and the sting of her emotional agony in his nose. "I only ever wanted somewhere to just be *me*." He rubbed her back, not real sure how to respond, so he kept his mouth shut. "I had it with my parents, and then I was a lone cougar in Alaska, but..." Moisture dropped onto his shoulder, and he wondered who else he could kill for her. Maybe those asshole seals in Alaska. He'd never eaten one. Probably pretty fatty, but he could— "I made a life for me. I was respected. I had a place in the world. It wasn't the greatest, but it was *mine*."

"You don't think you have a place now? Aw, sweetheart..." He hated this heart-to-heart crap, but he'd deal with it if it meant stopping her tears. He pulled away and cupped her cheeks, forcing her to meet his gaze. "I don't know what happened to your parents and I'm sorry for it. As for Alaska, you say the word and that entire herd is gone. The world doesn't need their shit stinking up the air. As for your job, that was just a paycheck."

One tear escaped the corner of each eye, trailed down her cheek, and rested on his thumbs. "But your place? It's right fucking here. With me. Do you understand?"

Abby's chin wobbled, and she shook her head. She was breaking his damn heart.

"You're gonna make me get all emotional and in touch with my feelings." He groaned and sighed. Declan bent his neck and rested his forehead on hers, their stares locked on each other. "From the moment I saw you, you were mine. Not because I wanted in your bed—because we both know I want to haul your ass into the other room and fuck you so hard you can't walk straight for a week—but because you just *were*. Wolf didn't care what had to be done. I didn't know it then, but you were *it*."

"It?"

"You're everything, sweetheart. You want a job, we'll find you one that keeps you away from UH assholes. You want a family, we'll work on making one. Start on this counter if that's what you want. I'm gonna make you so fucking happy, and I don't care who I have to kill to do it. But no matter what, at the end of the day, you're my mate and I'm fucking keeping you."

"Cougars don't mate."

Declan snorted. "Apparently cougars *do*. Your parents did."

Abby shook her head. "My mom was a cougar and my dad was a wolf. They only mated because Dad was old-fashioned and wasn't…"

"Call it old-fashioned if you want, but he wasn't gonna let her go. Wolves find a mate; wolves keep a mate. And then they mark their territory. Make sure every male who even gets a hint of our mate's scent knows she's taken." She was quiet for a second, just staring at him, and he needed her to understand. "Abby?"

"Yeah?"

"You're taken."

Her breath hitched "I..."

A new scent teased his nose, one that had his wolf wanting to sneeze. "Abby?"

"Yeah?"

"The bacon's burning."

CHAPTER THIRTY-NINE

*B*acon's burning?" As cliché as it sounded, Abby could get lost in Declan's eyes for years—forever. She swayed in place, mind clouded by her fiery arousal and the pulses of need that attacked with every beat of her heart. She took a deep breath, seeking out his scent, and got...a lungful of smoke. Her cat sneezed and she coughed. She pulled away from Declan while she alternated between choking on the clouds of smoke and waving the worst of it off while she transferred the hot pan to another burner to cool.

She shoved Declan aside and raced to the kitchen window. She flicked the latch and shoved the thing open further to let in more fresh air and push the dark clouds *out*.

And Declan...just laughed.

She glared.

He laughed harder.

"Like a friggin' hyena," she grumbled, and passed him again, snatching the dish rag from the counter and wrapping it around her hand before she grabbed the handle of the frying pan.

"Nah, I'm all wolf, sweetheart." He murmured, laughter still in his voice while he reached around her, took the pan from her grip, and nipped her shoulder.

His voice, that nibble, sent a tremor down her spine, the sensation followed by an overwhelming wave of desire. For him and only him. Forever. Even if cougars weren't a "let's get mated" kind of species.

"Declan." She'd somehow managed to turn his name into both a plea and a scold in one.

"'Declan, you're right'?" He slipped his arm around her waist, his solid front to her back. "'Declan, I don't want to live without you'? Or 'Declan, I want to get mated'?"

Abby wanted to throw caution to the wind, to throw her hands in the air and say "screw it," but...

The cougar told her to shove that "but" up her butt.

Did she want him? More than anything in her life. Mentioning the fact that cougars didn't mate was just an excuse. Some did. Some were driven to find that *one* person and claim them before anyone else could. Her parents had been like that, and since meeting Declan, Abby realized she was like that as well.

He released her and moved to the sink, dropping the sizzling pan while she went to the front door of the small cabin and pulled it open. A cross breeze would get the place aired out and—

And she found herself wrapped in his arms once more, carried to the comfy couch, and he dropped onto the soft cushions, her sitting across his thighs.

"Did you pick one yet?" he murmured, and that talented mouth found hers, teeth nibbling her lower lip.

"Pick what, now?" A sting zapped down her spine, and she melted against his chest, relishing that snippet of pain. Her cat liked it, liked being submissive to the wolf. Though it was quick to point out the submission was only in the bedroom. She was a modern cat, after all.

"I'm right. You don't want to live without me. You want

to get mated." He lapped at her lower lip, soothing the sharp sting he'd caused.

Abby shook her head, trying to clear away the sensual spell he wove around her mind. "No, you don't. You only think you want me." It didn't matter that she craved him more than air. "The thing with UH and your team and Pike..." She hated the way he winced. "You want something to cling to, Declan."

He pulled back, those sparkling blue eyes on hers, and she melted beneath his sensual stare. What he wanted was there, plain to be seen by anyone—everyone.

"Because Pike betrayed me? Betrayed SHOC? Shifters?"

Abby nodded, and he shook his head, but she wouldn't be brushed aside. "You lost your brother, and now you need something to hold on to."

It was why she'd kept her distance. She wasn't going to be used like a comfy blanket and tossed aside when his emotions recovered.

"For a smart woman, you're very dumb."

All right, getting sexy wasn't at the top of her list any longer. Declan tucked a lock of hair behind her ear, his stare turning intent, his teasing smile gone. "I can't claim to know Pike's thoughts, but if he was going to truly betray our kind, the SHOC compounds would have been hit already. That would have been followed by council headquarters. What he was doing there is something he'll have to deal with, but he didn't betray SHOC."

"He betrayed you," she whispered. "And I won't be some substitute—"

"For the love of bloody, rare deer, woman," he growled, and bared his fangs, the teeth growing longer and longer until they resembled the wolf's.

A quick flip found her on her back, Declan hovering above her with his hips snug between her spread thighs. The hard ridge of his arousal nestled along the juncture of her thighs, the hot hardness stoking her arousal once again.

"I'm gonna say this one more time. You listening?" A light dusting of gray fur slid along his jaw, and blue eyes flashed yellow.

Her breath caught, heart racing with a combination of desire and worry. Which made her want him even more. It felt good—this contrast between need and fear.

"Listening?" He growled deeper, his whole body shaking, and his dick vibrated against her center.

Abby swallowed hard and nodded. She was listening. Ish.

"Pike is an asshole. My team can fuck off, and if UH even *thinks* of coming near you again..." His growl intensified, more fur sliding into place. "You. Are. Mine. You run, I'll chase you. You hide, I'll find you. You even *think* about another man, I'll kill him." He rocked his hips, a roll of his hard length along her cloth-covered slit. "Everything that's happened since I met you has been *for* you."

Her body warmed, not just from desire, but from another emotion as well. Caring? Hope? Soft tendrils of love?

That last thought had her freezing in place for a moment. They'd known each other for a handful of days and he was talking about mating and claiming and...

Declan lowered himself, more of his weight resting on hers, and she widened her legs further, wanting him as close as possible. She craved the feel of his soft fur on her skin, craved the closeness that would come from mating.

Mating. Her human mind still balked. Cougars didn't... The she-cat reminded her that her parents *did*. Because her mother was a cougar and her father was a wolf who refused to let her out of his sight.

He looked at her the way Declan looked at Abby. A little creepy, a hint psychotic, but beneath it all was an instinctual need to simply *have*. All of her.

Abby's inner animal told her that it felt the same. It needed Declan.

"I don't know what to say." She cupped his cheeks and lifted her head, meeting him halfway when he lowered his own. She brushed her mouth across his, a caress of soft flesh that she gradually deepened. He took more and she gave it, opening for him when his probing tongue demanded entrance.

He swept into her mouth, and she savored his taste. Abby entwined her fingers behind Declan's neck, firm hold keeping him close while their kiss continued. A brush of his chest on hers, teasing her hardened nipples. The rocking of his hips so his cock taunted her hidden depths. Then the way his hand... He skated it down her side until he reached her ass. He cupped the right globe, gave it a hard squeeze, and then moved on.

He gripped her thigh and squeezed, then pulled and opened her to him even more.

Her whole body shook, her clit twitching and pùssy growing heavy with wanting. She needed so much. Him inside her, him claiming her, him...

Abby rolled her thoughts back. Claiming?

Yes, her cat hissed. She wanted to be claimed by Declan, and she wanted to do some claiming of her own.

That realization, the confirmation of her feelings that'd prodded her only a day or two ago, forced her to tear her mouth from his.

"Declan," she gasped, and he growled.

"Mine." He took her lips once again, the kiss turning dominant, punishing. He lifted his mouth and tipped his head, going deeper, taking more. *"Mine."*

On his next change of position, when he next put more than a hairsbreadth between their lips, she rushed out a single word. One that would irrevocably change their worlds forever. One she no longer hesitated to use. "Yes."

"Oh, *fuck no*." A familiar voice, one that belonged to a soon-to-be dead man if Declan's sudden snarl was any indication.

Her mate—or soon-to-be mate—ripped his mouth from hers, lifted his head, and bared his teeth at the person near the door. She had a suspicion, but she hoped she was wrong.

Abby turned her head and released an annoyed huff when she saw who lingered. She'd just gotten her head wrapped around the mating thing and now they were interrupted. "Hi, Ethan." Her attention drifted to the men crowded behind the lion shifter. "Hi, guys."

The four members of Declan's SHOC team waved. Well, Ethan waved while he shook his head. Birch looked everywhere but at her and Declan. Grant simply gave an absent nod as he stomped past them in search of the kitchen because "something smelled good." While Cole stared and wiggled his eyebrows, before asking, "How would you guys feel about a threesome?"

Which officially ended any chance of their mating occurring in the next several hours.

CHAPTER FORTY

*T*wo hours and no sex later and Declan was ready to kill them all. Starting with Birch and his idea that agents should bunk with other team members.

Birch wanted him and Ethan to share a room, as if they were kids needing to learn to play well with others.

"You can fuck right the hell off." Declan shook his head. He ignored Birch's nod as well as Abby's soft squeeze of his hand. "The answer is no."

"What he said." Ethan pointed at Declan, but his attention was on the grizzly. "I'm not sharing a room with those two. Do you know what happened the last time we shared a space and the asshole brought some chick home? I didn't get to sleep for *days*, Birch. They fucked for *days*. You know my cat gets pissy when he doesn't get his sleep, and coffee doesn't do shit for my whiny bitch."

"If you'd stop calling your lion a whiny bitch, maybe it'd stop being such an asshole," Declan drawled, and he tried to pretend Abby's growl wasn't vibrating through him. The asshole just *had* to mention a woman from his past. He wasn't sure which one Ethan was talking about, but bringing up any of them in front of Abby was a dick move.

Even if her growl made his dick hard. Not that he could

do anything *with* his stiff cock with the team hanging around.

"Both of you, shut it." Birch growled low, his deep rumble filled with frustration and menace. The bear focused on Ethan. "The team bunks up. Always has." The glare turned to Declan. "Always will."

"The team hasn't had a mated member before," Declan pointed out. He wasn't having a fucking unmated lion in the same room as his mate. He was only bunking with one person and that person didn't have a dick.

"You're not mated, are you?" Birch quirked a brow, and Declan glared at the man.

"I was gonna take care of that—"

"Gonna isn't done." The grizzly cut him off.

"I'll show you *done*," Declan sneered, and curled his lip. His wolf paced just beneath his skin, hunting for an opening so it could pounce. He wanted to work off the energy coursing through him, and taking it out on Birch was as good an answer as any.

"Okay, then." Abby stepped between him and Birch, her hand on Declan's chest to keep him still. The only thing that saved Birch was the fact that she didn't touch the bear. "Let's just calm down."

A snort came from behind them, Grant strolling forward and joining their small group. They'd been having the same argument so long, Cole had started the grill. Now he shoved a paper plate of food at Grant. This was Birch's attempt at having just a regular, relaxing barbecue.

Though the meat wasn't exactly cooked—just a little seared.

"Just let 'em fight it out." Grant spoke around a bite of his burger. The wolf needed to learn some manners and not talk until he was done chewing. "The winner gets his way."

Birch sighed. "They both want the same thing."

Grant shrugged. "Then let 'em have their way."

"Grant, it's important to—"

"Have a happy, cohesive team in order to effectively protect and care for our kind. We're given a great responsibility as SHOC agents, and we can't betray the trust of our people by fighting among ourselves." Grant took another bite of his burger. "I know. You say that every time." He shrugged and kept chewing. "It'd save you a few minutes to just tell us 'same shit different day.' Save even more if you shorten it to 'SSDD.' We've memorized it; it doesn't need to be repeated." The wolf waved his plate toward Cole standing near the grill. "You know, Cole does the best impression of you." Grant yelled to the tiger. "Yo, Cole, come show Birch how good you make fun of him. Do the happy, codependent speech."

"Children. You're all fucking children." Birch pinched the bridge of his nose, closed his eyes, and sighed.

"With guns." Ethan grinned and rocked back and forth. "Big ones."

Abby sighed. One of *those* sighs. Dammit.

"Sweetheart..." Declan murmured, and placed his hand over hers.

"I thought you were calling her 'baby.'" Cole joined them and stood beside Grant, eating a mostly rare burger, as well. Then the tiger turned to Birch and dropped his voice. "We have to form a happy, cohesive team in order to—"

Birch pointed at Cole. "Shut the fuck up."

Cole shrugged and bent his head to take a bite of potato salad from his plate. Without a spoon. Then his attention came to Declan. "Baby?"

"She doesn't like me calling her 'baby.'"

"Can I call her 'baby'?" Cole waggled his eyebrows,

and Declan's wolf surged. His skin rippled, his beast's nails scraping his muscles and stretching his flesh. He pulled on the animal, yanking and tugging it away from the edge of his control. It was so close, so near to busting free, but a fight with Cole wouldn't solve his problems.

It would make him feel better though, so maybe...

"No, you can't, and if you even think—" His arms stung, fur sliding free of his pores, and a growl built in his chest. One that vanished beneath Abby's soothing caress. She traced circles on his chest, a soft *shhh* escaping her mouth.

"He's just messing with you," she murmured.

"And I'm *just* going to mess with him." Hard. Declan's human half still felt the urge to kick Cole's ass.

"Okay, I think we're getting off-track here. Let's refocus on the problem and discuss what can be done." She laid both hands on his chest. She had to really want to redirect him if she was willing to get back to the "fuck no Ethan isn't sharing a room with us" argument. They'd been having the same one for nearly two hours.

"There's nothing to discuss," Birch growled. "We work as a team, we live as a team—"

"We survive as a team." The rest of them chorused, and Birch growled louder.

"Even after you all find your mates? Have pups and cubs? I mean, sharing a cabin on the lake is one thing, but what about when you're at the home base and waiting for an assignment? How big of a home do y'all plan on building to house everyone?" Abby's soft questions—true confusion in every syllable—silenced Birch. "And where?"

Their leader shook his head. "We're not 'mate' kind of shifters."

"Speak for yourself." Cole spoke around a mouthful of burger. "Some of the other teams have families and crap.

They have houses close to each other, but they each have their own. This asshole is no better or worse than the rest of us, and Abby is willing to overlook the guns and killing and shit." He shrugged. "I don't see why we can't find someone if they're willing to keep an open mind."

"Aw," Ethan drawled. "Cole wants a girlfriend."

Cole swung at Ethan, plate balanced in his other hand while the tiger and lion sparred, trading insults and blows. The four of 'em just watched those two go at each other, alternating between laughing and growling while they fought.

Birch released another sigh—this one bone-tired. "We're not like other teams. We do the jobs they won't. We take the risks that send other teams running."

Grant coughed and spoke low. "Pussies."

"We don't take mates because any-damn-one deserves better than a future cut short by tying themselves to an agent from Team One."

Declan grunted and Grant did the same. Yeah, they did. Declan hoped Abby never realized the kind of wolf she tied her life to and the heartache that might await her down the road.

Abby withdrew her hands, and he slid his arms around her waist, unwilling to let her go far. She turned in his embrace to face Birch, and her next words came out as a soft whisper. "You see yourself as a poor choice, but any woman would be lucky to mate one of your men, Birch. Life is a risk. Mating an agent on Team One is the best mistake a woman can make."

Birch gave her a questioning look, one eyebrow raised. Yeah, Declan wanted to know what she was talking about, too. Or what she was smoking.

"You take orders from SHOC, but you also ignore them

when they go against what you feel is right. You're all loyal to each other—to the point that you were ready to go rogue for Declan . . . and me." She fell silent for a moment, and he lowered his head, pressing a soft kiss to her crown. "If that isn't happy or cohesive, who cares? You're dedicated to each other and doing what's right. You've done bad things, but you're not bad *people*. You take the jobs others won't because you're better than them."

Grant grunted. "What she said." He took another bite of potato salad. "Does this mean I can get the fuck away from Cole's rank ass?"

"I don't smell!" Cole had one arm wrapped around Ethan's neck.

"Your boots, man! Get some insoles or something. Put those little odor eliminator balls in them. I gave them to you for Christmas and I still have to deal with your stink," Grant called out, and Cole released Ethan, turning his anger on the wolf instead.

"How'd I get a bunch of babies instead of killers?" Birch grumbled.

"Aw, you know you always wanted to be a big papa bear," Declan drawled, and Birch flinched, an old pain flitting across his features. Fuck, he was an idiot. "Birch, man, I'm sorr—"

The bear waved him off. "It's fine. I'll talk to the director. Find us a few options for a home base. See what's available across the country and what it'll take to get us set up somewhere. If we've gotta build six homes from scratch, it'll take time, but maybe we can—"

"Six?" Abby voiced the same question he had. "I thought SHOC teams were five-shifter teams. I don't want my own house or anything." She chuckled, and Declan echoed her, but he didn't take his eyes off Birch.

Which meant he saw the emotions that slipped over his features—guilt, worry, unease, regret...

"Birch?" Declan's wolf added its own hint of a rumble to his voice.

"About that..." Birch hedged.

"Yo, Birch. I didn't realize you'd talked to Dec and Abby about Pike already." Ethan was still bent in half and wheezing, not that Cole let him breathe. "He coulda flown in with us."

"Pike?" Declan's snarl was all wolf. All furious beast anxious to rip out throats and shit on bodies. *What about Pike?*

Declan followed the direction of Ethan's gaze across the yard until his eyes landed on what—*who*—had captured the lion's attention.

Pike—brother, enemy, dead wolf walking.

CHAPTER FORTY-ONE

*T*here was knowing that Abby was missing part of Pike's story and then there was *knowing* she was missing part of his story. She was still stuck on the first knowing, which was why her anger flared white-hot in an instant.

The man had threatened her, scared her, and hit her. *More than once.*

All while working for Unified Humanity.

Yes, there might be wholly justifiable reasons for his behavior when she'd been his captive.

Unfortunately, now that she was free, standing among shifters who'd risked everything to keep her safe, she kinda...forgot. Just for a moment, just a split second when her human mind experienced a distracting jolt of fear, which gave her cougar a chance to snatch control. The cougar didn't care about anything but the fear and pain. It only remembered the fight to ground Declan, to stop his wolf from taking over completely and turning him feral.

Pike hurt her. Stupid or not, the cougar wanted to hurt him back.

Declan released her, his arms withdrawing, and his wolf's nails caught on the shirt she wore. Already his beast was on the surface and ready to tackle Pike. Abby would simply have to be faster, and her cougar leaped to her aid. Her body strengthened, legs adopting the power of her cat. And the agility.

The agility that let her dart ahead of Declan, quickness that let her duck his snatching grasp, and push of strength that allowed her to leap and pounce on the wolf from twenty feet away.

Snarls and growls came from behind Abby, but she only had eyes for Pike. She struck Pike's chest, sending him falling backward, and she straddled his body. She dominated him, wrapped her claw-tipped hand around his throat until they penetrated his skin, and hissed once more. The coppery scent of his blood hit her nose, and her cougar purred. Pike had drawn her blood, and now she did the same.

Her other half gave her more power, infusing more of her body with the beast's presence. Now she waited. Waited for his retaliation. Waited for him to throw her off and attack. Waited for him to...

Well, she sure as hell hadn't been waiting for him to bare his throat. He turned his head aside, gaze on the ground while he also attempted to expose more of his throat. Then...a whimper. A whine. A wolf's plea for...forgiveness?

No. She shook her head with disbelief, but her cat released an encouraging trill inside her mind. The beast recognized something Abby didn't, but if identifying what the animal saw meant she didn't get to cut Pike into tiny pieces...

Well, she didn't want to know.

He made the sound again, more of his neck bared, his head turned as far as he could. Exposed. Submissive.

A stupid freaking *apology,* and now she didn't feel quite so justified in her attack. It was no fun beating up someone who wouldn't fight back. Abby huffed—frustrated and annoyed—before moving to sit beside him.

A hiss reached her ears, the sound purely feline, and she knew one of the others had shifted—Cole or Ethan was delaying Declan. That was the only wolf who'd be fighting to get to her and Pike so hard.

"Don't release Declan!" Birch roared the words, and Pike flinched beneath her.

"Dammit, kid. I told you to stay put until I had a chance to talk to them," Birch snarled. He growled as he approached them, fury in every stomping step, as if he were about to dive after Pike, too.

Well, she wasn't done yet.

"Hold it, Birch." She held out her hand, warding him off. Off-white cougar's nails tipped her fingers—sharp and deadly. "Only one person gets to kick Pike's ass at a time, and it's still my turn. You can yell at him in a minute."

Brass ovaries . . . she had 'em apparently.

"It's fine. He's right," Pike whispered, and she could see the pain lingering in his eyes. "Birch told me to wait, but I wanted to explain."

"Explain what?" Declan snarled at Pike and then at her. "Abby, get your ass over here."

Instead of moving, she took a deep, calming breath so she didn't try to kick all their asses at once. "No, I'm not. I'm not done fighting Pike. It's still my turn." She glanced at her mate, and Declan looked like he couldn't decide if he wanted to strangle her or fuck her. Abby knew how she'd vote, but only when they got rid of their audience.

"Pike, I'm the team alpha for a reason. I make plans; the team executes." Birch pointed to himself. "I say jump . . ." He gestured at the team. "They don't have to ask how high because they listened *the first fucking time I gave them an order*."

Abby shifted slightly, wiggling closer to Pike and farther away from Birch. Apparently Birch was slightly miffed at Pike, too.

"He's not on the fucking team," Declan snarled. "He's a traitor. You fucking—" Her mate's eyes blazed with his wolf's presence. *"You gave her to them."*

"You're not team alpha." Birch's glare moved from Pike to Declan. "You don't get a vote."

"I've wondered about that. I think we should be able to vote on shit. Like, when it comes to choosing our base when we're on assignment." Grant was still noshing. "The take-out on the last one was gross. *I* didn't even want to eat at some of the places." The wolf shuddered and then gagged.

And the tension popped *like that*. Grant was intelligent, deadly, constantly hungry apparently, but at his core he seemed like a peacekeeper. Of sorts.

"This isn't a conversation I wanted to have yet." Birch glared at Pike, and Pike winced again.

"I couldn't let Declan think that—"

"That you betrayed me and *my mate*? That I should—"

"Enough." The word whipped through the air, a wave of dominance and pure strength in those syllables. Her cougar flinched, recognizing a stronger shifter nearby. One who demanded obedience.

She generally wasn't an obedient kind of girl.

Birch propped his hands on his hips and dropped his head forward. His shoulders rounded, and the man looked like he carried the weight of the world—beaten and dragged down by responsibility.

The team alpha straightened and stared at Declan. "Pike was freelancing. For me."

More growling from her mate—his amber-eyed gaze moving between Pike and Birch before finally settling on the wolf at Abby's side. "You told them about the house. You're the reason Abby got shot. And then you told them about the island." Declan surged, and Ethan and Cole tightened their holds, pulling her mate back again. "You little shit..."

"He's also the one who made sure she suffered minimal damage while Unified Humanity had her," Birch countered.

Abby wouldn't call it "minimal" herself, but she supposed it could have been worse.

"He told them where to find her in the first place." Declan snarled once more, and both Ethan and Cole struggled to hold him back. "He—"

Birch held up his hand. "On my orders. Everything he did—everything he revealed to Unified Humanity—was at my direction." He rolled his shoulders. "Twitchy, remember?"

"All your 'twitchy' bullshit got us was Abby hurt."

The bear shrugged. "Maybe." Birch tipped his head toward Pike. "And maybe not. That's not a discussion for right now. As team alpha I'm telling you he's our sixth man. The rest will figure itself out."

"As long as it gets figured out before my balls explode, I don't give a fuck," Abby heard Declan mumble, which meant *everyone* heard Declan mumble, and she groaned.

"Declan..."

"It wasn't me." He snapped his gaze to her, eyes wide, the picture of innocence.

More than one of the men snorted.

The snort turned into a cough, which turned into several coughs, and they all looked anywhere but at her.

"All right. So much for a fucking barbecue." Birch clapped his hands. "Let's break for the day. Get settled in your rooms and then do whatever you want. We're having a run in the north quarter tomorrow night. No excuses. Everyone's wearing their fur. You can make fun of me if you want, but it's a damned team-building exercise. We can't have a happy—"

They four men finished it together. "Cohesive team in order to effectively protect and care for our kind. We're given a great responsibility as SHOC agents and we can't betray the trust of our people by fighting among ourselves."

Birch sighed, the men laughed, and Abby just smiled. They were dangerous—deadly—but they were still just men. Ones who liked to laugh, joke, and…

She met Declan's gaze and felt his heated expression all the way down to her toes. She knew he wanted her—she craved him just as much—but beneath that was something she wanted to call…love.

CHAPTER FORTY-TWO

Declan sighed and leaned against the nearest tree, crossing his legs at his ankles. Bark dug into his bare shoulder. On the outside, he appeared relaxed and content. On the inside, he wanted to run across the clearing and snatch Abby away from Ethan, Cole, and Grant's reach. If he didn't mate her soon, he'd kill someone.

But that wasn't exactly "team building." Team destroying, though... That could be fun.

He sighed. Again. Where the hell was Birch? They couldn't get their shit-show into the forest without him.

The snap of a twig, the crunch of leaves, and a gentle wind from the south announced the newest member of their group. One who had him torn in two—alternating between kicking the asshole's ass and whacking him for being so stupid... before kicking the asshole's ass.

"Lazy," Declan murmured as the newcomer stepped into his peripheral.

"Cautious," Pike countered.

He grunted. "I didn't cut your throat last night."

"Because Abby wouldn't let you."

Declan shrugged. It was the truth, after all. The only reason he hadn't done anything to Pike was because Abby had wrapped herself around Declan and fallen asleep the moment her head hit his shoulder. Even now he was certain she'd been faking, but he wouldn't tell her that. He wanted to mate *eventually,* and pissing her off would only delay them *again.*

Quiet blanketed them, two brothers standing side by side, but Declan felt as if thousands of miles separated them. They'd always been close, but now he wondered if it'd all been fake.

Abby's laugh reached out, her pure happiness acting like a soothing caress to his wolf. She was alive and whole. She wanted to be his. He wasn't sure what he'd done to deserve her, but he wasn't letting go. He hadn't done a good job of keeping her safe so far, but he'd do better. He had to. He couldn't live without her now.

"I'm sorry." Pike's voice was low, raspy.

"I know." He did know. The wolf knew, too. That didn't diminish its desire for vengeance though.

Pike slumped, shoulders curved forward, spine rounded. If he'd shifted, his tail would have been tucked between his legs, too.

Declan's wolf growled and shoved. It wanted him to snarl at the pup at their side. Show him the error of his ways. It wouldn't mind killing him either. But Declan kept it back. Not because he wasn't furious, but because Pike was his brother.

"Why?" That was Declan's only question.

"Birch—"

"I'm not asking Birch. I don't give a damn about the grizzly's twitchy bullshit. I'm asking you—*my brother*—why you betrayed me." He shook his head, the pain of his brother's treachery throbbing in his chest.

"You're not the only one driven by the past, Dec." Pike sighed. "You don't have a monopoly on pain."

"You?" Declan snorted, and pointed at Pike. "You left the pack voluntarily after the alpha died. I didn't force you to follow me."

"You mean after you killed the alpha?" Pike hissed. "You're my *brother*, Dec. I wasn't about to let you leave without me."

Declan ignored him. "I've done everything for you—given you anything you've ever needed. What do you know—"

"I know." Pike rasped those two words, his brother's agony more than evident. "I know that before you joined SHOC you'd spend months on a job. You'd come back for a few days and then leave on another. You think I just sat around and twiddled my thumbs while you did that shit?" Pike shook his head. "I had my own life. I had my own experiences with Unified Humanity. When Birch contacted me, I didn't hesitate." His brother looked him in the eyes, meeting Declan's hardened stare without a hint of a flinch.

"I'm sorry things played out the way they did, but the result was worth it."

Declan's wolf snarled and pulled at him, fighting to tear free of his human skin and sink his claws into Pike. "She shielded you."

"I know. I thought she was going to rip out my throat when she pounced." Pike rubbed his neck.

"No, in that room—at Unified Humanity. I was going to…" He ran a hand down his face. He was so fucking tired, and he knew they'd just go 'round and 'round with the argument. Declan *knew* he was right and Pike…fuck. Pike might have been right, too. "You were unconscious, and I was going in for the kill. She jumped on top of you so that I ended up with her neck between my jaws. You hurt her and she still saved your ass."

"I didn't realize."

"Yeah, well…" Declan shrugged.

"She saved me twice." A hint of awe filled Pike's tone, and he wasn't sure he liked the way his brother stared at Abby.

"She did." He shook his head. "She's the strongest shifter I know. She's been through so much—growing up and with us—but she's still over there laughing with the team."

"Stronger than you?"

He glanced at Pike, wondering if the kid was joking, but he looked honestly curious. "Killing's easy. Surviving, though, that's hard."

"Declan?" That soft voice, the delicate scent of her skin, and the soft padding of her bare feet on the grassy earth announced Abby's approach—and the end of his conversation with Pike.

They still had shit to figure out, but Declan had calmed enough to put off killing his brother… for a little while, at least.

He turned his head and watched her come toward him. She was his, in mind if not in body quite yet. Every curvy inch of her five-foot-eight frame. Every part of her would be his—soon. Fuck, he hoped *very* soon because he thought he'd go crazy without her. Neanderthal him wanted to *own* her down to her soul. He wanted to be her first thought of the day and last just before she fell asleep.

Because he sure as hell didn't want to be the only one going crazy in their mating. She already had him wrapped up in knots to the point that his wolf couldn't think of anything *but* her. Her smiles, her laughs, her kisses, her touches...

"Is everything okay?" She nibbled her lower lip, uneasiness in her expression while she flicked her attention between him and Pike.

"It's fine, sweetheart," he murmured, and held out his arm.

He tugged her close the moment her fingers wrapped around his. Once those curves were snug to his side, he gave her a kiss on her temple. He couldn't trust himself to kiss her anywhere else. Once he got started he wouldn't finish until he was *finished*. He was almost to the point that he didn't care who happened to be standing around watching.

Abby placed her hand on the center of his chest and tipped her head back to meet his gaze. "You sure?"

Maybe he could kiss the tip of her nose and be okay. He did just that and drew in a deep breath at the same time. Yeah, he wasn't okay. His cock went hard with that single hint of her scent, and he closed his eyes, trying real hard not to come in his jeans.

And his mate knew it. She wiggled her hips, body caressing his firm length while she gave him a knowing smirk. Even Pike could tell, his shithead little brother laughing like a damn donkey.

Declan reached out and whacked him in the back of his head. "Shut up, asshole."

"Declan," Abby admonished him. Of course.

"You can't expect me not to hit him. I didn't kill him, did I?" Yet. "Besides, he's my brother. I've been hitting him for more than twenty years. I can't stop now. It'd hurt his feelings."

Abby snorted. So did Pike. Declan had the urge to

glare at them both but settled for Pike. He still wanted to get in her pants and his fangs in her shoulder. Hopefully tonight. He knew the perfect spot just at the bend of the creek, and he'd already warned the team off. That area was a no-paw or -human-feet zone until sunrise *tomorrow*.

That'd give him the rest of the afternoon and all night to sate himself. Or at least take the edge off.

Declan licked his lips, imagining losing himself in her. In his fantasy, she'd shift back to human when they reached the creekside. He'd lay her down on the soft grass and take his time with her. Trace her curves with his tongue before he buried his face between her legs. Cats weren't the only species that liked cream, and he wanted all of Abby's. Then he'd settle between her legs and—

Poke.

Hell, no he wasn't poking. He was smoother than that.

Poke. Poke.

What the—

Poke. Poke. Poke.

Declan shook his head and rapidly blinked his eyes before turning his attention to the small finger poking his chest. "Huh?"

"Birch is here. He wants to get started."

He stared at her a moment more, trying real hard to figure out what the hell she was saying. "Huh?"

A large—familiar—hand whacked him in the back of the head. "Get your mind off your dick. Birch is ready to run."

Declan swung his arm out, fingers curled to form a fist, and aimed for his brother. Who ducked out of reach with a smile and a laugh before he jogged off to join the rest of the team. There was still a small hitch in Pike's step, but a shift would take care of the remaining injuries, putting him back together. At least physically.

"You sure I can't kill him? If I do it in his sleep, he won't feel a thing."

Abby just chuckled and gave him a soft kiss on the chin. He figured that meant no. Dammit.

CHAPTER FORTY-THREE

*A*bby held Declan's hand, his touch a comfort, while they slowly padded toward the rest of his team. She squeezed his fingers a hint tighter, a tremor of unease sliding into her blood, and she pushed the feeling aside.

"Sweetheart?"

She glanced at him, giving him a soft smile. "It's been a while since I've participated in a group run. In Alaska, gatherings were more like group *swims*, and before that, it was with my parents, so..."

"Eh, we're not all that organized. We'll shift, run as a group for a little bit, and then break off. Birch likes to find a cool cave to nap in. Ethan has a favorite rock where he can pretend he's got a pride of pussies waiting to lift their tails. Cole will fish a little in the creek. He just likes us to share the forest when shifted so our animals are familiar with each other."

"And the wolves stick together? You're like a mini-pack."

Declan snorted. "*Pike and Grant* can go run together."

"And us?"

"*We* will go exploring. I'll show you some of my favorite spots." He tugged her close, his hardness—including *that* hardness—pressed to her.

"Your favorite *private* spots?" Heat flushed her face, and a war roused inside her. She wanted to mate him—there was no disputing that—but in the middle of the forest during a run? Did she...?

Declan's eyes darkened, a deep amber replacing the bright blue. His wolf was out, peering at her through his eyes, and she recognized that look. Simply because it matched her own. Yes, the wolf wanted to mate. Now. In the forest. During the run.

Where anyone could come upon them while they solidified their connection.

Abby's center grew heavy and ached, that part of her already eager for his touch. Arousal blossomed and spread, reaching out from her core to consume her body. Her nipples hardened beneath her thin cotton shirt. She hadn't bothered with a bra or panties since she'd have to strip for her shift. They would have been just another layer to discard.

"Yes." He growled the word, deep rumble sending yet another jolt of need down her spine.

"Are you two coming?" Grant called out and then grunted, whispering "asshole" to someone before he yelled again. "I don't mean *coming*. That's later. I meant are y'all gonna strip and shift already. You're taking forever, and my balls are getting cold."

They were naked already? Abby turned her head, wanting to both confirm her suspicion *and* get a peek at the team, only to have Declan place his hand over her eyes.

"It's not cold, asshole. Summer hasn't been gone that long. Turn around."

"Does she want a look at my ass? She just had to ask." Grant's grunt that time was quite a bit louder.

"Turn. Around." Declan growled at the team, and the

texture of his skin changed, the wolf easing forward and taking over.

Abby turned her head slightly and rubbed her temple on his palm, her cat's attempt to soothe their angered mate. "It's fine," she murmured. "I don't care."

"*I* care." He grumbled. "Turn or lose your eyes."

"Do I get a look first? I need a good memory to carry me through the rest of my blind life." Grant had to keep pushing.

Her mate took a step toward the group, and she wrapped her arms around his waist, placing herself between Declan and the team. "Hey. He's just pushing your buttons."

He huffed and puffed—but there were no houses to blow down—and kept his gaze trained on the group at her back. "I'm going to push a button through his skull."

"Can you do that tomorrow? If you blind him now it'll annoy Birch and he's already agreed to let Pike bunk with the others, which means..."

Wolf's eyes met hers. "Alone."

"Yeah." Anticipation stirred her blood and her clit twitched, body anxious for him.

"Mate."

She nodded. "Yeah."

And she wanted it—him—so bad. Nothing else in her life had ever felt so right as being with him. She'd go through it all again—the pain, the fear—if only to end up with Declan once more.

"We turned around," Grant grumbled, though Abby was beginning to think the wolf just liked giving Declan a hard time. This time his words weren't followed by a groan, but a high-pitched whine.

Declan looked past her and then gave her his attention once more. "Strip."

If only they were in a bedroom...

She stepped away and then whipped her head over her shirt and tossed it aside, her shorts soon following, and then the cougar was there.

She embraced the cat, welcoming the animal with open arms and no resistance. Her transition slipped over her in a ripple of fur and flesh, bones and muscles reshaping to turn her into a glorious, golden beast. What used to hurt when she was younger didn't even warrant a flinch, nerves accustomed to the shift. Pale skin became sun-kissed fur, hands and feet turning into paws tipped with deadly nails, and bulky muscle swelled to replace her curves.

She dropped to four feet within a second of welcoming the cat, and Abby whipped her tail back and forth. Then she moved into a stretch, extending her forelegs first and digging her claws into the dirt before rocking forward and stretching one back leg and then the other. Abby turned her head up to the sky, enjoying the warmth, and she breathed deep to draw in the scent of her surroundings.

But her first scent wasn't of the grass or the trees. It didn't include nearby prey, or the aroma of the team. No, the flavors that consumed her were from one wolf—one specific, delicious wolf.

She lowered her head and looked to her left, searching for the source of that tempting aroma, and he was right there—at her side in all of his massive, midnight, dangerous and deadly glory.

A rumbling growl came from behind her, a sound the cat didn't recognize as Declan's, but she *could* identify the species.

Bear. She'd fought bear in the past. Fought and won, and she would again and again. She'd fought to survive in the past just so she could escape Alaska. Now she'd fight to keep the new life she'd only just tasted. A life of happiness even if it was occasionally bloody.

She settled into a crouch, claws firm in the dirt and grass—prepared to launch herself at any threat. She opened her mouth, fangs exposed, and released a long, threatening hiss. One warning was all it would get before she...

Declan chuffed and nipped her ear, the slight sting hardly worth thinking about because the cougar was still trying to understand... Two wolves. A lion. A tiger. A bear.

Oh my?

She shook her head. She wasn't in the wilds of Alaska. She wasn't fighting a polar bear for her life. She was in North Carolina with her mate and his SHOC team. They were going for a run, and then later...

Later she'd mate.

Abby nuzzled Declan in return, assuring him she was fine, and added an extra purr to make sure he understood. She was content. No, more than content. She was happy.

Another growl followed by a huff and she turned a glare on the bear—on Birch. The bear was Birch. The tiger was Cole, while Ethan was the lion. The two wolves... One resembled Declan, only slightly smaller in size. That had to be Pike.

Which meant the pale gray wolf was Grant. Grant with his tongue lolling out, tail wagging, and general look of play covering every inch of him. He was ready for fun, and Abby realized... so was she.

Now.

Abby nuzzled Declan once more, giving him a low, questioning trill, and then bolted for the tree line. Not just any part of it either. She sped across the ground, claws flinging dirt into the air with every long stretch, and she launched herself up and over the group of males. She landed with a *thump* on the other side, sliding sideways for a moment before she righted herself and glanced at the group.

She flicked the tip of her tail, waiting to see who would be the first to break ranks and chase her. With a howl and a leap, she had her answer, Declan's call echoing through the trees, and he grunted when he landed nearby.

The others released their own calls, snarls, roars, and growls in response, but Abby only had eyes—and ears—for Declan. The second his lupine gaze met hers, she was off. She broke into a sprint, cat's agility allowing her to bank right, then left, and then right again. She darted through the forest, embracing her beast while she simply enjoyed the act of running with a group. It was not a normal pack or a pride, but she figured they were better—a growly, grumpy, dangerous-as-hell, badass family.

And she was part of it—them—now. Or would be once she mated Declan.

A sharp nip to her hind leg grabbed her focus, and she shot a glare over her shoulder at the dark gray wolf keeping pace. The others crashed through the brush as well, a widely spread line of deadly predators wreaking havoc on nature.

But the wolf nipped her again, and she hissed at him. She was enjoying her run, dammit. The freedom of warm air in her fur, the breeze stroking her whiskers, and the joy of simply being a cat.

If he did it again, she had half a mind to finish the damn run in the trees. It'd been a while since she leaped from branch to branch as a way to travel—she was a hell of a lot heavier now—but she'd do it. *Just watch.*

The wolf didn't bite her again, though. He *pounced*. He took them both to the ground in a roll of fur and fang, slipping across the leafy forest floor. Soon their momentum gave out and they slid to a stop. Declan held her there, dominating her and yet not, while the rough sounds of the team's race slowly faded. When they were barely more than a whisper on the wind, he released her and hopped back.

Apparently, now he wanted to play—with her.

He bent down, forelegs nearly flat against the earth while his ass remained high, his tail rapidly wagging back and forth. He darted forward and then hopped back. Then he jerked left and right and left again, his mouth open wide and tongue lolling out. He barked at her, two short yips, and pounced on her again.

Or tried. She-cat would take it once, but not twice. She ducked out of his path and prepared herself to run. He wanted to play? He could try to catch her. But this time she'd known what kind of game they were playing.

Though it seemed he didn't want to chase; he wanted to *be* chased. Which was fine. Once she caught him she'd make him tell the team that cats ruled and dogs drooled.

CHAPTER FORTY-FOUR

*D*eclan put on more speed, his longer strides helping him keep ahead of Abby. Even with her cat's natural quickness, he managed to outrun her through sheer reach. It paid to be larger than her agile feline.

He darted left, leaped over the next log, and landed with a heavy *thud*, his gait not faltering. But hers did. A scramble of leaves, breaking twigs, and then a snarl told him she hadn't fared the jump as well as him. He didn't get a whiff of her blood on the wind, which meant her body wasn't hurt—just her pride.

He made a sharp right at the next rock and used the thick layer of leaves to help him spin to face her. He slid in a whip-fast circle, and suddenly he was eye to eye with her, the furious cat glaring at him with frustration and a hint of menace. Oh, his mate wanted to pounce on him. Good thing he *wanted* her to pounce.

He yipped and barked, tail wagging, front legs lowered. He wanted to keep playing—needed her to keep running. Just a little farther. The direction of the wind changed, a hint of fresh water carried by the breeze, and his wolf howled within his mind. Joy overtook the beast, knowledge that they'd soon claim their mate suffusing him.

He hopped left and then right, a sharp bark at Abby that earned him a darker glare and a flick of her tail. Sure, the narrowing of her eyes showed anger, but he knew Kitty wanted to play.

And he had the perfect spot for them to enjoy.

He hopped forward and nipped the air, his teeth audibly clicking together. Then he whirled once more, taking off deeper into the trees. He kept one ear focused on Abby's movements while he kept watch on the rest of the world around them. Sure, the creek was near, but he needed to make sure no one else was in the area, too. If one of those assholes thought they'd get a show...

A sharp jolt of pain tweaked his tail, and he glanced over his shoulder to find a grinning feline just behind him. She'd caught up while he was worried about other males ogling her and she made it known.

Just wait until he got her naked.

The bubbling creek was soon within earshot, the gentle splash of water acting like a siren's call. It lured him forward and he went—gladly. He flew over the last of the forest's shrubs and landed with a grunt on the wet dirt just beyond the line of trees. The moment his paws hit the moist ground, he danced in a circle, making sure he didn't expose his back to the little she-cat.

Abby was right behind him, her golden body easily clearing the brush, and her feline's grace made the leap seem effortless—beautiful. She was solid muscle and fierce power, a powerful cat that rivaled his own wolf's strength. She was a worthy match to his own beast. Size separated them, but the power their beasts held was so very close.

At a glance, anyway. The wolf still wanted to play. He wanted to pounce and roll and see who came out on top... before he made sure Abby was on the bottom.

She paced back and forth, tail flicking, the darkened tip revealing her cat's agitation. Declan was getting ready to agitate her a little more. He wouldn't hurt her, but...

He pounced, jumped across the feet separating them and shoved her sideways. He knocked her off-balance and she stumbled, losing her footing. She rolled across the wet dirt, snarling and hissing with each shift of muscle. He kept pace, joining the tumble until he was sure she ended up beneath him.

Which was when he realized his error. When he realized she was beneath him, all right. And also on her back. She pulled her legs close and then planted them on his chest and belly, shoving him from atop her furred form. Her fierce shove launched him into the air a couple feet before he landed with a bone-jarring *thud* of powerful werewolf muscle and bone.

Embarrassed werewolf muscle and bone.

I am alpha wolf. Watch me get my ass handed to me by a cat.

A cat who thought she was hilarious and quickly rolled to her feet before breaking out into some awkward feline dance. He could practically hear her thoughts. "Neener-neener, look who's a wiener."

He'd show—

Abby pounced next, taking *him* down in a pile of claws, fur, and fangs. She nipped his shoulder and curled her nails around his legs. She tangled them in his fur, as if clutching him close even as she fought to push him away. Then he felt it, the shift of muscles and the subtle change in her force.

She wanted to be on top and his wolf... wasn't opposed to the idea. It meant she could do most of the work while he simply—

She nipped his ear and he yelped, her fangs pinching the

thin skin and zapping him with a spear of pain. Dammit. While he'd been imagining her riding his human form, she'd managed to pin his mangy ass. Stupid wolf.

The wolf didn't argue but reminded him that he was thinking more with his cock and balls than his brain. Her ferocity made him crave her, and if Declan didn't understand that...

Yeah, Declan's human mind understood.

He understood and decided that it was his turn to regain control. Those feline eyes were a little too happy about getting him on his back, and he simply couldn't have that.

Another roll, another change of position, but this time he didn't follow the quick move with a snarl. No, he cooed, whimpered, and whined. He lapped at her muzzle and nuzzled her jaw, wanting her pale skin and two-legged form to return. He licked her once more and then pulled back. He met her stare and tipped his head to the side in question, wondering if she wanted the same as him. They had privacy. They had each other.

And then they'd have a mating.

Her cat mirrored him, the angle of her head the same as his, and he lowered his nose to rub it on hers. He whined again, rubbing his snout on her lower jaw once more before meeting her gaze again.

Her purr began low, almost inaudible, but quickly grew in volume. It increased until it vibrated through his whole body. A sound of contentment, happiness...willingness? Her gaze darted up and down the bare banks of the creek, and he pictured what she saw. They were at one particular, sharp bend. An area that curved so tightly that they were out of sight from anyone up or down the creek. It was a private, yet exposed place.

And so help his team if they intruded.

Declan retreated, easing back so she was no longer pinned beneath him. Then he went further, not stopping until she was out of his reach. He didn't want her to feel pressured, but damn...he wanted her.

The wolf retreated, giving way to his human body. Naked. Exposed. Anxious for her cat to let go already.

"C'mon, sweetheart," he murmured. "We're alone. Wanna make you mine."

She gave him a questioning trill, a soft roll of her cat's tongue, as if to ask him if he was sure.

"That I want you? Or that we're alone? I'm sure about both." He padded to the edge of the cool, gently flowing water. "Gonna rinse off this mud, and then I'll see about licking off every drop of water on your skin. How's that sound?"

That earned him a purr, a delicate sound from a dangerous beast, a contrast that made him want her even more. She was a contrast, softness that made him want to take care of her. At the same time, she retained a fierce strength that made him feel sorry for anyone who faced her. It was easy to kill. It took a lot to survive.

And she had. Through everything life threw at her, she'd survived. She'd overcome the worst. Now he only wanted to give her the best.

After he sank his fangs into that pretty shoulder and marked her so one and all knew she was taken.

Abby's shift was effortless, a flowing retreat by her cat and a gentle emergence of her human form.

"Abby," he murmured, and held out his hand, waiting for her to make the next move. He knew he didn't deserve her—not after the life he'd led. But if she'd let him, he'd take her and never let her go.

"Declan"—she took one hesitant step and then two— "what if...?"

"I'll kill 'em."

Her lips quirked into a tiny smile that had an extra dose of need sliding into his blood. "You threaten to kill your team an awful lot, but I haven't seen too much of that going on."

"You just have to bust my ass." He shook his head and kept his gaze trained on her. On the sway of her hips, on the subtle bounce of her breasts while she approached. The moment her hand touched his, he curled his fingers and enclosed her hand with a firm grip. He wasn't losing her now that he had her in his grasp.

Declan tugged, and then he had that damp body flush with his own, and her tempting scent surrounded him, blocking out all other aromas in the area. She was wet for him already, anxious for his possession. Her need spurred his, desire stirring in his balls while his shaft hardened.

Her hips wiggled slightly, just enough to caress his quickly hardening dick. She smiled wide, lips pulled back to reveal a hint of her cat's fangs. Then she bent her head and scraped a single fang over his chest.

"Fuck," he rasped, cock reacting to her whisper, her tease. "Abby, I won't be able to control myself if you tease me like that. I'll lose it, and I want to make this good for you. If you…"

She repeated that scrape, and Declan was man enough to admit that he whimpered.

"Just being with you will make it good," she said.

The wind picked up. It swirled around them, bringing forward more of the flavors of her arousal. Hot. Slick. Salty musk.

He ached to taste her, touch her, fuck and claim her.

Declan lowered his head, resting his forehead on hers. "Gonna rinse this sand off you, and then I'm going to claim you. Got that?"

"Better get started, then." With those teasing words, she tore from his arms and darted to the water's edge.

She splashed into the low waters with a joyous laugh, one that was so lighthearted and carefree that it washed away more of the darkness in his heart. She'd been brushing away those spots minute by minute, hour by hour. Even as he killed, it was on her behalf so dark stains on his soul never formed.

If he had a purpose, if it was for her, he didn't suffer. Further proof that she was his and his alone.

With a growl, he followed, baring his fangs and adding a snarl. The chilled water lapped at his heated skin, but it couldn't diminish his desire. Not when her hands slid over his body.

He did the same, tracing her form, exploring her with a desperate touch. He wanted to learn all of her. He wanted to know the meaning behind every sigh and each moan. He was desperate to understand what each groan meant and exactly what could be done to make her shatter in his arms.

And when he washed away the last streak of mud, he knew it was time. His wolf spurred him into action, encouraged him to sweep her into his arms and cradle her against his chest. He turned and strode to the water's edge and worked to ignore her tempting lips wreaking havoc on his neck and chest.

Abby nibbled his wet flesh, tugging on his skin and nipping him with her cat's fangs. She released a soft whine and wiggled in his arms, the feline asking for more. More than he'd give to her. Soon.

"There's a blanket over here with our name on it. Once I lay you down, you won't be getting up again for a while."

CHAPTER FORTY-FIVE

*A*bby didn't think she'd want to get up for a long, *long* while. And then his words penetrated her passion-glazed mind.

"You planned this." She murmured the words against his shoulder, then licked away the nearest drop of water.

Declan snorted. "Can you blame me?" His deep tenor slid through her and caressed her spine from inside out. "I want you to be mine, but we're surrounded by the team twenty-four seven."

She grinned and nipped his shoulder blade, licking away any sting as soon as she was done.

His pace slowed, and she lifted her head from his shoulder, turning her attention to her surroundings and the plush blanket resting on a sun-dappled patch of grass nearby. A few colorful pillows added to the alluring picture, along with a basket she hoped contained food...for later.

For now she wanted to gorge herself on Declan.

He lowered to his knees in a smooth move and then laid her on the soft blanket before taking his spot beside her. They remained close, his heat searing her nude body, yet she still had room to look her fill.

"Can't stand having those unmated males near you." His

words were gruff and low. Almost so garbled she couldn't understand him, but the message came through.

"They weren't ever going to take me from you." Abby lifted her left hand and caressed his biceps, stroking him from elbow to shoulder and then across his collarbone before slipping behind his neck. "From the moment you caught me, I've thought of nothing but you."

That was only a tiny lie. She'd thought about pain and death, too, but Declan had always been at the top of her thoughts.

His eyes darkened, a deep amber overtaking his vision. "No one will ever hurt you again."

She ran her fingers through the hair at the base of his skull, soothing the growling beast. "I know."

"No one will take you. No one will scare you." More of the wolf came out, his obvious fury still present.

"I know." She tugged, but he didn't budge, so she pushed to her elbow and went to him instead. She inched closer and brushed her lips across his as she brought their bodies together. His thick hardness nudged her hip, proof of his desire.

For her. Only for her.

Her core ached, her own body making its need known. She wanted him just as badly, wanted to be possessed and taken by him. Their hearts beat in time, their souls calling to each other, and their bodies were desperate to tie their futures together.

Now.

"Mate me, Declan. Mark me so everyone knows I'm yours," she whispered against his mouth, carefully slipping her fingers from his hair. She ghosted the tips over the flesh at the juncture of his shoulder and neck. "And I'll make sure everyone knows you're mine."

He shuddered, and his length twitched, throbbing, while a drop of moisture escaped the tip to decorate her skin. He was on edge, not far from finding that ultimate bliss.

A bliss they needed to discover together.

"Abby..." All he said was her name, but there was so much more in his tone. A warning and a plea in one.

She hooked one leg over his, sliding her knee higher and foot along the back of his thigh. She opened herself more and more to him, not stopping until she was wrapped around his hip, heel coming to rest at his lower back.

"Come to me, Declan." She nipped his lower lip, but he remained motionless.

"We..." He shook his head. "I'm..." The cool scent of his doubt drifted to her, suffusing her with the flavors of his emotions.

"Perfect for me." She gave him a gentle, openmouthed kiss. "Everything I've ever wanted." And another. "My mate."

He shuddered once more, and she sensed his control faltering. He acted like a demanding, grunting male who wasn't about to give her a choice, but he still fought to give her a chance to deny him.

As if she ever would.

Abby tightened her grip just enough to hold him, to pull him atop her when she rolled to her back once again. This time his hips settled between hers, skin to skin, bare hardness nestled to her slick heat. He shuddered with the new, intimate contact and she did the same, that single touch enough to push her near the edge of release.

Declan stared down at her, eye color flickering between amber and blue, his two halves battling for supremacy.

"Claim me, Declan Reed." She forced herself to remain immobile, to cease teasing him and give him a chance to move away.

"Last chance to run, Abby. Once I make you mine I won't let you go."

He growled the words as if they were a threat, and it sent a tremble of need dancing over her nerves.

She quirked her lips in a soft smile. "And once I make you mine, *I* won't let *you* go."

She rolled her hips, rubbing her slick, bare center along his firm length. She shuddered with the caress, the feel of his veined shaft stroking her intimate flesh, and whimpered as the pleasure gathered inside her.

"Fuck." He spat the curse and shifted his hips, that hardness changing position while he lifted away from her. He stared down at her body as the head of his length nudged her opening. "You're so beautiful. So perfect." He rolled his hips, gently sliding no more than an inch of his cock in and out of her.

The shallow penetration drew moans from deep within her chest, her whole body aching for more, aching for him. And then he gave her exactly what she craved.

Declan didn't stop with his next thrust, didn't cease penetrating her in a slow, tormenting slide until their hips met. "So mine."

Abby moaned deep and grasped his shoulders, the cat's claws emerging to scrape at his damp flesh. "Ahhh!"

Her sheath rippled and squeezed him, trembling around his thick, pleasurable invasion.

"Tight. Wet." He adopted a steady pace, a gentle glide of his length in and out of her center. The rough and tumble assassin made love to her, his passion a series of gentle rolling waves.

Not the rough, feral passion she'd expected from him.

She met his stare, and the reason was quickly visible in his eyes. He worried for her, worried about her response to his rough need.

"Declan, give me all of you." She scratched his back, knowing she left bright red lines in her wake. "Everything."

"Abby." His eyes seemed to glow, his wolf tugging at the end of its tether.

Next she broke skin, piercing the hard flesh of his shoulders with a small prick. "You won't hurt me. You never could."

She met his every thrust, bodies moving in a gentle glide and careful passion. She tightened her grip on his shoulders and lifted herself from the ground, then captured a bite of his flesh between her teeth. She bit down, not piercing him but showing him she was just as much an animal as he was. She had a cat inside her. A cat that was desperate to be his.

"Mate me." She murmured the two words against his chest and then repeated the harsh nibble. "Take me or let me go."

It was the push he needed, the final nudge that sent him over the edge into the uncontrolled passion she craved.

"Mine." The voice was Declan's, but the harsh rasp and growl was all wolf. The wolf who refused to let her go. Good thing she wanted to stay.

Abby fell back to the blanket and let Declan take control. She allowed herself to be swept away by his punishing pace, by the bliss he gifted her with each and every flex and relaxation of his muscles. His thrusts increased in power and rhythm, the slap of their bodies echoing through the clear forest air as they both sought release.

A release that would soon come. Her body shook, nerves alight with impending ecstasy and overwhelming pleasure. Her sheath rippled and squeezed his long length and hard thickness. His veined shaft caressed the most intimate part of her, the head stroking her G-spot with an accuracy that drew cries from her with every thrust and retreat. She sobbed his name, begging and pleading for more and more from him.

And he gave her what she craved. His pace turned into a punishing race, their fight to the ultimate pleasure increasing with every beat of their hearts. She whined, begged, and pleaded for more, aching to reach the pinnacle with Declan at her side.

With Declan inside her.

He gripped her hip with one hand, holding her steady and forcing her position to alter just enough to...

"Declan!"

Enough to give her G-spot a hint more pressure, to give her a hint more ecstasy that had her hurtling toward the edge. She stood at the brink, at the delicate line between need and possession.

"Give it to me, Abby." He growled and bared his fangs, the long white lengths of his wolf's teeth shining brightly with the sun's rays. "Now."

He wanted her—all of him wanted her—and she was prepared to accept him.

Accept and take him.

She released the thick leash she had wrapped around her heart long ago, during her life of turmoil and pain, and let it fly free of her body. Now she embraced Declan, drew him to her chest, and accepted every battered and bruised inch of his soul. He was her mate.

Hers.

With that acceptance, she cried out his name, head thrown back and shoulder exposed as the ultimate pleasure overtook her. It suffused her blood, stroked her nerves from inside out, and stretched to possess every inch of her trembling body.

Then he gave her more, he gave her everything. Declan

struck in that moment, in that very second she flew off the cliff of pleasure. A vicious pain tore through her, the jolting stab of agony breaking through the rising pleasure. But only for a moment. Only for a split second that stole her breath while he gave her what she'd craved for so many years. Fangs sank through flesh, teeth tearing into skin and muscle until he'd bitten as deep as he possibly could.

And he remained there, his body still drawing out her final release, his teeth in her shoulder and his mouth sucking at the wound he'd caused. Her cat roared in joy, the beast purposefully refusing to heal the damage. It had more important things to do. Such as copy Declan's actions.

Just as soon as she was done coming. Her orgasm continued on and on, his every thrust and every suckle spurring the ecstasy to rise higher and higher. And she embraced it. Embraced the pleasure and the pain and the extra pleasure the pain gave her. Her body tingled and throbbed with the overwhelming joy, with the maddening, ultimate relief until...

Until his strokes faltered, until his rhythm stuttered and he whipped his teeth from her shoulder. Blood and saliva dripped from his lips, the ferocity of his beast right beneath the surface of his skin. Wolf's eyes met hers, nothing but the beast in his gaze while he whispered a single word.

"Abby."

He wanted it—wanted to be claimed—now. His body was there, dancing on the precipice just as she had. He held himself back, watched and waited for her, and she couldn't help but give him what he craved.

Her cat rushed forward, fangs dropping in an instant as she rose and struck. Between one heartbeat and the next, blood filled her mouth, the bitter, coppery fluid pouring from his wound and sliding over her taste buds. Hints of his animal's muskiness and the man's pure sweetness flowed down her throat, coating her from inside out just as...

Just as his hips jerked once, twice, and with the third, he froze. His hips remained flush to hers, his roar filling the air while his seed filled her body.

The cat purred and chuffed at the idea, at the thought of carrying his cub or pup. It made her grip him tighter, pull him more firmly against her center so she didn't lose a drop.

Abby slowly withdrew her fangs and lapped at the wound, licking away the trickling droplets that swelled along the wound. Now they could never be separated.

Ever.

Declan slipped out, and she whimpered with the loss just as Declan groaned. His breathing came in harsh pants, his chest heaving and brushing her breasts with every inhale. Finally he fell to the side with a groan, dragging her close as he dropped to the blanket. She curled against him, body slick with sweat and coated in his scent.

"Damn," he wheezed, and lifted his head, kissing her forehead. "Just..." He inhaled deep and slowly breathed out. "Damn."

Abby hummed, unable to say anything just yet. She would. At some point, she was sure. Just...not yet. For now she wanted to glory in the feel of his damp body on hers, the aroma of their passion, and embrace the knowledge that she had a mate. She had one person dedicated to her and her happiness just as she was dedicated to his.

No matter what the future held, they had each other.

A bellowing roar split through their content quiet, the bear's fury followed by a chorus of barks, and then came a lion's objection as well.

So, they had each other and his SHOC team.

"I'm gonna kill 'em," Declan slurred, a hint of a growl

in his threat, but she knew he was just as drowsy from their lovemaking as she was.

"After." She sighed and snuggled closer.

"After?" He tightened his hold with a hum.

"Uh-huh. After a nap. And then after you claim me again. Maybe after you claim me twice." She nuzzled his chest and then relaxed with a sigh. Yes. A nap and a couple more rounds of claiming sex sounded like a very, *very* good idea.

He squeezed her tight and hauled her atop him, tugging until they were nose to nose. "Wolf has never wanted anyone other than you, Abby." He lifted his head slightly and brushed his lips across hers in the softest of kisses. "He never will."

Declan looked at her with smoky eyes that promised her the world. The same way her father had always looked at her mother.

Everything was okay—everything would *be* okay. At least until Unified Humanity decided to strike again. For now she'd take her joy—and Declan—and hold both close to her heart.

EPILOGUE

It looked like Birch was going to let Declan's post-mating glow last only until eleven. He'd roused Declan and Abby fifteen minutes ago—ordering Declan to get his furry ass moving. Now the team alpha had a look in his eye that said the team was about to be smothered by a load of Unified Humanity–Shifter Operations Command bullshit.

Declan held his mate close, one arm firmly around her waist, while she sat across his lap. He hadn't let her get more than an arm's length away once he'd gotten his fangs in her pale flesh. The wolf finally had her, and the beast wasn't about to let her escape.

The team sat around a table on Birch's back deck—the *entire* team. Which included Pike. Pike, who made sure his ass was next to the team alpha and as far away from Declan as he could get.

Abby had told Declan he couldn't kill his brother. He wondered if she'd let him rough him up a little though.

"Now that the happy couple has joined us," Birch drawled, "here's where we stand."

Grant raised his hand. "I'm sitting. Does that mean you want us to stand? Is this gonna be like church with all the praying and the 'please rise, please be seated, amen' shit? Because if it is, I'm gonna need a sandwich."

Birch sighed. "Fuck my life."

"Abby, will you make me a sandwich?" Grant flashed what Declan could only describe as "sad puppy" eyes.

Declan growled low, his wolf prowling and anxious to pounce on the male who dared ask his mate for anything. "Grant…"

"I wouldn't mind a sandwich," Ethan added.

"Potato salad, maybe?" Cole put in his own order.

"My mate is not cooking for anyone." The deck vibrated, and his roar echoed across the lake, the still water shimmering with the sound.

Abby stroked his chest, her small hand tracing circles on his pecs, as she whispered, "Shh…Calm down."

And as it always seemed to do, his wolf calmed with her touch.

"I called it. She's a dick whisperer," Pike murmured, and that had Declan's fury rising once again.

Declan ignored his brother's whisper and kept his attention on the team alpha. The quicker Birch spoke, the quicker he could drag Abby back to bed. "What's going on, boss?"

The team alpha took a deep breath and released it slowly. His gaze touched on each of them, attention even landing on Abby as he sought out the rest of the team.

"Quade is no longer a threat to Abby."

Cole snorted. "He never *was* a threat to Abby. One of us would have killed him if he'd tried to go after our kitten."

Declan's wolf bristled at the nickname, and he let a low growl escape his throat. "Cole…"

The tiger waved him away. "Down, boy. Bad dog."

"The director," Birch growled between gritted teeth

while he glared at Cole, "is under the impression that Grant was able to piece the tablet back together and part of the data was recovered. It reveals exactly what Abby reported—FosCo wired money to Unified Humanity. He's withdrawn his request to speak with her in light of that as well as the fact that she's now fully mated to a SHOC agent."

At least Declan wouldn't have to waste time killing Quade now.

"You going to share your 'twitchy' feelings with the class?"

Birch ran a hand through his hair and then gripped the back of his neck, massaging the muscles. The wind changed direction, a gust that snared Birch's scent and blew it in their direction. Declan pulled apart the different flavors, quickly identifying each one...including the last. The one that had his stomach clenching and his heartbeat stuttering.

"Aw, shit," Ethan mumbled.

"That bad?" Grant whined.

"Motherfucker," Declan growled.

Cole groaned. "I need to order more C-4, don't I? With or without notifying SHOC?"

Abby frowned, brow furrowed, and her attention drifted across the team before returning to Declan. Her sparkling blue eyes were clouded with confusion. "What?"

"Birch doesn't get worried, but right now he's worried."

"Concerned," the grizzly snapped, and curled his lip, flashing a fang.

"*Concerned*, then," Declan drawled, rolling his eyes.

Birch curled his lip a little higher before speaking again. "Over the last several years, tips about Unified Humanity and assignments to take them out from headquarters have tapered off."

Declan nodded. They had lessened over time. "Because we've been making a difference." Pike snickered, and he shot his brother a dark glare. "Something to share?"

Pike remained silent.

"There's someone inside SHOC feeding information to Unified Humanity. That same person is limiting what information agents receive."

Declan's heartbeat stuttered, and his lungs froze. Abby shuddered in his arms. He pulled her even closer, tucking her head against his shoulder. The others...weren't happy.

To say the least.

"What the fuck?"

"Fuck that."

"No fucking way."

Birch held up a hand to silence them all. "I had my suspicions, which is why I sent Pike in to UH." The grizzly nodded at the other wolf. "Pike gave me—us—the tip on FosCo. Our arrival, Abby's discovery, and SHOC's response prove there's someone on the inside feeding intel to Unified Humanity."

"Who?" Declan wanted to bathe in their blood and feed their bodies to natural predators.

"We don't know," the grizzly snarled. "Yet. Foster's death meant we couldn't get any info from him, and he was the closest link between SHOC and UH. The traitor is safe—for now. He—"

"Or she," Ethan grumbled, and everyone focused on the lion with narrowed eyes. "What? Why are you looking at me like that?" He frowned at them all. "The chicks in the pride do the heavy lifting and conniving. Never met a bigger group of feline bitches in my life. They will tear your shit up and smile while doing it. Just sayin'."

Birch picked up where he left off. "He *or she* is out of

reach right now, but FosCo wasn't the only big business wrapped up in Unified Humanity. Pike gave us another name—a name that won't go past our team until we figure out what the hell we want to do next."

"We?" Declan raised his eyebrows in question.

"We." Their team alpha gave Grant a blank stare. "We're going to talk about a democracy since going against UH while there's a traitor in SHOC might end up with some of us six feet under."

"Sweet." Grant punched the air. "First order of business, I want to be in charge of location selection for all future operations."

"Grant," Birch snapped, and the wolf immediately straightened, any hint of a smile vanishing from his expression. "This isn't the time for fun and games. We do this, we do it knowing that shit is gonna keep getting flung at the fan and we're the fucking fan that's gonna end up covered in it."

"I'm in." Abby's voice didn't waver, and she straightened in Declan's lap. "I know I'm not an agent, but if you're taking votes, then I'm in."

"Abby," Declan murmured, wrapping both arms around her and pulling her close, but she wouldn't have it.

"No." She brushed off his hold and turned to face him. "Unified Humanity needs to be stopped. If there's someone inside SHOC helping them succeed...we—you guys— have to do this." His mate lowered her head, soft forehead pressed to his own while she whispered. "There can't be any more children like me, Declan. Not if there's something that can be done to stop them. Can you imagine another child out there in a burning house? Praying for their lives while they're locked in a cupboard? The fire..."

"Shhh...sweetheart." He cupped her cheeks and brushed

away her tears. Declan lifted his head and let his gaze sweep the others, satisfied when they all gave him a brisk nod. "We'll do what we can to stop them and find the traitor." He directed his next question to Birch. "Where are we looking first?"

"Foster supplied the cash to Unified Humanity. Thanks to Pike's intel, we're going after the brawn next. We're hoping that will lead us to the brains. Somewhere in there, we'll find out who in SHOC is blocking us at every turn." Birch leaned over the table, gaze intent. "Take some time to get your head on straight because once we're back on deck, things are gonna get real ugly, real quick. This shit ain't gonna be easy."

Declan grinned, and the team spoke as one. "But it sure as fuck is gonna be fun."

Dangerous, too, but at least he'd have Abby at his side. He could face anything as long as he had her in his life... and in his heart.

READ MORE OF THE
SHIFTER ROGUES SERIES BY
CELIA KYLE IN:

TIGER'S CLAIM—Cole & Stella's story

ABOUT THE AUTHOR

Celia Kyle is a *New York Times* and *USA Today* best-selling author, ex–dance teacher, former accountant, and erstwhile collectible doll salesperson. She now writes paranormal romances for readers who:

1) Like super-hunky heroes (they generally get furry)
2) Dig beautiful women (who have a few more curves than the average lady)
3) Love laughing in (and out of) bed.

It goes without saying that there's always a happily-ever-after for her characters, even if there are a few road bumps along the way. Today she lives in central Florida and writes full-time with the support of her loving husband and two finicky cats.

Learn more at:

Twitter: @celiakyle

Facebook.com/authorceliakyle

Looking for more romantic suspense?

THE BASTARD'S BARGAIN
By Katee Robert

Dmitri Romanov knows Keira O'Malley only married him to keep peace between their families. Nevertheless, the desire that smolders between them is a dangerous addiction neither can resist. But with his enemies circling closer, Keira could just be his secret weapon—if she doesn't bring him to his knees first.

THE FEARLESS KING
By Katee Robert

When Journey King's long-lost father returns to make a play for the family company, Journey turns to the rugged and handsome Frank Evans for help, and finds much more than she was looking for.

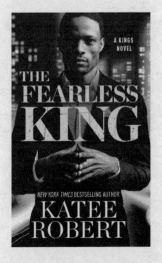

Discover exclusive content and more on
forever-romance.com.

FIERCE JUSTICE
By Piper Drake

As a K9 handler on the Search and Protect team, Arin Siri needs to
be where the action is—and right now that's investigating a trafficking
operation in Hawaii. When an enemy from her past shows up bleeding,
she's torn between the desire to patch Jason up or to put more holes in
him. Then again, the hotshot mercenary could be the person she needs
to bust open her case.

TWISTED TRUTHS
By Rebecca Zanetti

Noni Yuka is desperate. Her infant niece has been kidnapped, and the only person who can save her is the private detective who once broke her heart.

Follow @ForeverRomance and join the conversation using #ReadForever.

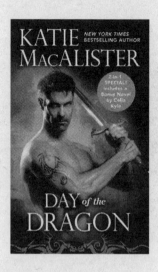

DAY OF THE DRAGON
By Katie MacAlister

Real scholars know that supernatural beings aren't real, but once Thaisa meets tall, dark, and mysterious Archer Andras of the Storm Dragons, all of her academic training goes out the window. Thaisa realizes that she really should worry about those things that go bump in the night.

TIGER'S CLAIM
By Celia Kyle

Cole Turner may act like a wealthy, gorgeous playboy, but he's also a tiger shifter determined to bring down the organization that's threatening his kind. Leopard shifter Stella Moore will do whatever it takes to destroy Unified Humanity, even if that means working with the undeniably annoying—and sexy—Cole.

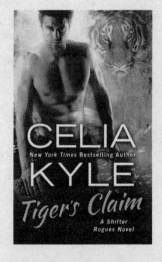

Visit
Facebook.com/ForeverRomance